A TWISTED FATE

Kristine Endsley

A Twisted Fate

The Exile's Paradox Series/Book One

www.kristineendsley.com

Cover art and design by Cristiana Leone

Editing by

www.arrowheadediting.com

www.markedandread.com

Published by KE Fantasy

ISBN: E-book: 979-8-9897685-0-9, Paperback: 979-8-9897685-1-6, Hardcover: 979-8-9897685-2-3

First edition: February 2024

*To the extraordinary women who helped make me who I am today.
Sue, Debbie, Cindy, April, Shannon, Carol, Fran, Deanna, Marj and
Doris*

CONTENTS

Index of Common Words

Aemina— Hally's elven country

Aeminan— Citizens of Aemina

Aemirin— Language of the Aeminan people

Ai— Expression or exasperation, like "oh"

Amura Ore— Governing council in *Aemina*

C'yo— Cuss word, equivalent to shit

Enda— Elf

Endae— The elven realm

Endaen— Elven

Imolegin— An *enda's* magical signature

Ja—Yes

Ma Colombe (French)— My dove

Meril— An *endaen* magical amulet

Muranilde— The soulmate like bond that Hally and Nolan share

Sae— No

Sajé— A comforting word/expression, similar to "shhh"

Savile— title of an exile (Hally)

Sitam— I know

Zayuri— Org. of samurai like warriors

<u>Word Endings:</u>

-ë— female

-o— male

-e— neutral or title

-i— plural

<u>Note:</u>

Remember! These are English translations for the convenience of English speakers. Please don't assume the characters are speaking English just because you're reading English.

A full *English-Aemirin* translations list is on my website: <u>https://kristineendsley.com/extras/</u>

1

Tattoos hurt. If you can't deal with that, don't fucking get one.

My client would have had a tattoo-tip-shaped gouge in his shoulder blade eight flinches ago if I wasn't used to men being such babies. I swallowed my laugh and wiped away the excess ink. The shop's bell jingled. My Mickey Mouse clock on the back wall said we were open for fifteen more minutes.

"Hello!" Lewis, my business partner and I called out at the same time.

My machine drowned out the visitor's response, but the tone of his voice held a hypnotic cadence, compelling me to relax, so similar to a spell I almost checked on them. I paused the machine and took a breath. They continued to speak, but the cadence was gone. Was I losing it? If I kept working, I'd forget the feeling. Sure, denial worked wonders.

"Hey, Hally?" Lewis's deep, mellow voice drifted back into my space.

"Yeah?" I wiped more ink from the tat and pumped the pedal.

"Got a guy out here that wants to talk to you."

"Who?"

"Won't say. Just that he knew you a long time ago."

A long time ago? Please. Humans didn't know the meaning of a long time ago. No way my six years in the States was that "long ago," as Lewis put it.

I lifted my machine and swiveled my chair around. "Mateo and Sam are picking me up at eleven fifteen. You know I don't have time to talk." I had to have time to clean after my client before then. Lewis knew all this.

Lewis leaned his dark, tattooed arms on the half wall separating the lobby and my studio. His eyes crinkled, and his lips twitched as he suppressed a smile. "Talk quick."

A lock of my black hair fell into my face from under my red cloche hat, ruining my glare. "Stop meddling."

"I'm not."

So convincing.

"Right. Have him make an appointment, would ya?"

"He says he really needs to talk to you."

"But he won't tell you his name? Have you considered he's lying?"

His lip ring twinkled as he shrugged his large shoulders.

"He French?"

"Got an accent, so maybe." Not meddling, my ass.

I lifted my eyebrows.

He lifted his.

He broke first, giving me that oh-so-innocent smile. Lewis was a six-foot-four, three-hundred-pound teddy bear that refused to mind his own damn business. He was also my very good friend.

"Girl, quit wastin' time. I'm not entertainin' this guy out here forever."

Sighing, I turned back to the tattoo, a black and white phoenix resting on my client's spine. "Fine. I'm almost done." I scratched my nose. "Shit," I whispered. "This better be worth it," I grumbled about the change of plans as I fixed my hair and replaced my gloves.

My customer chuckled.

"Don't start," I mumbled, tapping the peddle a few times before adding more ink to the needle.

He chuckled again. "I'm not saying nothing."

I lifted my machine and sat up. "Remember, I'm the one drawing your tat, mister. You don't want to piss me off."

He shut up.

I took a breath and imagined my jumbled thoughts leaving me as I worked. How long ago did the visitor mean? Everyone I'd known in Seattle since I'd last lived here was either dead or dying. Neither one of them had any business in a tattoo shop. I smiled at the thought of dead people crawling in here to get tattooed.

My Mickey clock announced the eleventh hour as my customer headed out to the front. After disposing the perishable equipment I followed him. When I pushed through the saloon doors, I found my client playing on his phone at the register. It hadn't taken *that* long. Attention spans were so short now. Rolling my eyes, I turned my attention to the rest of the room.

Thoughts about phone and attention spans scattered at the scene before me. The saloon door swung forward, smacking my back and I stumbled.

Lewis sat on one of our ugly brown couches, scowling at the chess board in front of him. He picked up the black rook, partially visible from my angle, set it down, then scowled again as his opponent proceeded to take a different piece.

The woman's back was to me, but by the look Lewis gave her—wait, a man had asked to talk to me, not a woman. When had she come in?

Two braids held back some of her long hair. Her cinnamon-red hair and golden highlights gave me pause. *Did* I know her? But Lewis said—

"Hally?"

Blinking, I looked away from the chess players.

"You want me to pay, right?" My client's eyebrows rose, the shadow of that chuckle he'd given me earlier still there.

"Oh, right." That sounded so stupid! I tried to ring him up without peeking over at the table. I failed—twice.

"Thanks. Love the tat. Looks like your night's gonna 'be worth it' after all," he teased, repeating my words from before.

He laughed at my flat look and made his way out the door. My attention went back to the couches. Checking her aura was out of the question. After my people had exiled me to this realm, I'd blocked my magic.

Sometimes I almost regretted my decision, but I didn't trust my magic. This was ridiculous. Nothing in the human realm warranted enough suspicion for me to consider checking her aura.

Lewis got up, shaking his tattooed head, frowning. He mumbled something as he rubbed the back of his neck and grabbed his black cowboy hat. His opponent stood next.

Whoa, not a she. And I hoped his front looked as good as his back. He was about as tall as Lewis—not a specific gender trait. Neither was the long red hair. How stereotypical of me. Jeez.

His Henley-style shirt...neither navy or royal blue—something...other. The hair and now the shirt? They nagged at my brain as I tried to recall where I'd met this person. I needed to pull it together and stop obsessing over this.

The visitor tugged his sleeves down, shrugged into his henna-brown leather jacket, and rolled his shoulders. Standing next to him, Lewis eyed me from under his tipped-down hat, smirking. Great. I couldn't stop my reciprocal smile, so I rolled my eyes and reached under the counter for my purse.

"So, Hally?" Lewis's voice reverberated around the small space, and my head hit the underside of the counter. He hissed in sympathy. "Ow. Sorry, Hally. Didn't mean to startle you."

With my stomach in knots and my hand on the back of my head, I stood up. My eyes peeked open, and my professional "hello" choked my throat. All thoughts of answering Lewis left me.

"No...Twy—Twynolan," I stuttered. The shirt, the hair, of course they looked familiar, damn it.

"Hello, Hally," he teased.

He pronounced the name correctly, Hal-ee, not Hail-ee, as some people did. But it sounded wrong coming from him. My real name is Hallanevaë, although to him I was always Hallë, like in the latte, with a whisper soft e.

My fists clenched until they shook. "What are you doing here, Twynolan?" I kept my voice steady and even managed to sound a little pissed off. Point for me.

Twynolan's face fell, and his ice-blue eyes darkened, before he went back to playing the "sad ex-boyfriend" card. He looked at Lewis, then back at me. "I—I must speak with you."

"Oh, is that all?" My stomach fluttered, but I shoved the nervousness down. Exile wasn't some prison sentence with visitation rights. The council could banish him for talking to me.

Lewis's lips puckered and he looked away. Did he see a resemblance? Something foreign, not human? No. Humans saw what they expected to see if not made aware of the oddity or without having something to compare it to, which was why Twynolan shouldn't be here.

"All right then, you two. I'll be seein' you, Hally." Lewis drew out his response and tipped his hat at Twynolan. He patted down his western-style vest and jeans pockets, then went back to the couch and grabbed his cell phone. "Nice meetin' ya, Nolan. Hally."

"Thank you for the company." Twynolan's dimple dented his cheek—adorable even after all the softness of childhood had left him. He hated that dimple.

My childhood best friend, not much of a bestie anymore, had an inviting, trusting kind of face. Which explained Lewis's immediate belief when Twynolan had said he knew me. That and it was the truth, broadly speaking.

Lewis put his phone to his ear as he pushed on the saloon doors. We waited, listening as Lewis prattled on the phone, until the back door clicked shut.

Once alone, Twynolan dropped his act. His light eyes contrasted with his golden complexion, but they grew neutral and assessing. I refused to squirm under his analyzing look.

Did I look immature? No. I looked like a kick-ass tattoo artist. The heavy makeup made my dark green eyes look exotic and hid my almost-black freckles. Tonight I wore my red cloche hat, angled to show off my awesome dragon ear cuffs, custom made for my pointy ears.

My long, black sweater with a blood-red cami underneath, black leggings, and black boots completed my badass, bitchy, artistic tattoo persona. The only thing not part of the costume was the leather bracelet holding a metal tag, etched with my foster sister's name on it. That stayed close to me always.

Alas, I had no tattoos. They were too identifiable. I lied to people and said I was allergic to tattoo ink because who's ever heard of a tattoo artist without tattoos? Not me.

Clearing my throat, I broke the silence. "So...no 'how are you?'" I shrugged. "Or a 'whatcha been up to in the past century and a quarter?' Usually, when people want to talk, they start with niceties. Humans *and* elves. "And I noticed your compliance spell you used on Lewis. I figured messing with people's free will was beneath you." The simple spell was used in defensive situations, not to make our lives easier.

He squared his shoulders and took a step forward. My hand shot out to stop him.

He sighed. "It has been one hundred and nineteen years, two weeks, and three days, actually. And explaining I come from the realm of *Endae* would have been awkward, would you not agree? Seeing as there are no other *endai* here."

Endai—what humans would consider elves. True, humans had no knowledge of different realms, elves, or magic.

"The spell was unnecessary. You're smart. You could have used your genius brain rather than magic. Again, why are you here? And so help me if you say 'I need to talk to you' one more time—"

"There has been—" He puffed out his cheeks. "There is some-one—I need—"

I'd never seen him so flustered under pressure. He always considered his words. Which, no doubt, was why it irritated me and my patience was growing thin. Pinching the bridge of my nose wasn't calming me down. Not from this. My hands flew up. "What the hell are you thinking? I'm in exile. Not that the last one hundred and whatever years without me clued you in. What did you tell me? Oh, right, I'm dead to you. Dead."

"Hallë, please—"

"Don't call me that," I hissed. "You forbade me to use your name. Same goes for me, buddy."

"*Ai*, Hallë—Hally." Twynolan licked his lips and looked at the floor. "*C'yo*," he cussed and shoved his hair back. "I am not leaving until we talk."

"Or what?"

"I will follow you around tonight. Bump into these human friends of yours." He clasped his hands behind his back and arched an eyebrow. "How long have we known each other, and did you ever once mention me?"

This was the kid who followed his sister and her friends to the lake when she told him he couldn't go. He hid their towels, replaced their dessert with silk dragon cocoons, and filled their bottles with lake water. That was not an isolated incident. Twynolan following me would be the least of my worries.

"Fine, but I'm not helping."

"We will see." He kept his arms behind his back and smiled a smug, dimpled smile.

I crossed my arms, waiting.

Twynolan leaned forward and opened his mouth, but the shop phone interrupted him. We stared at each other, listening to the ring.

"Are you answering that?" he asked after the fourth ring.

"It's not important."

Twynolan furrowed his brows and shifted to look at the phone behind the counter. "How would you know without answering it?"

"Twynolan." I clenched my jaw. "Focus."

The answering machine beeped, and my friend, Mateo, rushed to talk. "Hally, *ojitos*, are you there? Sam and I are running behind. Pick up the phone."

"Crap." I marched over and pushed aside the saloon doors. Cleaning my area would have to wait for tomorrow. Damn it.

Twynolan's long legs brought him up to me in seconds, matching my steps, something he always did to stay beside me. "Ah, yes, the friends…"

I glanced at the clock, Mickey's little tail swinging back and forth. The more of my human friends he met, the more excuses and lies I'd have to use.

"I wouldn—*net*, would not mind meeting them." Whelp, I found his English problem. Contractions. Betcha that annoyed the hell out of him. Good. "Oh, come on, Hallë—Hally, I can play nice."

I snorted. "Sure." I shoved the office door open and made a beeline to my cubby.

"Hallë?" he whined, and I rolled my eyes. "Why not?"

"They'll notice we both have pointy ears and weird-colored eyes. They're very smart people. Now shut up so I can talk to them."

"I do not think your eyes are weird."

I couldn't stop myself from scoffing as I lifted my eyes from the phone. "Well, your opinion doesn't mean shit."

"Hurtful, Hally." He held his hand to his chest, mock pouting. Jeez. "Shh."

As he opened his mouth, my cell phone rang. I raised a finger. After raising an eyebrow in challenge, he chose to turn around to face the artwork on the walls. I used to be just as obstinate as him. Wow, how annoying.

"*Ojitos!*" Mateo's energy exploded through the line. "Did you get my message?"

I jumped, and the corner of the cubby bit into my shoulder. Twynolan turned, and his eyes brightened with amusement. I jeered at him.

"Heeeelllo? You still at Yula's Quill?"

"Yeah, yeah, I'm here. Mateo—"

"Great. We're running about five minutes late. You good there? I figure it'd give you or time to clean." I liked to make sure my area was as clean as possible.

Crap.

"Mateo, listen. I can't go—"

"Oh no, you don't. You promised to come out tonight. How many times have you stood us up this month?"

"Three," Sam said in the background.

"Did you hear that? Three, Hally. That's every Friday this month. You can't back out."

"I didn't stand you up. I called and canceled for legitimate reasons. If I had stood you up, I wouldn't have called."

Twynolan arched an eyebrow, an unconscious tick when amused or challenged. Was there any chance he wouldn't use this to his advantage? No. No, there was not.

Mateo hummed to get my attention.

"Seriously, I'm sorry. Something came up, or rather someone. An ex-friend came in tonight. Some crap's going on at—" At what? Not home, not anymore. "—with his family."

Twynolan's movement caught my attention as he examined my poster "All the Things I Need to Know I Learned in Kindergarten." I held my breath. Could he read English?

"Then he can come, too."

"No way." I glared daggers at Twynolan's back.

"Come on. Besides Charlie, we've never met any of your old friends. And she's your cousin. She doesn't count."

He was such a drama queen. My head dropped back. The ceiling revealed no helpful solutions.

"I do not mind meeting them, Hallë," Twynolan interjected, loud enough for Mateo to hear. The hypnotic cadence was back in his voice, like reciting a poem to lure you in. I held up my finger as a warning to shut up and not use that spell. He shrugged, oh so scared of me.

"Is that him? He sounds nice," Mateo said in his matchmaker's voice that he'd been using a lot this month.

Twynolan laughed, getting Mateo's meaning regardless of the language/culture barrier.

"No," I answered Twynolan, but it could have easily answered Mateo.

Mateo's hints to start dating again was the main reason why I hadn't been going out with them. Well, with Mateo. Sam and I went to lunch yesterday. He kept his opinions to himself, most of the time.

"Oh, I like him already," Mateo said.

This wasn't going well. I closed my eyes. "I hate you both."

"See ya soon, *ojitos*. This'll give you more time to reacquaint with your ex-*friend*."

"No. Mateo? Crap, he hung up. Come on, No—Twynolan. We have to go. Now." I grabbed my coat and hauled ass to the back door.

"*Ojitos?*"

"None of your business." A nickname for pretty eyes that Mateo's mom started. Mateo loved it because I hated it. He had a Seattle accent, so I hadn't even known he spoke Spanish until his mom's visit.

"Where will we go?" Twynolan perked up, full of genuine curiosity.

I released my tight jaw and blew out though my pursed lips. "Somewhere we can talk away from them."

The cold February air hit me, stealing the breath from my lungs as I shoved the door open. My thin coat was the wrong choice for this weather, but the temperature wasn't supposed to drop until tomorrow night. That's what I got for trusting a weather app.

Twynolan stopped under the doorframe and looked down at me standing behind him, waiting for him to walk through. "Because you do not want your friends to meet me?" He held his hair down as the wind tugged at his intricate *Aemiran* braids. He inched forward enough for me to close the door, but that was all.

"Exactly."

"Because there are no *endai* here."

"Yes."

"Do you truly believe that would be a problem?"

Ushering him away from the building wasn't working. I dropped my arm and my anger for a moment. "I've witnessed what humans can do to each other. I am terrified of what they'd do to me if the wrong people found out."

"Do you think your friends would harm you?"

"No. But the more people who know, the likelier it is that the wrong humans will discover me. You have to be careful and have an explanation for everything."

After about ten seconds, he dipped his chin. "Very well, Hallë." He stepped three steps into Post Avenue.

"I've told you to stop calling me that." I turned to face the door, key in hand.

"Hally."

Okay, maybe not. The name sounded wrong coming from him.

The stubborn bolt constantly refused to lock without a good amount of jiggling. At last, I won the fight and turned to the dark, urine-scented avenue. Twynolan stared into the shadows. The next street over was visible at the end but did nothing to brighten the old alley-turned-road between the two historic buildings. He held his hands behind his back, relaxed except for the slight furrow in his brow and the tightness around his eyes. Nothing seemed out of the ordinary to me. "Everything okay?"

A moment passed before he looked at me and tipped his head to the side. "Why would things not be?"

I opened my mouth to give him a smart-ass remark but decided not to. Yesler Avenue was a hundred feet to our left, and he fell into step beside me, but not too close.

"Do you think he would like me?"

I stopped and turned to him, my coat snagging on the bricks of the old building.

"What?"

"Your friend, Mateo. He said he liked me already. Do you think that would be true if I was to meet him?"

Scoffing, I started moving again. "Of course they would, No—Twynolan." That was the third time I'd almost used his nickname. Not that he wasn't likable. I was just pissed that he was here. And frustrated. And, hell, this wasn't good. When I turned to go up the hill, he got in the way. I tried to step around him, but he blocked me.

I crossed my arms.

He looked down.

I looked up.

He smiled a stupid, condescending smile, irritating the hell out of me. His damn adorable dimple showed, too.

"We're going this way." I pointed up to Seattle's Pioneer Square and the pergola. "Are you going to move or what?"

"How far do you plan to go to avoid your friends? I must talk to you, but we cannot stay out here. It is too cold."

"I..." I pressed my lips together and looked toward the Pioneer Building. "I'm taking you to the coffee shop. There." I pointed up the hill again.

His eyes lit up, and I caught myself before I smiled. I was pissed, damn it.

"No magic. I know humans won't recognize a simple compliance spell, but don't do it. You are risking my safety."

"I see." Nodding, he stepped to the side. Letting my curiosity get the better of me, I hesitated, but no. I refused to make him elaborate. We stared at each other for a beat. Groaning, I gave in and started moving.

Twynolan reminded me of home, of our families, of what happened. They exiled me when I was one hundred and twenty-seven, an adolescent in our realm. We'd grown up together, looked after each other, stood up for each other...until I screwed up.

We waited for the walk signal at the corner of Yesler and First Street. Twynolan stood two or so steps behind me with his hands behind his back, watching the cars drive around us.

With my hands shoved in my pockets, I tapped my foot. "When did you get here?"

"At ten forty-four, remember?" He chuckled. "When Lewis was meddling."

I groaned.

"We played a lovely game of chess, by the way."

The signal turned.

"When did you get to Seattle?" In the middle of First Street, I spun around, pointing my finger. "No, wait. How long have you been in this realm?" Half backward, I hopped on the curb.

"*Hallë, quessa. Emelasi coja muranildi juetera? Ne—*" *May we speak as muranildi now?*

"Twynolan!"

He tore his eyes away from the globe lights in the pergola behind me. Lips parted, he stared down at me wide-eyed.

"It's been a hundred and nineteen years since I've spoken *Aemirin.* I doubt I'm good enough to carry on a conversation. And I don't want humans to hear you speaking it. Speak English."

His smile dropped as he listened to me, his brows pinched. "What a shame. Our language is much more fluid." Twynolan brought his hand out from behind his back and reached out to me but stopped. He dropped his hand and licked his lips. "Very well, but give me one thing."

I cocked a hip and crossed my arms. "What?"

He leaned in. "Call me Nol," he said, voice lowered. "We are *muranildi*, are we not?"

Muranilde, our soulmate-like bond—which doesn't always equate to lovers. No, our bond went further. If one died, the other would follow within a decade. We felt hints of our past lives: lovers, we thought a parent and child one time, siblings two or three times, but mostly...lovers. This time around, if I hadn't left—

I swallowed hard as I realized where my thoughts had strayed. I turned away from him. I would not cry, refused to. This was my own doing, and I wouldn't wallow in self-pity.

"Hallë—"

I swallowed the lump in my throat. "Why? I'm *savilë*." My voice warbled and my eyes closed on their own.

"So? Calling each other by our *Muranilde* names has nothing to do with *Aeminan* laws."

A warm weight settled on my shoulder, but I didn't jump. His fingers squeezed gently. With our bond, closeness felt natural, comforting, even after so long, but no, I didn't deserve it. He tried to pull me back, as if the century apart didn't make us strangers. In this life, we were strangers. As *muranildi*, we weren't. Too much had changed.

The wind blew my hair into my face, and I tucked it back under my hat, itching where it had tickled my nose. I looked down at my feet and shook my head. "How can we be *muranildi*?" I pulled my arms tighter around myself. "You broke our bond."

He let go and dropped onto a bench under the pergola, muttering in *Aemirin* about stupidity. The absence of Twynolan's hand left me colder than before, and I shivered. "*Ai, Hallë lacar upastira.*" *You are still so stubborn.*

"Yeah? Well, it's kept me alive. If it's not broke, don't fix it." I sniffled. My nose was going numb.

He rested his hands on his stomach and dragged his feet under the seat. "Words cannot break the bond our Mother gave us and you know it. I was angry and hurt. Do you blame me?"

"Hell, no. I deserve what I got." But he had still broken my heart.

"No, you were too young. The punishment was too harsh for a child."

"I've made it this long." A cop car went by us up the hill.

"But at what cost?"

My throat tightened.

"They miss you. It was unfair—"

Twynolan's soft words brought me back around to face him. "Shut up! I *killed* them. I deserve this." I squeezed the cuffs of my sleeves until my fingers ached. If it hadn't been for the *Muranilde* bond, they would have sentenced me to death for killing with magic. "What in the realms is so bad that you'd risk asking for a *savilë's* help?" My voice broke at the end. I pressed my sleeve to my mouth. Did he even care how much his words hurt me? He lifted his head, and his lost look sent chills up my spine. "Wait, we need to go inside. My nose is about to fall off, it's so damn cold out here."

"You have at least five more minutes before that happens."

Smart-ass.

He smiled wide enough that his dimple showed, and I couldn't help but smile back. Between one blink and the next, he was standing beside me. I squared my shoulders and stepped away from him. How the hell had he gotten so fast?

"Amazing how quickly we are becoming familiar again, yes? See? *Muranildi.*"

"You're so full of shit. I don't know you at all anymore." Or what he was hiding.

He shrugged. "That will change."

My eyes narrowed. "Why? How long are you staying?"

"As long as this takes, but you said you wanted to go inside?"

Oh, yeah.

As we walked out from under the Pioneer Square Pergola, he matched his steps with mine. His arm brushed my arm. When I moved over to give us more space, he moved over, too. The little shit. Telling him to knock it off would only encourage him.

Along with the frosty air that filled my lungs, the scent of home invaded my senses: our realm's ancient trees, similar to Earth's redwoods, but bigger, and the fragrant clove and orange scent of the blossoms near his parents' house. To keep from breathing in the smell, I held my breath and sped up. The blossoms brought back happy childhood memories that were buried so deep I never dreamed about them. Damn. Just as I had started to calm down, too.

"Hallë…" Twynolan drew out my name. Before I got even six steps away, he grabbed my hand. I jerked back, but his warm fingers wrapped around my cold ones. "What is wrong?"

"Nothing." I shook my head.

He tipped his chin down, and arched his eyebrow, challenging that single word. There was no fooling him. I let the hurt fill my eyes, and he stopped.

"Come on. I need coffee, and you can tell me what the hell is going on."

Since he refused to release my hand, I pulled on him until we were moving again.

"The explanation will be difficult to discuss."

"And that's why I need coffee."

2

THE HIGH-PITCHED WHIR OF the coffee grinder filled the stairwell in the Pioneer Building. The smoky aroma wrapped around me as we walked through the door of my favorite coffee shop: an old, eclectic, laid-back place where customers could chat or sit alone. Pictures of old Seattle throughout the years covered the walls, as did local musicians: The Wailers, Jimi Hendrix, and Nirvana, to name a few. They let pets in here for Pete's sake!

Twynolan tightened his grip on my hand and refused to walk farther than the entrance. With a final tug, my shoulder was against his chest. He glanced at me, looked up and around, licked his lips, and swallowed.

"You want to talk in here?" he whispered while gripping the doorframe.

I almost felt bad for him. Almost. He deserved this and more for coming to me.

"Yep. Let's go."

Grounding his teeth, he gave the room one more scan. "Very well."

We weaved through the tables, passing the couch where two young people sat with their dog, enjoying their drinks and each other. A study group gathered around the largest table. Books, papers, and laptops were scattered all over the top. Perfect. The loud patrons and the espresso machine would drown out our conversation.

The far-left table in the back was wobbly and no one seemed to like the dark corner except me. I'd brought my ex here to break up with him so he wouldn't make a scene. My coat slid across the table, and I turned to get in line. Two young women walked in the door, talking and paying no attention to anyone.

"What are we doing?"

"*I* am getting coffee before I listen to your bullshit. *You* are crashing into my life with no regard to the repercussions I could face if you act like yourself and get noticed."

Twynolan blanched and crossed his arms. "I do not get noticed."

I stared up at him. He couldn't sneak his way out of a deaf and blind man's house.

"You always do, either from your clumsiness or your annoyingly magnetic charisma." I left him pouting at our table to get in line before the two new girls sidled up there.

"Not unless I want to be noticed." Twynolan bumped my shoulder as he lengthened his steps to beat me to the line.

"Fan-freaking-tastic," I muttered.

One of the students at the study table let out a high-pitched laugh as I walked by. Another threw a paper wad at a third. Distracted by the kids' outbursts, I walked right into Twynolan. My hand came out to catch myself and settled on his back. His leather jacket, worn and well used, was still cold from the freezing February night.

We both teetered forward but didn't fall in a heap. I stared up at him, dumbfounded. The students laughed, and he looked over my head at them. His dimpled half smile peeked out. Tipping his chin down, he met my eyes, proud of himself.

"See, I am not so clumsy now, am I?" he murmured in *Aemirin*.

He used to stumble over nothing as a kid because his muscles were always playing catch-up. Stepping back, I pushed off him, a small part of me hoping he'd topple over. No such luck.

Righting ourselves, I looked ahead to Nettie, the usual night barista, taking the drink orders of the customers ahead of us. I jumped when Twynolan leaned in to be heard over the espresso machine. "What is a mocha?" He pronounced mocha with the "cha" sound.

"It's a mocha," I said, emphasizing the hard "c."

His brow furrowed as he considered my correction. Leaning over again, his jacket brushed my cheek, and I breathed in the spicy smell of *Aeminan* leather conditioning oil. Without permission, my father's smiling face surfaced from way down in my memory.

"But I learned the c-h produces a *cha* sound in the English language."

His words wiped the image away. I uncrossed my arms and shoved them in my pockets. Damn him. The two ladies behind us giggled, and when I glanced back, I knew they had heard our discussion. Great.

I turned to face Twynolan, still leaning over. He smirked. My breath hitched at his roguish expression. I was sure he did that to all the girls. It might have worked for a second, but I saw through it. I cleared my throat and lifted my chin, refusing to back down. Still close to me, his face fell, and then he gave me an unguarded smile, which was far more attractive than the trying-too-hard look.

"So?"

What had we been talking about? Mochas, right. I looked ahead of us instead of at his too close face. Why was he making this awkward? "There are many exceptions to the rules."

He stood there silent, as if waiting for something. I glanced at him. Did he want me to give him an English lesson here?

He tilted his head. "But what is it?"

Oh right, that. I huffed. "Coffee with chocolate and milk. Would you like to try that?"

The espresso machine screamed. "Do you like it?" His face stayed near my ear to be heard over the noise.

"Sometimes." I raised my voice instead of turning.

The leather oil, combined with the smell of the coffee beans, had a vertiginous effect. I wondered if I could ever smell coffee again without thinking of *Endae*. Irritated with myself or him or the situation, I started tapping my foot. "Why not something simple, a black coffee, and if it's too strong, you can add stuff to it."

"What kind of milk is in a mocha?" Again with the mocha!

I closed my eyes and counted backward from ten. Couldn't he just go away, leave me to my exile, and stop reminding me of how I'd lost everything? Was that too much to ask?

"Am I annoying you?"

"Very much so."

"I am very sorry," he teased.

"No, you're not. You're acting like a child because I brought you here and won't let you meet my friends."

He huffed. "Fine. Black coffee."

Surprised by his snippy answer, I opened my eyes to check on him. Had I pissed him off? Why did it matter? He rocked up onto his toes with his wrists clasped behind his back. His damn dimple showed with his "gotcha" grin.

"Your dimple is showing," I said.

He shifted and almost covered his cheek before realizing what he was doing. He pouted for a second. Another point for me! I stepped up to the counter before he could say anything.

"Hey, Nettie."

"Hi," Nettie said, as perky as can be. She really was perky most of the time. Her Cookie Monster-blue nails clicked on the counter. She jutted her thumb at Twynolan and wiggled her eyebrows. "He's new." While her flirting was always over the top, Nettie was a keeper. To her, all kids were munchkins and deserved free cookies. Plus, her grandkids were adorable.

"Yep, and you'll never see him again."

Nettie stuck her lip out at Twynolan while fluttering her mascara-caked eyelashes at us—mostly Twynolan. "What can I getcha?"

"A twelve ounce dirty chai latte, breve, and an eight-ounce decaf drip for him." Who knew what he'd do on caffeine? Nettie gave Twynolan one last look, which might have held a hint of sympathy. I dropped my change into their tip jar.

"Why did you do that?" Twynolan whispered, his chin touching my shoulder.

"It's a tip. When you feel they've done a good job, that's how you show them."

"Does she not get paid? That is what they do here. Yes? They use currency?"

He knew the answer. If Twynolan's English was any indication, he'd spent some time around humans, and he was nothing if not observant.

"No—" I paused before using his nickname—again. "Twynolan, stop. Do this shit on your own time, with someone who'll believe your naivety."

"Own time? They believe you can own time in this realm?" he whispered again, though not as close anymore.

I turned and gave him a flat look.

Twynolan smiled and tapped my nose as he had done when we were kids. I covered my face and laughed.

He came close again. "*Esmë'a, ësmem tiar dunyairi'ar äsanë mico naura.*" *My dear, I love to watch your eyes shine when you laugh.*

That made me stop laughing as I tried to work through the possibly intimate sentence. *Esmë* depended on the rest of the sentence to determine how close they'd meant the endearment. Twynolan waited, eyes bright and mischievous, as he saw me working it out.

"Not funny," I grumbled as we went to the other end of the counter to wait. "And quit talking in *Aemirin*."

"I find this quite entertaining, actually." He pulled my hat up and gently pinched my ear. "Your ears are red. You should practice your *Aemirin* and you may figure it out."

I swatted at his hand, then tucked my ear back under my hat. He'd never teased me like this before. Many things were different now.

The barista made a fern leaf in my foam. Usually, the cute coffee art cheered me up, but tonight the leaf reminded me of *Endae*. I snatched Twynolan's drink without thinking, and the coffee burned my fingers through the paper. I gasped as my fingers let go of the lidless cup. In slow motion, a hand dove and plucked the cup out of the air before it hit the floor. Without spilling a drop.

"Whoa, dude. Nice reflexes," one of the students called out.

The world came back to life. Murmurs of conversations. The espresso machine.

Twynolan held his coffee out, all proud of himself, his head two sizes bigger thanks to the kid's compliment. Jeez. That must have been a spell. No one was that fast. I bit my tongue. He'd saved the coffee from scalding my legs, so I let it slide.

Lesson learned, I grabbed two paper sleeves and headed to the condiment table. Twynolan leaned over my shoulder to see what I was doing. My elbow connected with his stomach to make him move. Out of the corner of my eye, I saw his hand sprawling out to grab the wooden stir sticks. All of them.

"Twynolan!" I slapped his hand away before he touched them.

He lifted his chin, daring me. Right. What could I do about it besides complain?

A middle-aged lady beside me laughed. I checked to see what was so funny and realized she was laughing at us. "Good luck, honey." She laughed again as she walked away. "Least he's cute."

Beside me, Twynolan chuckled. I elbowed him again, and he grunted. His eyes lingered on the students we passed. As we sat down at our table, he was listening in on their conversation.

"You know it's rude to do that, right?" I took my first sip of yummy, delicious coffee—the best type of therapy.

He looked at me, eyebrows high. "Do what?"

I tipped my head toward the kids.

Twynolan twisted his cup around and pressed his lid down. "If they wanted their conversation to be private, they should have picked a private place."

Hint, hint? Whatever. "You have until I finish my coffee."

Twynolan continued to mess with his cup. "I do not know what—"

"You know damn well what it means. Start talking."

"Hallë, please stop being so hostile." He leaned closer to me. "I've been trying to lighten your mood this entire time, yet you won't calm down," he spoke low in *Aemirin*. "You said you'd listen, yet you've formed your opinions prior to what I must say. How can you give my circumstances an unbiased consideration if you won't lower your defenses?"

I took a swig of my coffee. "English, Twynolan." Was I hostile? Did I want to gouge his eyes out? No. But his presence hurt, and no amount of teasing would make it better. Even if messing with me in line reminded me of old times.

Twynolan huffed and sat up straight. "*Ai, quturode racar omeya'a.*" *Ai, you're a pain in my ass,* he muttered.

"Not as much as you are in mine," I touted our normal comeback to each other, in English.

Amused, as I took another sip. Twynolan sank down and folded his hands over his stomach. Sitting like that, he looked more human.

I tapped my fingers on the table. "Well?"

His smile dropped, and the familiar crease formed between his eyebrows. I used to smooth that crease out with my thumb when he got upset.

"I looked through your artwork. You are very talented."

"Twynolan."

"I never imagined you would be an artist like your mother."

My eyes narrowed. "What do you want?"

He dropped his eyes to the table. "More time? To have a pleasant conversation with my *muranildë—*"

"Knock it off."

"One which does not involve such dire circumstances."

"Twy—"

A heartbeat later, he was leaning over the table, an inch from my face. His eyes grew colder, harder. All the playfulness had left him. No emotion. "For you to stop calling me Twynolan. I will continue to annoy you if you will not call me Nol. We are *muranildi.*"

My body tensed, the hair on the back of my neck stood up, and I started shaking. His words weren't threatening, but the dead look in his eyes scared me. Twynolan's stare broke. Life crept back into him. His eyes softened as he roamed my face, and then they lowered to my hands around my cup.

"Hallë," he breathed. Making no sudden movements, he settled back into his chair. His arms slid off the table. In hushed *Aemirin,* he continued rambling, "I...I'm sorry. I didn't mean to startle you. Please, forgive me."

We sat in silence. The sounds of the café filtered into my awareness. His eyes flashed up to look at me, then back to his lap. I don't know how long we sat there with the sounds of the café dividing us. For one small moment, my *muranildo* had frightened me.

"I just..." He swallowed hard. "I need to hear...Our bond goes beyond this lifetime." He scowled. "You do not understand. People talk about it as if what happened was some romantic tragedy. They do not understand what the *Muranilde* bond is for us. People say Hallë and Nol, and I hate it. Those are our names for each other, not theirs. They do not know who we were lifetimes ago."

"You told me I was dead to you."

"I know."

"You told me never to call you Nol again and broke our bond." Which was impossible, but the statement had broken me. "I can't—" My throat constricted, and I looked away. The lady from the condiment table sat two tables away from us, drinking her coffee and reading a book.

"Please? I have missed you."

His words brought my head around. He *missed* me? How could he say that? I had no one here and he had everyone. I missed my parents, my friends...the schoolmates I killed. Why did he have to come here? My eyes welled and my throat closed up.

He reached for my hands, laced together in front of my coffee, but I pulled them back before he grabbed them. Yet not fast enough that I didn't feel his calloused palms on my knuckles. The quick movement made a tear fall. No more. I rubbed my hands together in my lap. Since when did a scholar have calluses?

"Hallë—" He sighed, his voice just loud enough for me to hear above the murmur of conversations around us.

I didn't need his pity, and I didn't need him. "I've worked hard to forget everything over there. Calling you..." I swallowed. "I can't. And if you won't accept that, we're done here."

He held up his hand to stop me. "No. Please. I will not ask again."

"Fine, but I'm halfway done with my coffee." A slight exaggeration. "I'm serious. The truth."

Twynolan rolled his shoulders. His eyes darted around the shop, then settled on me. "A mage who escaped from prison in *Atrau* has run to this realm."

Atrau, the capital of *Aemina*, in *Endae*. "What does that have to do with me?"

"She has killed thousands of our people and she has come here looking for you."

A chill ran through me. So many questions ran through my head, but I couldn't decide which one to ask first. "Are you sure?"

"Yes."

"Do you think she's here to kill me?"

"I do not think so." He licked his lips. "I believe—"

"You don't think I've talked to her, do you? Or that I'm hiding her? Does *Aemina* think that?"

"No—"

"So, you're here to warn me about her?"

"Yes, I—"

"Are there *Zayuri* here? Is your uncle here? Is he going to come talk to me?" His uncle was a high-ranking officer of the *Zayuri*, the most honorable league in our realm. Think bounty hunter with a samurai twist. Almost everything about them was a mystery. Oh, and his uncle was scary as shit.

"No, Hallë, please stop asking questions. Aswryn is powerful. Not like you, but she is very dangerous. If you come in contact with her, you cannot trust her."

"Okay, but if she escaped and came here, why aren't the *Zayuri* here to apprehend her? It's not like they'd send *you* to fetch her." Twynolan would prefer to research a fugitive rather than help catch one. "Wait."

If he'd discovered somehow that this mage, Aswryn, had fled here, and no one believed him, it would be just like him to come himself to prove them all wrong. "Does your uncle even know? Or did you figure it out and come here on your own?"

While Twynolan had inherited the magic of his *Zayuri* family, he'd vowed never to become one. No matter how much his uncle and mother pressured him.

"My uncle knows, I swear." He fidgeted. Not a lie, but there was something he wasn't telling me. "After she escaped, I saw her vanish, and because I know her *imolegin*, I followed her here."

I swallowed, the coffee turning sour on my tongue. None of this made any sense. "What the hell? Why would he let you come here without him? And how do you know this mage's *imolegin*?" Sure anyone could feel magic, but identifying someone's magical signature required time together.

"That is for another conversation once you agree to help me and when we are out of here."

"If." I held my finger up. "Hang on, what do you mean, she vanished? You need a *meril* to travel." Not even I could travel—before I blocked my magic— without an amulet.

He exhaled slowly, annoyed that I'd interrupted again, but I couldn't help it. "Also for another conversation."

I took a long drink of my coffee, glaring at him over the lid. How many "other conversations" did he think we'd have? The pain in the ass knew how to scare the crap out of me, though. And I couldn't stand how vague he was being, damn it.

"Okay then, why do you think this asshat's looking for me?"

He tilted his head. "What is an asshat?"

I pursed my lips. "You gonna answer my questions, or what?"

Twynolan's expression grew distant as he focused on his stirrer spinning on its own. The stupid genius. I clamped my hand on top of his cup, the stick trapped between my fingers.

"What do you think you're doing? I told you no magic, and that includes Sandra Bullock impressions with your damn coffee."

Twynolan frowned, his cinnamon eyebrows pinched. "I—I am sorry. I did not realize—"

"Of course you didn't." I sighed, letting his cup go. He was a genius, but that came with annoying habits, like zoning out while deep in thought. "Just be mindful of your actions."

"I will. I am sorry." He inhaled as if to speak, but instead took his first sip of coffee and then sputtered it out. "*Ai*! This is disgusting."

My head shot up, and customers' heads turned our way. At the scowl on his face as he brushed coffee off his jacket, I burst out laughing.

"It is not that funny."

I wiped the moisture from my eyes. Taking pity on him, I waved my hand toward the front. "Go get some cream and sugar. It'll help."

He kept scowling at me like the coffee's bitter taste was my fault.

My snickering stopped when he stepped in front of me. I leaned my head back. "What?"

"*Dunyairi'ar carasanën.*" *Your eyes are shining.* He arched an eyebrow, the mischief in his eyes again.

I wrinkled my nose at his smug face. The ass.

"Yeah, well, your dimple is showing."

His hand shot out, and he thumped my nose.

I growled and covered it. "Do not start that. We aren't kids anymore."

Since we were little he'd thumped my nose, claiming he was just trying to help me get rid of my dreaded freckles. Twynolan knew I hated my dark freckles and green eyes, so different from everyone else. That and I looked exactly like my grandmother and wielded the same magic as her—again, different from all other *endai*.

Twynolan and I had been in each other's lives since I was born, and countless lives before this one. He knew who I used to be, not who I'd become.

I propped my chin on my palm and waited for him to fix his coffee. People stared at him as he walked by. Could they tell he wasn't human? No. They watched him because he kept his head held high, even though he'd spilled coffee all over his front.

What was I doing? We weren't here to catch up. I needed to find out why this person was here looking for me, or at least why he thought so. He'd called her Aswryn? Why was she killing *Aeminani*? Why was she in this realm? Or at least why did he think she was after me? I hated to admit it, but Twynolan was usually right, but he was being so vague! I checked on him across the café.

My ex-best friend had grown so much. He'd always been tall, lanky, and clumsy. Well, he was not clumsy anymore, as he'd demonstrated earlier. As a matured adult, filled out and all, I saw a fair amount of his mother's and father's sides. His hair color, lean muscles, and height were from his mother's side and so much like his uncle. He also had his father's broad shoulders, smile, and sense of humor. But that damn ability to go from sly smirk to trusting smile—that was all his own.

"Is everything all right?"

Twynolan stood in front of me. I straightened and blinked a few times to get my head back into the here and now. When had he come back?

"Oh, um...just lost in thought." About a murderous mage here, the possibility of *Zayuri* showing up at my house, nothing big. I paused. "You're not keeping a low profile with that coffee stunt you pulled."

He grimaced, then lifted his hand about chest high and made a small gesture like flicking a bug. The humans who were still staring looked away. I refused to argue; he'd done it to irritate me.

"There." Once he sat, Twynolan took a small sip of his coffee. "Better. I might try that mocha later." Again with the *cha*.

Pain in the ass.

"So..." I urged him to continue.

"Yes?" He blinked.

He took a hesitant sip. Nothing. Another sip.

After too many minutes—okay, more like seconds—of silence, my patience broke. "Fine." I closed my eyes. "I'm sorry for laughing at you, okay?"

He kept drinking, all calm and collected. I squeezed my cup to restrain myself from yanking the thing out of his hands.

"All right, you are forgiven."

I prayed for patience. "So, why?"

"You know the answer. Stop and think."

"I don't want to think. I want you to tell me why she's after me."

"Come now, there is no other *enda* more powerful than you."

I rolled my eyes. He and I both knew that wasn't true. My magic was different, more organic—and gone. That last part wasn't his business, though. Was my magic strong? Yes. Most powerful? I doubted that. But maybe this Aswryn person believed the rumors and thought I was the most powerful *enda*.

"That's not—"

"The way you and your grandmother can wield magic without spells or *merili* gives you...opportunity? Yes that is the word, an opportunity no other *enda* has. You have freedom, without—" He licked his lips, trying to find his English words. "—learning how to—"

"You don't need to explain my own magic to me. Yes, we don't need to learn spells, but that doesn't mean we can do anything we want. We still have to understand the process of what we want our magic to accomplish." That was why I found casting spells that other *endai* created so difficult.

He pressed his lips together. "Yes?" He drew out the word. "That is why I came to you. Her vanishing is a problem with all *endai*—"

My stomach dropped.

He held up his hand, eyebrows going high when he saw my expression. "And with Aswryn looking for you—her biggest mistake ever—you can...stop her."

If Aswryn had killed people, her sentence was death. Our *Muranilde* bond was the only reason I was still alive—banished and alone, but alive. I began to put two and two together, and I wasn't liking four. My thumb rubbed across the worn down etched names in the metal tag of my old bracelet.

As always, it grounded me. I forced myself to exhale and started counting: *one, two, three, inhale.* The couple with the dog was leaving. *Four, five, six, exhale.* Nettie laughed at something, the espresso machine screamed again, and nothing was calming me.

Every fiber of my being wanted to scream, to jump across the table and slap him. Looking at him without reacting was impossible, so I focused on my bracelet. Hundreds of possible responses bounced around my mind. None of them were nice.

"Hallë? Did you hear me?" Twynolan asked once I reached twenty.

"You're both here because I'm *savilë.*"

"No—"

"You want me to kill her, don't you? What better person to do it. I mean, I've killed with magic once already. What's one more? You know the damn *Zayuri* assassinate *endai* all the fucking time. Do you see any of them getting banished? No."

Twynolan stiffened, emotionless as I bashed his uncle and those like him. "The *Zayuri*—"

"This is bullshit." I had to whisper or I'd scream. "I vowed never to use my magic on another person again. *Ever.* I can't believe you—"

"That is not what I said." He reached across the table and touched my arm. I jerked away.

"No." I stood and grabbed my jacket off the chair.

"*C'yo, Hallë nas nú*—"

"English."

He shoved his hair back in frustration. "Aswryn will come, and I—"

"I'll deal with her in my own way." I clenched my teeth. "Non-lethally."

"*Ai,* I must have said this wrong. Please be patient with me?"

A quick glance around the shop assured me that no one had noticed our argument. His spell still held, small as it was. All of them were completely oblivious to their surroundings. In my peripheral vision, Twynolan's arm moved to smooth down the front of his jacket. He lifted his head and saw me watching him.

"Hallë—"

"Don't." I held up my hand to stop him. "Stay away from me, Twynolan."

I turned on my heel and left him at the table. Before I got halfway across the room, my best friends, Mateo and his fiancé, Sam, walked in. Twynolan came up behind me, and my friends blocked my exit. Tables and chairs were to my left, and the counter was to my right. Trapped. Great.

"Ha, I told you she'd be here, Sam." Mateo grabbed Sam's coat sleeve and shook it. They took all of five steps to get to where I stood glued to the floor.

Mateo left Sam's side and wrapped his arms around my stiff shoulders. Cold water droplets from his black coat wet my cheek; at his five foot ten, my chin didn't reach his shoulders. His expensive aftershave mingled with his mousse, creating the scent that was Mateo. He pushed on my shoulders and gently shook me. "I knew you'd be here."

"Sam? Seriously?" I looked at the reasonable, down-to-earth one of the pair.

Sam shoved his hands into his brown wool coat and shrugged. His golden curls brushed his olive-green scarf and his cheeks turned rosier by the second. "Sorry, Hally. I kept him back for as long as I could, but he wouldn't stop until we came. You know how it goes."

Yeah, I knew.

"Don't be so negative." Mateo looked behind me, and his rich brown eyes locked on Twynolan's pale blue ones. "And you must be her *old friend*." He let me go, stepped back, and hooked Sam's arm.

"Guys, this isn't—"

"And you must be the friends Hallë did not want me to meet." Twynolan's arm brushed mine as he stepped in close behind me.

Mateo reached his hand out and grabbed Twynolan's. "I'm Mateo Sanders and this is my partner, Sam Decker."

"Hello." Twynolan began, but Mateo didn't stop.

"I love your accent. Are you from France, too? I bet you are. You gotta tell us all your stories about Hally. All we know is what Charlie tells us, and you know how . . ."

"Mateo—" I muttered.

"...she's always working. So are you going to introduce him or what, Hally?"

"You need to give her a chance to talk first, dear." Sam nudged his partner, then brushed his hand through the back of Mateo's short black hair.

"He's not my friend."

"My name is Nolan. We did not part on good terms, so I knew this was the only way for Hallë to talk to me."

"I love how you say her name. So much softer. Isn't it, honey? Ha-lay." Mateo softened the beginning as Twynolan did, but the end was too harsh.

Sam nodded, but Mateo didn't notice.

"It was a slip. She asked me to call her Hally—sorry. The name is...hard for me."

"How long are you here for? Maybe we could meet up somewhere tomorrow."

"No, Mateo," I said as Twynolan said, "Sure!"

"No." I turned and glared up at Twynolan. "We're done. I am leaving. Without you."

The crease between his eyebrows appeared as he frowned. "Hal-lë—Hally, please?"

Sam said Mateo's name, and I turned back to them. He had his hand on his partner's shoulder, looking up at him. "Let's leave them be." Sam flipped a loose curl off his glasses as he twisted to look at me. "Sorry, guys. We thought it would be fun to crash the party."

"Don't worry, Sam. In fact, do you guys mind giving me a ride?"

Sam's hazel eyes grew intense with concern. "Yeah, we—we can do that."

"As for you." I pointed at Twynolan's chest, my teeth clenched. "Don't come near me again."

His lips parted as he realized I was serious. My friends moved to let me pass. Once down the stairs, I went to pull on the front door, but it didn't budge. Above me, Twynolan's hand kept the door closed.

I stared at the door. "Let go."

"Hallë, please understand, Aswryn is...*C'yo*! Dangerous and—" He grumbled another swear in *Aemirin*.

Someone made a shushing noise. Behind us, Sam, stoic and hard to read, stood on the lowest step. Mateo, on the next step up, held onto the railing, worrying his bottom lip between his teeth.

My attention returned to the *endao* blocking my escape. "Move."

"Nolan." Sam came over and touched Twynolan's arm. "I'm sorry, but you need to let her go."

The two of them locked eyes for a beat. Twynolan's shoulders slumped, and he gave me a forlorn look and dropped his arm. I yanked the door open and hurried out.

"She killed An'di, Hallë." Twynolan's words echoed around Pioneer Square.

I'd reached the trees in the Square before his words froze me.

"That is why I am doing this."

I turned and stormed toward him, while Mateo and Sam stayed in the doorway, stunned. They'd never seen me so angry.

I pointed at Twynolan. "You don't get to come over here and lay that on me. I am *savilë*. None of you care about me. Why should I care about any of you?"

"You do not care about An'di?" His voice trembled. Fucking A, he was telling the truth. That bitch had killed his big sister.

"Of course I..." With my throat tight, I had to focus on keeping my words steady. "I'm sorry for your loss, but I've left that world behind me. I can't." I shook my head, pressing my lips together.

"Hallë, please?"

I squeezed my eyes tight as his voice broke. Mother help me, but I needed to end this. "Revenge never solves anything. Let your uncle find Aswryn."

My eyes sprang open when a warm hand touched my shoulder. "Come on, Hally. I'll take you home." Mateo's gentle voice was my undoing, and I turned away so Twynolan couldn't read the lie on my face.

3

"Never?" Mateo asked.

"No," I said, laughing. "We were only ever friends. I swear." Somehow, no matter what, Mateo always made me feel better. He refused to accept that my childhood relationship with Twynolan had been strictly platonic. I shifted my hips, and the slight movement made my bedroom hammock swing.

"Why the hell not?"

"We were kids, for one. Second, we never felt that way. There are such things as close platonic friendships with the opposite sex."

Mateo tucked his pillow farther under him and propped his chin on his palms. He'd messed up my bed, wrinkled all the blankets, and pulled out both pillows. His *Legend of Zelda* socks tapped on my headboard.

The metal tag on my bracelet flashed in the moonlight shining through my window and onto my hammock. My thumb brushed the engraved name, worn with age but still distinguishable. I dropped my arm, and the bracelet dipped into the darkness that was most of my bedroom. Like my life, such a small part lived in the light. I sighed. If Twynolan was right and Aswryn had found me, she could expose everything.

"Are you sure you don't wanna give this guy a chance? I mean..." He waggled his eyebrows.

"Mateo! Knock it off." I threw one of my little pillows at him. It missed the bed and landed on the floor. "He yelled across the Square that his sister was dead. Why would that warrant a chance?"

"I bet that was just as hard for him to tell you as it was for you to hear it."

"Yeah," I whispered.

"You should call him," he whispered back.

"I told you, I don't want him in my life."

"Life's too short for grudges." Mateo knew what he was talking about. His family was full of them. He reached behind him and pulled out his phone. The artificial light paled his brown complexion and darkened everything around him.

"What are you doing?"

Instead of answering me, Mateo put his phone to his ear. He tapped his fingers on his pillow. "Hey, honey, did you, by chance, get his phone number?"

"His phone number?" I asked, throwing my blanket off, but my legs got tangled as I stood. The hammock swung, and I flipped onto my face with an "oof."

Mateo plugged his other ear. "Okay. What time did you end up leaving him?"

I froze, still tangled in blanket. To have left him implied he had been with him at a previous point in time. Fan-freaking-tastic.

"Okay, I'll tell her. No, she's feeling better. All right. Love you, too." Mateo looked at his phone and pursed his lips.

"Sam talked to him?"

"They talked for an hour. I am supposed to tell you Nolan likes mochas." Mateo chuckled after saying *mochas* with the *cha*. He got off my bed and tugged on the hem of his designer shirt.

"What the hell? Why would you two go behind my back like that?"

"Sam stayed to make sure he didn't follow you."

My shoulders dropped, and I looked down at my feet, half in shadow. I was so screwed.

"Nolan's staying in Seattle for the week. He told Sam you'd know how to get a hold of him. The person Nolan is looking for sounds like bad news. If Nolan's as gentle as you say, he might be in over his head. You should talk to him before he picks a fight."

I scoffed and rolled my eyes. "Twynolan couldn't fight his way out of a cardboard box."

He raised his dark eyebrows. "Exactly." Mateo grabbed my shoulders and gently shook me. "I know you. If your old friend ended up in a ditch somewhere, you'd be devastated."

My body went cold as visions of him dead in a ditch played in my head. There would be no way to tell his parents or bring his body home. His parents had lost one child already. Twynolan needed to let the *Zayuri* handle this.

Mateo kissed my temple, pulling me out of my thoughts. "Think about it, 'kay?"

I nodded and followed him out of my room.

The hushed silence in the upstairs hall felt eerie yet fitting for tonight. The creak of a board echoed around the wide-open hallway when Mateo stepped in the wrong place. I would have laughed at the look on his face if it hadn't been for my sleeping roommates, Charlie and her daughter, Ray. They were also my adopted nieces.

Everyone used the back door—well, everyone we knew. Mateo and I slid our shoes on and grabbed our coats. My fingers brushed the cold keys in my pocket, jingling them as I hesitated. There was no reason to lock up the house. We were only walking to Mateo's car. Habit won, and I locked the door.

On the porch, the frigid air took the breath from my lungs, reminding me of earlier. I ground my teeth. Mateo walked ahead of me, animated about something. The nerve of Twynolan asking me to kill someone.

"So what do you think?" Mateo's question pulled me out of my head.

"Oh, sure." I hoped that was the right answer to whatever Mateo had been talking about. I knew better than that.

He nudged my side. "Hally, were you even listening?"

Frosty, exhaust-tainted air filled our lungs as we walked out of my backyard into the alley behind my house on North Beacon Hill. "No. I'm sorry. Lost in thought."

"I'll forgive you. Tonight's been a little overwhelming. So, about Sam's birthday present, you already know I'm getting him that suit we saw—"

"No!" I came around in front of him. "I told you to get the watch he didn't get for Christmas."

Mateo winked. "Gotcha."

I laughed and tapped his arm. "Thanks."

"No probs, *ojitos*. Christ, it's cold out here. The car seems ten times farther away when it's this cold." He blew into his cupped hands as we walked.

Mateo had parked at the end of the alley since every parking spot was taken, all the good humans tucked into bed. Most of our neighbors owned at least two cars and parked them behind their homes instead of in their garages, thus no guest parking. I didn't have one. Garage, I mean.

"Yeah, just make sure you're careful driving home, okay?"

"Why is it you sound more like a mom than Charlie?"

I laughed. "It's all in your head."

The Crayola-yellow lights of Mateo's car flashed against a fence as he unlocked his sedan. He leaned his arm on the doorframe. "Want me to drive you back?"

"We're like five houses away!" I nudged him. "Get in your car, you big baby. Tell Samuel he's on my list. I know he means well, but I can't, I just can't deal with...Nolan."

"I'm sure he knows he's in trouble. Shit, it's cold. Bye, Hally."

He ducked into his car and shut the door. I waved as the bright red taillights disappeared around the corner. What was with this Aswryn person? Well, if she did find me, she was going to be disappointed. My magic was gone. No magic, no power. I shivered and shoved my hands into my coat pockets.

My mind kept going back to An'di. She'd been as much a big sister to me as to Twynolan. He was right. I could never be mad at her. The day they banished me, An'di hadn't even been at home.

The sound of my shoes scraping the icy cement brought me back to the present. I kicked a bottle cap toward a dumpster. A loud crash from across the alley made me jump. A few raccoons chittered from the same direction, and one fat raccoon ran out in front of me. To my disgrace, I yipped and jumped backward as the thing ran past me. After a few deep breaths, I laughed at myself. At least no one had witnessed my not-so-brave moment.

Then a voice echoed around me. "*Hallanevaë, rei fayib luba.*" *The stars guide us together tonight.*

A shock ran through me. Once again, Twynolan was right. I swallowed my rising panic and answered in *Aemirin* as best I could.

"The star...path is bright tonight." I turned a slow circle in search of her to no avail. "Who are you?" My voice wavered with my uncertain *Aemirin.*

"I seek an audience with you to discuss a vital matter in *Aemina.*"

Her voice seemed to come from everywhere. My heart raced. "*Aeminan* matters don't concern me. I'm *savilë.*" Yeah, good going, Hally. That would fix the problem. I'd told Twynolan I could handle this, and I would, damn it. But how? I wouldn't kill her. Death is not a punishment. Living a long, lonely life knowing you failed is a damn good punishment, I'll clue ya.

"A plague has ravaged our people. They are sick and dying—"

A plague? That's not what Twynolan had said. "They are all dead to me. You will not sway my...decision. Leave me alone." I started walking away, but I didn't know where to go. Not home. That would be stupid.

"Hallanevaë, stop."

A wave of nausea doubled me over. An acidic smell stung my nostrils. "What are you doing to me?" My words vibrated in my head. I was going to be sick.

"Nothing. I have only checked my ward so the humans can't detect us."

"You're doing something to make me sick, and that doesn't bode well for you." That sounded right, hopefully.

"I swear, the only spell I have done is my ward. Will you permit me to come close and examine you?"

"Not on your fucking life." Oops, that was English. "Stay away from me." Back to *Aemirin*.

"I can't aid you if you won't allow me to help."

"Did I ask for your help?"

"Fair, I suppose," she conceded.

"How do you know I won't lash out and kill you? I have nothing to lose."

"I believe you care about your family's health and well-being. And your own."

"Are you threatening me?"

"Not at all. As I said, people are getting sick. If your *muranildo* dies, you die, too. So this is also self-preservation."

She had me there. My senses were out of whack. Aswryn said my name again, and her voice bounced around in my head, jumping off my eardrums like a trampoline.

"The *Amura Ore* claim the plague is a curse I created." The plot thickens. Why didn't my *muranildo* tell me any of this? Who was lying, or was the truth somewhere in the middle? "I believe the *Amura Ore* sent a *Zayuri* to speak with you. I am sure they have told you conflicting information about me."

But she messed up, skewing her facts. The *Zayuri* didn't follow our government's orders. They *would* follow the royal family when called upon, however. Aswryn should have known I knew this. *Keep it together, Hally.*

I started to shake my head but stopped and held my head to keep my brain from sloshing around. "No *Zayuri* has come to me." My *muranildo*, not any *Zayuri*. I prayed my half-truth would convince her I knew nothing.

"Very well." She sounded confused. As the seconds ticked by, I began to doubt she believed me. "They have sent the *Zayuri* to hunt me, but killing me will solve nothing. This is a cursed plague of epic proportions, and the *Amura Ore* wants to use it to destroy me."

"What did you do to piss them off?"

"I was born, and I am powerful. Stronger than them. Sound familiar?"

"They bred me to be strong." I swallowed and tried to focus. "They used my grandparents to get my level of magic, but I'm not what they expected."

"And they got rid of you for it."

"No. They got rid of me because I killed my friends. Their plan was to marry me off and keep trying to create the perfect puppet."

"And you were going to stop that, weren't you? Join the *Amura Ore* and destroy them from within."

"I was going to work within the system to change their range of power."

She laughed. "Is that what you told everyone? Come with me, Hallanevaë. We will—"

"What is it you think I could do? Even if I could help you, how do I know what you claim is true? You expect me to believe you on..." What was the word? "...good faith? With nothing to support your claim. Leave me to my exile."

The streetlights began pulsing. Wet, cold metal touched my thigh—the black van three houses down from mine. My hand rested on the ice-crusted hood, and I sank down to sit on the bumper. Water seeped through my pants. A loud crunch on the cement came from my right, but the lights were still too bright for me to see anything.

Hands grasped my shoulders and gently pushed me back against the van. "You're getting worse." Her *endaen* eyes reflected amber in the streetlight. If I squinted, Aswryn stayed still. Sunken yellow orbs stared at me from mere inches away. She had a harsh look about her. Dark taupe skin and wrinkles, probably from stress, not age. She didn't look old—no older than six hundred.

"Back. Up." My teeth stayed clenched, so they didn't chatter, but my words held a threatening ring. The acidic smell was getting worse. Gross.

She furrowed her brow, and her thumbs pressed on my temples. "I don't understand how you are so sick. This started when I approached you? Have you tried to create a personal ward? That may help."

"I can't—" I hesitated as my voice echoed. "My health is my own. You've discussed your vital matter. My decision stands."

"Something is missing."

Oh, crap.

"That's not right. I feel your *imolegin*, but...it's buried."

"You have no right—"

"Brace yourself, child."

Pressure built inside me, like a boa constrictor around my torso, in the core of my magic. I squeezed my eyes so tight I saw stars.

"Stop!" My knees buckled and I slid off the bumper.

Everything intensified, my head spun, and the smell...I couldn't catch my breath. Memories of those long dead clouded my thoughts. France, my sister dead in my arms, bodies littering the front line. Shit. Breathe. Focus. I was where? Cars. Blinding streetlights. Gritty, icy cement. Seattle. The alley behind my house with an *Aeminan* murderer. Pain. When had I fallen? My knees stung.

I couldn't stop shivering, even with my jacket on. My ears rang so loudly that I wondered if Aswryn heard it, too. Her boots were in my line of sight, six feet in front of me. I raised my head. Aswryn held her right hand out in front of her, left held against her temple. She dropped her hands and grabbed my arms. No one besides me could undo my spell.

Aswryn frowned. I tried to pull away but failed.

I forced as much venom as I could muster into my voice. "Get away from me!"

Her eyes flew open, shock rocking her back. "Impossible. How dare they do this to you!"

"They didn't do it. I did!"

"Why? Mother Anara, gave you a gift, Hallanevaë. To neuter yourself is blasphemy. How are you alive?"

I swallowed hard, unable to look at her. The process had hurt. A lot. But if I hadn't blocked it, I would have used it eventually, or humans would have put me in a lab to try to access it or, for all I knew, weaponize it. Still, our magic was a gift from Anara, and she was right.

"Come, we will free you. Then, with your magic, I—we can work out my curse's immunity problem." Aswryn dragged me behind her, although I couldn't remember standing up. She pulled me closer, but I leaned away.

"Let me go." Like hell I was going to *Endae*. They'd kill me.

"Hallanevaë," a cold, emotionless voice called. "I warned you she would come. Do not trust her words," Twynolan said in English. I looked over Aswryn's shoulder and saw him standing across from us. His hands clenched and unclenched at his sides, like a cowboy waiting to draw his gun. Oh good, time for that "other conversation."

Aswryn stopped and tried to push me behind her.

"Are our people sick?" I asked as I struggled against Aswryn. "You said she's killing people. Did An'di get sick? Is that how she died?" My voice wavered at the end.

"As you informed me tonight, you do not care."

His words shattered me. My jaw dropped. I had no room to argue. That's what I'd led him to believe.

"If you go with her, I must conclude you are conspiring together."

"Conspiring? I just met her. Where'd you get this half-baked idea? You two are nuts." And this coldhearted, zero-emotion act was his uncle talking right there.

"She is coming with me, Nolan."

Aswryn yanked me off-balance. I pulled back but was too sick to do much good. Her arm wrapped around my waist, and she gripped my wrist. Gritting my teeth, I kicked her shin.

Something slammed into my chest. Aswryn's grip slipped and pain shot through my arm and shoulder. My back slammed against a dumpster. My nose stung with the reek of garbage and the smell sent me over the edge. I vomited until my coffee was gone.

Everything looked like fuzzy blobs with little black spots. As my heartbeat slowed, noises filtered back in: the shuffling of feet, a grunt or two, and a few incantations I didn't recognize—not that I'd memorized many. I used the dumpster to stand and walked to the end of a truck.

A good hundred feet farther from my house were the vague, blurry shapes of the two *endai* fighting. They threw spells at each other, some yellows and reds from the harsh ones—curses from Aswryn. Most were felt as a shift in air pressure. Thankfully, Aswryn's ward kept my neighborhood oblivious.

After what felt like forever, the fighting duo became less fuzzy. I jumped back when an arc of blue-black light flashed in front of the taller figure—Twynolan. The smaller figure staggered and fell to the icy ground. Twynolan didn't wait for Aswryn to recover. He ran up and shoved a spell into her chest. Aswryn fell flat on her face. Twynolan flipped her over and wrenched her arms back.

Then Aswryn disappeared.

Gone.

What the fuck?

Something threw Twynolan backward. He doubled over, holding his middle, and then Aswryn reappeared ten feet away. She stalked toward him and flicked her wrist. Twynolan fell.

"No!" I screamed. My palms slapped the ground when I tripped. "Aswryn, stop!" Hands still stinging, I pushed myself up.

Twynolan sprang into a fighting stance. I'd felt Aswryn's power, and not only had Twynolan stood his ground, but he was fighting back. My nerdy, clumsy bookworm friend—ex-friend—was standing his own against this powerful *endaë*.

A flash of blue-black light hit Aswryn.

She countered with a spell.

Twynolan dropped to a knee, otherwise appearing unfazed. He stood back up and rolled his shoulders back.

Twynolan countered another spell. Their spells collided. The force of the collision shook the laurel hedge next to them and blew past me. Nausea sent me spinning.

"Let the rest of the *Amura Ore* fall. They don't need the *Zayuri*'s protection."

What did Aswryn mean by that? My grandparents were assembly members.

"You are still wrapped in your own delusions, Aswryn. You are failing."

Aswryn roared and threw another spell. A car window broke.

Ignoring the pain inside and out, I continued making my way toward them. My foot slipped on a patch of ice and down I went again. With my ear pressed against the wet cement, my attention stayed on them. I got my ass back up and kept going. Two cars left to go.

Twynolan shoved his arms forward, palms close, and black light threw Aswryn backward. She stood and smiled. My head vibrated with her creepy cackle, like spiders crawling down my back. To steady myself, I leaned on the car next to me.

Aswryn held her hands out, ready. Light whipped out from Twynolan's arm again. Aswryn dodged it. She threw a spell that pushed Twynolan back a foot. How much longer could he stand this? He had better balance now, and even more strength. That didn't mean he had built endurance. I'd bet my best hat he'd studied these fighting spells and techniques. Studying them, though, didn't give him the stamina of a seasoned fighter.

"She knows you killed my sister, Aswryn. She won't help you," Twynolan said in *Aemirin*. He turned as Aswryn moved to stay facing him. She sighed, loud enough for me to hear from fifteen feet away.

"I suppose you told her about her father as well?"

My head stopped spinning for a moment. I waited for Twynolan's retort. My father wasn't dead. He couldn't be. Twynolan would have told me.

"Nol?" I called around my tightening throat as I slid to the ground, too dizzy to stand anymore.

He turned, and focused his neutral expression on me. Who was this strange *endao*? This couldn't be my *muranildo*.

Yet...he was.

Enough of this bullshit. We were going to have this conversation now, right after he got Aswryn under control. And there would be no killing. None. My fingertips dug into a crack in the pavement.

The stinging helped clear my head. I was still dizzy and shaking, and everything narrowed down to moving forward. I dug into my coat pocket for my keys. Without hesitating, I ran straight into Aswryn. The force moved her backward. Aiming the keychain pepper spray bottle at her face, I closed my eyes, held my breath, and sprayed.

Everything next happened within seconds of each other.

Aswryn knocked the bottle out of my hand. It landed a good six feet away. Their spells, meant for each other, hit me. One in front, one in back. Twynolan yelled my name.

Moving and breathing were impossible. Stars crawled across my vision.

Aswryn sat on her ass, ten feet away, wheezing and coughing. She noticed me looking at her and started laughing between coughs. Her eyes weren't swelling up. I hadn't sprayed her long enough.

Twynolan stepped up to Aswryn and bent her arm back at a bad angle. All the while, Aswryn kept looking at me and laughing, interrupted by heaving coughs.

"Get up, Aswryn," Twynolan said.

"Will you let her die?" she wheezed. "Or is your mission more important?"

Twynolan stopped pulling on her and looked at me.

"Hallë? Are you all right?" Twynolan's voice echoed through the alley.

Did he really expect me to answer that? I wanted to tell him I was okay and to take Aswryn back to *Aemina* where his uncle could arrest her. That I would be fine when this wore off. Hopefully.

Aswryn wheezed and cleared her throat—or tried to. "You will regret your choice, Hallanevaë. Wait and see." With that vague threat, Aswryn vanished, and Twynolan held nothing in his arms.

"Hallë? Hold on, I'm coming," he said, in *Aemirin*. Twynolan was beside me in a heartbeat, his knees skidding to a stop against my side. He squeezed my arms. Held my face between his hands. Checked my pupils. Grabbed my shoulders. Lifted my head.

I wanted to tell him to stop shaking me. To let go of my face and, for Pete's sake, stop shouting. Twynolan leaned over me and listened for my breathing.

"I can fix this, Hallë." One hand made an arc over my chest, casting something. The other made a cup above my stomach. A blue-black speck of light grew brighter in his palm. He pushed the light into me while making another arc. Like before, when both spells hit me, every nerve in my body screamed.

Then nothing.

4

"*Dono unara. Jeme!*" *You must wake. Please!*

What was happening?

Something shook me. My arm hurt. My palms hurt. I couldn't open my eyes. I couldn't talk. Colors exploded behind my eyes as the voice yelled in my ear.

"*C'yo! Jeme, sye voida vimun. Mina...Osyem mewara wey.*" *Shit. Please, don't die. I...I can't lose you, too.*

The voice sounded familiar. Was that *Aemirin*?

They shook me again, which helped me focus. Now I remembered.

Twynolan shook me a third time. "Hallë, wake up."

Why was he yelling?

At first, my voice failed, but as he shook me for the fourth time, I grabbed his wrist. "Nol. Stop." I licked my lips and raised my voice. "I'm awake."

He hugged me, his weight crushing me. "Hallë," he cried against the crook of my neck.

Without thinking, I responded like before, pressing my hand against his back. His familiar soft hair slid under my palms. Since I was little, I'd wished I'd had his hair. Silly, but true. Tears stung my eyes, but I had no right to shed any. *I* had chosen to cast the spell that banished me. *I* had decided to block my magic. *I* didn't get to have a pity party.

Twynolan sat up, taking his familiar warmth away. His beautiful hair slid between my fingers.

"Are you in pain?" He switched to English as he grabbed my face.

"Just stop yelling. What happened?"

"The spells were violent. I—you fell unconscious." He lowered his voice. "I have been trying to wake you."

My eyes widened. "What!" My scream echoed through the alley. "Are you kidding me? You *do* want me to kill her." I shot my hand out, pointing to where Aswryn had been. "Otherwise, you'd have followed her to wherever she went this time."

"*Hallë.*"

"Don't lie!"

His eyes filled with panic. "*Sae, osyconëm flunic genjara,*" No, I couldn't just leave you. "*C'yo,* you have no idea."

I pressed my lips tight and glared at him. "Then go after her now. Go on!"

He shook his head. "*Sajé,* I will not leave you to freeze to death."

"Sure you can." I slapped his hands away as he tried to inspect my pupils—again! "I'm fine." Except for the lights and sound making my head pound. The nausea. I was fine.

"There is no need to run after her. She will be back after she recovers from the potion you sprayed on her. For now, where do I take you?" Twynolan gave me the most stubborn look, and I knew he wouldn't budge.

I huffed. "My house, I guess."

"*Astur.*" Okay. Twynolan started to gather me in his arms.

"What the hell are you doing?"

He scoffed. "I have grown stronger over the years. You do not weigh much at all."

"I can walk."

"You tried to sit up and fell back down. I think walking is not an option." With that, he stood. Okay, so he had gotten stronger.

"Whatever," I mumbled.

For a handful of heartbeats he stayed still as we looked around the empty alley. "Which way, Hallë?"

Oh, right. "At the brown Volvo."

"The what?"

I pointed ahead of us. "Six lights down on the right."

He sighed and began walking. An awkward silence settled over us.

"You never answered me," he said.

"What?"

"Are you in pain?"

"Oh. No," I lied, which he saw through. He was my *muranildo*, after all.

"Your hearing?"

I shrugged. "Everything is loud." Like the deafening sound of the pebbles under his shoes.

"And?"

Was he making a checklist? "That's all."

"*Etwa.*" *Whatever*, he muttered.

The awkward silence loomed once more. He shifted me, scooting me up enough for me to rest my head on his shoulder. I felt awkward doing it, but my head weighed, like, fifty pounds.

"What she said, about Laro?"

Twynolan glanced down at me. My father was dead. Twynolan saw my face, and his expression softened. "Yes, your father was infected—recently. You were asking so many questions in the café and the noise and...I would have told you if you had stayed."

"Infected? Like a virus or something? Or a curse?"

"Both. They are connected."

"How long does he have?"

"Possibly a year. I am sorry. I will tell you everything once we are inside."

To keep myself from freaking out before I knew the details, I searched for something else to talk about. Anything but silence. "Are you mad at me?"

"Yes."

"Because I told you I won't help you?" Did he think Aswryn and I were working together?

"No, that disappointed me."

"Because I said I don't care about An'di?"

"No, that hurt."

"Then—"

"Is this your house?"

We stood in front of my eight-foot-high arched wooden gate, the laurel and lilac bushes reaching over the fence. "Yeah."

He stepped up to the gate, but when he couldn't figure the latch out, he rotated his index finger, casting a manipulation spell. A wave of nausea rolled through me.

"Let me down. Let me down! I'm going to be sick."

"*C'yo*, I might drop you."

As soon as he set my feet on the ground, I pushed him away and reached for the fence. The ice-cold boards soothed my raw palms. After thirty seconds or so with my forehead against the fence, my breathing evened out.

"Crap, I was just beginning to feel better," I mumbled.

"We need to get you inside."

"Give me a second."

"Now, Hallë."

He grabbed my shoulders, but I pulled away and waved him off. "Would you give me a minute? Jeez."

He crossed his arms and waited sixty seconds. "Better yet?"

"Let's find out." I pushed off the fence but kept my hand there to steady myself. He reached around my waist to pick me up again, but I twisted away. "I can do it."

"Let me carry you."

"I got it."

"I do not want you to fall."

"No! I can do this." I took a few steps and found I wasn't lying. "See?"

"*Tullaca, la upastira.*" He cussed and complained about stubbornness.

Instead of starting the pointless argument, I focused on making my slow way through my backyard. My lot was the largest on the block and the oldest. An old-growth hemlock and a redwood I'd planted in the '20s resided there. I'd built six raised garden beds to keep them company.

Twynolan didn't try to pick me up again, but I felt his hand on my back when I stumbled. We triggered the automatic floodlights, and I would have fallen on my ass if he hadn't caught me.

"Is that supposed to happen?"

"Yeah. Come on." I tugged on his arm to guide him up my steps. The keys slipped from my shaking fingers at the back door. "*Putain*," I cussed under my breath in French.

"That did not sound nice." Twynolan leaned against the doorframe and dangled the retrieved keys in front of me.

"*Pilassa.*" *Shut up* I growled in *Aemirin* that time.

He smirked and watched while I opened my house and walked in from the cold. My stomach twisted—apprehension over what he'd tell me now that we were inside, but I needed to know. Whatever he said, with his vague explanations in the café, could I believe him? I wanted to, but if I did and it was a lie...I wasn't sure my heart could take that betrayal.

Every part of my body protested when I moved. My fingers shook as I unbuttoned my coat. Boots in hand, Twynolan inspected my mud/laundry room instead of taking off his coat.

I hissed as I slid my arm out. "How long do we have before she shows back up?"

"Worry about that later. Right now, I must know you are safe with no ill effects from the spells you jumped into without thinking." He looked down with no emotions. How was he this calm? "I was also hoping you might have some bandages I could use?" He winced and held up his hands to show me the cuts he'd earned in the fight. There was a bruise forming on his cheekbone and a road rash on the left side of his jaw. When had he fallen?

I inhaled and held it. Was this really the best idea? "Don't talk and follow me. The floor creaks in some places."

He nodded.

As we walked into the main house, the familiar lemony scent of Murphy's oil relaxed the tension in my shoulders, and my shivering subsided. My head still throbbed, my palms and knees stung, and—oh, who was I kidding? Everything fucking hurt. We passed the stairs, and out of the hall closet I grabbed a cardigan, which belonged to Charlie. It was big on me, but I couldn't care less at that point.

The first aid kit was under the sink in the tiny toilet room across from the closet. My reflection in the small mirror startled me. My makeup was smeared and made my green eyes look like empty sockets. I squeezed my eyes shut for a second and looked away. Talk about creepy.

"Perhaps if you drink something warm, you might stop shivering." Twynolan leaned against the doorframe.

"I told you not to talk. I can't wake up my roommates."

"Ah." He put a finger over his lips. "But tea could help," he whispered.

I rolled my eyes, and he raised an eyebrow.

"Fine."

We walked out of the hallway, turned left, and left again to the kitchen peninsula. The moonlight shone through the sheer white curtains, lighting up the entire front of the house. It's funny how you don't realize your house is messy until company comes unannounced. A board game and Charlie's sweater lay on the dining table. Ray had a doll and stuffed white bunny sitting in a chair. The first aid kit went on the peninsula while I went to fill the kettle.

Twynolan roamed the dining room. At first, he picked up Ray's My Little Pony from the counter, examined the pictures on the wall, and even played with the game pieces.

"Do you want some tea?" I couldn't *not* offer. That would've been rude.

"Only hot water, please. I have my own."

Oh, well, weren't we just prepared?

The kettle clanked against the bottom of the cast-iron sink. The noise seemed three times louder than normal. This tea better fucking work. I was done with this jittering and aching crap.

Taking a deep breath, I asked, "Are you sure—"

"You seem to be feeling better." Twynolan set down a Candy Land game card.

I pressed my lips together. Had he interrupted me on purpose? "Sure. Aswryn?"

"Yes?" He settled his hands behind his back and kept roaming the dining room.

"Twynolan," I growled. "How do you know she'll be back?" I shivered, remembering her threat.

He puffed his cheeks out. "Aswryn is a planner. She attacks, vanishes, waits until we least expect it, and attacks again until she has worn her opponent out. This is what she has done countless times and which is part of why she is so difficult to catch."

I turned off the faucet and looked back at Twynolan shaking the saltshaker on the table. Lovely.

My hands shook carrying the kettle to the stove, but I managed.

"Why are you heating it with the stove? We are the only ones here and you still will not use your magic?"

"I told you I don't use magic."

"*Tanwalu?*" *Truly?* "Not once?"

I turned with my hands on my hips. "Stop avoiding my questions."

Twynolan stalked into the kitchen. "What did Aswryn tell you tonight?"

"You first." I stomped my foot and balled my hands into fists.

"We have a few days. Not tonight or tomorrow. Now, what did Aswryn tell you?"

I lit the pilot light and adjusted the flame. "She *told* me people are getting sick and the *Amura Ore* are blaming her. They're saying it's a curse she created."

He leaned against the edge of the range, six inches away from me. I stepped back to lean against the counter on the other side of the range—giving myself space.

"But she messed up..."

That relaxed his shoulders.

"She told me she wanted me to work on an immunity problem of *her* curse, after she...When she..." My throat closed up as I tried to tell him how Aswryn had invaded me and discovered my block. I couldn't see the horrified look in his eyes as well. "When I refused to go with her."

He nodded and gave me a bit of room. "The *Zayuri* are immune. She has been trying to solve that for some time."

"I'm not conspiring with her," I whispered.

"I know."

"You thought I was."

"I know you did not—"

"But you said it."

"Hallë." He leaned over until our eyes were level. "I believe you."

Did he? He didn't believe me tonight with Aswryn. Did he doubt me before, too?

He saw the doubt on my face and hung his head. "*C'yo*, it was an accident and you never should have been exiled."

"Yes, I should have."

He growled. "*Majut*," he cussed and continued in *Aemirin*. "No, they were wrong. It was a stupid prank. I told you not to use that spell."

"Don't you dare get into that. You are here because of Aswryn, not to dredge up the past and throw it in my face. Now I'm done playing twenty questions. Tell me everything."

"Oh, so you will let me finish a sentence?"

I leaned back and shook my hair out of my face. "Well, if you weren't being so vague about the whole damn thing, maybe I wouldn't have had to ask questions."

"*Ai*, Hallë." He turned away and found the faucet to play with for a second. "You thought I would tell you everything in public? In English? And do not tell me you cannot understand *Aemirin*, you are a language protégé."

I balled my hands into fists against my ribs. "Yet, you yelled across the Square that Aswryn killed An'di. Your English was just fine there."

"*Sye voida tullacen godurenco.*" *Don't be fucking ridiculous*, Twynolan growled, giving up and switching to *Aemirin*. "*Jato!*" *Yes!* "I panicked. Still, I didn't *want* to tell you in a fucking café. A café, Hallë. Truly? How am I supposed to tell you anything that would upset you in public? And how do you expect me to tell you everything in English? I'm slow, and I can't form contractions right. I don't speak it 'just fine,' as you say. I sound absurd. An accent," Nol tutted. "I was surprised your friends understood me."

"Nol—" But he didn't hear me.

"I've been worried about you every day since you left. We've been trying to get an appeal to stick." He shoved his hair that had fallen out of his braids. "I want to curse the day the *Amura Ore* banished you. But if they hadn't, you would have died. The curse attacks magic, Hallë. It's debilitating. Your grandmother says it is a twisted fate that brought you here, and I agree." He took a deep, shuddering breath and turned away from me.

"The *Amura Ore* left everything to us because we are immune. They expect me to capture her because I can sense her *imolegin*. I can't do it alone."

"You mean the *Zayuri*—"

He stopped pacing and thumped his chest. "I'm *Zayuri*, Hallë. And a damn good one," he said in *Aemirin*.

My stomach lurched, and I grabbed the counter so I wouldn't fall, but my knees wobbled, and Nol reached out. His speed, his strength, and his change of emotion made sense now. He was *Zayuri*, even though he had vowed never to take that path.

"*C'yo*. This is why I didn't tell you in the café."

"Let me go," I demanded the moment my feet were off the floor.

"I will. Quit whining." Nol's voice was calmer but still low with anger. He set me down on a kitchen stool at the peninsula and propped his arm on the counter, less than a foot away from me. He reached for the first aid kit, found the latch, and rifled through the contents.

"What kind of healing kit is this? No bandages. No medicine. What are these paper things? *C'yo*, I don't understand humans."

"Here." First I took the box away from him, then pulled out a paper-wrapped gauze square and an alcohol wipe. I shook the packet and ripped it open. "See, they're in the paper. If you'd slow down, you'd notice that. Gimme."

My fingers brushed over Nol's rough palm as I took his hand and pressed it flat on the counter. The calluses made sense now. He hissed when the wipe touched his knuckles. I stifled my laugh.

"Do you laugh at your clients like this as well?" he grumbled as he took over cleaning his cuts.

"Sometimes." I laughed again. "The big *Zayuri* whining over a scrape."

"*Hinam Zayuri.*"

"Even more pathetic." *Hinam* was the equivalent of a captain, if I remembered right.

"*C'yo*, I am sorry. I should be speaking English."

"You can speak *Aemirin*. But you must speak English around humans."

"I need to practice." His breath shuttered as his tension deflated.

He *was* slower in English and I knew he'd find the contractions frustrating. Plus, he was right, I found languages easy to learn. I used to speak four *endaen* languages and I'd picked up ten languages on Earth. So being fluent in English and *Aemirin*, I wasn't noticing him reverting to an *Aemirin* word to alleviate the problem every time.

"Got that all out of your system?"

"Not the least, but that helped," he said.

I smirked. As kids, I could get him to tell me anything once he got into one of those rants. Nol touched my face, and I jumped back. He pulled his hand back but held it up in front of me. A black drop hung from his thumb. Oh yeah, my makeup.

"It is black. This makes it hard to hide them from me."

"You need to give me space, Nol. We're not close anymore. I know you're looking for comfort, but it's been too long."

He frowned. "You are the one who seems to need comfort."

I cleared my throat. "Well, people get the wrong idea."

"When have they not?" He puffed out his cheeks again. "It has been hard, and with you beside me again—" He grabbed another alcohol packet and tapped it on the counter. "*C'yo*, I cannot promise not to reach out. You are right. The bond seeks the comfort."

The kettle whistled, and Nol jumped. The reaction was so unexpected that I laughed.

Scowling, he lightly pushed my shoulder. "That is not funny. I did not know that thing screamed."

Nol got up and pulled the water off the stove. The knob was beyond him, though. Reining in my laughter, I went and saved him—or the stove. Whichever one needed it more.

"Did I not just sit you down?"

"I'm not a child, Nol."

"I noticed," he grumbled in *Aemirin* as he stepped back to let me handle the stove.

"What's that supposed to mean?"

Nol swore under his breath. I caught "ridiculous" in there somewhere.

I shuffled around him to reach the mugs and didn't say anything, not wanting to start up another argument.

I grabbed my "Inking before coffee is dangerous" mug for me and the Maxine the Hallmark lady one that read, "I couldn't care less, but I'm working on it" for him. Out of the corner of my eye, I noticed Twynolan watching me. So, I cocked a hip and glared him down with the mugs in my hands.

He'd propped himself up against the counter, his arms folded over his abdomen and ankles crossed in this nonchalant, "cool guy pose". Jeez. He studied me with a look in his eyes that made me fidget. Puffing out his cheeks, he looked at the ceiling as he muttered something else. "*C'yo*, I...see you are not a child."

"You sure? 'Cause you're chastising me like I'm one."

"I do not understand that one. But in...safe—" He shook his head. "In...trust. No, that is not right either." Nol sighed and gave up. "*Nuedellen tätar esmem sye voida eycam enfaenërb ladori.*"

Translating that took a moment because one of those words couldn't mean what I thought it meant. *Enfaen* with *esme*, love and affection? No. I shook my head. "That...I don't know what that means."

"*C'yo,*" he growled, rolling his eyes. "You—it is obvious you grew up. You became a beautiful—*attractive*—" His eyes went wide as he shrugged. "*Endaë.* Do not look at me like that. Take the compliment and shut up."

As he flustered through his explanation, my smile kept getting bigger.

He tsked, and as I laughed, he plucked both mugs out of my hands before I even realized he'd moved.

"Hey!" I exclaimed, forgetting to be quiet.

"*Sajat.*" *Quiet.* "Your roommates, remember?" he whispered, too close to my face, and I gulped. Then he thumped my nose and chuckled.

I tried to push him, but he moved away too fast. I leaned against the sink. The cold ceramic soothed the road rash on my palms. He brought both mugs to the counter by our chairs, grabbed a small canvas pouch from under his coat, and rummaged through it.

"Tea?"

I turned my nose up. "I have my own."

"This will help you heal better than those stinging paper things of yours."

"This isn't your mom's tea, right?"

He snorted. "*C'yo, sae.* It is a mix of An'di's. This is more effective and tastes better. Even my *murë* admits it."

Whoa. His mother admitting that something worked better than her medicine was high praise. Nol tilted his head as he held tea leaves above my water. I nodded, and he dropped in a large pinch.

"Come, sit and talk."

"You gonna tell me everything?"

He rocked his head from side to side. "*Wana.*" *More or less.*

"No, all. Even if it's hard. I still haven't said yes."

"Not with words."

He had me there. Aswryn considered me an enemy now.

"She said I'd regret my choice."

"Yes, she did."

I pushed off the sink and sat back down on my stool. Silence settled between us, not awkward this time. Aswryn had taken An'di from him. I couldn't let her take my family. He leaned over and nudged me with his shoulder, pulling me out of my worry.

"What?"

"You are calling me Nol," he said.

The night had been a roller coaster. "I guess I have been."

"Thank you."

I nodded. "So—"

"Are you disappointed?" Nol winced as he shifted on the stool.

"What? Why?"

"*Zayuri*?"

I balked. "Why would my opinion matter?" I huffed out a laugh. Once my eyes refocused, Nol's glare made me shiver. I had to swallow before giving him a serious answer. "No, of course not. How did it happen?" Not all children of *Zayuri* families were born with the special magic. His uncle and mother had pushed him to follow the *Zayuri* path until he vowed never to hold a *Zayuri* blade.

"I wanted to fight back." Nol slumped over. "Aswryn found Gileal and An'di while they were working—Gil is our curse expert. I followed their trail, which I later realized was a trap, and Aswryn took me. She takes and uses people as test subjects. I was very new in my *Zayuri* training."

I nodded my understanding.

"My uncle found us a week later. But that time with her allowed me to learn her *imolegin*, and I will use it against her now. What is the word in English?" The lack of emotion as he explained such a horrible experience, and in a foreign language, probably had more to do with grief than his *Zayuri* training.

"Irony. And An'di?"

He stuck his pinky in his water, muttered the incantation, and it began swirling. "Aswryn was hunting healers—" He swallowed hard.

He didn't need to say anything more. I closed my eyes.

"How did Aswryn escape?"

"Some one helped her. My uncle is investigating *who* helped her. We cannot rely on the *Aeminan* guard. We are certain it was one of them."

"Aswryn has us isolated, Nol. Tell me you see this. You—to test her curse on. Me—to perfect it."

Nol shrugged. "Yes, but I either follow her or let you face her alone. She is manipulative and ... convincing? No. There is something more than—" Nol made a fist and reverted to *Aemirin*. "*C'yo*. She's conniving and her curse is intricate, how it attacks magic and the accelerated range of infection. All evidence leads to an illness, but An'di never found one. Until the day she died, she believed Aswryn had attached it to an—do you know what an *alosmiato* is?"

He wasn't surprised when I shook my head. I knew he was simplifying his *Aemirin* for me, but some words I figured out by the way he used them.

"I have not found another English word for it besides *plague* It is very small. She believed Aswryn bound the curse to it. Gileal is our curse expert, but there are no healers to help him find a cure. We must break it."

But to break a curse, if the creator wouldn't break it, the person had to die.

"Who is Aswryn? Why is she doing this?"

"Aswryn, from what has been found, she was a *Mellorian* diplomat's daughter. There was a raid at their home, but then there is nothing on record after her mother died."

"The *Mellorini* have supplied you with this information? Are they immune?"

"They are, but our political relationship with them is..."

"Precarious. But she doesn't *look Mellorian*."

Nol's eyebrow lifted. "Are you sure?"

"Their people have golden eyes." The richer the gold, the "purer" their blood was. "No. She can't be mixed race, can she? That'd be—"

"A death sentence for her mother and her, according to their law."

"Our realm is so screwed up. Although this one isn't any better, I'll clue ya."

"Gileal thinks her father is an *Amura Ore* member and the curse is revenge for her mother."

"Then why would she develop a curse to infect all our people? Not the entire *Aeminan* population is to blame."

"I believe there are others with their own agendas helping her. Aswryn may have created the curse, but others helped her cast it. Your grandmother agrees."

My breath caught in my throat at the mention of my grandmother. "Is...How is she?"

"Your grandmother is safe and living with my uncle. They are quite a cute couple."

"Good for them." I smiled.

Nol smiled back. "Yeah."

"So." I took another sip of tea and steeled myself. "Is Gil..."

He lifted his chin. "Zella refused to let him come. Your grandmother knew if Gileal saw you, he wouldn't return."

My shoulders relaxed. Thank our Mother Gileal was alive.

"He refused to talk to me before I left."

"Oh." I bit my lip and racked my brain for something to say.

"You are already looking better," Nol said.

"I am? I don't feel anything."

He still had most of his tea. The bruise on his cheekbone had faded, and the cut on his other side was almost gone.

"I don't know what I can do to help you. I won't help you kill her to break the curse. Besides, I can't use my magic."

"I would never ask you to kill her. She is already after you, and I am not certain how safe Lewis, Mateo, or Sam are, or even these roommates of yours. She said you would regret choosing me, and she does not hold empty threats. Act normal, and when she comes for you again, I will be there. You will *not* jump between our spells." Nol's glare made me shiver. "Stop her from vanishing. I will arrest her and take her back."

"So the *Amura Ore* can sentence her to death?" Like I would have been if not for Nol and our bond. Our laws were clear: use magic to kill another and our lives were forfeit.

"Tatie?" The voice of Ray, my three-year-old niece, echoed through the house from the stairwell.

Nol jumped, knocking his tea over. Not very *Zayuri*-like of him.

"One moment. That's my roommate's daughter. She must have heard us," I whispered.

"Tatie, are you down there?"

If his blood hadn't drained from his face, I would have teased him.

"Hey?" I whispered, grabbing his arm as I walked past him. "You okay?"

Nol swallowed, smoothed down his jacket, and nodded.

I squeezed his arm once and went to Ray.

"*Ma colombe*, what are you doing up? Go back to bed," I said to her in French as I took her small shoulders and turned her around.

"Is Uncle Mateo here?"

"*Non*. Come, Tatie will tuck you in." I patted her back as she walked a step ahead of me. I noticed Charlie's door was open as we walked by. Once in Ray's room, I tucked her in and kissed her little nose. "Now, you go back to sleep, and I will see you tomorrow."

"In the morning?" she said, her voice hopeful.

"No, I must leave early."

"When the sun gets up?" she asked, stalling.

"Probably."

"In two minutes?"

I smiled. "I will see you after I come home from work."

"Can I go with you?"

My chin dipped. "No."

"I'll be quiet. I can color on the couch."

I kissed her forehead. "Sleep."

Ray huffed and turned over. Going back down, I made sure both my girls' doors were closed. When I came back to the kitchen, I found Ray's pink pony on the counter in front of Nol and his mug was in the sink.

"How old is she?" Nol asked, composed again.

"Nol—" I bit my lip, playing with my lip ring. Aswryn could very likely hurt Charlie or Ray to make me help her. I shivered at the thought of losing them. "Okay."

"What?" He sat up straighter, a bit uncertain.

"*But* she must live and face her failure. Death is a release, not a punishment."

"Aswryn will not break the curse out of the kindness in her heart. Come up with a different way, and I will take it. I swear. But you must prove it works to the *Zayuri* and the *Amura Ore*."

"How will I show them when I'm *savilë*?"

He smirked. "Leave that to Gileal and me."

I covered my mouth and muttered, "If he ever talks to you again."

"He will, since I have news of your safety and what a pain in the ass you still are." He laughed and continued to laugh after I shoved him off his stool.

5

"CRAP," I SAID AS my laptop bag slipped off my shoulder. Nothing was cooperating. Giving up, I set my latte on the ground to retrieve the shop keys. After unlocking the door, I reached down for my coffee, and the door opened, hitting me. My coffee rolled into the middle of the road. Wonderful.

"Ow, Hally! I'm sorry, kiddo. Not again, girl. You're gonna need to get that checked out if you don't stop smackin' yourself upside the head. What the hell you doin' down there anyway?"

"Getting my coffee." We looked at the settling coffee cup in the road.

Lewis opened the door wider for me. I picked up my now empty cup and threw it into the trash bin next to the door, then set my laptop bag down on the computer desk.

"I'll go getcha a new one later, 'kay? Spiced amaretto?"

"Yeah, that would be great if you could. So, did I beat Agent Zack-ass here?" I shut my cabinet and looked around our small, empty back room.

"No, Special Agent Zack Thomas is right behind you," the worst, most annoying prick of a DEA agent said in his weasel-toned voice as he stepped into the back room.

"Oh, lovely," I said in a sweet-as-honey voice. He knew I hated him. "Then you can buy me coffee. It's your fault."

Agent Thomas snorted. "How's that?"

"You called Sam at seven and demanded we be here at eight. I need coffee to function." Sam had more or less appointed himself my lawyer, due to this asshat. But he had to work this morning, so he'd asked Lewis to go, which happened on occasion.

Zack sat down on the love seat. "I'm not buying you shit. You're late."

"So? You know I take the bus."

I bet he thought I'd meant to be half an hour late out of spite. Tempting, but no. In truth, my bracelet was missing. Reluctantly giving up, I'd scribbled a note for Charlie to keep an eye out for it. If only my sister were here now.

"Any responsible business owner should drive their own car. You have that Volvo. Use it. I'm amazed you still get customers. Not only are you late, but your bedside manner sucks. How many—"

"Agent Thomas, you called her here for a reason, right?" Lewis interrupted before I said something stupid. Our conversations still got heated, but they were nothing like they'd been before Lewis, Sam, and Mateo came into my life. "Not to harass her? Unless you changed jobs and are workin' for the Better Business Bureau."

Lewis's sharp tone shut up the puny agent. He didn't look the part of a mellow person, with his large size, piercings, and tattoos, but the one and only time I'd witnessed Lewis livid in the almost four years I'd known him was in my defense against Zack.

Zack shifted on the love seat, fuming. "Yes, I did."

"Did what? Change jobs?" I asked

Zack's cheeks flushed. The dark bags under his eyes darkened. "No."

"Then get on with it," I said as I sat down at the dining table. "Please," I added, sweetly.

I didn't need this. Aswryn could show up anywhere, and Nol was MIA. When I woke up, my hammock was empty, and Nol was gone. Not even a note. What the hell, right? Couldn't I get one fair ride at least once in my life? Of course not.

"Hally, acting bi—rude to Agent Thomas won't get us anywhere." Lewis sat relaxed, leaning back in his computer chair. His clenched jaw told me Zack was irritating him too, though.

"Thank you, Lewis." Zack nodded and came to sit across from me at the table. He sighed as he settled in, believing he'd won. "Have you heard from Ian?"

"Nope." My response came without thinking. "They monitor the prisoner's calls." I tilted my head and narrowed my eyes. "Don't they?"

Zack leaned forward and tapped his fingers on the table. His upper lip curled. "Of course they do."

Had I hit a nerve? I mentally rubbed my hands together. "Then you already knew my answer." What a joke of a DEA Agent.

"Has anyone from Ian's operation contacted you on his behalf?"

Be the bigger person, Hally. Be the bigger person.

"Why would anyone do that?"

"Yes or no."

I looked at the ceiling. "I am not, nor have I ever been, part of Ian's drug 'operation.' Which sounds ridiculous because we both know it wasn't *his*. Ian is too stupid to organize anything other than a box of crayons. He had a boss. We went over this. Clue in. I'm not your man. Go find Ian's people."

"You haven't answered my question."

"What?"

"Have you been in contact with anyone affiliated with Ian?" Zack asked.

I looked at Lewis, the only other sane person in the room. He closed his eyes and shook his head.

"No!"

"Agent Thomas, what's with all these questions about Ian?" Lewis sat up and uncrossed his arms. The tattoo on his neck pulsed.

"Ian skipped his parole."

I counted the time down. He still had six months left on his sentence. My testimony had sent him to jail, so the state had to notify me of his release, right? My coffee threatened to come up, and I waited for my stomach to settle.

"He's supposed to be in for four years. How is he out so soon?"

"He got out early for good behavior."

There must have been more than that going on. Ian wouldn't know good behavior if it bit him in the ass. "Those must be some pretty lenient 'good behavior' guidelines. You think he's coming for me?"

"I was thinking more about Katie and Seamus." Zack shrugged. "When was the last time you heard from her?" Crap, Ian's ex and his kid.

"Katie? Jeez, I can't recall."

"She contacted me."

"About Ian?"

"She had something to show me, and I think you might know what she's talking about." Zack pulled some papers out of his bag and laid them face down on the table. "I think she's protecting you, but I'm hoping you'll give me a straight answer for once."

"Okay." He'd piqued my interest. A first.

"Katie ran into some of Ian's people last week. They had a few strung-out teenagers with them. And, well, Katie recognized one of them. A kid they trafficked down in Arizona."

"Nice story. What does it have to do with me?" Katie had helped traffic people?

"I'm hoping you'll recognize him, too."

"Like, from Ian's shop?" Maybe I could help with something. All kinds of people had walked through Ian's door.

"No, in Arizona."

Well, there went that idea. "I've never been to Arizona."

"Yeah, I thought you'd say that," Zack mumbled.

Zack flipped over a photo: a boy, maybe seven or eight, standing outside on a field with a football. Desert-hardy shrubs and various cacti were in the background behind a chain-link fence. The red-orange Arizona desert dirt covered the kid, the ball, and between the dried patchy grass.

"This is the kid Katie swears she saw a week ago. Derrick Polanski. This was him in ninety-nine. And this one is Katie's picture." He flipped over another photo.

Ian had his arm over Derrick's shoulders. They stood in an airport, next to gate twenty-two. Ian was a fridge of a man with platinum blond hair and a goatee. Derrick was a few years older in this one. His eyes were red-rimmed, one cheek was puffy, and his hair was disheveled.

"Katie took his picture, hoping to free him one day. She tried her hardest."

I nodded and leaned over to grab the photo. "When was this again?"

"You tell me. You were there."

I lifted my eyes from the picture to meet Zack's. "Excuse me? I told you I've never been to Arizona. Ian doesn't have his spiderweb tattoo, and he got that before I came to the shop. Did Katie tell you I was there?"

Zack licked his lips and flipped over the last paper. Another photo with the same tones, so probably another photo of Katie's. This one showed Ian and the boy sitting in the boarding area. Ian was looking out at the plane, with the boy looking at his shoes.

"So?"

"Look who's sitting across from them." Zack tipped his chin at the picture.

On the right side, in the other row of chairs, a young woman with black freckles looked past Katie. Curly black hair, twisted into a '90s updo with a large clip, fixed so my ears weren't visible. I wore a *Clueless* inspired monochrome sage mini dress and cream Mary Jane pumps. Lewis pulled the picture over to look at it. He looked up at me, then down at the picture again.

My stomach churned. I had left Paris in 2002, flown to Québec, Canada, gotten bored, and went to visit the grave of my foster sister's daughter in New Jersey. An elderly couple had recognized me from the last time I'd lived there in 1922. All three of us had frozen. Her husband had gotten one word out before I'd bolted: "How?"

My layover out of New Jersey had been in Arizona. How in the realms could my luck be so bad that they'd been trafficking a kid on the same fucking day I was flying to California?

"Hally?"

"What?" I snapped.

"Did you hear me?" Zack asked.

Lewis sat back up and crossed his beefy arms. His eyes looked straight ahead to the posters and sketches on the wall above the love seat. He had no need to look at the photo anymore. He knew.

My eyes shifted to Zack sitting back all proud of himself, thinking he'd finally tied me to Ian.

"Hally?" Zack called my name a second time.

"No." I shoved my hair back and dug deep to stay calm. "No, sorry. That...person looks like me, but that isn't possible. I was fifteen and still living in France. Remarkable resemblance, but—"

"Don't start."

I heaved a big sigh to look bored and fed up. Well, I was fed up. There had to be a way to convince Zack and Lewis that it wasn't me in the picture.

"What are you suggesting? If this was Hally from a decade ago, she'd be in her thirties now. Does Hally look like she's in her midthirties?"

But...had I read Lewis wrong? He'd looked convinced it was me earlier.

"That's what I thought. How do you explain this photo, though? Some people do look younger than they are." Zack stuck out his lip and tossed his hands up. "I dunno."

"That's not me. I—I was in France."

Liar!

"Okay. I did some digging and found you—Nevaeh Bercot. I tell you, it wasn't easy."

I tried to stay calm as I scrambled for a logical answer. "Charlie Bercot-Roux is my cousin. Maybe this person is a relative on our grandfather's side."

"Your freckles even match. Tell me the truth, Hally—or *Nevaeh.*" Zack leaned over the table. "Come clean. You did the right thing by turning Ian in, but I need to know all you know about the trafficking."

"Like I've told you, I was never part of Ian's drugs, and I certainly did not know about the trafficking. I never saw Ian or—wait, Rob came in with two kids on separate occasions. I thought they were his sister's kids. I gave them stuff to color on."

"I think you can do better than that. Rob is obvious. He was Ian's shadow. I'm not saying you helped, but I know you were part of Ian's crew."

"As soon as I found out what Ian really was, I reported him. Our paths crossed in two thousand four. He liked my artwork and offered to teach me the trade. That's all."

Agent Zack-ass shook his head. "You were running his drugs—"

"I was not!" I sat up and slapped the table.

"Then what is this?" He pointed to the photos. "Give me something I can believe."

"Fine, fine." I crossed my arms and slouched in my chair. "I'm a two hundred and forty-six-year-old elf who was exiled from my realm for using magic to kill two other elves." Telling them the truth in this bullshit way was pretty damn easy and something I'd never tried before. I scowled like an irritated young twenty-something; at that moment, I couldn't remember how old Hally Dubois was supposed to be.

"That's not funny."

"I've been here for a century, traveling the world, but mainly France because I like the crepes." Okay, the last part was stupid. Sue me.

"This isn't a *Dungeons and Dragons* game."

"Agent Thomas, I know you've been looking for the rest of Ian's guys, but I've told you time and time again I was never part of it."

"Then how do you explain the airport? That's some crazy coincidence for you to be there at the same time." He tapped the photo of me.

"That wasn't—" I started to argue but stopped. "That's it. I'm done arguing." Sam always told me I didn't have to answer Zack's questions if I didn't want to.

"I want you to sit down with me and Katie to look over her pictures and the documents I've got. You two may not know where they all are now, but—"

"I did not know them at the time of this picture. I'm done with this."

"It's better to give me the truth now. With the photos Katie submitted, in addition to other evidence, this is now an open investigation with Homeland Security and the DEA. If you're not careful, one of their agents will be on your ass. You hate me, but you'll hate them even worse. Give me the truth. Tell me what you know and let's get these victims home."

"I would help if I could. I'm genuinely surprised at your professionalism today."

"Come on—"

Lewis fidgeted, which distracted Zack. I looked over too. He locked eyes with mine. Then he blinked slowly and glanced at Zack. The message was clear. He had my back if I needed him.

"Agent Thomas, I'm sorry I can't help. If Ian gets in touch, I will contact you."

Zack touched his tongue to his teeth as if counting them, seeking patience.

"Time to leave now, Agent," Lewis said.

Zack looked from Lewis to me. "This isn't over. Me and Homeland wanna know how you got in this picture since you claimed to be in France. Let me tell you something, though. You don't look fifteen in this picture. Just sayin'."

My eyes flicked to Lewis, and my stomach cinched tighter. No, I looked exactly the same age. Lewis watched Zack as he packed up the photos.

"This is happening, Hally. Watch your back, because I will be."

I rolled my eyes.

Lewis went to the back door and held it open. "Goodbye, Agent Thomas." Zack looked at me for a moment longer, then left without another word.

Lewis and I stared at each other for a moment before he moved away from the door and went to sit behind the desk. "Hally—"

"That isn't me." That sounded so convincing. Everything started closing in around me.

"You wanna tell me what's goin' on?"

"You're doubting me?"

Lewis's eyebrows shot up to the top of his forehead, and his lip ring caught the light.

"I'm serious." I sounded like a whiny child, but damn it!

He shut his eyes and took some deep breaths. "I am your friend. I'm not gonna go reportin' you to that dick of a cop."

Damn, this was so unfair. "I have never run drugs."

"I don't doubt that," Lewis said, and I heard the truth in his words.

"Or trafficked for that matter." I shuddered.

"Mm-hmm."

"But I—I am—I'm older than I look. Okay?"

Lewis looked down at the desk. He opened his mouth and shut it again. "This friend of yours, Nolan?" He paused again. "He knows, doesn't he?"

I waited too long, giving Lewis his answer.

"Hot damn. I'm still callin' ya kiddo, 'cause there ain't no way you're older than me." Lewis stood up. "Two hundred and forty-six, my ass." He moved over to the cabinet and grabbed his coat and keys. "Elf." He snorted.

"Where are you going?" My voice trembled.

"To get you your coffee. Maybe you'll calm down after that."

"Lewis?" I stood up as he grabbed the door. "I'm sorry. I just can't—" Wringing my hands, I tried to think of a way to explain myself. My heart hurt as I told him what I needed to say. "If you want me to leave, I will."

The whites of his eyes stood out from his dark skin as he studied me. "No," he said at last. "No, I don't want you to leave. I just don't understand why you don't trust me."

Relieved, I released the breath I was holding. Lewis turned back to the door and opened it, but he stopped at the threshold. "Are you in witness protection? That's why you were shocked to see that Nolan guy. He's from before."

I'd never thought of that. I plopped down on the love seat and stared at him. I closed my mouth and swallowed.

"That's fuckin' awesome."

"I can't—"

"Hey, I know you can't say no more. Fucking cool! I won't tell nobody. I think you should tell Sam, though. He's been there for your lawyer stuff with Zack and all. You owe him that."

"Lewis, please—" But what did I say to that?

"I'm gonna go, and I promise, I won't say a word." He paused again. "Well, maybe for a mil." He smiled so big his eyes became slits. "So fuckin' cool."

"Lewis!" I balled my hands into fists.

He laughed and left.

"Well, at least you're not mad at me," I mused to an empty room.

I considered what Zack would do if I said I was in WITSEC. He'd call my bullshit as soon as he went looking for proof. I got up and went to splash some cold water on my face.

If I said I was thirty-three, I'd need to leave much sooner than I'd planned. I hit the edge of the sink. Damn it, this was so screwed up. I wiped my face on a paper towel and fixed the minimal amount of makeup I'd applied before rushing out of the house. The eyeliner was awash, but of course, glitter never really went away. Always a speck of it in some place or another.

Keeping my history in the past was becoming more difficult with each new life. With fingerprints, DNA, pictures, and a whole host of other technological crap, changing identities was a damn near impossible task. If all else failed, living in the Himalayas as a monk sounded promising. That ought to be fun. I'd have to shave my head, but I bet I'd still find the fucking glitter.

6

AT 6:05, RIGHT AFTER sunset, the last light still touched the bricks on the old hotel building across from Yula's Quill. Not enough to penetrate the tinted windows, though.

The last chorus of Evanescence's "My Immortal" played, and Lewis was humming along as he sketched on the opposite couch, even though he claimed to hate everything but country.

The events of the last twenty-four hours gnawed at me. My stomach growled, but I couldn't even eat my lunch earlier, the nasty lettuce notwithstanding. My head popped up at the jingle of the lobby door.

"Oh my gosh. Katie?" I shoved the laptop away and got up to give my friend a hug.

Katie squeezed me back. "Hello," she said in an airy voice that always danced on the air currents.

"Look at you!" I pushed her away to take full notice of her.

Her layered wheat-blonde hair reached all the way to her waist now. In California, she'd mostly been a walking skeleton. Katie had filled out all her curves and looked so much healthier. Her skin, the parts not covered in clothes or tattoos, didn't look deathly white, more pale peach now.

Katie wore a gray wool coat down to her knees, but her Japanese koi scene tattoo peeked out from under the collar. The piece, which Ian had done, came down and around one shoulder, and featured a sakura tree over a pond over a full back piece. A full sleeve of swimming koi on her left arm, which Ian and I both worked on. One of my first big pieces.

I lifted her hair and held her face in my hands. "You are so beautiful. Seattle agrees with you—must be the rain."

"Yeah, that must be it. Not that I've been clean for over three years now."

I turned back to Lewis, who was still sitting. "Lewis, it's K—"

"I know. Nice to finally meet you." Lewis waved from his seat.

"You too. I've heard so much about you." From behind Katie, two little hands slipped around her waist, and a little blond head poked out, complete with freckles and a button nose.

"Is this Seamus? He's so big." I bent down to his level. "I knew you when you were a baby."

His deep blue eyes were so like his father's but held his mother's warmth. He stared at me for a moment before he hid behind his mother's hip.

"Seamus, I have some coloring books and games to play with if you'd like?" I told him.

The four-year-old looked up at his mom. Katie nodded. He grabbed her hand, and they followed me over to the coffee table where all the kid stuff was stored. Seamus immediately pulled off his orange-and-blue winter coat, dropped it on the floor, and went for the puzzles.

"Sit, sit."

Katie settled down beside me and slid her hands under her thighs.

I scooped up all my art supplies and laptop and dumped them on an end table. "So, I don't think this is a coincidence—"

Her hair swished as she shook her head. "I wanted to tell you that I told Zack you're not involved. He's really got it in for you."

Lewis snorted. "You got that right." He swept something off his paper.

"Zack told me you said that. He said he thinks you're just protecting me."

Katie rolled her eyes and waved her hand. "Still, I'm sorry. So he told you about Ian, right?"

"Yeah. Have you heard from him yet?" I looked down at their son.

Katie followed my gaze. "No. I take it you haven't either?"

"No."

Katie leaned over and patted Seamus's back. "He hasn't seen Seamus since he went in. I love that you still keep puzzles and stuff."

"Mostly just Ray plays with them, unless her uncle Lewis has bought her another pony to play with."

"That's what uncles do." Lewis stuck his lip out, his eyes bright with fake innocence. "D'ya like toys, kid?" He gave Seamus the stink eye.

Seamus giggled and nodded big.

Katie laughed as I jabbed my thumb in his direction. "See what I have to deal with?"

Her eyes widened in mock horror. "Horrible."

She reached for my hand and squeezed. Wrapping my fingers around hers, I squeezed back. We hadn't done much laughing in Ian's tattoo shop. There hadn't been many girls either.

"I'm sorry I didn't keep in touch," I said.

We let go, and Katie slid her hands under her thighs again. "No, it was me. I had family matters to take care of. I didn't tell them about Seamus, and well, my family is...There're family traditions and Seamus is behind because I didn't bring him sooner."

"Sooner than one?"

"They didn't see him until he was two, but yeah. It seems silly. Gaelic traditions."

"Oh." I'd never heard of any Gaelic traditions like that, but then I'd never studied them either. "Family is important."

"It's everything. I am grateful they accepted me back."

"Because of Seamus?"

"Partially." Katie looked down at her knees and hunched in on herself.

"So...the boy?" I rushed to change the topic. "From Arizona? I don't remember him ever coming in." Throughout my two years in Ian's shop, a few kids had come in, some more often than others.

"They sent him to Seattle soon after Ian and I took him from Arizona. Didn't think I'd ever see him again. I took pictures of every kid I knew about. I gave police information when I could. No one ever did anything until Zack."

"Yeah, but Zack?" I leaned back. This sounded nothing like the DEA agent we knew. "You're telling me, of all the cops you've told over the years, Agent Zack-ass was the one to look into it?"

"Yeah. Right? He had a cousin taken when they were kids."

"No kidding?"

Katie nodded. "If I'd known then, I'da told Zack a long time ago."

Seamus came up to Katie and showed her his finished puzzle.

"I wish there was something useful I could do."

She kissed her son's head and set the puzzle on the table. "I dunno much either. We've both been out for too long."

"I couldn't go to the sentencing," I said.

"Right. You went and got your sister?"

"Cousin and her daughter—"

"Weren't they in an accident or something?"

Wow. That Katie remembered at all showed how much she'd recovered. Although, by the time of the trial, Katie had been clean for six months. Once she found out she was pregnant, she quit cold turkey.

"Yeah, Charlie's husband died in a car crash, and she wasn't coping well. We need to exchange numbers and schedule a playdate for the kids."

"Yes, that would be wonderful. Seamus doesn't have many friends outside of the family."

Another jingle brought our attention around to the entrance. The newcomer stood right inside the door, and the fluorescent lights made her wavy blonde hair look a harsh, dark yellow. She stood at about five-ten, and the pallor of her olive-toned skin made me think she didn't go out in the sun much. Clean but ripped jeans and a T-shirt that read, "Did you turn it off and back on first?" made me smile. I liked her already.

"Hello," Lewis and I said in unison.

"Oh, hello? I'm Dana. I have a seven o'clock appointment with Hally? I'm early, though."

"Totally fine." I couldn't place her accent, maybe an Eastern European one. Things had changed so much since the wall fell. I couldn't keep up.

Katie grabbed Seamus and pulled him close. "Hally?" she whispered and pulled on my arm. Her whole demeanor had changed, and for the first time this visit, I saw the old Katie. The scared-for-her-life Katie. We got up together, and she pulled me around Lewis, circling toward the door. If not for the fear in her eyes, her behavior would have seemed comical.

"What's going on?"

Katie's eyes flashed behind me to my new client. "Do you know her?" she breathed. She put a finger over my mouth and shook her head. So, instead of speaking, I shook my head no. She studied me for a good thirty seconds, tilting her head to look at my ears, then back to my eyes.

"How did I not see it before?" She licked her lips. "You're my friend, so I won't tell them, but you're not safe here anymore. You should go."

"What are you talking about? Is this about Ian?"

"Don't be coy, Hally." Katie touched my cheek, her eyebrows furrowed and her mouth set in a firm line. "Don't let them find you."

"Are you okay, Katie? Do you need me to call somebody?" She gave no signs of using, but her behavior had changed so fast.

"That's the last thing you want me to do." With that, Katie ushered her son out the door and turned right toward the viaduct.

"Holy hell." I couldn't move from my spot.

"What just happened?" Lewis said as he walked up to me. We stared into the night activity outside my shop. "She was doin' fine. That ever happened before with her?"

"She's had problems in her past, but I thought she was better now. Lewis, I'm scared she'll hurt herself or Seamus."

Lewis nodded, looking as shocked as I felt. "I can find her before she gets too far. You go on and talk to Dana here."

"No. Call Zack. The way she was acting, I don't think she'll calm down if we go after her. Zack can call her, or he can find someone who can get to her. I didn't get her phone number for a playdate either." I wrinkled my nose and slumped.

Lewis strode over to the register and grabbed the phone. "Sounds good."

I nodded and took a steadying breath. "So Dana? Can I get you something? Coffee, tea? A stiff drink?"

"Do you have any stiff drinks?" She laughed, which made me laugh as I shook my head.

"Seriously, though, do you want to reschedule? That was so bizarre."

"My flight home leaves Wednesday, so I won't have any other time."

"Oh..." With what had happened, I didn't think I was up for tattooing for the rest of the evening. "Okay. Let's go sit down and see what we can come up with."

Dana sat next to me, and a whiff of tree sap came up out of the old cushions. This was where Nol had sat. Where was he? Something rolled around in me. Not exactly like last night, but if it went on for too long, the dizziness would come back. No nausea yet. Something more subtle, perhaps a residual effect.

"Are you all right?" Dana touched my arm as I sat down.

"I...I feel a little off, but I can manage. Did you get a chance to look through my portfolio?"

"Oh yes, they are very beautiful. Your art is like magic."

Her choice of words gave me pause. "Did you—did you see anything you like?" I cleared my throat and tucked my hair behind my ear, brushing the edge of my hat and ear cuff. "An idea of what you want?"

"Oh, yes. I want an orange moon."

"Orange?" I hesitated. "The color orange?"

She nodded, satisfied with her answer. "Yes. When the Earth goes in front of the sun?

"Oh, a lunar eclipse." Well, color me stupid.

She furrowed her brow. "Will that be possible?"

"Yeah, that's fine. I just—"

"Thought you two might like somethin' to drink." Lewis came in, pushing the saloon doors with his back while holding three mugs in his arms. Where'd the time gone? "All we got is herbals, and Hally, I don't wanna hear you complainin' 'bout not gettin' coffee. Chamomile is gonna do you some good. Agent Thomas said he'll go check on her."

"Thanks. Do you think he'd give me her phone number?"

"Dunno. Worst he could say is no." He sat down with his *Blazing Saddles* mug and pulled his drawing pad onto his lap again.

My head continued to swim, but maybe the tea would help. The warm liquid coated my throat and my empty stomach. Well, shit. That salad was the only food I'd had today. Note to self: eat more. "Let's go ahead and get a rough draft started. Where do you want this done?"

"My neck." She placed her palm on the left side of her neck. "Here to there." From just under her ear to the bottom of her neck. Oh boy.

"Have you considered a secondary place?"

"No. It must be on my neck."

"It's just, a big orange dot—"

"That is where I want it."

"Okay." Maybe she'd change her mind later. I started sketching, shadowing the moon, and making the craters. "What about something else to go with it? Trees or birds flying through?"

"No trees or birds." She smiled and leaned toward me until her knee bumped my thigh.

"Clouds across the bottom, like fog?" I reached for a graphite pencil from the coffee table. My vision swam for a moment as I straightened. "It's just your moon would look like a big orange dot without anything else."

"What do you think would be best?" For a second, her caramel eyes with honey-yellow flecks were all I saw. Everything appeared larger than normal and slow. She moved, cupping her pointy chin, and things began to go back to normal. I blinked a few times, and my pencil tip came into focus, then the sketchbook. What the hell?

"Sorry." Clearing my throat again, I looked down at our sketch. The dizziness was getting worse. She'd asked a question. Right. "Maybe—"

"What about something circling it?" Lewis suggested.

"Like what?" Dana turned her shoulders toward Lewis and, in the process, bumped my leg. She was way too close, but every time I shifted away, she would come closer again. I'd have said something, but the weird, hazy feeling kept me from asking her to back up.

My mind drifted back to last night again as I drew: the curse, Aswryn, my grandparents, Laro, Nol, *Zayuri*—Dana's sharp intake of breath startled me out of my thoughts. The start of a dragon now circled the orange moon.

"A dragon, yes." Dana mostly breathed the words. "The way you have the wing dipping toward the middle is perfect."

"Thanks."

"It's coming along great, Hally." Lewis had crept up on us and was standing behind me, studying Dana, not my sketch.

"Thanks."

"You alright? You're actin' weird."

"I'm not feeling well. Everything feels slow." The lights and colors flickered brighter for a second. "I didn't get much sleep, either. Nol and I had a lot to discuss."

"Ah, 'Nol' now, is it? Spent the night, did he?" Lewis smirked.

"Don't give me that crap. We talked. That's all. Then he slept in my hammock. I'm gonna help him out this week."

"Sure, sure."

"Let's schedule this now," Dana blurted.

Lewis's eyes narrowed as he turned toward my client.

I reached for my phone to look at my calendar, and nausea lapped at the edges of my stomach. I started shivering. "You said you leave Wednesday. How about Tue—"

"Tomorrow. In the morning."

"That might work." I hesitated. What day was tomorrow again?

"We're closed tomorrow and Monday," Lewis answered.

"Oh, right." Sunk back into the couch, too dizzy to see the screen.

"Then Tuesday. Nine would do."

Lewis grunted and said something under his breath. Something nagged at the back of my mind about this week, but I couldn't remember. I squeezed my eyes shut and took a breath.

"Um, I..." If I could see past the glaring white light of the app to see my schedule. "Hang on. I'm trying to look at my calendar."

Dana's sigh vibrated through my head. "There is no other time that works for me."

My vision started to sharpen, and my screen came back into focus. "I guess that'll work."

"Hally? We're not open 'til noon, though."

I shrugged. "It'll be fine." She needed nine, so we'd do nine on Tuesday. No biggie.

Lewis frowned and rubbed his bald head. "Hal—"

"Fantastic. I'm excited to do this, Hally." She jumped up and bounced on the balls of her feet. Instead of shaking hands when I stood, Dana hugged me. Not what I'd expected, but whatever. "I can't wait to see you then."

We said our goodbyes, or I thought we'd said them. Through the dizziness, everything felt only half real.

"That woman rubs me the wrong way." Lewis's comment pulled me out of my fog.

"What?"

He followed me around as I cleaned up, grabbing his stuff as well. As he talked, my brain slowed its spinning. "I can't believe you let her push you 'bout your schedule. Didn't let you finish your sentences. What the fuck, Hally? And you'd just got done sayin' you were gonna help Nolan this week."

Oh, right. I shook my head. "If I need to, I can reschedule. I'll figure it out. Right now, I'm so groggy. I think Katie threw me off."

"It's okay. Like you said, you can reschedule. And if not, screw her. It's your art."

"Yeah." Still, something inside me worried about disappointing Dana. "I think I'm gonna call it a night." I closed my toolbox drawer with my hip. "I'm not feeling like myself at all. Do you think you'll be fine by yourself?"

"I dunno, kiddo. We're pretty busy," he mumbled as he gestured to his empty workspace across from mine. Lewis's office skeleton, Wyatt Earp, stood in the corner, watching us, wearing his cowboy hat, Mardi Gras beads, and temporary tattoos. "Wyatt might want another tattoo."

I grinned. "Smartass."

Tattooing needed to be done in a sterile environment, and while my area was clean, it still needed a thorough wipe down. And I felt guilty for not cleaning last night. Three-quarters of the way through, a group of young navy sailors came in, loud and boisterous. They talked to Lewis and sat down on the couches.

"You a tattoo artist?" One of the sailors had snuck back and found me.

"Uh, yeah?" What else would I be?

He smiled a toothy smile and leaned on my flimsy cubicle wall. "You don't seem too sure about that."

My dirty rag made it into the bleach bucket as I stood. "Yes, yes I am. Sorry, I'm cleaning."

"Yeah, I see that." He tipped his chin up. "I'm Justin."

Please don't ask me out. Please don't ask me out. "I'm Hally."

"Like Halle Berry?"

"Who?"

"*Perfect Stranger*?"

The movie didn't sound familiar.

"Storm in *X-Men*?"

"Oh. Sure, I guess."

Justin settled his chin on his hands. "So, I thought tattoo artists were supposed to have tattoos."

"I'm allergic to the ink. Got a scar and everything." I pulled my T-shirt off my shoulder to show him a few of my shrapnel scars, which I claimed tattoo ink had caused.

He whistled. "Wow. So what do—"

"*Bonjour*!" a familiar voice called out from the back. Charlie to the rescue. My niece wore one of her many little black dresses. This one touched above her knees, the hint of sequins catching the lights as she moved. Her long chestnut hair was arranged into a messy chignon, with wispy tendrils in front of her ears.

Physically, she took after her father: broad shoulders, taller than me (but who wasn't?) at five-eight, olive skin, dark brown eyes, and full lips. Tonight, she'd applied her makeup more dramatically than normal to match her evening attire. I didn't remember her having any plans for the night. Not that she needed to tell me, but my niece normally told me of her plans so I could watch Ray.

"Good evening, Lewis, Hally." Charlie acknowledged us in English.

"Hey, girl!" Lewis called from his studio. "Damn, Charlie. You look *good*."

"*Merci*, Lewis." Charlie greeted me with air cheek kisses.

"Thank the Mother you are here," I spoke in French. "Save me from breaking this poor sailor's heart."

Charlie's lips curled up in a liquid, flirtatious smile. She stepped in closer and placed her hand on my upper arm. "Come, Hally. I need to talk with you about tonight. Excuse me, please. I must steal her away."

Out of the corner of my eye, I caught Justin watching us, slack jawed. Once the break room door closed, she giggled.

"I'm not too sure that dissuaded him, Charlie."

"Eh, let his imagination run wild." She skipped to a black garment bag draped over the computer chair, her black heels clicking. "But I'm serious. We need to discuss tonight."

"Oh? I assume it has something to do with what you are wearing?"

"Yes, plans have changed. Mateo called me and told me you stood them up last night—"

I groaned. "I did not—"

"—to meet a hot guy named Nolan. An old friend from Europe. Mateo assumed I knew him." Charlie raised her eyebrows and paused, waiting for an explanation. "I had to pretend to know him." Again she paused, but I kept quiet. "Well?"

I shrugged. "Well, what?"

"Is this Nolan your ex from Spain? Can I meet him?" Charlie pouted, her brown eyes going round and sad. "Please, Tatie. I never get to meet anyone from your past." She sounded like Mateo.

"With good reason. But no, this isn't him. That was Daniel, and he won't ever get on a plane."

"So who's Nolan, then? When will I meet *him*?"

"I don't think—"

"Come on!" She pouted like a child instead of acting like a twenty-eight-year-old.

"He left already, love. Now, what is this you have?"

She perked up, Nol forgotten, and placed her hands on the garment bag. "This is your outfit for tonight."

"What? Where's Ray?" My stomach flipped as I thought of Aswryn.

"She's spending the night at Nat's—while you go to Cinder with Mateo and Sam to make up for last night."

Clubbing at Cinder meant dancing and drinking until closing. Then a sleepover at Sam and Mateo's house. I wouldn't get home until two p.m. If Nol came back before then, he wouldn't have a clue where to find me. Then again, he hadn't told me where the hell he'd gone either. The ass.

Then I remembered Charlie's plans! Doug! They had tickets for a show, and the plan was for me to watch Ray.

"Charlie, I've felt like shit for the past hour."

"No excuses."

A small black wad of cloth came flying my way, then another with straps. Lingerie, lacy bikini panties, and a lace push-up bra with an extra wide band that reached the bottom of my ribcage. Almost a midriff tank top.

"Ta-da!" Charlie turned with a black, sheer dress of mine from a year or so ago.

"Where's the slip for it? Did you bring leggings?"

She dropped her arms and groaned. "Tatie, don't be such a prude."

I gasped. "I'm not a prude. I'm just not a hooker."

"The bra is long enough to be a tank top. Now go put it on."

"No. I refuse to wear this in public."

"You will see how good it looks once it's on. Now go."

"When did you get so bossy?"

"What are you talking about? Everything I know I learned from you."

Giving her a sneering scoff, which had no effect on her, I folded the dress over my arm.

"Go. I promise the dress isn't as sheer as you think."

"Bullshit." But I went anyway. Once she saw how see-through it was, we could go home and at least get something more presentable.

7

THE DRESS COVERED MORE than I remembered and it wasn't as sheer as I thought. The front went low, but the back went up and wrapped around my neck as a choker. Charlie had thought to bring pantyhose and knee-high suede boots. If I moved the wrong way, my ass would show when the fabric swayed. Charlie mumbled that I knew how to move without anything showing, which I did. Again, I am French—well, for the past century. That counted in my book.

Sam came in soon after I got out of the bathroom, and things went too fast for me to argue. Cinder featured a fantastic view of Elliott Bay and Sculpture Park, visible from both two-story windows. Tall tables lined the walls in alcoves. Neon lights lit up the bar, making the bottles glow.

Mateo's spiky hair bobbed ten feet from the bar into the crowd of dancers. Sam had already apologized for not being at the meeting, several times throughout the day. He knew about Zack looking for Ian, but not the rest. He hadn't had time. Mateo gabbed about our night out the entire way there, providing no chance to bring up Zack.

The three of us had taken three shots each within the hour since we'd come in. The bartender came back with my drinks: a shot of tequila and a glass of water. Breathing heavily, I nodded and passed him a bill. I'd told myself I would drink more water than this. Whoops.

Three-quarters through my water, Mateo sauntered over, hips swaying, and grabbed my lace gloved hand. He didn't even try to talk—no point with the booming music.

On the floor, someone tugged my arm, and another someone shoved my shoulder. Sam was swaying in time to the music. Mateo pulled me close and began dancing again, the three of us forming a triangle. Every few seconds, I would feel a body press against my back as so many people danced together.

Dancing took me away more than any drink, but mixing in a few shots with my friends made the night that much more distracting, giving me some headspace not to think about the crap of today and yesterday.

Mateo grabbed Sam's hips and pulled him in for a kiss, going a little deeper than Sam usually allowed. He blinked shocked eyes at Mateo. Bumping Sam's shoulder to catch his attention, I shrugged, pulled him in, kissed his cheek, and twirled him. That got a laugh out of the two of them.

After a while, I pointed to the side of the floor, then to Mateo, and to me. We had drifted to the front of the club. Dodging a few people, I made my way out. I almost ran into two women holding drinks. How they'd managed to maneuver through the throng of people without spilling took massive skill.

The heavy lobby doors moved slowly, heavier from my intoxicated state, no doubt. A rush of refreshing cold air blew my hair back and flew through the thin fabric of my dress. I shivered.

The absence of everything but the beat took a moment to adjust to, almost like adjusting to dry land after a boat ride. I wobbled in my heels twice, damn maybe I was more drunk than I thought. I didn't fall in though! On the way back into the club, the wall of noise hit me harder than I expected.

Someone pushed back on the door, but I pushed harder and stuck my head in, about to yell at whoever to move off the fucking door. Who I saw made me swallow my words. What was this? Screw with Hally weekend?

The worst person imaginable blocked my way into the room. His evil, taut smile closed my throat. Not good. Ian's lips turned up at seeing my fear. He knew he had me.

A scar on Ian's cheek ruined his most prized tattoo: a spiderweb that expanded out around his ear, with a large skeletal spider smack in the middle of his cheek so the legs reached out to his eye, nose, and chin. The scar sliced through the abdomen. I would have winced at that damage if my body hadn't frozen up.

Ian stepped forward and used his chest to make me step back. Jolted by Ian's movement, I shoved back as hard as I could and slipped through, right into the mass of people. If I could make it to the bouncer, I'd be fine.

Ian grabbed my upper arm and squeezed. I ran into three people as Ian dragged me off the dance floor. He whipped me around against the wall next to the balcony door. I tried to punch him in the throat, then knee him when he dodged my fist. No luck. The icy air on the balcony shocked me as Ian shoved me through. I had a moment of sheer terror as I imagined him pushing me over the railing and down onto the large rocks of the waterfront.

"Scream and I'll snap your arm," Ian growled in my ear. I smelled the liquor on his breath. "Surprised to see me, bitch?" He shook me and slammed my back against the railing.

"Not really. Agent Thomas told me you got out." There was no way I'd mention Katie. His pinpoint pupils confirmed he had something else in his system besides alcohol. That made him unpredictable and dangerous. "You skipped your parole. I'm honored you'd risk more jail time for little ol' me."

Ian shook me a second time. My lower arms tingled from lack of circulation. "Shut up."

I rolled my eyes. "You are so predictable, Ian." Again, I provoked him. I needed to take Ian's advice and shut up. "They know you left California, and Thomas knows you're up here. I bet he's watching me right now." Where the hell was my smug attitude coming from? Was I that drunk?

"Not in this crowd he ain't. We need to talk."

"Everyone's wantin' to talk to me this weekend. What do *you* want?" I blurted with no regard for self-preservation. Aswryn must have knocked the sense right out of my head.

"Where's Katie?" Ian tilted his shaved head. His white, bushy eyebrows scrunched together like fuzzy albino caterpillars.

I giggled at the thought.

"What's so fuckin' funny?"

I shook my head, but I couldn't stop smiling. "I'm a tad bit drunk. Please disregard the stupid things I say or do."

The caterpillars pushed against each other. Ian gave me a hard shake that hurt my neck. That wiped the smile off my face. "You owe me a lot of money, Hally. A lot."

Gaining some inner wisdom, I kept my mouth shut.

A slow, evil smile threatened to split his face. "Either you tell me where Katie is, or you work off what you owe me. How many languages do you know, again?" I could almost see the steam rolling out of his ears as he squinted in thought. "More than me." Ian pushed his index finger against my chest. "Me and my new partner came up with how you're gonna pay me back." He wagged his finger in front of me, tapping my nose on the last wag. He let go of my left arm to use his right hand. "All you gotta do is travel. So which is it gonna be, bitch?"

That must be where Agent Zack-ass had gotten the idea of me running drugs across borders for him. "Fuck you," I spat in his face and shoved my thumb in his eye socket.

Ian growled, wrapped his fingers around my wrist, and yanked. His elbow hit my forehead, and then he slapped me across the face. My ears rang.

"You fucking little bitch." He leaned his head against mine. "You wanna play this game? Fine. You fuckin' cunt. You're gonna take me to Katie."

So, which was I? A bitch or a cunt? I almost asked him but held my tongue. Ian yanked me around, and I dropped in front of him like a deadweight. Which was a bit unfortunate because he tripped over me and fell on his face.

No fucking way would I let this moron get to Katie and Seamus.

Ian's lower body fell on me, so even if I had been sober, it'd have taken a while to untangle myself. But with Ian's graceful face-plant, we got the attention of the club's other patrons. Two came to me, and two went to Ian.

"Dude, you okay?" one guy, still holding his Corona, asked Ian. He wore a shiny clubbing shirt, but with a Hawaiian print. Cute.

Someone grabbed me by the upper arms and helped me stand. The girl was taller than me, with adorable, tightly curled dark hair that came to just above her shoulders. Her olive-green dress complemented her warm bronze skin, just a tad darker than Nol's. She wore yellow, pink, orange, and an assortment of other colored bands around her arms that reminded me of rainbows. She, too, held a Corona.

"Help," I whispered to her. "Get a bouncer. Hurry." Her light brown eyes went wide, but she set her jaw.

She looked up at the girl that could have been her sister next to her, and nodded. The other girl went running into the club while the guys helped Ian to his feet. Both men only came to about Ian's chin and were half as bulky. They wouldn't stand a chance. Ian stared daggers at me, while one of them tried to get his attention. He knew I'd dropped on purpose.

"Let's get you inside."

"He won't let me leave without him."

"Pat?" Rainbow Girl looked over at the trio standing five feet in front of us. "Pat," she yelled louder over the music.

The young man with his arm around Ian's looked over at us.

"White tanker."

Whatever that meant, he took her meaning and nodded back.

"Come on. They got this. We'll take the other door," Rainbow said.

"There's another door?" I asked, looking around the deck. Sure enough, all the way to the left, a door led inside.

"Don't you fuckin' take her anywhere. Let go of me."

I looked back in time to see Ian hit Pat in the stomach and shove Pat's friend aside. "Run," I told the girl. "Just run."

Her friend was getting the bouncer. This brave girl didn't need to stay with me. Ian's arm snaked around my waist and pulled me back to him.

"Hey, asshole!" my savior in rainbow armbands yelled. She set her feet shoulder-width apart, with her hands planted on her hips. "Let her go."

Ian laughed. "Or what?"

I stomped on Ian's foot with the heel of my boot. Ian picked his foot up and jumped back. I kicked his shin and backed up toward the brave girl who'd stood up to Ian, a man three times her weight.

"Let's go!" I yelled before I stumbled. She caught my arm, and we ran to the other door just as two bouncers came through it to get Ian. We stood there, clasping arms, this stranger and me watching as Ian argued with the bouncers pushing him toward the door.

"Hally! You tell me where Katie is right now."

"Or what, Ian? You're gonna threaten me with all these witnesses around? Really? Right after you broke parole? I knew you were stupid, but this tops the cake."

"You fuckin' bitch!"

"Get a new line!" I yelled as the bouncers dragged him through the door. "Thank you," I told the girl still clasping my arms. "That was—" I swallowed before continuing. "That was very brave of you."

Pat and his friend came up next. "How ya doin' there?"

"Good, all thanks to you four. Where's your friend?"

"I'm sure Jess will be here soon. You wanna go inside? Do you have anyone else with you?"

I let out a short bark of laughter. "I wasn't with him. He found me."

"I see."

"But yes, I came with friends whom I must find on the dance floor and ruin their good time."

"I'm sure they won't mind after they find out what happened," Rainbow said.

"Probably not."

The three of them walked back inside with me after grabbing their Coronas, plus Jess's, off the railing—couldn't forget those. Unfortunately, Ian's outburst hadn't ended outside, and many people had stopped dancing to watch as the two employees dragged a red-faced, white-eyebrowed fridge of a man, this close to kicking and screaming, out the front door.

Mateo's styled dark hair, atop a worried face, came bobbing out of the crowd. Sam's golden curls came into view next to Mateo's shoulder as they got past most of the lookie-loos.

"Mateo! Sam!" I called out and waved them over before I smiled at my saviors.

"Hally! Oh my God. How did Ian get in here?"

"Like everyone else did, Mateo," I teased and set a hand on his shoulder.

Mateo pulled me in and hugged me. The cologne, hair products, and soap that made up Mateo wrapped around me. My body stopped shaking, and I relaxed against him. I let go of Mateo and hugged Sam. Being the same height, his hair got in my face, and I smelled the conditioner and cologne mingling around his neck. Jeez, I loved these guys. And Aswryn could take them away at any moment. Nol had said she wouldn't try again for a few days, and I believed him. But would she attack me or try to take my loved ones?

"We need to go, guys."

"Agreed. Call Zack in the car. You wanna come home with us?" Sam slipped his arm behind my back and went to pull me away.

"Just a sec." I turned to the crew who'd saved me. "Thanks, you guys. The world needs more people like you."

Rainbow hopped once and came over to hug me, her hair bouncing along with her. "You take care, and I hope you never have to see that asshole again."

Mateo wrapped his arms around each of us, and we made slow progress through the crowd abuzz from the big event. How embarrassing. At least no one was looking at me. We got to the door, and one of the bouncers stopped us.

"You okay, ma'am?"

"I'm fine, but don't call me ma'am." I winked at him, which made him show off his pearly whites.

"Okay. We're gonna keep him here. You said something about parole?"

"Yeah, he skipped parole to come find his ex and kid up here."

"Okay, we'll get on that."

Sam held his hand out to shake the man's hand. "Thank you. I don't want to imagine what could have happened." Sam took a shuddering breath.

I smiled at the bouncer. "You don't have to, Sam. It's gonna be okay."

The bouncer held the door for us, and we could hear Ian yelling from the staff lounge. We grabbed our coats from the closet, and I fished my phone out of my pocket.

Next on the agenda—calling my least favorite DEA agent.

"Hally, you wanna go to our house?" Sam asked again.

"No, I'll be okay. Ian's gonna be picked up and taken in soon, which makes me feel great." I looked down at the bright screen and flipped through my contacts to find Zack's number. "I'll text Charlie. She might stay at Doug's tonight, though." I swished my hair out of the way and put the phone to my ear, a habit of many decades with long hair.

"Hally?" Zack's gruff voice made me think he had been sleeping. Oh well.

"Hey. Ian showed up at Cinder tonight."

"Cinder? What's that?" He woke up pretty damn fast.

"A dance club on Queen Anne Hill."

"When was this?"

"The bouncers grabbed him when he tried to take me. They're calling the police. You're right. He wants Katie something fierce."

"Great. Thanks, Hally."

"Um, you're welcome?" That was the absolute first time I'd ever heard the big T from him. Ever.

"What? I can say thank you."

"I didn't know it was in your vocabulary, honestly."

Agent Thomas snorted. "Whatever." The line went dead on my end this time.

"He said thank you."

"It's something people usually say when they're grateful," Mateo said.

"Not Agent Zack-ass Thomas."

"To be fair, dear, Agent Thomas and Hally don't have the best of relationships." The scent of real leather wafted out as Sam opened my door while looking at his partner already sitting in the car with the door open.

"That's an understatement." Mateo pulled his phone out, checking whatever computer scientists checked while on vacation. Wait—

"Is that a house? You're not moving, are you?"

A large, brown, two-story house, with a bright green yard and palm trees, flashed up on Mateo's screen. Not that I made a habit of looking over people's shoulders.

Mateo tsked. "No. Vacation homes." He showed me his screen. Nice. Seemed reasonable, and so not my business.

"Sorry, Mateo. I didn't mean to look. It was just there when I glanced over."

"It's okay, *ojitos*." He touched my fingertips holding the back of his seat.

I dropped back into the comfy seat of Sam's Audi A8. "Second night ruined in a row."

"Girl, whataya talking about? Last night was a treat. That Nolan is a cutie. We better see him after he gets his ass back here—and after you ream it for not telling you where he went, of course."

Not a chance, but I couldn't keep from smiling. "Sure." Absolutely no way.

"Let's getcha home." Sam smiled at me from the rearview mirror.

He needed to know about the photos, but that conversation would happen when I had a better excuse than Lewis's WITSEC idea. The guy who watched everything to do with the Wild West would come up with *that*.

"What's so funny?" Sam caught me smiling about Lewis in the mirror again.

"Something Lewis said, had to have been there." If Zack pressed this Arizona thing, I would need to leave. There were no two ways about it.

Mateo, Sam, Lewis, and his girlfriend, Yumi, had become closer to me than most friends through the years, besides my foster sister's family. Aswryn found me here and I was sure she'd follow me. The sooner I left, the less chance Aswryn would discover my friends.

"You okay?"

"I'm just tired, Sam."

"And worried about Mr. Cutie?" Mateo twisted around.

"That, too. He is so getting the longest lecture of his life if he comes back."

"He seems like good people, Hally. You don't get too many of those in life."

"Then how'd I get so lucky to find four of them here?"

"Ah, shucks." Mateo laughed.

And I'd be leaving them soon. What a horrible friend I was. One thing was for sure, I was too drunk to make any solid decisions tonight.

8

"Tatie!" Charlie's yell woke me too damn early. Hadn't I just fallen asleep?

"*Quoi*?" *What*? I mumbled into my pillow. I turned my head and peeked around the room. Sunlight streamed across my ceiling. Sunrise. So about seven? I groaned and burrowed into my blankets. I hated mornings.

"*Tatie, réveiller!*" *Auntie, wake up.* "Sam is on the phone for you," she said in English to include Sam.

That brought my head up. "What?" I had a limited vocabulary before coffee, and my head hurt. Charlie's silhouette twirled across my room.

I covered my face with my arm and squeezed my eyes tightly, which made my head pound worse. This better be important, like death or fire important, because I'd only gotten three hours of sleep, if that. And I was still hungover.

"Oh good, she's awake. Sam needs to talk to you about that guy..." She paused. "Right? He said Nolan called him a few minutes ago."

"*Quoi*?" I bolted upright, trying to ignore the pressure between my temples. See, low vocab. "*Donne-moi.*" *Gimme.* Eyes closed, I held out my hand.

Charlie handed me the phone with a "Here she is" before flopping down on the bed over my legs. I mumbled something—in French, English, or something else, I had no clue.

"Hally, Nolan just called from the West Seattle police station. They're holding him over there because he doesn't have his passport."

"What the hell?" I pulled my legs out from under Charlie and flung my blanket back. I paused to gather my thoughts, making sure I spoke the right language and didn't mumble. "Why the hell did he call you?" Did I mention I'm not a morning person?

Familiar with my morning attitude, Sam didn't sound offended, nor did he sound hungover. "He doesn't have your number, and I gave him my card Friday night, remember?"

No, I did not. "'Kay—"

"I'll meet you there. Did he leave his passport at your house?"

"Um." Such a massive extent of a vocabulary. "I dunno."

Sam stayed silent for several breaths. "Okay. Let's just focus on getting him out. They can't hold him without charging him, but it's not like they'll inform him of this."

"Wonderful."

"Stay positive. You'll get through this."

I rolled my eyes. "Have you met me?"

Sam chuckled. "Oh, and lay the accent on thick. I think Nolan's playing the 'not much English' card. He hasn't answered their questions, and they're irritated with him 'bout it."

"Crap. Thank you. You're the best."

I tossed the phone on the bed and caught Charlie staring at me with her big brown pouty eyes. She was already dressed in black jeans and a soft gray sweater that went past her wrists and covered most of her hands. Her dark brown hair lay loose over her shoulders. Her makeup, impeccable as usual, looked almost non-existent, but the look was actually harder to achieve than you'd think.

"Don't start." I pointed at her and went into my closet to pick out clothes.

"Come on, Tatie." Charlie followed me.

"Do you need the car today?" I shoved my clothes around on the hangers.

She leaned against the doorframe. "I have to pick up Ray before dinner, but we've got time."

Crap. Dinner. I forgot about Sunday dinner with all our friends. All we needed were people coming to the place Aswryn had found me Friday night. Fan-freaking-tastic.

"We? Charlie, you aren't going. This is private. Something I want everyone to stay away from—"

"Too late for that. Who is Nolan?"

I sighed. Charlie, and my entire human family, had more of a right to know about this situation than any of my friends here. My family knew almost everything about me. I met Charlie's great-great-grandmother, Emmaline, almost a year after arriving in this realm. Her family took me in, adopted me, accepted me, and kept me alive. Emma sensed I wasn't human as soon as we met and each of her descendants had the same sixth-sense. The second Charlie met Nol, she would know he was an *enda*.

"And do what, exactly?" Charlie continued. "Where's he live? What's he want? Mateo said something about him needing your help. What with?"

I registered Charlie had been talking for a while now. She resembled my foster sister in her extrovertedness and persistence. And they were both smart as a whip. I froze pulling my shirt off the hanger. Nol had those same qualities. Well, I'll be damned.

"Tatie, are you even listening?" She stood in the doorway still, back on the frame, playing with a lock of her hair.

"Of course, love. How could I not? There is no ignoring you."

"I know. I'm good at being annoying. Spill it, lady!" She tossed her hair back.

I'd grabbed one of the first shirts I'd seen, my cream doily blouse. Cute as hell. Lace cotton, like a doily, and wavy cuffs on the short sleeves and at the midriff hem. A low-cut neckline with padded cotton lace buttons.

"Um, no, you are not wearing that."

I looked down at my outfit. "What's wrong? You love this blouse."

"I mean the slacks. You aren't going to a business meeting."

My shoulders dropped. She was right. I picked black jeans that had more rips, buckles and zippers than fabric. And of course I wore my favorite rose-embroidered black Docs.

"Better?" I scowled.

The corner of Charlie's full pink lips twisted, a little quirk of hers when contemplating. She stretched her arms above her head. Her stomach peeked out under her gray sweater. "You'll do. Now get a move on." She grabbed my arm and pulled me toward the bathroom. "You've got five minutes."

"There is no way I can be ready in five minutes, Charlie."

"You'll manage."

I stopped at the bathroom door and turned to face her. Charlie stood at the top of the stairs and smiled a conniving, evil smile. She'd never have gotten away with that sassy comment as a child.

I shook one finger at her and pursed my lips, which only made her smile bigger. My tactics weren't working.

Charlie giggled. "Hurry, or I'll leave without you." With that, Charlie headed downstairs with a spring in her step. Being so chipper in the morning should be outlawed. "I haven't heard the door creak. Get in there, Tatie."

Growling, I swung the door enough for her to hear the creaky hinge and the click of the latch. No time for a shower, so I wet my hair down and put conditioner in it; otherwise, I'd have a big black puffball on top of my head.

My mind kept drifting through scenarios that explained the series of events that had brought Nol to the station. I eased up on my toothbrush. What the hell was he doing at a police station? And a passport? Of course Nol didn't have that.

I lowered my mascara brush and sighed at my reflection.

It looked like I had to call my forger, and buy Nol a freaking fake passport. I paid the guy enough to keep his mouth shut, but as far as illegal dealings went, David wasn't that bad of a guy.

"Tatie!" Charlie yelled, her voice echoing up the open stairwell and through the bathroom door. "Let's go. I'm sure you look great, as usual."

A little bit of pale champagne shimmer power over my freckles would do it.

"Tatie Hally! Come on!"

Makeup done, teeth brushed, I threw the door open, made sure the handle didn't hit the wall, and headed to Charlie, my Docs tromping all the way down the stairs.

"So, who said you were coming with me?"

Charlie leaned against the doorframe to the laundry room, swinging the keys around her finger, a mischievous twinkle in her brown eyes. "Me. I'm meeting this guy, no ifs, butts, or nuts."

I smiled. "It's no ifs, ands, or buts, love."

Charlie shrugged. "I like mine better." Which translated to: she knew but didn't care. Charlie never aimed to play down her French heritage or remember American slang. I'll admit, I'd seen guys fawn all over her when she messed up her words.

"Whatever, love. I am too tired and hungover to object to you coming this morning."

She pulled the laundry room door open, tossed the keys up, and snatched them. The winter sunrise, through the large back windows, cast an orange glow on Charlie's hair, turning it mahogany. "Don't think I'm dropping this subject."

"I have no idea what you are talking about." I looked away and held my chin up.

"Bullshit you don't. We have roughly fifteen minutes before we get there. Plus the time it will take to find a parking spot. You have ample time to fill me in." The icy air slapped our faces as Charlie opened the back door.

"You might not like it," I warned as I adjusted my favorite red and black swallow-tail coat, then stepped out onto the porch with her. The bitter cold of the railing bit into my palm as I descended.

Charlie spun around at the bottom of the stairs, jumping on the balls of her feet. "Just tell me."

"Give me the keys. I'm driving."

She narrowed her eyes. I gave her my best parental look. Resigned, knowing she'd never win against her Tatie Hally, she harrumphed.

Her warm breath billowed around us. Charlie dropped the keys in my hand, then cocked a hip and jutted her chin out. She gave me one of those quizzical, guarded looks, waiting for my answer. "I'm not going any farther—"

I smirked and crossed my arms. This oughta be good. "Nolan is Nol."

She didn't register my words. "Okaaay, that's grea—wait, what!" Her doe eyes flashed bright.

I couldn't hold in my laugh.

She set her hands on her hips. "Don't bullshit me. Really, who is he?"

I hooked her arm and guided her through our backyard. "Twynolan, my one and only *muranildo*."

"Not funny, Tatie. Where's this coming from? You never joke like this."

"I do not. He has asked for my help." I patted her arm. "Come, love. I'll explain in the car."

"Wait, you're serious? I get to meet Nol?"

I nodded, grinning at her stunned expression.

"Nol? *The* Nol? Your Nol?"

"Mm-hm." I kicked a frozen piece of dirt off the cracked cement.

"But how? I mean, why? What—"

I opened the gate and guided her through first. "Are you going to let me explain, or are you going to pepper me with questions?"

Charlie shut her mouth, did a little skip, and hurried to the passenger door, squealing. Where did I start?

SEATTLE DID NOT DISAPPOINT in downtown traffic congestion. What should have been a fifteen-minute ride turned into half an hour, allowing more time for questions I had no answers for such as plague symptoms, points of infection, and if it was a virus or bacteria or something unknown in this realm. Oh boy. Sam texted me twice for ETA updates.

We found parking on Stewart, down and around the block. The Volvo's engine pinged, and the pitter-patter of ice drops tapped the faded brown hood. Dark clouds threatened to dump more freezing cold rain upon our heads if we didn't move our asses.

"Sam is saying the police want a passport and visa," I said instead of getting out.

"What are you going to do?"

"Get papers for him, I guess."

She looked out the windshield. "Shit."

"Exactly." I bit the end of my thumbnail as I watched cars pass the intersection we were facing.

"How will you do that with Agent Thomas watching you?"

"Do you think that will matter?"

She shrugged. "What do the Americans say? Cover your ass." Charlie puffed out a breath and leaned back again. "Why everything at once?"

I threw up my hands. "That's what I said!"

"You can't call the forger on any phone Thomas knows about."

"Good thought. How about you go get me a cheap one while I'm in there?"

She narrowed her eyes. "Fat chance. Let's go." To drive her point home, she shoved her heavy door all the way open.

"You are as stubborn as your pepé."

"Heard that one before," Charlie mumbled.

"I will love you forever and ever. Besides, what is there for you to do here?" I gestured to the large police station.

She clicked her tongue. Specks of ice clung to her hair as she twisted her lips, considering. "You'll leave with Sam."

"I will not. I promise."

Charlie shifted her weight and adjusted her purse strap. "Fine."

"Thank you, Charlie." I pulled her in to kiss her cheeks. "Whatever you want for this."

"Full backstory. I want to know everything. Plus, he has some explaining to do. He thinks he can waltz into your life after what he said to you?" She noticed my sharp intake of breath. "I will behave, Tatie. What he told you destroyed you, but I have always wanted to meet him. Do you think he'll let me take some cell samples?"

"I don't know. He doesn't know that my magic is blocked. I don't want him to know—"

"*Pourquoi*?" *Why?* Charlie flung her arms around as she talked in typical French fashion. "He's going to find out! You're crazy if you think you can hide that from him."

"Yes, but I—I want to tell him." I shoved my rain-damp hair back and looked away. "I just don't know how. I tried, but the words wouldn't come out." I stepped closer to her, pleading. "Please? Let me tell him when I'm ready."

Charlie looked up the hill, licking her lips in contemplation. Her warm breath drifted away. "You have until tonight."

"That's not long enough."

"If he's as smart as you say he is, he may already suspect it. Tonight after dinner."

I sucked in air. "What do you think the chances of canceling that would be?"

"Not one, Hally Dubois."

Groaning, I hugged her again, rising onto my toes to rest my chin on her shoulder. "I worry this won't go well. Something doesn't feel right."

She nodded her cheek next to my temple. "Yes, me too."

My insides tightened. With her family's second sense, the ominous feeling solidified in the pit of my stomach. I had a fleeting thought to snatch Charlie and Ray away before shit hit the fan, but that wouldn't work. Fate had a way of finding you wherever you went. And with that wonderful thought, she took the keys. It only occurred to me after she'd left that she could have dropped me off at the front. We were both a bit preoccupied.

The almost complete silence of the West Police Precinct replacing the downpour of rain left a ringing in my ears. The rainwater dripped off me onto the Seattle Police logo. Hollywood lied. The police station looked nothing like in the movies. The lobby had a bulldog statue and two glass boxes with books or something in them. Hmm, most impressive. My Docs squeaked on the concrete floor and echoed around the space. Two officers with squawking walkie-talkies walked around me, deep in conversation. A woman stood in a corner closest to the welcome desk, talking on her phone. She didn't sound too happy.

One person walked out of the women's restroom and passed me going to the seats against the left wall. I walked up to the welcome desk. The police officer behind it had to be north of fifty, and she reeked of cigarettes.

"Ahem?"

The desk officer looked up from her computer screen.

"I'm Hally Dubois—"

"Sign in on this and take a seat, 'kay, hun?"

"I believe my lawyer is back there with my friend."

She focused her green-blue eyes at me, clear and bright with wisdom. "Your no-English-speaking friend?"

I slumped. She smiled, her smoker's yellow-tinted wrinkles folding together, crinkling into her laugh lines. "Guess you're here to translate?"

I didn't answer.

"Sign in and I can get someone to take you to them."

She nodded after I'd signed in and pointed to her left. My eyes followed her finger to the door a police officer had just walked out of. Behind that door was what I imagined a police station should look like.

With so many voices and phones, I couldn't tell what anyone was saying. A sea of cubicles filled the large room. Officers sat staring at screens or talking on phones. Some stood talking to their buddies or civilians. A few of those civilians had handcuffs on, too. A kid in a flannel shirt and baggy jeans and a woman with a huge purse nagging about him being grounded until graduation walked past me and through the door.

"Dean?" To my left, the front desk officer looked somewhere beyond me. No one turned toward her. "Officer Dean," she called a little louder.

A uniformed officer about ten feet to my right with a coffee in her hand perked up. "Yeah?" She used a tone that some *might* have considered respectful.

"Help this girl. Please." It was not a request.

Officer Dean turned to me, a bored look in her low-lidded brown eyes. I saw a hint of Asian ethnicity in her dark straight hair and cheekbones. She said something to her colleague, who sat in front of his desk. She lifted her chin in my direction. The officer's hazel eyes assessed me. Neither of them approved of what they saw.

Understanding dawned. My hair was sopping wet, dripping between my neck and coat collar. My jeans were wet above my boots. I was sure I looked like a drowned little punk, with all the zippers and rips in my jeans and Doc Martens.

Then I realized my swallowtail coat looked a little...unconventional, if you would. Add to that my dragon ear cuffs, silver lip ring, and black eyeliner. Perfect for a gothic, badass tattooist, but not so good for grown-up first impressions. For a moment, I felt embarrassed, but then I stood up straighter. Their opinion of me did not matter, and I'd be damned if I allowed these people to make me feel inferior.

Since Officer Dean seemed incapable of walking toward me, I went to her. Neither of them talked to me when I got there. The other officer—Officer Miller, according to his name tag—had a blond Marine-style buzz cut. Neither of them looked older than thirty.

Going for bitchy and laying the accent on thick, I lifted my chin and stared them down. "I am Hally Dubois. I'm here meeting my lawyer, Samuel Decker, and we are here for a friend whom you have kept here for far too long. Where are they?"

Officer Dean's shoulders hunched. Still, she said nothing. Officer Miller, on the other hand, stood up straighter. He had an incredible smile and a dimple on his chin. I bet he got a lot of girls with that smile. "Well, I guess we can go see what's goin' on, ma'am. I'm not too familiar with the situation. Dean, you wanna go ask the sergeant?" Miller had a slow southern drawl. Texan, I decided.

I nodded. "Good, but don't call me ma'am." I lifted an eyebrow at Dean until she got a move on.

"I don't know how long your friends will be, so how 'bout I show you where you can wait?"

"Why would it take so long to find someone?" I shrugged and tipped my chin down. "This place isn't *that* big."

"Like I said, I don't know the situation, and we're busier than we look."

Irritated, I pursed my lips, waited a few seconds, then nodded again. I waved my hand for him to go first. "Are we going, or are we waiting for your co-worker?" These people were going to get a bad review on Yelp if they weren't careful.

"Oh right. Sorry, ma'am."

Once on the opposite side of the room, we passed a beverage station, complete with sugar, creamer, napkins, and sticks. The coffee smelled burnt, but if this took too long, I'd be willing to take my chances. Six plastic chairs lined the wall to face the precinct.

My hands slid down the backs of my thighs before I perched on the edge of the last seat. Officer Miller shifted next to me. Was he waiting for a tip or something?

"I need to get back to workin' on my reports. The paperwork is never-ending."

"You weren't doing your paperwork when I came in." Yes, I was laying the bitchiness on thick, but they'd pissed me off. Still, all of this before coffee.

"You just wait here now, ma'am." With that, he left me to my own thoughts.

My phone chirped. Charlie had found a phone, and she was on her way, except she'd used a lot of acronyms and emojis. I rolled my eyes and sent her an OK.

"Hallë?" Nol's sharp tone made me jump. "What are you doing here?" he snapped in *Aemirin*.

He was mad at me? Shocked at his attitude, I couldn't come up with a response. Why the hell wouldn't I be here?

"*C'yo.*" He paced while he muttered in *Aemirin*. "I called Sam to help me. I can't believe I was allowed to leave at any time. What a joke. They treated me as if I were guilty before asking me anything. Such incompetent, irritating officers. What the fuck is a passport and visa?" Nol growled.

He stopped pacing and dropped into a chair next to me. Brooding, Nol leaned back, lounging in the chair with his long legs crossed at the ankles, and rested his hands on his stomach. Pouting, he glared at the people working behind their desks as if they were personally responsible for his issue.

I shook my head.

"*Mannan?*" *What*, he snapped.

With that attitude, would he throw a fit or close down if I told him why I was pissed? My lips turned up in a sneer.

"Nothing."

"What? Tell me." Nol sat up, annoyed and offensive. "*Hallë.*"

"Do not get me started on all the shit that is wrong with this." Too pissed to care, I didn't bother to keep my voice down. Two officers stood up and peeked over their cubicles. *No concern of yours, people. Get back to work.*

Nol dropped back against his chair, hard enough to make the connected chairs move. "*Endaë,*" he sighed, the equivalent of "women."

A short, harsh laugh escaped me. "You're being a dick, you know that? You are too smart to be this stupid. The Nol I knew would have figured this out on his own. The Nol I knew would've considered other points of view and understood what you pulled is wrong." I stood up and began walking out to put distance between us before I screamed at him and his clueless face. Unbelievable.

Of course he followed me. So not the right thing to do. Once I entered the lobby, Nol tried to grab my arm. I yanked it away and reared on him. "*Sye voida devin.*" *Don't touch me.* My harsh words echoed around us.

Nol stepped back, more confused now than angry. "How do you expect me to understand if you won't tell me?" he continued in *Aemirin*

"I shouldn't have to," I hissed back. "Have you listened to yourself? All you can do is complain about how the police treated you."

Nol still looked clueless.

Giving up, I blew up at him. "You left Friday night after you convinced me to help you. Gone. No note. Nothing. Then you show up at a police station two days later, and all you tell me is you're irritated with the police?"

"Hallë—"

"Don't 'Hallë' me, Twynolan."

"You are angry because I am irritated?"

"Did you hear anything I said? I'm not angry that you're irritated. On the contrary, I would be too if they'd kept me here as long as they have."

"*Mina*—" I

"Why, hello." Mateo's voice echoed through the lobby.

Both of us stood stock still as Mateo walked toward us, his hands in his pockets, the door closing behind him. How the hell was he so awake this early? Only one reason. He hadn't gone to bed yet. Like me, Mateo was not a morning person.

"Where did you come from?" I leaned in to give him air cheek kisses.

"I came with Sam. Waited out in the car trying to catch some sleep. Sam texted me that you two went into the lobby." He waved his arm around, encompassing the entire station in case we didn't know what he meant. "You, Nolan, are lucky Hally has a phenomenal lawyer friend."

"I aim to please." Sam came up behind us. "Good morning, Hally. You good, Nolan?" Sam came up beside Nol and placed a hand on his arm.

"I cannot thank you enough, Sam. I am sorry I had to call you."

Sam waved his hand. "Nah, I gave you the card for a reason. I will need to get some details about what happened, though. And you have to find your passport."

Nol rolled his shoulders back and nodded in agreement. "Very well. I would be happy to talk to you any time."

"I need breakfast," Mateo announced, coming up beside Sam and grabbing his arm with both hands.

"Great idea," Sam agreed, shifting his weight before Mateo could pull him off balance. "You two can eat while I talk to Nolan."

"Guys, I'm in no mood to go out to eat. Can you not see I'm pissed at him?"

"Oh, trust me, I heard you. You've been pissed at him since he got here. I kinda get why you'd be pissed at him this time, though," Mateo said. "I mean, dude, leaving and making her worry all day yesterday? It scared all of us when the police called and said they had you. Jesus Christ. We thought you were dead."

Nol's blue eyes widened, making them look darker. His lips parted as he finally got it.

I needed coffee, but there was coffee at home. We could talk at home, and I could yell at Nol to my heart's content.

"I would love to eat, Mateo, for this may be my last meal once Hallë has finished with me." Nol winked at Mateo, and his dimple showed.

"That settles it. *Ojitos*, you're outvoted. So, unless you wanna walk your grumpy ass home in the rain, you're gonna have to give up and come with us." Mateo waggled his finger toward the floor near my feet.

"Charlie and I drove here. She'll be here any moment. How the hell are you two not hungover?"

"We didn't drink as much as you did," Sam said.

The white noise of the rain on the pavement filled the lobby. Charlie walked through the front door with her hood up. Tendrils of her brown hair stuck to her face and rain jacket.

"Hi, guys! What'd I miss?" Charlie smiled, brightening up the whole room. Her eyes turned to me, then up and behind me. Her lips parted. She swallowed, then looked at me for the confirmation she didn't need.

"We're going to breakfast!" Mateo announced, startling Charlie.

She swallowed and turned to Mateo.

"Oh?" She glanced at us again. "Where would that be?"

I groaned.

9

Nol stared, unblinking, at his plate as our server slid a tall stack of sweet-smelling pancakes in front of him. Five of them, to be exact, with a side of stuffed hash browns. The frying oil on the potatoes turned my stomach.

Mateo and Charlie were sharing an eggs Benedict and some sides. Sam was still waiting for his omelet, which the server promised would be right out.

This white porcelain mug in front of me was all that I needed. The coffee—Folgers, I was sure—needed extra sugar. I shook a second sugar packet and focused on the granules spill into the blackness.

We sat at a curved booth against a window. I ended up, by Mateo's design, next to Nol so we could chill out and make up. Right, like sitting next to each other would fix our problems. I'd used my purse to put space between us on the seat.

"Did you tell them you saw the attack?" Sam asked Nol, returning to their conversation.

I lifted the maple syrup and drowned Nol's pancakes. He watched me kill them in stunned silence. I shrugged. What would he do? Not eat them? Like I cared. I wondered if I could get him hooked on sugar before he left.

Nol unglued his eyes with a long blink and went back to his legal conversation. "I tried, yes, but when I answered too slowly, they directed me to their car, asking about passports."

They kept talking, but Charlie's giggle distracted me. Mateo placed a grape in her mouth, and she fluttered her eyelashes at someone in another booth. The guy, who had stunning hazel eyes and firm, full lips, gave her a lazy smile. Oh, jeez.

Nol's conversation drifted in and out again. "I must admit, by that time, my English was fading."

One of the servers walking past filled my coffee mug without asking me, and I could have kissed him.

"*Merci beaucoup.*" Only after he'd blushed and shuffled away did I realize I'd said thanks in French. Oh well.

"Hallë." Nol's breath tickled my ear and startled me. "What are you doing?"

"Anything I can do to not fall asleep," I grumbled and inched away a little.

"If you are going to flirt with the boy, you should order something as well."

I opened my mouth to argue, but only owned it. "Flirting is not a crime. I'm French. It's what we do."

"I've noticed. The both of you." He waved his hand toward Charlie.

"Get over it. I'm not a child anymore. Stop telling me what to do."

He sighed heavily. "Obviously. I am merely asking you to eat something."

He gave me that pouty look that used to always get me into trouble. I growled and grabbed his fork with the pancake bite he hadn't eaten yet. "Happy?" I asked with my mouth full of sweet pancake and sweeter, almost too sweet, fake maple syrup. Ew.

Nol's jaw dropped as I raised an eyebrow and gave him a quick sneer. I reached over, closed his mouth with a finger to his chin, then went back to my coffee. A movement across from me caught my attention, and I found Charlie silently laughing. She gave me a thumbs-up. I hid my smile behind my mug.

Sam said something about the police using the excuse of the station's network being down. "If you can find your passport..." Blah, blah. I lost interest again. More boring lawyer stuff. Once I got Nol away from the others, I planned to throttle him.

I sipped my coffee and people-watched. The little girl at the next booth peeked her head over the bench for the third time. I scrunched my nose, and she copied. Her mom scolded her. A flicker of something caught my eye out the window. Well, the rain had stopped, but flecks of snow made their happy little way to the ground. Lovely. That, however, didn't mean the snow would stick.

I fished my phone out of my purse to check the time. 8:24. To think, only four measly hours ago, I'd been crawling under my covers after taking some Aleve—for the hangover and Ian.

Maybe Nol would give me some more of An'di's tea. I closed my eyes, elbows on the table and coffee mug at my chin. Ian and Aswryn all on the same weekend, and I couldn't protect my loved ones. I shouldn't have let Charlie come live with me. While she'd needed the change after her husband died, she and Ray were safer in Paris than here, threatened by those two lunatics.

The counter bell dinging, the murmur of conversations around us, and the freezing air blowing in as the door opened—everything shifted me back into the here and now. Whoa, where had I gone? My eyes flew open as our server stretched her arm around me to set Sam's omelet on the table.

"Anything else?" the server asked.

"Hally? Haaaally?"

I swallowed, smiled at the server, and shook my head. "Yes? Sorry, Mateo. Evidently, I haven't had enough coffee." I lifted the white porcelain to my lips.

"No worries. Nolan, you'll fit right in."

I narrowed my eyes at Mateo, and he winked.

"This, please?"

I looked to see what the hell Nol was talking about and found him pointing at a picture on the menu. He arched an eyebrow at me, then went back to Sam's conversation. The server set a yogurt parfait in front of me five minutes later.

"You're such a pain in the ass," I mumbled again as I stared down at the berries and yogurt.

He thumped my nose. "Not as much as you are in mine," he whispered in *Aemirin*.

"There's no way I can eat this, you know? My head is killing me."

"You shouldn't steal my food then."

I grumbled but didn't say anything else because, well, he had a point. Instead, I stomped on his foot. He made a fake "oof" sound and gave me one of his teasing smiles. I stuck my tongue out.

"You said they picked you up at three?"

"About that time, yes."

Sam typed something into his phone, nodding.

I stirred my frozen fruit around, creating little lines of blue in the white yogurt as I tried to put Nol's timeline together. "Where were you yesterday, though?" Immediately, I wanted to retract my absent-minded question. His answer could involve magic or *Aemina* or Aswryn. "Never mind. That's none of my business."

"There was a situation with work I needed to deal with, and they wanted an update. I didn't want them to think I was—what is the word? Skirting my duties?"

I stabbed at a berry as Nol shoveled forkfuls of hash browns into his mouth. He went back to *Endae*? Would he have gone if he'd known he'd left us vulnerable? Charlie was right: he needed to know I'd blocked myself.

"Wish you would have said something." I kept my eyes on my food. I didn't have much of a right to ask this of him, but I complained anyway. "You know, since you want me to help and all." My eyes darted toward him.

Nol opened his mouth, but Sam interrupted. "I think we're about done. We should get some sleep before dinner tonight." Sam pointed to his very sleepy partner.

"I'm awake," Mateo mumbled.

"Hallë." Nol leaned over to whisper in *Aemirin* as Charlie got up to let the guys out of the booth. "I warded your house. You and your friends were in no danger."

Mateo kissed Charlie's cheek before she sat back down. Then he bent over to kiss my forehead. "See ya tonight, Nolan."

"Yes, tonight." Nol quirked a corner of his mouth.

"Oh, so that's what that was about. Doesn't matter? Really, Mateo?"

"Not my fault you weren't listening. Night night. See ya later." Sam held the door open and guided Mateo out the door.

"I love those two. I'm so glad you met them, Tatie."

The two of them walked up the sidewalk to Sam's car where Sam held the door open for his partner.

"They are pretty amazing, aren't they?"

Charlie made an agreeable *hmm*.

"So, Charlie, Hallë said you are her roommate?"

"Yep." She played with her parsley. "With my daughter, Ray, who you will meet tonight."

"Exciting. Has Hallë mentioned why I am here?"

Charlie rested her chin on the back of her interlaced fingers, her elbows propped on the table. "Somewhat." Her eyes twinkled with mischief. Jeez.

Nol nodded and took another sip of water. The server set down our ticket, distracting Nol for a second. She took all the plates but left my parfait.

"Hallë, I need to go back to where the police took me from."

"For what?" Charlie fluttered her brown eyes up at Nol, all sweet and innocent like.

Nol shifted. "Well, I hope to find my belongings. Perhaps they were not taken."

I covered my smile with my mug. What would be his next bullshit explanation?

Charlie looked at me, her eyes filled with laughter. "Oh, I doubt that. If you left your stuff, someone already took it. Did you have your passport in your wallet?"

Nol looked at me for help. He got none. "Yes, of course."

I held my breath to keep from laughing. No way could a passport fit in a wallet. I shoved my parfait away and propped my head on my hand. "I can't do it. I can't watch you drown."

"Aw, Tatie. This was just getting fun."

I licked my lips. "So..." I started, uncertainty slowing my words, "remember when I told you that, um, no one knew about me?"

Nol's light blue eyes narrowed.

"Well, I kinda...lied."

Nol blinked and didn't say a damn word. I refused to break our stare first, or swallow, fidget, or anything. I was not losing this one. The happenings of the place swirled around us. In my peripheral vision, I saw the little girl peek over the booth again. Some dishes crashed to the floor in the back, but I didn't flinch.

"Sooo, are we going to have a problem here, Twynolan?" Charlie's question broke the silence between us. "Pardon my mispronunciation."

Without even a twitch of his eyebrow, Nol looked across the table.

She hesitated for a moment, then sat up straighter and continued. "Are you expecting her to elaborate? An apology? Excuse? Or are you waiting for her to give you a full report of the hundred and nineteen years she's been here? She doesn't owe you one god damned explanation."

Nol rolled his shoulders back and fidgeted. Let him stew. I sat back and let Charlie continue. She'd always been good at back talk.

"Tatie is a very private person, and she has every right to be."

"Yes, I agree." Nol kept his voice cold, full *Zayuri* style.

"Well, that's not how you're acting. She has gone through hell. Don't get me wrong. She told me about your situation. And my condolences on your sister."

Nol dipped his head in thanks.

"If you trust and respect your *muranildë*, then accept that Tatie trusts me to know the truth about who she is and why she's here. And she will, if she so chooses, tell you in her own good time. Now a few more things. I've also wanted to kick your ass for saying what you said to her, and I have always, always dreamed of meeting you. However, for now, we need to get back to the situation at hand."

Nol still sat frozen and emotionless. "How much do you know?"

She tossed her hair back. "Assume I know everything, and I'll ask if I don't understand."

"Do you know *Aemirin*?"

Charlie waggled her eyebrows. "Maybe." She did not, but her feistiness was showing.

"You could have told me, Hallë." He sounded offended. "I will protect her and her little one from Aswryn. *Idorem'a,*" Nol said, giving his word of protection.

My heart leaped into my throat. With his oath, I knew he understood how important Charlie and Ray were to me.

"Thank you. I wouldn't have…" I searched for the right words, but they kept getting mixed up.

Nol snatched my hand up before I could pull away. "They are special to you. They are special to me, then."

"They are my family." I chewed my lip, weighing whether to tell him more. I pulled my hand out of his. "And, um, well, they're not the only ones."

Nol's eyebrows shot up, his lips forming an "o."

"But you won't meet them."

"Hallë, I will—"

"No, I mean, they live far away." I took a deep breath. "So let's get back on topic."

Nol sighed. "Yes, I suppose. If only the situation were different and I could visit with my *muranildë* and her family."

What was I supposed to say to that? He'd given the oath to protect them, but that didn't mean all was good between us. I realized he was stalling again.

"You know you're still on my shit list, right?"

"Still?" He wrinkled his nose. "I was hoping that would work."

Charlie laughed, and I shook my head. "Nope. Now, I assume you're the reason for the network being down that Sam mentioned?"

"Yes, their electric grid is not magic based like ours, but simple enough."

"You have electricity?" Charlie asked.

"Hallë never told you?" Nol's eyes grew round as he looked from her to me.

Charlie stared dumbfounded.

"Why is this surprising? Electricity is not a newly found concept," Nol explained with impatience. "Without it nothing would exist."

"I know it's just—"

"We aren't a primitive world like your fairytales lead you to believe, love." Although some descriptions were oddly similar. "Our advances have been developed with magic *and* science."

"You've just said so little about it."

"You read too much fantasy. So," I turned back to Nol. "What's this about going back somewhere?"

Nol clasped his hands together on the table and shifted. "I went to check in, although Gileal is not my superior. He likes your idea, Hallë."

"You went to Gil and didn't tell me you were going?"

"You whine like Gileal. When I came back to your house yesterday, no one was home. Then I felt Aswryn's *imolegin*—" He switched to *Aemirin*. "Her magic tugged on my awareness."

"How? You can't just—"

"There's a *Zayuri* spell. That's all I can say. Aswryn was assaulting a human in the corner of a park. Once the man fell, she grabbed a large bag and ran. I injured her." He turned to Charlie. "And I see you do not understand *Aemirin*."

Charlie winked. "You don't know that." She sat up and pointed at him. "Hey, you spoke *Aemirin* on purpose."

His mouth curved into a wide grin. "Honest? I am tired, and I am forgetting words, but in part, yes." Nol frowned and came back to me. "As I was saying," he said in English, "when I wounded her, she ran up a hill around the forest of buildings. This city is very confusing."

"'Forest of buildings.' Accurate, actually," Charlie said.

I squinted at him. "You agreed not to kill her."

"And that was not my intent. There is something at or near the park she wants, and I stopped her. Will you take me there or not?"

Charlie groaned and slid out of the booth. "It's too cold for this. You both owe me, big time. Blood samples and *Aeminan* science."

"*Aeminan* science?" Nol muttered to me as he rose from the booth.

"She'll explain." I gave the little girl a wave and paid while they went to the car.

10

Nol grabbed the oh-shit handle as I turned the corner on West Lake Avenue.

I snickered.

"I do not find this funny at all, Hallë. This metal box is too big for you to control."

"I've been driving since nineteen twenty-seven. There is nothing I can't drive." I made a turn on red. Some asshole pulled out in front of me, and Charlie and I cussed the dude out. Too bad they couldn't hear us.

"Okay, we're at Valley and Westlake. Where'd they pick you up?"

"There is one of those organized car stations—what are they called? And it is near some very odd-looking boats. They looked to be standing on the water, with two feet and two long arms. Forgive me, I have no idea what they were."

"Seaplanes," Charlie said. "Over there, Tatie." Charlie pointed north to continue up Westlake.

"There, within those trees. Aswryn ran—" Nol twisted toward the driver's side. The light turned red, and I stomped on the brakes. Nol flew forward, the seat belt jerking on his shoulder.

Nol rubbed his collarbone, grumbling, "You meant to do that."

I didn't argue.

I chose the parking spot closest to the north tip of Lake Union Park. A seaplane tour business shared the "organized car station," as Nol had called it. Too damn funny.

The engine pinged as we stared out into the cold, wet cement and grass. I tutted. "This is tiny, just a little strip of grass and a wide, curvy paved trail on the lake. How can they call this a park?"

The only visitors to the small grassy area were two old people feeding birds on a bench at the water's edge.

"What now, Nolan?" Charlie said. "Are you going to do a little mojo and run after her?"

"I'm calling David before anything else happens. You can go play outside if you want."

Nol raised an eyebrow as he leaned back and closed his eyes. "Will it be a long conversation?"

"Maybe," I evaded.

Nol grunted, pulled the seat lever, and leaned back, and I swear he fell asleep. Like that, between one second and the next, he was out. I rolled my eyes and dialed David's number. His voicemail picked up as it should, and I left a brief description of what I wanted.

"That is all? How many times have you talked to him?" Nol mumbled.

"Why? Is it really any of your business?"

Nol muttered something under his breath, his eyes still closed.

Charlie sighed. "Well then, I guess it's either take a nap or get this over and done with."

Nol sat up, his lips tipped up at the edges, his dimple showing. A small shift in his expression, something indescribable, told me his idea. I hummed my negation, and his smile flattened.

"As a reminder, there will be no magic. Do you see those two people over there? Do you see the hotel behind us? There is no way to know how many people could see you cast a spell."

Nol checked his bag on the floor, adjusted his leather jacket, and rolled his shoulders. He brushed his hair out of the way, touched the middle of his back, and rolled his shoulders again. If I asked what he was nervous about, he'd deny it, so I didn't ask.

"Hallë, again, I am *Zayuri*. We have our ways. Do you see that stone in the distance? With the park name on the face?"

Neither Charlie nor I answered. I saw grass, water, a beach, trees, and a bridge.

"Come, I will show you." Nol opened the door, and cold air rushed in to take his place.

Charlie and I climbed out of the car. The snow had stopped again but could start again at any moment. Ice covered the ground, though. We followed Nol across the bike path toward the curve in the pathway he had mentioned. Once closer to the street corner, I saw a thick stone slab toppled over, sliced smooth at an angle. Walking even closer, I noticed the engraved "Lake Union Park" sign.

Nol reached the toppled sign first. He knelt and placed his hands on the base. A faint white cloud billowed around him as he let out a long breath and bowed his head. A sour taste filled my mouth.

My warm breath blinded me, and my almost-not-there headache came back with a vengeance. I started shivering. Nol showed no indication he'd even cast a spell. Anyone around us would think he was inspecting the broken sign. I only knew because of this damn reaction.

"Tatie? Are you all right?"

I flinched when Charlie touched my hand. Pins and needles bit into my skin where she touched, as if my hand was asleep. I tried to shake off the feeling, but that only sent little bursts of pain down my arm.

"I'm a little lightheaded. Maybe Nol was right about the eating breakfast thing." I backed up to the grass, ten or so feet away, and crouched. Frost had stiffened the blades of grass that I brushed my fingertips across. A scuff of shoes on the pavement broke my concentration.

"Do you feel anything?" Nol asked, his tone hopeful.

"No." Clenching my jaw enabled me to stand without throwing up. I demanded my body to suck it up and ignore my nausea. "What happened there?" I pointed at the broken sign.

"Aswryn threw a spell at me. She shoved the man against the metal bar near the bridge. I came up from the...What is this white strip on the street?"

"Crosswalk," Charlie said. "A spell did that?"

Nol didn't answer as his attention turned to something in the soil a few yards away from me. He picked up an object the size of a marble and lifted it toward the sky.

"Hallë, I think this is blood." He spun around and shoved the thing too close to my face.

I grabbed his wrist to bring the small object into focus. Yellow and green smoke churned inside the small translucent black pearl.

"Holy shit. She dropped a *meril*? Do you think that's how she vanishes?"

He shrugged.

"You said she ran away from you, right? It makes sense."

"What's a *meril*?" Charlie leaned in to look at the little pearl as she asked.

"An amulet that holds magic."

"Oh."

"Wait here." Nol tossed the *meril* in the air, then slid it into an inside pocket. "I doubt Aswryn is around, but keep alert, Hallë." Nol bent down until we almost touched foreheads. "You may not want to, but to protect Charlie, you will need to use magic if she finds you."

"I ca—"

"Do not argue this. People will—*C'yo*." Nol gave up and changed to *Aemirin*. "Humans will rationalize what they see if anyone happens to be watching. You are protecting your family. The percentage—"

I stopped him before he started spouting off the statistics and probabilities and other such smart stuff I didn't understand. "Just hurry your ass up. I'm cold." I gave up trying to explain. He'd only interrupt me again.

"If I sense her *imolegin*, I must pursue. If that happens, I'll meet you at your house later. I promise," he told me in *Aemirin*. Without waiting for a response, he stood and left at a trot.

"You need to tell him, Tatie. You're putting us both in danger."

"I tried. He's not in the right state of mind to listen to me." I reached over and snaked an arm around her waist. "Come on. We'll go sit in the car."

She watched Nol a second longer then let me guide her back. "What did he say to you?"

"Oh, he lectured me about refusing to use magic."

"He thinks you can fight this *endaë* girl? I mean, if she's so strong that Nolan can't suppress her with all his fancy *Zayuri* magic, what makes him think you can?"

"I—my magic—" I twisted my lips. I'd never talked about my magic, and doing so seemed wrong. "—is different. Aswryn doesn't understand it."

"But Nol—sorry, Nolan—does?"

"More than anyone but my grandmother and father, yes."

"And he thinks you can help him?"

"As bait since Aswryn is already after me. It makes sense, really. He also thinks I can stop her from vanishing."

"But if that amulet is what makes her vanish, he doesn't need you to do that."

"True."

Engrossed in our conversation, we were at the car before I remembered to get my keys out.

"Finally, you got away from the redhead."

Charlie and I stopped in our tracks.

"You're supposed to be with Agent Zack-ass. What the fuck, Ian?"

With four hours of sleep and Nol's magic wreaking havoc on me, I didn't feel scared of Ian at all. Nol was still on the other side of the bridge, examining something on the ground. He couldn't get here in time to help unless he figured out how to vanish like Aswryn.

Ian stood less than fifteen feet away from us, on the curb next to a tall stone art piece in the park. We couldn't outrun Ian. He'd run track in high school—I'd seen his trophies.

"I dunno. He never came. Something with the computer systems screwin' up all night. Couldn't hold me any longer. I know my rights. I was surprised to see you at the precinct as I got out, though."

Unbelievable. The spell Nol used to disable the power grid had worked in Ian's favor, too. What the hell had I done for the universe to screw me over with all this? I mean, come on, so many others did so much worse.

"I don't give a shit if you mind or not, but you're takin' me to Katie. You can go, too, if you're a good girl." He winked at Charlie, kissing the air.

"Go screw yourself," Charlie yelled at him from right behind me.

"Ian, this is stupid. I don't even know where she lives. You'd be better off asking Drake."

Ian jolted back. No one mentioned Drake, like, ever. While the man had helped Katie and me move up here, there were rules in place.

"What Drake doesn't know won't hurt him."

"Oh, he'll know if you get close to Katie. Go back to California. Better yet, give Zack information on that Derrick kid, then go back to California."

Ian tilted his head, those white caterpillar eyebrows scrunching up as he tried to think past his brain capacity. "I dunno what you're talking about. Let's go, Hally."

Ian reached back and pulled a gun out from behind him. Great. Ian with a gun. Just what we needed. My heart dropped to the cold pavement. Guns and Ian did not mix. The last time he'd kept a gun in his shop, it had backfired on him the one and only time he'd tried to use it.

"Now, Ian, where on Earth did you find that?" I swallowed hard, trying to push back all the really, really bad what-ifs that my mind threw in my face. Shit. "Did your new friend not hear about what happened the last time you had a gun?"

"Fuck you, Hally. Get in the car."

Movement behind Ian caught my attention, and I tried not to react to Nol's stealthy approach. More what-ifs popped up. Did Nol know what a gun was or how to handle a situation with guns?

"Ian, you should put the gun away. Do you even know how to tell if the safety is off?"

He didn't. His "crew," as Zack liked to call them, did not let Ian handle handguns. Shotguns, sure. Drugs, yes. Not handguns. They were beyond him.

"Of course I know."

"Really? You should look again, dipshit."

"You can't see it from there." But he turned his wrist to look at the gun anyway.

I glanced behind Ian, imploring Nol to keep a low profile.

He gave me no indication he understood me, his emotionless, ice-blue eyes flicking quick glances my way as he got closer. "Hallë's logic does seem sound. Ian, is it?" Nol stood about six feet away from Ian. Nol was taller, yet at a glance, one could overlook that with Ian's much bulkier arms and shoulders. "Put your gun on the ground and step to your left."

Ian swung around, gun out, not paying attention to where he pointed that thing. "How the fuck did you get back here so fast?"

Once Ian's body was out of the way, Charlie and I could see Nol behind him, legs wide and on the balls of his feet, ready to lunge forward at any second. A faint black glow pulsed at the end of Nol's outstretched arm as he twisted his wrist right, then left. The *Zayuri*'s magical dagger, an *Azaye*.

"Is that a fucking toy lightsaber?" Ian snorted.

"I assure you it is a real metal blade, and she can cut your gun in half without any hesitation."

"Nol, stop!" Both man and *endao* stopped and looked at me. Huh, guess my voice did have some authority. "He isn't worth enough to wipe that blade clean with, let alone stab him with it."

Ian, still staring at me, didn't notice Nol move in. One moment he was a body length away, and the next, an arc of black light curved toward Ian. Charlie let out a small scream as something black dropped into the juniper bushes next to them. A blink later, Nol was standing eight feet away. Any doubts about his *Zayuri* claims evaporated.

Ian turned his head back and forth between the three of us, unsure of what had happened. As Ian worked through the situation second by second, his face got redder and redder. Poor Ian.

Another piece of the gun fell to the ground. Nol's blade had sliced the gun into three pieces. Ian yelled and threw the remaining part of the gun at Nol, which Nol dodged with a slight slip to the left.

The huge idiot rushed forward, reaching out to strike. Nol moved much quicker and Ian stumbled forward. He whipped his head around to keep his eyes on Nol. With his front foot, Ian pivoted and bolted forward. Another step to the side and Nol was out of Ian's reach again, but this time, Ian cried out.

Oh no.

"Stop." I rushed toward the idiot, praying Nol hadn't done much damage.

Ian doubled over, cussing about his arm being cut, while Nol appeared in front of me. "He is alive, Hallë. I merely scratched the inside of his arm." Nol pointed to where Ian's cut was on his own arm. "Shall we go, or would you rather wait and call the police again?"

"He's okay?"

Nol placed his hand at the base of my neck and squeezed. "I promise. My blade burns when it cuts—when I command it to."

"You cauterized the cut?" Charlie asked, still beside me.

"I do not know what that means." Nol shook his head, frowning at Charlie.

"It burns. Is it bleeding or—"

"Ah, that. It will heal soon. Trust me, I know how to use my weapons." He smirked at Charlie, which shut her up.

I laughed at the effect Nol's flirting had on her. Oh boy. Should I put rules in place? They were both adults, and Nol wouldn't be here *that* long. But still. Groaning, I headed to the car and looked at Ian over the hood.

Ian was looking on the ground around where the barrel of his gun had landed. Ian did a double take, glancing from the gun to Nol and back. Yeah, the smartest thing he'd done in his life. *Don't mess with the Zayuri, asshole.*

I banged on the hood to get Charlie's and Nol's attention.

"Are we going or what? I'd prefer not to wait around until numb-nuts over there loses more brain cells and decides to run at Nol."

Charlie did a sort of hop-step, and walked up to the car, Nol in tow. He was not looking at her butt, was he? Mother help me.

Once off West Lake Boulevard, I texted Agent Zack-ass about Ian's whereabouts and asked why the hell he wasn't in his custody. I also had one unopened text. David agreed to meet at three.

11

"So…" CHARLIE LEANED BACK into the sofa. "What if it isn't just a curse?"

Nol lounged on one of our living room wingback chairs, in his signature pose: legs straight out, ankles crossed, and arms across his abdomen. Still looking at the ceiling, he inhaled slowly and puffed his cheeks out.

"Hear me out, this is my area of expertise. Diseases, not spells," Charlie said. She'd already told him she was an epidemiologist at the University of Washington. "This sounds exactly like a virus. They infect and attack various parts of the body." Nol went to say something, and she waved at him to stop. He didn't listen.

"You are not trying to say magic is not involved, are you?"

The two had been discussing everything science related since we'd left the park. All of it was way above my comprehension. When we got home, Charlie had shown him pictures of blood and tissue cells of all kinds.

"No, there is, but the symptoms you described sound like a really aggressive virus. If I identified the compromised ME cells, I might see the culprit. I could get a better idea of what you're dealing with." She pointed over at her home lab in what used to be the formal dining room. Yes, I'd bought her a home lab.

Nol's expression grew more and more frustrated, but he kept quiet, per his normal reaction. "Compromised, culprit, ME cells…" Nol

murmured under his breath. The crease between his eyebrows deep-
ened.

"You won't get this right away. Give it some time," I said.

"If you would translate what she is saying, I would understand
more. The words are complicated, cells, and ba-cer, but..." He growled
in frustration, not able to pronounce or know the terms.

"We are not a...What is the word? We are advanced, just not in the
same manner as here. We do not need to cut or poke into a body to
heal anything. I do not understand how you can *see* magic. Magic is an
energy our bodies make.

"That is why we tire after casting too many spells. Curses give off
light, yes, but that is not the magic itself." Nol batted his hand around.
Our healers—doctors—had all sorts of advanced medical spells. Sure,
we had medicine, like An'di's tea, but magic was always involved.

"Nol—"

"*C'yo*, this is bullshit!"

"No, it's not."

He scowled at me. Now who was acting like a child? "She's not
saying humans are more advanced. She doesn't know what you do and
don't know."

"I don't need a fucking lecture. I know this all. Magic is..." Nol went
off speaking words I didn't know and probably would have learned if
I had stayed in *Aemina*.

Charlie frowned, but I just shook my head to tell her to ignore him.

"Listen," I tried to plead with him, understanding his pain. "I'd
translate if I could, but I don't know the words."

Nol slumped further. "*Sitam*." *I know.* Even as an adult, he looked
adorable when he pouted.

I tried to hide my amusement as Nol could only stare at her as she
rushed to explain everything at once.

"I've identified the cells that hold energy. Your spells, your magic,
are a product of that energy, okay?"

Nol nodded slowly, his eyes flicking to the side as he tried to keep
up.

"Slow down, Charlie," I told her. "You're gonna lose him."

Charlie couldn't stop though, her hands, and eyes getting more animated as Nol nodded and listened. "That light is the flame that the energy gives off."

"You call them ME cells, yes?" Nol asked, following way better than I ever could.

Charlie nodded and took a drink of her coffee in her periodic table mug: CaFFeINe = LiFe. "It's easier to understand if you saw them yourself. Come in here and I'll show you." Charlie stood, leaving her mug on the table.

Nol stayed seated, watching as Charlie walked to her lab. He scowled and whispered to me in *Aemirin,* "I don't need to see these cells. It's a curse, Hallë, and we need to discuss the next few days."

"Nol—"

"I must stay out of sight yet be able to get near you when Aswryn approaches you. If this *meril* is her *vamameril,* that's a boon for our—"

I clamped my hand over his mouth and glared him down. "You are being rude, speaking in *Aemirin* in front of Charlie."

Nol pulled my hand off of his mouth and narrowed his eyes. "You speak in French in front of me. Plus, she doesn't need to be involved in our plans."

They were our plans now? This *endao!* This morning he was pissed because I went to the station and now we were making *plans*? I counted to ten. "Stop and go look at what she wants to show you. She's very proud of her work, and she has no one but me to talk with, and I'm not smart enough for her research."

"Hallë—"

"Humor her for fifteen minutes. Please?"

His frustrated expression lifted at the time frame. "Fifteen minutes?"

"Yes."

He puffed out his cheeks again and looked toward the lab. "Very well."

For the love of Pete! "Twist your arm to go learn something," I mumbled, teasing him.

"Under normal circumstances, I would enjoy spending time learning this, but we must find Aswryn."

"I know. Now get your ass up and go look at Charlie's research."

Charlie gave a fist pump and opened her lab doors when Nol stood. "You're going to love this."

Everything was set up exactly how Charlie wanted it, move it at your peril, so I was going to watch how long Nol fared.

After getting a coffee refill I poked my head inside. Nol stood in the middle of the small room with his arms raised to the ceiling light, squinting at a tiny glass rectangle. He could have pressed his palms on the eight-foot ceiling. Charlie pressed a finger on each book on her bookcase, reading the spines. She pulled out a huge blue-and-pink book with a picture of a molecule on the front.

Tables lined the wall to the right, with gadgets and machines. Some cabinets stored beakers and other glass stuff, and a large refrigerator with two glass doors hid in a corner on the back wall.

My designated chair was tucked in a corner in the front. That way I could sit and drink coffee and talk to her while she worked. I stepped around and leaned my back against the doorframe. Wrapping my hands around my warm mug.

"This is from Hallë's blood? I do not see any glowing here, besides the light shining through."

Charlie and I homed in on what he held in his large hands.

"I'd prefer you not rummage around, please. Not to be rude, I just like to keep my lab in order and—" Wonderful, he'd managed to get into trouble in under three minutes.

"No, I understand. I apologize." Nol went over and slid the little slide back into a box.

"Oh, those are dry samples." Charlie looked at me, her eyes wide. She mouthed "sorry" to me for some reason. "So, no, you won't see the cells glow. That slide identifies the ME cell. If you noticed, I have them circled. Here, come check out this book. Can you read English yet?"

"Some, and I can write as well. Many rules seem to be allowed to break. I do not understand why there are rules if you are only going to break them."

"Those are the best kinds, I guess," I informed him.

Nol grunted without looking up from the book Charlie had set in his arms. He flipped through pages, mumbling a word here and there. He squinted at a picture. "Is this real?"

Charlie came over and peered at the book. "Yep. It's using a high-powered microscope to show you a bacterium. This one—" Charlie flipped through a few pages. "—is a virus. A cytopathic virus."

"What does pathogen mean?"

"That's a—"

Nol flipped through the book, ignoring Charlie. "Disease-producing..." He continued to mumble to himself as he went to find answers for himself and ignored any of Charlie's attempts to explain—now this was the Nol I knew.

"Well, considering that...A pathogen is *alosmiato* in *Aemirin*. Why do they divide them into different agents when every *alosmiato* has their own features? This is my sister's expertise." His brows knitted together as he began muttering again, back and forth between *Aemirin* and English. "Gileal needs to be here."

"Because a virus isn't really considered alive and a bacterium is," Charlie continued to explain.

"Your book says it is not agreed upon. We consider both alive—"

"They can't reproduce, for one thing. Or—"

Nol held up a finger, then continued to flip through his book. "Hmm, alive. Are they both not, what is the word?" Again, he flipped to the back. "*Ai.*" He sighed like he was bored and harrumphed in annoyance, mumbling in *Aemirin*.

"I thought you said you didn't know this stuff." Charlie threw up her hands and glared at him.

"You gave me a very informative book," he offered, not understanding why she was upset.

"Charlie—" I tried to intervene.

"Yeah, and you've had it for, what, a minute? I thought you said you can only read some."

"Yes." Nol looked over at me for help. "Reading definitions of words helps me understand more. I do know these...things, but I do not know the words in English."

"Then how did you *not* consider this a virus before?"

"We did, in the beginning. An'di could never find one to prove if Aswryn had tied the curse to one. Wait—" He flipped through the book some more, then set it down on the table for Charlie to see as well. "Your machines, do you think they might see one?"

"I have a microspore at work strong enough to see one." Charlie crossed her arms, still annoyed with the speed at which Nol had grasped the concepts. "If you can bring me samples."

Nol went rigid. "I will not bring an infected *enda* here and risk Hallë's life."

"We don't have to bring anyone over. I could go over and take—"

"No," Nol and I said together.

She chewed on the inside of her lip, thinking. "We could cure this. No magic, no killing Aswryn. Let me help, please?"

Charlie fidgeted, unable to contain her excitement as she saw Nol cracking. "You could bring me some blood samples. I could teach you how. It won't take but a few hours at work. Nolan, what do you have to lose? I'll check to see if you're right, if there's magical energy in the virus."

"Yes, speaking of that, may I see these ME cells you have named?" Nol changed the subject without Charlie noticing or agreeing to anything.

"Yeah!" She went to her microscope and flipped it on.

Nol touched each part of it, messing with the knobs. "Amazing, and magic is not used to create this light scope?"

Charlie chuckled. "No, definitely not."

"Not all devices have to have magic to work, Nol. Even in our realm."

Nol turned to me and did a double take like he'd only now realized I was here. He raised an eyebrow, and his eyes followed my mug while I took another sip.

I gave him a slow smirk, just a little one. He swallowed, looked away, and turned around. I hadn't meant to flirt, but maybe that would make him stop treating me like a child.

"If there is no magic used, I must know the inner workings of this device."

"Which would you rather do, Nol? Look at the cells or take apart the microscope?"

"There will be no disassembling of my equipment," Charlie snapped.

I held my mug up. "She has spoken."

Nol grabbed something beside the scope and fiddled with it until Charlie snatched it. She grabbed a lancing pen and readied a slide. My sneaky niece snagged his hand and jabbed his finger. Nol hadn't been prepared for the small prick, and he jumped, jerking his hand out of her grip.

I almost spilled my coffee laughing; this was too much fun. Nol narrowed his eyes, which only made me laugh more.

"*C'yo*, a warning would have been nice."

"You big baby," I teased.

Charlie laughed at us as she concentrated on getting drops of Nol's blood on the slide.

Nol scowled at me, then examined his finger.

"Here, Nolan, come check this out." She set one of her slides under her scope and bent over the lens. Her hands twisted a knob on the side, and then she got out of the way.

Nol bumped his eye into the lens, stood up, and rubbed both of them. "How do I see out of this thing without injuring my eyes?"

Once Charlie and I stopped laughing, which Nol joined in on after a few seconds, they got down to examining the cells. After a few moments, I went to sit in my lab chair to watch them "ooh and aah" over his blood. Charlie lifted her eyes from the microscope and looked at me.

"Tatie, tu dois venir voir ça. Ça expilique tellement." Tatie, you must come see this. It explains so much.

I sighed and got up, setting my mug on the little table beside the chair. I'd seen my cells before. What could possibly be so different? I ducked between them and adjusted the lens until I got a clear image.

Nol said something, but I didn't hear. What I saw under the microscope stole all my attention. The white light looked similar to nerves firing off, yet the cells weren't the same shape. Each one of his cells pulsed, like Christmas lights, but not in unison.

The light would expand out of the cell, and once they bumped into each other, they'd glow together. Like they were sharing their light. Mine did not do that.

My cells pulsed a faint glow inside each ME cell and did not share in any way, like little stars twinkling in space, doing their own thing. I tried not to choke up, but I realized, at that moment, how much my block affected me, neutered me.

I reached for my bracelet for comfort, and my heart sank further when I only felt my skin. I sniffled and closed my eyes. A hand touched my hip, and I felt Nol's arm against my back.

"Are you well, Hallë?" He pulled me in for a hug. Before, I would have gone to him and let him hug me, felt his chin on top of my head. I still craved the comfort of my *muranildo*, but I couldn't depend on that again.

"Yeah." I shifted away from him and didn't look up. "They're beautiful. I love seeing them, is all." I turned my head the other way and found Charlie watching me.

She frowned, worry lines appearing on her forehead.

"Excuse me." I grabbed my mug and left the room. I wanted to run but forced myself to walk away.

How my block affected my body rattled me and, frankly, scared me, yet Nol's ME cells had left me in awe and inspired. I grabbed my sketchbook and ducked into my art studio to be alone.

The idea of my ME cells drifting in space alone and Nol's sharing that light fired off sketches in my head. I sat and focused my attention, drifting off into the place I went when I drew.

"That is beautiful, Hallë." Nol's voice made me jump, bringing me back to the here and now.

Had I fallen asleep? I flipped the picture over and tried to slow my breathing as he talked. My studio was my private place.

"Sorry, I did not mean to startle you. We need to leave."

"I...Out, please." I pushed him out of the room and shut the door behind me.

"I did not mean to upset you." Nol wouldn't let me push him any farther once we were out of the room. He reached for my face, and I turned my head. He let out a harsh sigh.

"You didn't know. It's private. It..." I struggled to explain, flustered and wondering how much he'd seen.

"I understand. A place all your own." He dipped his head to make me look at him.

I tried to give him a nod and a small smile. Nol reached for me again, and I shook my head. So instead of reaching for my face, he moved to grab my shoulder. I turned away from that as well.

Nol dropped his arm. "*Ai,* come here, Hallë, please."

I swallowed hard. We'd been so close as kids, always leaning on each other for comfort or sanity sometimes. I didn't need him now, though.

"Let me hold you," he pleaded. I knew he needed this, too. Comforting me comforted him and vice versa. Our bond called for nearness.

I took a breath to steady myself and turned away toward the open hallway. Nol grabbed my hand and stepped close. When I looked back to tell him to let go, he hooked my jaw with his finger so I had to look up at him.

"Fine, but know this." He raised his eyebrows and looked at me sternly. "Your sketch is beautiful."

Frustrated, I looked away, since I couldn't turn my head.

"I think that would make a great tattoo." I tried to laugh off his compliment, but he pinched my chin. "Look at me, please. I am serious. I would like that as a tattoo."

I scoffed. "Sure."

"I would so!" He laughed. "Why do you doubt me? I love it."

I pushed him away. He didn't move, and when I looked up, I caught that same roguish grin he'd given me Friday night at the café. I hiccuped.

Um... "Nol?" I fidgeted, as seconds passed. Had I gone too far flirting downstairs; Please, Mother, no. His smirk turned into a frown, and his eyes dropped below my eyes.

"Did you get more freckles?"

A shiver ran through me, expelling my nervous energy. The pain in the ass.

"You did! I must name them." But his expression told me he'd meant to unnerve me. He went to touch one.

"Don't you dare. I don't have any new freckles."

"Then, perhaps they look out of place because you hid them Friday night."

"They don't look out of place, Twynolan."

He chuckled, let go of my chin, and tapped my nose. "How would you know? Do you see yourself the way I do? The way anyone does? I think not."

Growling my slight frustration, I ducked and spun away from him before he could do something else. "Enough about my freckles. Let's get going."

He scooped up my hand and held it. This time, I didn't pull away.

"Thanks, Nol." He'd gotten my mind off what I'd lost and comforted me in another way.

Knowing what I meant, he squeezed my hand. "Of course. You are my *muranildë*. I will always find a way to comfort you. I am serious, though. I want that tattoo."

"Your mother would kill you. No, she'd kill me, or she'd want to."

He shrugged. "I am an adult."

"Yeah. You say that now. Wait until she sees it."

Nol's stride brought him in front of me, and he tugged me toward the stairs. Off to buy an illegal passport. Yippee.

To be clear, there were no new freckles.

12

"And you are sure this man is trustworthy?"

"For the umpteenth time, yes!"

"I am hungry."

Nol skip-hopped a few steps ahead of me. We jogged across the 112th Avenue intersection toward the Bellevue Library.

"You had a huge breakfast." We'd passed a bakery so that must be where he'd gotten his hungry idea.

"Yes, and I am hungry again. Are not you—no, *arrrant* you hungry?" He sounded like a pirate. "These contractions are odd. Ours are fluid and roll off your tongue."

I stayed silent, enjoying his annoyance. He tsked and attempted again. I hoped David could do this today. I shook the little envelope with Nol's passport photo, which we'd bought at the Walgreens Charlie had dropped us off at before going to pick up Ray. I wondered how much money I'd have to shove at him.

"I-i-iy-d," Nol tried. "That is not correct. Hallë, stop laughing and help."

"You're trying too hard." I attempted to help him to shorten the words and practice breaking words into smaller parts. The struggle was real, people.

We crossed 110th Avenue and stopped in front of the corner entrance of Ashwood Plaza. Nol stopped practicing and stared up at the brick building and surrounding grounds. The whole library included the plaza and a large playfield. Together, they took up an entire city block.

"Here is where we are meeting David. The Bellevue Public Library." I smirked as I watched his reaction.

"A library?"

"Yep." I hitched my purse up on my shoulder and kept moving. Feeling his absence, I looked back to find him staring up at the structure.

The three-story brick library wasn't that impressive compared to the Seattle skyscrapers or many of our structures in *Aemina*. Nol used to stay in the library for as long as they'd let him, reading whatever snippet of information he had learned about that week. Seeing the younger, innocent Nol peeking out made me smile more.

We'd be late if he stood and stared any longer. I trotted back and grabbed his sleeve to tug him up the long ramp and through the tall glass doors. Nol stumbled once as I guided him up the steps and past all the aisles he wanted to stop at. I did not laugh—out loud at least.

David worked on the second floor in the computer lab. We found him at a librarian's desk, with a pencil between his teeth, too engrossed in his work to notice anything.

Once at the counter, I rested my chin on my hands and waited. David saw the movement and looked over. A flicker of recognition. He went back to his computer.

"Just a sec, Hally. Gotta do this first. Then I'm all yours." He winked.

"No problem."

The harsh white light of the computer monitor made his light brown skin paler and his brown eyes black. David frowned again, pressed enter, and pushed his black, round, wire glasses farther up his nose.

He took the pencil out of his mouth and tucked it behind his ear, hidden by his black, curly, jaw-length hair. His Star Wars T-shirt was worn, but the stubble on his face was barely there. For an IT librarian guy and whatever else he was, he didn't look unkempt. Or perhaps that was a requirement of the job. Either way, he looked good.

David's focus shifted to Nol, who had shouldered up next to me. His eyes hardened on Nol for a second, and then he looked back at me. Trust didn't come easy for David, which made sense, considering his side job. But hey, it paid his student loans. He stood and folded his arms on the counter across from me.

"Your order sounds a bit..." He looked up at Nol again, this time more assessing. "Detailed."

I shrugged.

"Let's go talk. Follow me."

We followed him through the computer lab door. Due to all the electronics, the room was warmer and smelled of heated plastic and ozone. The bolt clicked as David locked the door.

Everything was set up like a classroom. Desks with computers faced forward, while a big teacher's desk was in the front in the far corner—not that the room was huge or anything.

"You said you needed this ASAP. How ASAP?" David asked as we walked to the front of the room together, Nol trailing behind us.

I looked over my shoulder. Nol seemed more interested in the whiteboard than in our conversation. I knew better.

I winced and couldn't help my sheepish expression. "Twenty-four hours, or sooner?"

David stopped and grabbed my forearm, halting me. His eyes bulged. "For all that? I got other things going on, Hally. Wednesday sure, but tomorrow?"

"I wouldn't ask if it wasn't really important." I tilted my head and attempted to look pathetic.

He tsked and looked down, biting his lip. His eyes traveled back up to mine. He squinted. "It's gonna cost ya." He pulled on my arm to start us walking again. "My other clients are important, too."

His normal fee was ten thousand, fifteen for a rush job. I hooked my incisor on my lip ring, thinking. "How 'bout eighteen?"

David leaned against the teacher's desk and crossed his arms. I picked a desk close to him to lean on and I watched him while he focused on my feet, thinking.

"You want a passport, visa, license—"

"No license," I interrupted. "A bank account is a must, though."

"I'd hafta stop everything else. Twenty-five."

I swore under my breath. "Twenty. That's five thousand more than your normal rush rate."

"Things are trickier nowadays with new technologies and stuff."

"Come on, David."

David took a deep breath, eyes following my body down, and slowly his gaze came back up. His mouth curved up. "If you only have twenty, we'll need to get creative."

Nol came to settle beside me. He crossed his arms and gave David his hard, emotionless stare. "What are you implying?" He lifted his chin and looked down his nose at him.

I shivered at the lack of emotion in his voice. I hated this side of him. "My friend has offered you more than what you charge. You want more, but do not offer another monetary counteroffer. That is quite...How do you say? Bold with me beside her."

My jaw dropped after a second as I realized what Nol meant. I elbowed his side and glared at him. He ignored me and kept his eyes on David.

David swallowed hard and licked his lips. "You may be the face on the ID, but Hally is the only one I discuss terms with. Stay out of it."

"Then show her respect and—"

"Twynolan," I growled under my breath. He stopped and looked down at me.

"Would you excuse us for a moment, David?" Without waiting for an answer, I pushed him back the way we came, unlocked the door and dragged Nol past the librarian's desk. "Stay out."

He lifted an eyebrow, but his expression stayed neutral. "Excuse me?"

"Never speak for me like that again."

"Hallë—"

"No." I pointed at him. "I can defend myself. That was totally uncalled for in there."

Nol leaned back, shocked.

"The person who didn't show me respect in there was you." With that, I spun around, walked back into the lab, and relocked the door.

"David? I'm so, so sorry. He can be really protective and—"

"Save it. Twenty-five thousand. And you better have a passport photo."

My shoulders fell. "Of course." From my purse, I fished out what I needed and paid half the amount we agreed on. We talked about names and birthdays, and all the while, David stayed cold and distant. And pissed. I'd been doing just fine before Nol's damn attitude got David's hackles up. Damn it. Men!

"I'll call you when it's ready. It'll be tomorrow evening at the earliest. And do not bring him with you."

I stared at his computer, not able to meet his eyes. "I won't."

David snapped his laptop shut and stood up. "Anything else?"

"I really am sorry. He hasn't slept in a while, and he overreacts."

David's brown eyes softened, and he sighed. "You sure about this guy?" He slid off the table, and we walked to the door.

"Yeah, he's...He can't get over the fact I've grown up."

"Oh, I think he has."

I laughed. "Look, I'll make it up to you. Send ya a few pizzas? Your normal ones?"

David hemmed and hawed. "You're moving in the right direction there." He clipped my chin and winked.

"Fine. Video games *and* food."

David laughed, and I left him at his counter to go collect my pain in the ass, overprotective, scary-as-shit *muranildo*. I found said pain in the ass in the foreign language section with an English-to-French dictionary. Fan-freaking-tastic.

He smiled, full-on, with a "nothing's wrong" expression. A complete one-eighty. And a complete lie. "Hallë, can you check this out for me?"

I yanked the book out of Nol's hand and set it on the book cart. Not giving him another look or waiting for him to follow, I marched to the stairs. He stayed right behind me and did not say a damn word while we walked out.

I expected him to tug on my hand or something after we left the building. Instead, he walked so close behind my left side that I could have elbowed him. I wanted to tell him to back off, but that would mean talking to him, and I wasn't ready for that. My steps jarred my teeth as my feet hit the cement a too hard going down the gradually sloping ramp.

Pissed at him or not, he was hungry, so I needed to find him something to eat. Once at the bottom of the ramp, I pulled out my phone to look for some nearby restaurants with good ratings.

In one fell swoop, Nol snatched my phone, and we were in the corner between the first- and second-tiered planters separating the street from the plaza.

"Nol!"

He picked me up and set me on the lip of the planter. My feet dangled above the ground. Nol grabbed my hands, placed them on the edges of the rough, cold ledge on either side of my thighs, and held them down. Bark and little rocks dug into my palms as he pressed his weight to keep them there.

"What the h—"

Nol bent over, almost eye to eye. He kept some warmth in his eyes, angry and irritated warmth, but at least it wasn't his emotionless stare.

"Be mad at me all you want. I can handle that. What I cannot stand is allowing men to treat you like a...as an object."

"That is—"

He leaned in closer. "No, my turn now." Nol's harsh tone, unlike his normal quiet anger, caught me off guard. "He was extorting you for sex. In front of me."

"He was not. He meant food and video games."

He put a finger over my lips. "He was. He did not treat you as a person. I do respect you. Under normal circumstances, I would not speak for you, but you were not stopping him, and he was doing it in front of me. That is as much of an insult to me as it is to you. You are such a strong *endaë*, Hallë. Also selfless. And you let—How did Charlie put it? You let people walk over you."

I'd left them alone for an hour and a half. Incorrigible, both of them.

"If I had not been there, he would have demanded sex for his services."

"How dare you. I've worked with him for four years."

Nol wasn't listening. I tried to wiggle my hands free, but he had them pinned.

"I wager my sword he does not want me there when you pick up the passport."

He waited for me to say something. He knew when I lied, or at least, he used to, and I didn't want to test that now. I'd have loved to slap him, though, and I suspected that was the reason for pinning my hands down.

He lifted an eyebrow. "You agreed to twenty-five thousand dollars, yes?"

I looked away. "You cost me five thousand dollars and at least a hundred dollars in video games. He might demand the newest game console this time. All because you didn't think I could handle one immature kid with a complex."

"Look at me and tell me you noticed him assessing you. Raising his eyes like he did, putting his hand on you. Look at me, Hallë. He thinks you are weak."

"And you made me look weaker."

He looked down and seemed to count to ten. "I am going with you to meet David. I do not trust him. This is nonnegotiable."

"I can handle myself."

"Like you did with Ian? What did you do to piss him off?"

"You think you have everything all figured out. Why should I bother telling you?"

"Tell me if Ian will be a problem while we hunt Aswryn."

I took a deep breath and decided to be a grown-up and look past my anger. For a minute. "Honestly? I have no fucking clue. He has nothing to do with you. It just so happens to be my luck that they coincide this weekend."

"Who is he, Hallë? Certainly not a past lover. He would crush you."

"Please tell me you did not just say that."

I wanted to plug my ears. This was about as bad as having a sex talk with your parents—no, worse. I had to look away from his accusing blue eyes. Damn, how could he make me feel guilty when I hadn't done anything wrong?

Coming up from behind Nol, two little girls, maybe two and three, in little pink coats pitter-pattered along the walkway up to the library. Their mother walked behind them, at the ready in case the younger one tumbled on her wobbly feet.

The mom looked up as she passed us and met my eyes. She smirked, her eyes darting to Nol and back. If only this had been as simple as a quarrel like it must have appeared to onlookers. I wondered if her life was simple, happy, and perfect. Doubted it.

"Hallë? Will Ian interfere with our hunt for Aswryn? And this Agent Zack, as well?"

"First of all, never talk to me about my sex life—including David. He'll demand more money and food. Second, Ian and Zack aren't your problems. I will deal with them." I shrugged at Nol's confused frown.

My problems had nothing to do with Nol, and he didn't need to butt in. My shoulders drooped and I looked down at my lap. "I can't guarantee they won't show up, though. That's out of my hands."

Nol looked across the field. No adorable girls to distract him. I watched my feet kick back and forth, my toes tapping his shins.

"Do you want me to take care of Ian?"

My feet stopped midswing. I swallowed hard and tried to slow my breathing. First, his plan to kill Aswryn, and now his offer to kill Ian. What had he turned into?

"Going around killing people is not a solution."

Nol laughed—a bent over, hands on his knees laugh.

"Really? You think offering to kill Ian is a joke?" I kicked him, my foot hitting his shoulder. "I can't believe you."

Nol stood up and walked back to me. I took the opportunity to smack him. The ass blocked me, twisted around, and held my wrist. "You'll have to be faster than that." His other hand came around and thumped my nose.

"Quit that!" I rubbed my nose, not that it hurt. More like I was protecting it from further thumps.

"Hallë, your innocence is endearing," he spoke softly in *Aemirin*. "There are other ways to eliminate a threat. *Zayuri* know other skills besides killing assailants."

"How should I know? *Zayuri* aren't exactly forthcoming about their skillsets." I shoved him with my free hand. "Stop laughing at me, you stupid genius. Everyone knows *Zayuri* kill people."

Nol lifted a shoulder and tried to keep a straight face as he looked back at me. His light blue eyes danced with laughter. I kicked him hard, the planter I was sitting on being the perfect height to get him in the shin. Nol jumped back. Still laughing! I waited until he came back and settled, his hands resting on the cement lip, before I kicked him again.

"Okay, okay. You win," he called out.

Nol scanned the park before locking eyes with me again. "My second point—if I see this Ian again, I will stop him, not kill. Again, non negotiable. My mission is Aswryn. Anything to hinder my hunt will be, um, dampened? No..."

"Suppressed," I corrected. "Even if that hinders my life here? If it threatens my safety after you leave?"

"I have my ways." Nol gave me an adorable smirk.

"Your dimple's showing."

Nol moved to cover his cheek, realized what he was doing, and tried to tap my nose. I squealed and ducked, slapping at his hand. Somehow, he trapped both my arms on the lip of the planter again.

He came in close, our noses almost touching. "Are we better now?" he asked low, trying to make it awkward again. I saw his game now and didn't react.

I leaned forward until our foreheads touched. "No," I whispered, "you were a dick at the station. And you are an ass for not leaving a note on Friday. And what you did up there with David was not okay."

Nol twisted his lips, stood up, and puffed his cheeks out. "I am sorry that I lashed out at you at the police station. Thank you for coming. I am also sorry I left without telling you. I did not think I would be gone for so long. But I am not sorry about David, and you will need to live with that."

I thought about his apologies, waiting awhile to make him fidget. Familiar with me, he saw I'd accepted his apology without me saying anything and poked my sides a few times. I couldn't *not* giggle, and he knew it.

"Come. We must catch this bus you talked about. I am very hungry and eager for dinner."

I considered his chances of survival as slim if I had to hear him bitch the whole hour-long ride home. "I should feed you first."

Nol perked up. Without warning, he lifted me up high and set me down on his other side, like a child.

"I can get down myself." I slapped his arm. "You need to stop treating me like a kid!"

He chuckled.

"How can I treat you like a child and flirt with you at the same time?"

"You're flirting with me to make it awkward in an attempt to get your way. Ergo, it's really not flirting."

Caught, he twisted his lips and thumped my nose again. I growled. He laughed and proceeded to pull me to the intersection, on a mission to find him some food. Mother help me.

13

A bright orange-headed Ray ran over and latched on to my legs, almost knocking me back out my front door. Ray and I would have tumbled back if Nol hadn't been standing behind me. I steadied myself and stepped inside before I picked her up.

As I walked farther into the living room, Ray bounced in my arms. "Tatie. Tatie, guess what?" She didn't let me guess. "Uncle Lewis brought me a new My Little Pony."

I rested my forehead on hers, letting our freckled noses touch. Lewis had promised not to buy any more. "Oh really? Uncle Lewis spoils you like crazy."

"Hey, girl!" Mateo called out from the kitchen.

Sam and Lewis were sitting in the living room, playing Scrabble on the coffee table. The Sounders game played on the TV.

"What took you so long? Mommy almost burned the kitchen down."

"Oriane Caroline Roux, that is not true," Charlie yelled from the kitchen. "Mateo, you stop telling my daughter bullshit."

Mateo cackled.

Ray wiggled out of my arms to go see Nol. He still stood in the entrance, staring down at my little red-headed niece. I squeezed my eyes shut. I should have warned him. An'di had almost the same color of hair. I was such an ass.

Ray grabbed his fingers. "Hello, I'm Ray. My real name is Oriane, but nobody can say it 'cept Tatie and Mommy."

Nol stood frozen, his eyes glued to her.

I grabbed his arm and squeezed. "Ray, this is Nolan. We were best friends when we were little."

Ray looked at me. "I *know*, Tatie."

"Why don't you let Nolan step in all the way?" I pulled her back by her shoulder and tugged on Nol's arm. That unfroze him.

He took a step forward, then knelt on one knee. She reached out and brushed Nol's hair back to touch an ear.

I crouched, resting my forearms on my knees.

She leaned in and cupped her hand against his ear so only we could hear. "I know you're like Tatie."

Nol swallowed. "How—how do you know that?"

"I feel it in my heart," she explained, shrugging. That was the closest explanation any of my sister's descendants could give me.

Nol lifted an eyebrow at me. I mouthed, "Later."

We jumped as Sam whooped with the crowd on the TV, cheering when our keeper blocked the ball.

"Are you gonna take Tatie back home?"

Nol licked his lips and swallowed hard. "Do you want her to come with me?"

Ray looked down at the floor, her hand dropping to his shoulder. She shook her head and leaned into Nol until she was almost sitting on his leg.

"I know your Tatie would be sad if she left you."

She thought for a moment, then nodded. "Maybe you should stay here and be Tatie's friend again. Mommy says you're gonna sleep over. Wanna sleep in my room? I got anodder bed."

Nol smiled and scooped her up. "We will see." He took her and sat on the couch while I stared at the two of them. "So, what is a My Little Pony?"

Ray had never warmed up to someone so fast. She slid off his lap, ran to her toy basket, and came back, shoving the pink plastic pony less than an inch from his face. "See, it has a tattoo on its ass."

"Ray! You don't say that word, young lady," Charlie snapped.

"Yes, Mommy. Sorry," Ray responded, more out of habit than a meaningful apology.

The first time I saw the ponies, I'd laughed so hard. I couldn't get over the tattoos on their asses. I mean, how perfect. Now the toys were Lewis's "thing" to give her. Not mine, like one would think. I couldn't recall how many she had, but she had a toy bin just for them. Charlie and I forbade him to give her more, but he kept a list, and his and Yumi's goal was to get every single pony.

Nol took the toy from Ray to examine the thing at a more reasonable distance. As Charlie came up beside me, Mateo put a wine glass in my hand. I kissed both their cheeks, and Mateo took his seat at the Scrabble game.

"How'd it go?" Charlie rested her temple against my head.

I took a sip and hummed behind my glass.

"That bad?"

We watched as Nol took another pony and had it galloping on the coffee table toward Ray at the end.

Charlie leaned against me. "*Elle est prise pour lui.*" *She's taken to him.*

"I think it's from your ability to sense my kind," I whispered in English.

"*Oui.* That must be it. I feel like I've known him much longer than a day."

Nol looked over at us, but Ray tapped his hand to keep him playing.

"He heard us?"

"Yeah."

"That's why you said it in English?"

"Mmm hmm," I hummed into my wine glass. I took a breath and found something else to focus on. "Is Yumi working, Lewis?"

Lewis didn't look up from the board as he answered. "Yeah. She says hi and sorry. I'll have ta leave 'bout nine, though."

We understood his girlfriend's odd hours at the hospital. "Well, don't leave without some dinner for her."

Lewis's lip poked out as he put a word on the board.

"That's not a word," Sam said

"Is so," Lewis argued.

Sam pulled out his phone, determined to prove Lewis wrong. "Christ," Sam whispered as he lifted his gaze to a gleaming Lewis.

"See?" Lewis gloated.

Mateo leaned over to rub Sam's back, but he saw it for what it was. "Quit cheating," Sam accused his partner, batting him away.

Mateo pressed his hand to his chest and sat up. "I never cheat."

"The hell you don't." Lewis bellowed, his laugh turning into a cough at the end.

Charlie choked on her wine as we both giggled at our friends.

"I'd never stoop so low." Mateo looked away, caught my eye, and smiled.

"Mateo James, you do too cheat. Tonight and every time we play Scrabble," I scolded.

"And Yahtzee," Sam called.

"Guys, look, Yedlin's going! Go, go, go!" Charlie cheered for our soccer team. "Goal! Did you see that play?"

"Yeah. There's no way the other team is recovering. Not at the eighty-ninth minute," I said.

"Depends on the stoppage," Sam argued. "They got another goal a few minutes ago."

The oven timer went off, and Charlie moved to take care of the food.

I touched her arm. "I'll go. Sit and rest a little."

"You sure?"

"You cooked all by yourself—"

"I helped!" Mateo added as I walked into the kitchen.

I turned to set the oven-hot dish down on the counter and almost dropped it. Nol stood against the peninsula like he'd been there the whole time. My eyes narrowed at his guilty grin.

"Why are you in here?" I set the dish down beside him.

He leaned over to smell the food. "To bug you." But he looked like he had a lot of stuff on his mind—sad and tough to talk about stuff.

"I'm sorry about Ray."

Nol's eyes shot up to stare at me. "What?"

"I should have warned you about her hair. It's the same color as An'di's."

He looked down at his feet, his cinnamon-red eyelashes hiding his eyes. "There is no need for that. She is lovely."

"How'd you get away from her?" I shut the oven door.

"Bathroom break."

"I can tell her to give you a break."

"No. I can pretend I am not here to hunt someone while playing ponies with her."

What did I say to that?

"Nolan, wanna see my star and blueberry ponies?" Ray came running in with four ponies now instead of two.

"Um, sure?" Nol dragged out his answer.

I snickered into my wine class. "Now you're in for it."

Nol frowned. She tried to climb on the counter, but Nol picked her up and set her next to him. Soon she'd have him over at her toy basket, introducing *all* her ponies. I set my glass down next to the sink and got back to fixing dinner. The room spun, the walls blurred, and I grabbed the counter before I fell. Not this again.

I looked over my shoulder at Nol and Ray still playing ponies. No magic was cast. Well, I hadn't eaten much today, and this was my second glass of wine. Yeah, that could do it. After grabbing a cheese stick from the fridge, I went back to work. A few minutes later, I nudged Nol and Ray out of the way to get under the cabinet for a gravy boat.

"Why don't you two go play in the living room?"

Nol tapped a pony on my head. "Because it is quieter in here."

I rolled my eyes and reached to take a sip of wine, only to find my glass empty. "Did you drink my wine?"

"No, I do not like red wine." Nol made his pony kiss Ray's nose.

Ray giggled and galloped her pony on Nol's jacket sleeve.

I poured myself some more. "Take your jacket off and stay a while."

"Where?"

"Coat hooks in the back?"

Nol didn't look up. "I would rather keep it close." He glanced toward the back then gave me an exasperated look. "My sheath is connected to it," he answered in *Aemirin*.

Oh. I set my glass down and grabbed the stepladder to pull the Sunday dishes down.

"Here, Hally. Let me help." Mateo stepped over and took my armload of dishes.

"Hallë, you could have asked me to help."

"Nah, you're having fun with Ray." I made it all the way to the floor before my head spun again.

"Besides, I like to help Hally. Makes me feel useful," Mateo said as he came back from the dining room.

"No, you're in it for the snacks." I took a deep breath, and the dizziness subsided.

"That, too." He kissed my cheek.

I huffed and grabbed a roll off the cookie sheet. When I reached for my wine, it was empty once again.

"Okay, Twynolan. You are drinking my wine."

"I am not. Ask Ray."

"Don't bring her into this. Open your mouth." He obeyed and there was no red on his tongue. I narrowed my eyes at him. "You better not be pouring it out."

Nol gave me the fakest innocent stare. Ray wiggled and tried not to snicker. I growled, turned with the glass in my hand, and collided with Mateo on his way to grab the last of the dinnerware.

Both of us reached for the glass as it fell in slow motion to the floor and made a marvelous shattering sound. Twinkling shards, big and small, lay around my bare feet.

Mateo jumped back from the mess. "Hally, don't move."

"Is everyone all right?" Charlie called from the living room.

"Hally dropped a wine glass. I'm gonna get the broom." Mateo dashed out of sight.

"It's okay, Mateo. I've got one in here! Nol, under the sink, I've got a dust broom—" A shard cut my foot, and I hissed. The little piece had embedded itself into my heel.

"Hallë, wait." Nol reached for the shard I plucked out of my foot. He held it up at eye level. Two fingers circled the piece as if following the rim of a glass as he cast his spell. The shards started floating. Sparkling points of light came together like puzzle pieces. When he opened his cupped hands, an unbroken, clean wine glass rested in his palms.

"Nol—" I faltered, shaking and dizzy. Oh, I wanted to kill him. Damn the stupid genius.

"I got it!" Mateo shuffled out of the pantry, broom and dustpan in hand. His eyes searched the floor. "Where's the glass?"

Nol spun to the sink with the repaired wine glass in this jacket.

"Nol used the little dust broom under the sink."

"That fast?" Doubt and confusion filled Mateo's brown eyes.

I forced out a laugh. "Well...it wasn't *that* fast. Sorry, Mateo. I tried to tell you not to worry, but I guess you didn't hear."

"No." Mateo pulled on his earlobe while he stared from the floor to me to Nol and back again. "I—I'll go put it back."

As soon as Mateo left, I rounded on a very guilty-looking Nol. "Do you realize what you just did?"

"Yes." He looked me in the eye. "Hallë, I am so sorry."

"Wow." Ponies forgotten, Ray, whiskey-colored eyes large as saucers, stared at the wine glass in the sink. "That was better than the wine magic."

"Wine magic?" I gritted my teeth. So that's where my wine had gone, and that explained why I felt like crap. Nol tried and failed not to smile. "Are you kidding me?" I hissed. "What if someone saw you?"

Nol's face sobered. "I am a trained *Zayuri*. Stealth is second nature."

"I told you—" I stopped, closed my eyes, and counted to ten. "We'll talk later."

Nol shrugged and lifted Ray off the counter. "I am sorry."

Oh, that solved everything.

Mateo came in through the pantry, his eyebrows furrowed, eyes on the clean floor.

"I think that's it, Mateo," I told him, my voice too high.

Mateo mumbled something. Crap. I began rambling about stupid stuff to distract him while we got everyone to the table.

Once seated, I caught Mateo looking past Charlie to where the glass had broken. He'd look at me, then away instead of meeting my eyes. After a few bites into my dinner, Lewis made things worse.

"So, Hally? Wanna tell Sam 'bout Zack yesterday?"

"Right," Sam said. "We never got to talk about the rest. Perfect timing, Lewis."

I glared at Lewis and mouthed, "Stop."

Lewis set his jaw and his eyebrows shot up, wrinkles moving his skull tattoo on his head. "So?" He waited for me to start, fork halfway to his mouth. "You gonna tell 'em?" Three forkfuls of potatoes later, he continued. "Zack-ass had pictures of Hally."

"Oh?" Sam didn't seem too concerned as he patted his mouth with his napkin.

"I'm—" How the hell did I start this? "Agent Thomas—I'm—"

"Hally's in WITSEC."

"I told you I'm not."

"And she's thirty-three."

Mateo choked on his wine. "Excuse me?"

"And these two know it." He pointed at Charlie and Nol.

They both looked up at Lewis. Charlie rested elbows on the table, her hands folded together under her chin. Nol had food in his mouth, eating like he hadn't been fed just two hours ago.

Sam set his fork down and put his arms on the table. "Tell me about these pictures, please."

"I—" I choked. Everyone except Ray was watching me. Charlie glanced at everyone. She wanted to help, but neither of us knew what to do. "Not right now."

Sam frowned. "It's okay, Hally. You can trust me. I am your lawyer."

I pulled my hands into my lap, again touching my bare wrist instead of my missing bracelet. "I didn't expect to talk about this at the table." Lewis got my best death stare. "I never said I was in WITSEC. You drew your own conclusion."

"You gotta trust us. Sam can protect you and get Zack to stop buggin' you."

My hands shook as I set my napkin down. My nose tickled, and my eyes started stinging. This was happening. My secret would come out, and I'd have to go into hiding.

"This is what you've been hiding?" Sam's shoulders dropped, and he let out a huge sigh. "Christ, finally."

They knew I was hiding something? "No."

"Hally? You don't have to deal with this on your own. Have you told the marshals?" Sam wasn't listening. "It'll be okay. We can go talk to your case manager. They'll get the pictures from Zack. He'll have to leave you alone."

"Hally, you gotta—"

I held both hands up. This had gone too far. "Stop. Please."

"Hally really is my aunt." Everyone focused on Charlie, and she paused. "Sh...she's had to hide, and when she came home to rescue me, it put her in a lot of danger."

"From whom?" Sam asked.

Charlie froze.

"How long have you been hiding? We can find you protection if you aren't in WITSEC—"

I shook my head. "It's nothing like you think. There's no way to help you understand." I covered my eyes.

"Give us a chance. We might surprise you." Mateo's words brought my head up. It was the first time he'd spoken since the glass incident. "You know me. I believe in just about anything. Aliens, time travel." Mateo shrugged.

"As your lawyer—"

I squeezed my eyes shut and shoved my hair back. "I never asked you to be my lawyer, Sam."

Silence.

My arms shook as I stood and pressed my fingertips on the table. I'd never yelled at any of them before. "I cannot believe I am being pressured into telling my friends things I'm not ready to talk about. I'm used to Zack doing it, but I never thought you guys would."

Everything was ruined. "Excuse me," I whispered as I forced myself not to run.

Ray started crying as soon as I was in the hallway. My feet shuffled through the house and into my studio to hide. I refused to cry. Breaking the friendship before leaving would make things easier anyway. Why had I allowed myself to get close to them?

My brain wouldn't settle on a single problem. Leaving. Protecting Charlie and Ray. Aswryn. Zack. Life. None were a match for my less than four hours of sleep and all the exhausting stress of the weekend. I curled up on my comfy chair, hugged a pillow to my chest, and rested my head on the armrest.

"Heléne! Where are you?"

Emma's terrified and panicked voice startled me awake. My ass hit the floor, and I looked around for her, only to find my art and the smell of paint, turpentine, and lavender spike. My lip trembled as the nightmare drifted away. I would not cry. I would not fucking cry.

I picked myself up off the floor and found my way downstairs. The bright white of the moon shone behind the white sheer curtains of the dining room. My sister's favorite tea was in the pantry. The rolls were in the bread box. I made two sandwiches while I waited for the water to boil.

There in the semidarkness, I sat on the counter, staring out the windows, holding on to her voice from a dream I couldn't remember. My fingers touched my wrist where my bracelet should have been. I had to find that bracelet. Everyone left me. Keeping her old luggage tag wrapped around my wrist gave me a little comfort, a sense that she hadn't left me, and now I'd fucking lost her. If I couldn't find it...I'd have no one.

14

Noon on Monday, Ray and I sat on the bus to Bellevue to visit David. He'd finished Nol's passport early. Bored, Ray handed me back my phone and turned around to bug an elderly lady. I tapped Ray's shoulder, and she huffed, slumping back in her seat. She kicked the seat in front of us, which I didn't care about until the suit in said seat gave me a sneer. *Come on, people. She's three.* I smiled and let her keep tapping away.

This morning, Charlie had rushed into the kitchen as I was pouring my first cup of coffee, hair and makeup done, jeans and blouse ready to go. She'd needed to run into work. Someone had broken in and attacked a colleague. Charlie didn't know much more. I'd shooed her out the door while she'd asked me if I could watch Ray.

After finding no Nol around the house, I found a note taped to the fridge. How sweet. Smart-ass.

Hallë,

This is your note. I am sorry I did not wake you, but decades of abuse from waking you up have taught me to let you wake up on your own. I am leaving here to meet Gileal. Together we will collect the blood samples Charlie wants. I will make sure Gil knows I am on your shit list, as you said. I should be back by tonight or at the latest early tomorrow morning. Do not go to David without me. Tell him we will meet tomorrow. I promise I will check in with you before I hunt for Aswryn if I sense her imolegin.

— *Nol*

Perhaps my choice to go this morning had been a bit hasty, but he'd pissed me off. Besides, I'd met David several times and in multiple places before this. Once at a buddies' house while they were playing a video gaming campaign or whatever it was called.

I didn't know which was worse: hearing that Nol had left to see Gil or knowing that Nol was going to see him. Our best friend was the only person who understood our bond. That and Nol thought I'd take orders from him like one of his *Zayuri* soldiers? Yeah right.

The recorded voice on the bus announced our stop. I held Ray's hand before she slipped jumping down the steps. As the bus headed off, I forced her back into her coat and hat in the thirty-degree weather. Finally done with that fiasco, she kept a few steps in front of me, dancing and humming.

According to my phone, we had a few blocks of residential housing to walk. Maybe she'd settle down. *Sure, keep dreaming, Hally.* My phone dinged, and I checked the map. We needed to go right. I brought my head up to check on the fiery three-year-old in her not-so-natural habitat.

"Ray! Come back here, *colombe*." She turned, skipped, and almost fell.

I hurried over and grabbed her tiny hand.

Once we were on the sidewalk again, Ray let me go, took two steps, and turned around. "Tatie? I'm hungry."

"This won't take long, *ma colombe*. I'll take you to lunch afterward."

"I'm thirsty, too."

"I'm sure David has some water. We're almost there."

We took a left toward the beachside houses that faced Mercer Island. This must be where people lived who couldn't afford Mercer but still had money. Too ostentatious for me.

My phone chirped with a text from Charlie.

"Ray, come back!" I called and only after three more times, she minded me.

"Be home late. Sorry," she texted.

When I looked up, Ray was crouched, picking the grass.

"Ray, your scarf is getting wet." I blew on her freezing hands and made her giggle. We had two houses to go.

"Maybe David will have cocoa."

Ray bounced on her tiptoes. "And marshmallows?"

I shrugged, not willing to make promises.

Ray went to run down David's steep driveway, but I snatched her hand. Grumbling, she stomped down the slick asphalt until we got about halfway, before she slipped. When we got to the door, Ray rang the doorbell and began fidgeting after a while, which, in three-year-old girl time, was thirty seconds.

A chain snicked, and David cracked the door open as if he wasn't expecting visitors. He looked down, saw Ray, then gave me a flat look.

"I didn't have a choice. You called early."

"You wanted it ASAP."

"Dude, do you want the rest of your money or not?"

David sighed and opened the door as I set my hands on my hips.

Ray began taking off her layers before David even locked the door and bolted the two chains, one at normal height and the second one a foot higher. Could I reach that? Should I check? No. I shook my head. Nol's warning was getting to me.

"Do you have any cocoa? Ray is thirsty and cold."

Ray gave me her coat, but David didn't have anywhere to hang it. In fact, his foyer didn't have much of anything. The stairs against the wall to the right led up to a dark second floor. On our left, the lights on the entertainment center glowed in the dark living room. While visible to me, I doubted Ray saw anything.

"I've got apple cider. She can watch some cartoons while we talk." He flicked the ceiling light on and grabbed a remote.

I clicked my tongue. "What's there to talk about?"

David lifted his eyebrows instead of answering me. What kind of answer was that?

"Come on, kid. You like Nickelodeon?"

"*Wonder Pets*?"

She followed him into his living-turned-theater room of sorts. Blackout curtains covered all four windows, a huge flat-screen TV hung from the far wall around an array of chairs and a couch with video controllers, and game cases littered everywhere. Talk about overkill—well, in my opinion.

"I dunno." David picked a cartoon channel.

Ray jumped onto the couch.

"Are you okay with her having apple cider in here?" I draped our coats over the back of the couch.

"My friends and I have beer, popcorn, and all sorts of other stuff in here. What's cider compared to that?"

"Point taken." I sat next to Ray. She seemed quite content watching her show.

David went around us and into the dark hallway. I heard some clanking and a microwave come on. The television sucked me in, and time flew out the window.

"Here ya go, kid." He set her mug on the table in front of her. At home, we still gave her a sippy cup. He had a lot more confidence in her than I did. Oh well.

"What's wrong with talking here?"

"Your papers are still up there." He jabbed his thumb toward the stairs.

We passed the upstairs bathroom and two other closed doors on the way to his office at the end of the hall. A small file cabinet stood behind a large L-shaped desk against the far wall of the room. Bookshelves lined the wall opposite the covered windows.

He took his seat in his swivel chair behind the desk and held up the documents. My stomach flipped, again with those damn pointless nerves, courtesy of Nol. Time to put on my big girl panties and shove my doubts aside. I pulled out the agreed upon money. David shook the papers in the air, but when I went to take them, he snatched them back. I shoved my money back in my pocket.

"This was more complicated than I expected." He tapped the envelope on his knee.

"If you aren't done, why did you call me here?" I crossed my arms, staring down at him, out of his immediate reach.

"I got to looking for Nolan's digital footprint. You know, to switch some names around?" He shrugged, still tapping the papers. "But there's nothing. Zero digital presence."

I dragged my fingertips on the edge of his desk and walked to the front to grab his mouse. "No offense." The little ball inside rattled when I shook it. "But maybe you're not good enough to find him."

David snorted and rocked back. The chair squeaked. "Oh, I'm good enough. I'm better than some NSA hackers, so if there was any trace of him, I'd have found it."

I doubted that. To appear bored, I set the mouse down and looked around the room. My fingertips skimmed the papers close to the edge of his desk. He had to turn his chair to follow me.

"I don't know what to tell you." Once the other side of his L-shaped desk separated us, I cocked a hip and crossed my arms. "Can I please have the passport?"

David leaned all the way back and stayed there, smirking at me like the Cheshire Cat. "That DEA guy is looking into you again. He found a picture of you."

"I know. It's taken care of."

"Since he found something, I thought I'd look, too. Maybe fix a few things."

"How thoughtful." An agent held a threat. Whatever David had found didn't matter one fucking bit.

The chair squeaked again. "I cannot find anything about your childhood. Did you know that? Not one grade school picture or even your graduating class."

"Of course you didn't find anything. You don't know my birth name." Childhood pictures had never crossed my mind. What interest would anyone take in me? "Do you want your fucking money or not? You're not the only person who makes fake identities."

"I've got everything from the States, Canada, France. How was Spain? When were you there again?"

"David, give me my documents."

"Oh wait, 1995 as Natalie Lombard, that's right. You went to the University of Salamanca. What's strange is you don't look a damn day younger than you do now. Shouldn't you have been, like, ten?

"I thought it had to be a mistake, but then you kept reappearing in France near the Bercot family. That's Charlie's family, right? Charlie Bercot-Roux. You were with the Bercots in 1978. A funeral for one Franny Bercot, daughter of Léon and Michelle Bercot. You didn't pop back up for a while after that."

Whatever David had found didn't matter. He couldn't do anything. Spots danced around my vision. Reassuring myself wasn't working. I swallowed and focused on filling my lungs, which didn't want to expand. David watched me, rocking in his chair, hands behind his head. Squeak, squeak.

My chest ached as I forced myself to breathe. To hide my shock and jitteriness, I searched for something to focus on. The pencil on the desk would work. I snatched it and tapped the mechanical thing against my bottom lip.

"Are you trying to threaten my family over some dumb-ass theory you've concocted? Relatives all have resemblances. You've been watching too much SyFy channel. What is that show? *X-Files*? This isn't like you, David. Is this all because Nolan was a dick? A little bit of editing of a family photo and, voilà, you got a perfectly believable Hally from fifty years ago. Real original."

"You know it's not fake."

"I'm not waiting around anymore. Hand over the documents now or give me my money back."

"No." His chair squeaked again. "I don't know how you're doing it, but wouldn't my NSA friend be interested in seeing what I've found? In fifteen minutes, my file will be sent to him unless I type in my password and cancel the command."

"Excuse me?" I threw the pencil on the table hard enough that it bounced off and landed in David's lap. "NSA friend, my ass."

"Are you willing to find out?" He ignored the pencil and stood up, but he couldn't reach me with the table between us.

The sound of me swallowing brought a smirk to David's face.

"We're going to have to renegotiate." He took a deep breath. His eyebrows arched into his curly black hair, and he shrugged. "Fifty thousand."

"For what? Not to tell your imaginary NSA friend? About an imaginary person? I'll take my chances. The passport, David. Now. Then I'll give you the other half—twelve thousand fifty."

"Fourteen minutes. It's right here, Hally. Wanna see?"

"Enough. I'm leaving." I spun and strode to the door because running meant fear, and I was not scared. At least that's what I told myself.

"You're not leaving this room until you tell me how you're not aging."

Five feet from the door, his hand touched my shoulder, but before he could squeeze, I slipped out from under him and turned around. He lurched off balance, his mouth a crooked oval.

While David stood at about six feet, he didn't have much mass. Controlling his movements didn't take a lot of effort, especially with some self-defense classes under my belt. I grabbed his hand before he could react and hooked his thumb backward into a lock.

He hissed and leaned forward, tipping him further off balance. My left fist slammed into his jaw with an uppercut, but with my other arm holding him in a lock, my punch had little force behind it.

That didn't matter. David spent his time behind a screen, not picking fights on the playground. A sweep down and around in a half circle and I had his arm bent the wrong way. David fell to his knees, and I grabbed his ear, still holding on to his arm with my other hand.

"Do you think I've lived this long without learning to fight?" I gritted my teeth.

"How did you know I was coming?"

"Superpowers. You're louder than Ray running through the house, you dipshit. What did you think you'd do to keep me here, huh?"

He didn't answer, so I yanked on his ear.

"I dunno. Tie you up."

"And I thought you were a pretty nice guy. Shows what I know. Don't expect another Fourth of July barbecue invite. I already had one psycho and one idiot attack me this weekend. You will not be the third." I racked my brain for a threat that wasn't empty. Nothing except pain.

Did I have it in me to break his arm? Yes. Yes, I did. Did I want to? My eyes closed as I thought about that. I was so done with being beaten up and threatened. With a fraction of pressure more, his bone popped, and he screamed. I let him go, and he dropped to the floor, cradling his arm.

Spittle flew out and landed on the carpet, and drool ran down his cheek. "You bitch."

"Yep." One last kick to his shoulder for good measure and I left him whimpering on the floor.

At the last second, I remembered the papers. I jogged back to grab them from the desk and dropped the money. As I ran back by, David grabbed my ankle and pulled my feet out from under me. My forearms slapped the floor. A second later, I stomped my foot down hard toward him, but he grabbed it before I could hurt him. He pushed himself up before I registered he'd stopped me and trapped my leg under his knee, pressing down on my ankle.

How he'd moved that fast I did not know. I didn't doubt it had something to do with the rage I imagined was coursing through his body, which wasn't unwarranted in the situation.

"You piece of shit," I growled. He held my legs down, and I did a sit-up.

With his hands occupied holding my legs, my hands were free to punch him a second time. I gave him a palm strike to the bridge of his nose. The cartilage crunched, and he yowled. The weight of his knee lifted off my ankle, and he'd already released my other foot. I scrambled to the door, slammed it and ran down the stairs.

"Ray!" I hissed. "We have to go."

"But..."

"No. Now. You can watch your show later." I grabbed our coats, then her arm.

"Tatie, I—"

"Don't argue, please."

I yanked on the door, but the damn chains kept the door closed. David stomped down the upstairs hallway, as my fingers were still fumbling with the highest chain. Why, oh why, did he have a lock so high? The chain slipped on the second try.

He tromped down the stairs, each step a hundred times louder than normal. I got the next chain and bolt unlocked in short order and flung the door open.

The cold air blew through my sweater, chilling me to the bone. Ray began to cry. She mumbled something, and I groaned in annoyance. Impatient, I picked her up and slammed the door shut. My boot slipped on the steps, but I caught my balance before we fell.

"*Je suis désolé, ma colombe.*" *I am sorry.* "We have to hurry."

I jumped over the last three steps. My ankle rolled, and we almost fell again. The side of my foot where David had pinned it to the floor throbbed. A shock went through me, from my hand to my heart, as my palm touched the frozen grass.

Instead of going down, I leaned the opposite way and launched forward in a sloppy runner's stance. With Ray still in my arms, I hit the driveway running and didn't stop until we got to the sidewalk.

"My shoes," Ray cried. "You left my shoes in there."

Shit. Now standing next to the mailbox, I turned around. David stood in the doorway. Blood dripped from his broken nose, and he cradled his arm. He didn't look too happy.

"We'll go buy you new ones. They were all scratched up anyway."

"But I want those ones!" Ray threw her head back and wailed. With her being hungry and tired and three, I should have expected this.

My body started shaking. The fear and adrenaline were catching up. Fucking A, why did Nol always have to be right? At least this time, he was only half right. No sex extortion, but I never should have trusted David.

"Ray." I shook her in my arms and yelled her name again. "Stop that this instant. There's no reason to cry. We'll buy you new shoes."

Her lips trembled, but her bawling stopped. I nodded once, then looked back at David.

"It's not a how. It's a what, David. Do you think staying young is all I can do? Come after me or my family and you'll find out just what else I'm capable of. Trust me, you don't want to know." Now *that* was an empty threat. Empty, but damn good.

I hitched a whimpering Ray up my hip and left the way we'd come. My ankle pulsed with every step, but there was nothing I could do about it. Once we were back to where we had to cross the street, I set Ray down on the cold cement and crouched to her level.

"I'm cold," Ray managed to say as her teeth chattered

Tears brimmed the edges of Ray's dark amber eyes. I set my coat on my knees and wrapped her navy-blue wool coat around her. She wore thick, light pink tights and a long sleeve pink sweater dress with ruffles on the cuffs and neck.

All appropriate little girl winter clothes. Ray's shoes weren't the only things missing. Her scarf and hat weren't in her pockets. I fiddled with the buttons, pressed the collar flat, and ruffled the flared hem.

"I'm sorry for yelling at you. Tatie shouldn't have done that. You were trying to tell me you forgot your shoes, and I didn't want to listen. We'll go shopping right now. How does that sound?" I tried to smile.

Ray nodded, and those tears fell, rolling down her face. "It's okay."

"No, dove, it's not. I was mad at David, and I took it out on you."

Ray's cold hand touched my cheeks. "Why are you mad at him? Did he make you cry?"

"No, he just said he was going to do something bad." Which was sort of true, right? I slid on my coat and picked her up.

"Oh. Nolan should kick his ass."

I stopped and glared at her. "Young lady, are you supposed to say that word?"

She shook her head.

"Exactly. So stop. And by the way, Nol does not need to kick his ass. I did."

She laughed. "Really?"

"Yes, I did. Punched him right there." I pressed my fist under her chin. "Ka-pow. And kicked him there. Hai-ya." She giggled, and I pinched her nose. "But let's not mention this to Nol, okay?"

Ray sighed and rolled her eyes. "Okay. But Tatie? I'm hungry."

She slipped, and I hitched her back up. "I know. Let's go shopping *and* eat."

15

Ray picked flats—pink, of course. Shiny Mary Janes with a bow. Not winter appropriate, but I didn't care. She pushed her two boxes of shoes up on the counter, one empty and one with unicorn sneakers.

Payless in the Westlake Center had a BOGO sale going on. Ray twirled around the store in her own little world, wearing her new Mary Janes. The lady behind the register checked the sizes of the sneakers and rang them up.

"Forty-one twenty-two."

My hand shook, but with concentration, I swiped the card. Nothing happened. The associate said something, and I swiped again.

"Ma'am? Ma'am?" The lady stopped me from trying a third time, her fingers covering my card. "That's your Costco card, ma'am."

Between her fingers and mine, I noticed the familiar black, red, and gold. That *was* my Costco card.

"Sorry, I..." I had to pause and think. "It's been—I had a horribly bad weekend."

"It's fine, ma'am," she said slowly, enunciating her words, as if treating me like I didn't know English would calm me down.

"Tatie!" Ray's high voice startled me. "Can I buy this bag? It's like Mommy's."

"*Non, colombe.* You have bags at home."

Ray ran over and grabbed the shopping bag from me. Whatever, they were her shoes. Once we were out of the store, I stopped and looked back. Now I realized why the lady had enunciated her words—I'd spoken in French half the time in there.

"Are you still hungry?"

Ray tugged on my arm. "Yessssss," she hissed.

"Let's go find some food, 'kay?"

Ray swung her bag, then my arm. "Thank you for the shoes."

"You're welcome, dove."

We made our way to the food court after buying a coffee, a cookie, and cocoa. Cash, no card mishaps that time. I forgot to add cream or sugar, but then figured the black coffee would settle my shaking hands and nerves.

"Okay, what do you want to eat?" I asked when we got to the center of the crowded food court.

"Can I go play?" Ray looked from me to the playground and back. She jumped up and down shaking cookie crumbs all over her coat and the floor.

"I thought you were hungry."

"Nope." She shoved her cookie up as close to my face as she could, which was at my shoulder.

"Fine." I scanned the sea of small tables and people, searching for an empty *and* clean one. One four-seater table a short distance from the play area sat vacant. "Run to that table there before someone gets it."

Ray bolted and flew into a seat on her tummy. How that didn't hurt kids was a mystery to me. "Can I go now?" she asked when I made it to the table.

Instead of answering her right away, I slid the shopping bag onto the table and slipped into my seat, all while watching her fidget in the chair. Only when I got settled and took a sip of coffee did I answer. "Eat the cookie and you can play."

She looked at the cookie. "I don't want it."

"Child, you are almost done with the thing."

Ray shoved it into her mouth. Her little eyes went wide after realizing she couldn't chew that large a bite. I drank my coffee without losing eye contact with her and her stuffed cheeks. Careful bites, and

I didn't say anything when she chewed a few times with her mouth open.

"I'ffffm dwwwone."

I raised an eyebrow, and she rolled her eyes. The little brat. She watched me until the last swallow. Oh, such torture! As soon as I nodded, she bolted to the playground, kicked off her shoes, and left them out in the middle of the entrance. I went to pick them up.

"Hally?" a somewhat familiar voice called out. I set Ray's shoes on her chair and looked around. The voice's owner, the client from Saturday, waved at me like a loon from the restaurant on my right. She came over, two large shopping bags hooked on one wrist. "May I join you?"

"Sure. Dana, right?"

"Yes! You remembered." She slid her bags near mine on the table and sat in the chair in front of me, obstructing my view of Ray.

"If you could move to this chair so I can face the play area? My niece is playing, and I want to keep an eye on her."

"Oh? Which one is yours?" Instead of switching chairs, Dana scooted around until our knees touched.

"The one with long red hair." I found her jumping and realized she'd dropped her coat somewhere. I twisted my lips but decided to leave her alone.

"Ah, the little ginger! Now I see why you couldn't work today! We must hold our families close and savor these moments, for we never know how many we will have."

I smiled. "That is so true." So far, the coffee hadn't worked on the jitters, and a headache was building behind my eyes. I placed my elbows on the table and rested the cup against my left temple. "I see you've been doing some shopping. How's that goin' for you?"

"Quite well, thank you. I've found a nice sweater dress, a neck pillow for the plane ride back, and new headphones"

I nodded, and then wished I hadn't. "I'm happy to see you enjoying yourself."

Dana grabbed my upper arm and shook it a little. She didn't let go until I shifted away. "And you, how have you been, besides enjoying time with your niece?"

I shrugged and turned my cup in my still-shaking hands. "The weekend's been pretty crappy. I have another headache, and I'm all jittery, but I'm hoping things will improve soon."

Again, Dana touched me, this time my fingers on my cup. "That's right. You weren't feeling well on Saturday, either."

My stomach turned queasy. Not again. I frowned and thought back. Everything seemed so jumbled together. "It's been a roller coaster, I guess." I lifted the cup off my temple and checked on Ray.

"Do you think you would be up to a few hours of enjoyment on Wednesday?"

My vision shifted like a kaleidoscope. As I tried to puzzle out what her question meant, I realized I had been squinting at her. She laughed and reached over to touch my elbow. "I'm sorry. I probably did not say that right."

"Oh, no, you did—"

"I'm sorry, I thought you liked..."

"No, no, it's okay. You caught me off guard. I don't—" When she'd made the appointment, Dana had claimed her flight on Wednesday left her no other time than this Tuesday. Now she had time on Wednesday to ask me out. Then what Lewis mentioned came to mind, how pushy she'd been during the consultation. "Since you needed to have your session Tuesday morning, I had to move things around. I've got a friend over."

"I'm sure you could sneak out for a little time on Wednesday after-noon."

Maybe Lewis was right. "I can't. There's just not enough time in my schedule this week." Yeah like helping a *Zayuri* (ex) best friend find a psycho rogue mage. The usual.

"We can do a few hours—"

"Dana, no, I can't."

Dana looked up, over toward the playground. "I see. Perhaps—"

Ray ran up to me, out of breath. She pulled on my sweater. My body swayed, and some coffee sloshed out of the lid.

"Ray! You almost spilled my coffee."

She stepped back, her little eyes downcast as she mumbled an apology.

"You're fine, dove. Just be careful." I pet her hair and pulled her in for a hug. "Now that you're here, I need you to find your coat." Her head followed where I pointed.

"My friend wants to know if I can have some of her candy." Young children made friends so easily. If only life were that simple.

"You have a new friend? That's great. No, though. You already had a cookie, and I bet you two didn't ask her parent."

Ray frowned and dropped her shoulders, but at my look, she didn't argue. She went to grab her cocoa and saw Dana sitting next to her cup. Her hand froze and she stepped back to hide behind me. In my peripheral vision, I saw her peeking out from behind my arm, staring at Dana.

"Ray, it's okay."

"*Je ne l'aime pas.*" *I don't like her*, Ray mumbled at my shoulder.

"Oriane Roux, that's rude. Why don't you go play while I talk to my friend? We'll leave in a little bit, okay?"

Ray glanced at me, then at Dana. "I want to go now."

"In a little bit."

"I miss Mommy."

"Mommy is at work. Ray, go play."

Ray huffed and opened her mouth to argue but thought better of it and stomped off.

"I am so sorry. She doesn't warm up to people quickly."

"Trust me. I understand." Dana looked away, holding her breath.

"I didn't mean to make things weird." That was a lie, though. I had pushed to see her reaction.

"Not at all." She rested her hand on my knee again. "Perhaps we can revisit this at my tattoo session tomorrow."

This time when I moved away, I made it more obvious. She didn't give me any indication that she noticed, except letting her hand drop.

A shiver ran through me. I set my coffee down and pressed my temples. My breath shook, in and out, then three more times. With every exhale, I imagined the pain and nausea leaving my body. No such luck.

"Are you okay?" Dana placed her hand on my shoulder. "Hally?"

She knew I wasn't. "I'm fine."

She laughed. "Perhaps you're allergic to me."

With my temples between my hands, I laughed, hoping the pressure would lessen the pulsing pain. "And what is the excuse for all the times you weren't there?"

"True, true." I dropped my arms and met her light caramel eyes. Her brow furrowed as she looked from one of my eyes to the other. "Will you be alright getting home? Don't give me a, what do the Americans call it? A blanket answer, either."

"I'll be fine, and that isn't a blanket answer. Ray needs an actual lunch, and I'm sure I will feel better once I have something in me."

"All right. I will let you get back to watching your niece." She stood, grabbed her bags, and held her hand out. Good manners made me offer mine.

She turned my palm up and rubbed the inside of my wrist with her thumb where my bracelet should have been. My arm jerked, but I couldn't pull away. Not that she held my wrist tight. I just *couldn't*.

"Until tomorrow, then." She dropped my hand and turned away without waiting for me to respond.

My chest compressed, and I couldn't take a full breath as I watched her walk away. My wrist felt warm and hummed like a current of energy under my skin.

"Tatie!" Ray dropped her coat in my lap, breaking my eye contact with Dana's back. "I'm hungry!" she yelled. "Tatie?" Ray grabbed my hand away from scratching my wrist. "I want chicken nuggets."

I took another breath, strong and not shaky at all this time.

"Tatie! Tatie, listen."

"Yes, Ray. Chicken nuggets. Stop yelling, please."

She put her hands on her hips. "I haven't aten in thirty years!"

"Do you know how many thirty years is?" I helped her into her coat.

"Yessss," she hissed wide-eyed and silly.

"I don't believe you because thirty is much more than three. You are three, aren't you?" I tugged her coat closed.

"Yes," she said as she giggled. Then Ray hopped to the table to pick up her cocoa. Settling my coat on my own shoulders, I reached for her hand and my coffee. "Tatie?"

"*Ma colombe?*"

"That girl? She's bad."

"*Colombe*, you don't even know her."

"She's a bad *enda*."

"Ray." I bit my lip trying to pull myself out of my jumbled thoughts. My head still hurt and I was nauseous. I knelt in front of her. "Why do you say she's *enda*."

Ray screwed up her face then shrugged her shoulders.

"*Ma colombe*, does she feel like an *enda* to you?"

She shrugged again. "I don't like her."

"Well, you don't have to like her. Is that why you say she's an *enda*?" Maybe with all the new excitement Ray was confused. I knew it wasn't doing my senses any good.

Ray shrugged again, unwilling to talk now. I'd ask her again later. Maybe after she'd "aten".

"Chicken nuggets, huh?" I stood up, and we found our way out of the middle of the food court. Chicken strips were close to chicken nuggets. "What about this one?" I pointed to one of the actual restaurants lining the court instead of the fast-food ones.

Ray ran ahead, but before she got three steps away, I snatched her warm little hand in mine.

While we waited, Ray fidgeted. Alex, our server, handed us menus, a coloring one for Ray and a laminated one for me.

"What do you want, dove?" I wiggled the menu in front of her while she opened her mini box of crayons.

Ray tapped the chicken and a bowl of macaroni and cheese with her red crayon. She waved her crayon above the menu, picked a picture, and scribbled the face red.

Her new shoes tapped me for the five hundred and twenty-seventh time before our server came around and took our order. By my second cup of coffee, my stomach started to settle. My headache left before we finally got our food.

Another server, not Alex, slid our meals in front of us. Ray picked up one chicken strip and dropped it back on the plate.

"Here ya go!" The server clapped once. "Anything else?"

"These aren't chicken nuggets," Ray stated, grumpy from so long without food.

The server's smile dropped.

"They're like chicken nuggets. I betcha they taste the same." I tipped my chin at the flustered young server.

She let out a breath, looked at Ray once, and left us.

I picked up a piece of blue cheese off my salad. The tangy ball melted in my mouth. "Do you want my olives?"

She shook her head and poked at her macaroni and cheese. They expected kids to eat all of that food?

Ray huffed and poked at her food again.

"You need to eat, Ray."

"The noodles are mushy." She took a bite of chicken, then a grape.

I slid an olive onto her plate and her mood brightened. "So, how was the birthday party?"

Ray's face lit up, and she told me about the presents, the birthday cake, and a fairy named Fred that came to visit. Odd, but sure. My phone buzzed in my pocket.

"N is bck. Whr r u?" Charlie texted.

I glanced down at the text again. Crap. Six thirty and we still had to catch the bus. I called for the check, and we didn't take any doggy bags for her soggy macaroni or my wilted salad. We made the six forty-five on the route with one transfer. We'd be home by seven twenty. At least something was going right.

16

THE AUTOMATED VOICE ANNOUNCED our stop, and I had to move a sleeping Ray over a bit to pull the line. An old man one seat ahead gave me a dirty look as I struggled to lift Ray into my arms.

Sure, I could have woken her up, but the house was a block away. An easy walk even with forty pounds weighing me down. Except the snow flurries obscuring my view. Ugh. It was sticking.

At the front door, I shifted Ray to my left to grab the freezing doorknob. The voices coming through the door stopped as I pushed it open. I couldn't look over Ray's frizzy hair, but I assumed the two of them were in Charlie's lab.

"Charlie, would you come take Ray so I can take my boots off?"

"Tatie…" Charlie hesitated. "I didn't expect you until closer to eight." She lifted her daughter from my sore arms. I shook them, stretching my wrists.

"I texted you. Once my boots are off, I can take her upstairs. I'm sure you and Nol are elbow deep in those samples." She let out a forced laugh, and I looked up, from loosening the laces of my first boot. "What's wrong?"

"Um." She looked over her shoulder at Nol, giving him a kind of panicked expression. "Tatie." She bit the side of her lip, a worried habit.

"Charlene Hannah Roux, tell me what is wrong right now."

She glanced at Nol again. From Charlie's hesitance, I knew he'd done something stupid again. "Twynolan, what did you…" My question trailed off when I looked across my living room.

Another person I'd never expected to see again stood next to Nol with a drink in his hand. His wide, non-human teal eyes stared back at me, brilliant against his oak brown skin. The tip of his pointed, narrow nose turned up at the end. Time had matured him. He'd cut his coarse, untamable golden hair midway up his neck. Then he smiled his adorable crooked smile, revealing his mischievous side.

I tried twice to say something, but words failed me. What could I say? I didn't know what to do, what to think or feel. The one person who had stayed by me when Nol had left stood there, smiling and fidgeting.

"Hallë." Nol hesitated. "Please, do not be mad. I can explain—"

"I'm gonna go ahead and take Ray upstairs. It might take a while." Charlie looked at the two *endai* behind me. "Good luck, guys."

No one said a word. The squeak of the top step released me from staring down the hall. I turned to look at the idiots in my living room. Then, without giving them an iota of emotion, I proceeded to take off my boots.

"Hallë? Would you say something?"

Standing up, I flipped my hair back and stepped on my heels to slide off my boots. Sighing, I tossed my coat on the couch's arm. "I need a drink."

Nol inhaled and started to say something, but I walked away before he had the chance. I poured a tiny bit more than two fingers of brandy and added ice. The two *endai* stood at the fireplace across from the front window.

To stay calm, I kept my movements slow as I walked back, sat on the couch, and leaned over my legs to rest my elbows on my knees. My drink clung to the glass as I swirled it. Over the rim of my brandy snifter, I watched them fidget like two guilty children.

"Well." I shrugged and took another sip. "Explain."

Nol's lips parted, but he stayed silent. I raised an eyebrow and kept waiting. Gileal elbowed Nol, who winced.

"We got permission for him to come."

"Oh? Did you now? To do what? Obviously, not to come visit the *savilë.*"

Gileal cringed at the last word.

"No. They knew that would happen."

Their eyes followed the glass as I took my third sip. "So?"

"He...he is here to help Charlie."

I inhaled sharply and ended this back-and-forth bullshit. "Would you please grow a pair and tell me what the hell is going on?"

Nol licked his lips. "Remember when I told you Gileal is our curse expert?"

I didn't respond.

"Since Charlie is looking for a cure, I suggested he come help."

"How long does he plan on staying?"

"Until Charlie finds answers."

"That could take a while."

Nol lifted one shoulder. "We are all prepared for that."

"We? As in everyone there. No one thought to include Charlie and me in that decision."

"No, we did not."

Gileal shifted toward me. Lowering my chin, I stared at him. He stopped, looking crestfallen. Of course they hadn't considered anyone but themselves. Sure, sharing knowledge with Charlie made sense. We had one problem, though.

"Fine, but he can't leave the house. No one can see him."

"*C'yo*, Hallë, not this again."

"No. Look at him." I held my hand out toward Gileal. "He looks the least human out of all three of us."

"*Maca los*?" What's wrong? Gil continued talking, but he spoke too fast for me to follow. He looked at me, his teal eyes pleading, asking me a question I didn't understand.

I held my palm out to stop him. "*Juete dugel, Gileal.*" Speak slower, Gileal.

He held his breath, frowned then turned to look at Nol. That's when I realized how slow Nol had been speaking to me. How much elementary vocabulary he'd used with me. I felt like an idiot. Of course they knew words I didn't know. Of course they spoke faster.

"Gileal, I haven't spoken *Aemirin* in a century."

His brow pinched, and he mouthed my words to figure them out. Damn it! He couldn't understand me. Nol translated, using a few different words.

I noted them and his pronunciation. My "e" and "ë" sounded almost identical, and I held my "s" too long. What else did I say wrong? How had Nol understood me all weekend?

Gileal's attention came back to me. "You're doing quite well, actually. I wouldn't remember a word, and you're talking in sentences."

"I sound like a fucking idiot," I mumbled into my glass in English. I already needed more.

"You don't, Hallë. Gil is right. What is the English phrase? Do not beat it up," he said the last in English.

I pursed my lips. "Don't beat yourself up. Now, back on topic. Gil doesn't look human, especially his eyes. No human has eyes like that. People will ask questions. I can't have that exposure, Nol."

"It's true. Gorgeous, but not human." Charlie came out of the dark hallway. "Told you she'd say that. Pay up, Nolan." Charlie held her hand out.

Nol groaned, dug into his pants pocket, then placed a bill in her hand. All the while, Gil snickered. I looked down at my glass of ice, but my head snapped up when Nol hissed.

Charlie laughed and plopped into her chair while holding out the bill for me to see. Twenty dollars. Where the hell had he gotten money from?

"Tell me what she said, Nolan," Gil demanded and pinched Nol's arm.

Nol hissed again and then grumbled out a quick translation, glaring at Gil as he rubbed his arm. Gil's beautiful teal—non-human—eyes turned to me and he proceeded to pout.

I sighed and sat up. "I'm sorry, Gil. Humans are..." How did I explain this? I'd seen the worst of humans, but evil wasn't exclusive to a species. "You may not be safe from them." Lame.

"Because of my appearance? I can fix that." He smiled at me, then at Nol. "I *can*." Gil sat in the chair across from Charlie and set his drink on the coffee table. He held out one hand, his fingers spread wide, and rotated his wrist, whispering something under his breath.

His magic trickled through me instead of slamming into me like Nol's and Aswryn's magic had. The dizziness lasted for a moment, reminding me of when Nol had cast the deflection spell in the coffee shop.

Nothing seemed to change. Nol and I looked at each other as Gileal smiled his crooked grin, waiting for something.

"Oh my god!" Charlie yelled, startling all three of us. She stared at Gil, pointing her finger. "Oh my god. You ch-changed."

I turned back to Gil, and my jaw dropped. The spell had dulled his eyes to look a human turquoise blue and his ears were rounded.

"You—what just happened?"

Oh, right. Charlie hadn't understood what we'd said. "He's trying to convince us to let him stay by casting this"—I waved my hand up and down in his general direction—"spell."

"*Ma—missä.*" Nol tried to find words. I guess Gil had been keeping secrets.

"What kind of spy would I be if I couldn't find a way to fit in?"

"*Evayuro?* You're a spy—he's a spy?" I asked them both.

Nol shrugged. "Is that a problem?"

"No, but I never pegged Gileal as spy material."

"See? I will fit right in." He sat up tall, proud of himself.

"What do you think, Charlie?" I asked.

"Tatie, you need to tell them about your magic before any of you make a decision," Charlie said in French.

I bit my lip ring, contemplating. Charlie was right, though.

"I need to speak English to complete my disguise," Gileal pleaded.

"That's not possible," I told him.

"For you it is," Gil argued.

Ah, crap. I went to pour more brandy. "I can't cast a spell to make him understand English."

"Why not? You've done it before," Nol said.

I stopped and squinted at Nol. "You're off your rocker. That's totally not possible."

"Remember when we went to see the dragons on your birthday?"

"Sure," I said as I sat down. How could I not remember one of the best adventures of my youth?

"When I got hurt, do you remember what you did?"

"I went to get one of Laro's friends. One of the *Terrin*."

"Yes, your father's friend. You and your father are the only ones who can speak their language in our city. Do you remember what you did so we could understand him? So he could teach An'di those spells?"

"I translated for him."

"No, you cast a spell so we could understand one another. So he could speak *Aemirin*."

Charlie choked on her drink. "She did that?" Her jaw dropped as she stared at me.

"Mhmm hmm." Nol nodded. "Not only understand, Charlie, but speak as well. She could do the same for me with French, if she wasn't such a pain in the ass." Nol flashed a teasing look at me.

Charlie snapped her mouth shut and met my eyes. She pursed her lips into a hard frown.

"This isn't—" I started.

"Please?" Gil's eyes pleaded with me.

Nol looked at the ceiling and groaned. "Hallë, come on."

I took a drink and leaned over my glass, swirling the liquid again. Why did people call alcohol "liquid courage"? There was no courage coming out of this damn glass.

"I can't."

"If Gileal could communicate with Charlie, they—"

"I can't." My heart pounded in my chest as I reached for the courage to tell them what I'd done. I couldn't bear to tell them, but I had to. Gil knelt in front of me, placing a hand on my knee. I hadn't seen him leave his chair.

"*Hally, jeme?*" *Please*, Gil begged. "Nolan told me they don't have magic here, so I understand you may be leery of casting now."

"I can't," I whispered.

"You mean you won't," Nol said.

"No—"

Gil grabbed my hand and settled beside me on the couch.

"When I came here I vowed never to use my magic again."

"We respect your vow—"

"Nolan, shut up and let her talk," Gileal snapped. He sounded so much like his father that I almost laughed.

Nol huffed and dropped into the chair Gil had sat in. He crossed his ankles and folded his arms over his stomach. "Fine. Continue," he grumped, waving at me to go ahead.

I took a deep, shaking breath. "I…" My heart was in my throat, choking me. How was I supposed to say this in *Aemirin*?

"I will translate." Nol's words were softer as he realized my problem.

Gil's hand slipped under my left hand, sliding past where my bracelet should have been. I jumped, unprepared for his touch. He refused to let go when I tried to pull my hand away. Instead, he squeezed and gave me another one of his smiles, but with his features dulled to appear human, the look didn't work like it used to. He winked, which made me smile.

With one last swallow, I set my glass down, glanced at the three people in front of me and settled on looking at my hands.

"I was ashamed of myself for what I did. I'd tried to stop my spell from hurting them, but I couldn't. I wasn't sure why—if I couldn't control my magic or if the spell was too advanced like you told me, Nol." I paused and waited until my breathing leveled out. "So, I took my choice to use magic away."

Nol finished translating, then frowned. "What does that mean?"

I raised my head and locked my eyes on Nol. "I blocked my magic."

Nol didn't translate. Instead, he kept searching my face. I waited until my admission soaked in. Nol turned to Charlie, then back at me.

"That is impossible."

Gileal flicked his fingers at him, casting a spell to poke him and get his attention so he'd translate. Nol glared at him and flicked one back at him. "*Mata.*" *Wait.* Nol searched my face. "How?"

"I found the core of my magic and…closed it off, shut it down. I don't know how to explain." I threw up my free hand. "You know my magic is different. I can't help Gileal understand English."

Nol sat back in his chair. His eyes stayed glued to me as if he were waiting for a "but" or a "ha, just kidding."

"I—I tried to tell you after you fought off Aswryn, in the house that night, but I couldn't."

"What is wrong?" Gil squeezed my hand as he grew impatient with Nol's lack of translating.

Nol narrowed his eyes, and the corners of his mouth twitched, giving me a ghost of a smile—more of a grimace. He huffed out a brief laugh.

I took a deep breath and tried to move the conversation forward if Nol wouldn't. "I was about to, but when I started, you wouldn't listen to me. Then Ray came down—"

"Do not," he said, keeping his words slow and controlled, "use Ray as an excuse."

He stood up and shoved his hair back before walking over to the wall, keeping his back to us "Everything makes sense now," Nol whispered in *Aemirin*. "That's why you didn't fight Aswryn. If I hadn't arrived when I did..." His cinnamon-red hair moved as he shook his head. "*C'yo*. What were you thinking, not telling me you can't access your magic?"

Gileal held his breath. For a moment, I feared he would push me away, but he relaxed and didn't move from my side. He began to rub gentle circles on my wrist with his thumb. My gaze rose to see Charlie staring at me with wide eyes. She didn't need to know *Aemirin* to understand the gist of Nol's words.

"*Miten voidacon zentar husoni mina?*" *How did you intend to help me?*

"Nolan—" Gil started.

"*Tanwalu, Gileal.*" *Truly, Gileal.* "Charlie is more useful to us than she is. That's why she didn't tell me. Hallë, what would you do if Aswryn came without me here? How would you protect yourself? The girls? Your pepper spray? You can't use that again. She's prepared for that now."

"Aswryn knows my magic is gone."

"Juanaconar ellë?" You told her? "Why in the starless abyss would you do that?" He squeezed his hands into fists.

"I didn't tell her. I mean, I was going to, but she kept talking over me. Then she—she reached into me and sensed the block. She was so shocked and I was scared to see the same look on your face."

I paused to calm myself. "Her magic is what made me sick Friday, when you guys fought. I didn't know that at the time, but every time you cast, I get sick."

No one said a word, so I looked up. Nol stood there staring at me, his fists still opening and closing. I had seen him this livid only once before. My stomach dropped. My breath hitched, but I refused to cry.

"I..." I steadied my voice. "I knew you'd be angry, but—"

"Yes, I'm angry," Nol interrupted me in *Aemirin*. "You should have told me at the coffee shop or Yula's Quill. But no. Because why? You figured I'd leave? I wouldn't want your help if I knew? What a selfish thing to do."

I couldn't bring myself to answer him. Before Aswryn's attack, I had told him I wouldn't help, so he hadn't needed to know. Out of habit, I reached for my bracelet, and my throat tightened from its absence. I would not cry, damn it.

"What in all the realms did you think you would accomplish by not telling me? You say you're an adult, Hallë, but you are acting like a child."

"Nolan—" Gil tried to interrupt.

"Nica tanwa, Gil." It's true. "If Gil hadn't come, you would never have told me, warned me. I would have found out from Aswryn as she was attacking me. While I held back because you don't want me to kill her. I'd have expected you to be beside me and you wouldn't have been there! Was it planned? I have half a mind to think you're working with Aswryn."

I couldn't stop myself from reacting. I jumped up and shook my fist. "You take that back." My first tear fell as my control slipped. "I didn't know how to tell you. You weren't going to tell me Laro was sick. That Aswryn's curse is a plague. You told me about An'di as a last resort."

"Tatie," Charlie called to me. I couldn't look at her, though.

"Those details were planned for another conversation. Giving you extraneous information would have drawn attention away from my initial request and compromised the mission."

"Compromised the mission? So, then you were..." More tears fell, and I began tripping over my words. I couldn't get enough air. I couldn't stop crying. "You were going to use me to kill Aswryn and leave without telling me anything. I bet you weren't even going to tell me goodbye."

"Bullshit." Nol paced back and forth across the living room. "You and the girls will not be on your own at any moment while Aswryn is still at large. Gileal or I will be with you at all times. That is not negotiable, and I don't care if you take that as an order because it is one."

I moved to get in his face, but Gil stopped me. He shook his head, a grave look in his eyes. He became too blurry to see, so I squeezed my eyes shut.

"I can't rely on you now that I know you can't protect yourself. And she knows you are completely vulnerable. What in the realms will I do now? I have to change my entire plan. If you had only told me Friday—"

"Nolan, please stop. Calm yourself and sit back down," Gil said.

I held my breath to keep quiet. I couldn't look at any of them, so I stared at the floor. Charlie said something, and someone may have responded. I wasn't sure. I closed my eyes and tried to control my breathing.

"I can't, Gil. I'm too fucking pissed. You are still so fucking reckless, Hallë. I thought you had changed. Why can't you ever think before you act? Like in the alley. Those two spells could have killed you. They almost did. Do you have *any self-preservation?*"

I couldn't take it anymore. With my arms around my middle, I took a step forward, then another. I needed to leave, go throw up, or lock my door and never come out again.

"*Sae, sae—*" *No.* Gileal snatched me back as I took my fourth step. He pulled me against his front and held tight. "Stay here, Nevie."

Again, he stayed with me, supported me while Nol...He was going to leave me again. Leave angry and—I couldn't hear those words from him, not again. I couldn't survive them a second time. Gil turned me around and rested his chin on my head. He kissed my temple and squeezed.

"Nolan, use your damn training and calm down before you ruin what you're still mending with her." Gileal shifted his weight, and I felt his warm breath against my neck as he exhaled. "Look at her. Listen to yourself."

"Aswryn could have *killed* her, Gileal. I left her with no magic to defend herself."

"I know. But this isn't helping. Where are you going? Nolan, stop."

"I have to think." His heavy steps hit the floor as he left down the hall.

How could he think I was working with Aswryn? Another set of footsteps, quicker and lighter, retreated a moment after Nol's.

"Nolan, wait a goddamn fucking minute. Where the hell do you think you're going?" Charlie's words echoed through the hall.

"Out. Away."

"I vouched for you, you son of a bitch. Not once have I ever seen Hally cry. She *never* cries. She's the strongest person I know, and within a few seconds, you broke her down."

"Move out of my way, Charlie, or I will move you."

"What would you have done if she'd told you Friday?"

"I don't know," he admitted after a few moments. "Move, now. I must go. I need to think."

Hearing the back door shut undid me, and my knees gave out. Gileal swore and grabbed me before I fell to the floor.

"Everything will be fine. He'll be back. I promise," Gil told me, but he couldn't know for sure.

The rest of the evening was a blur. Gil helped me up the stairs; he knew I hated being carried. The next thing I remembered was Charlie telling Gileal to help me into my bed as if he could understand her. She kissed my forehead and apologized. Gileal lay down beside me over the covers and wrapped his arms around me.

Someone placed a warm washcloth on my cheek, most likely Charlie. My crying stopped soon after that, but I couldn't stop those stupid childish hiccups.

After Charlie left, Gil kissed my head, and he told me "this will work out," or "he's coming back," or "I'm here with you," or some other comforting crap I didn't need but took anyway. I fell asleep in Gileal's warmth, smelling of home.

THE CLICK OF MY door latch startled me awake sometime later that night.

Gil patted my back. "*Sajë*. Just listen."

"Gil?" I held my breath to hear Nol's voice.

"What are you doing?" Gil whispered back.

"I talked to Charlie. Well, rather, I got lectured by Charlie. I will go to her lab with her tomorrow with the samples. You go with Hallë to work." Nol's order lacked emotion. Where had that been before? I would have preferred his icy, unemotional *Zayuri* self over what he had done earlier.

"I planned on it," Gil said.

"How is she?"

Gil didn't answer. Silence fell long enough that I thought Nol had left.

"I screwed up," Nol said.

"Yes, you did."

"I'll talk to her. But I need to calm down more."

Silence again.

"Good night, Gil." A second later, the door clicked shut.

"See, he didn't leave you."

"He thinks I'm working with Aswryn."

"*Sae—*"

"Yes, he keeps hinting at it. I'm not, Gil. I'm not."

"*Sitam.*" *I know.* "He knows, too. Trust me, he knows. *Sajë*, go to sleep, love. I'm here, and he hasn't left you."

But he would. They both would and I'd have to find a way to survive alone again. It was the exact reason I hadn't wanted Nol to stay in the beginning. I settled in and listened to Gil's heartbeat until I fell back asleep.

17

THE SUN BEAMING THROUGH the open curtain—jeez, I needed to close those things—woke me. Gil's eyelashes shone a golden blond in the deep yellow of the morning. If only last night wasn't the reason he was in my bed. If only money grew on trees.

"I always dreamed of waking up beside you in the morning."

I rolled my eyes. "Still the romantic," I replied in *Aemirin*.

"Only you." Gil squeezed his eyes shut and stretched, reaching out and pressing the headboard. "How are you feeling?"

I wrinkled my nose. Hollow, sad, broken, nervous. Nothing came to mind.

"That bad?" Gil asked. "I wish we could stay here together and forget the world."

"We can't do that, can we?"

"You would? With me?"

Oh, crap. "Um...maybe I said that wrong."

"You didn't. I'm teasing you. But we must discuss one thing before anything else."

"What?"

"What kind of name is Hally?"

Unable to keep my laughter quiet, I rolled into my pillow. The anchor holding down my memories, or rather the feelings behind those memories, lifted. I would have cried again, if not for Gil's hand on my cheek, his teal eyes roaming my face, my hair. He kissed my nose.

"You don't like my name?" I stuck my lip out.

"*C'yo*, has my Nevie learned to flirt?"

I laughed again, softer this time, and gave him a one-armed shrug. "Don't use Nevie—"

Gil pressed a finger to my lips. "*Sitam*." *I know.* "I won't, but Hally is too harsh for you."

I shrugged again. "So did you bring clothes and other..." I let my sentence trail because I couldn't remember the words.

"Yes, downstairs."

"How about you get your bag while I find clothes and take a shower, hmm? We can meet in the kitchen later."

Gil raised an eyebrow. "In a moment."

He pushed me onto my back and kissed me. When I didn't object, he climbed over me, and we continued. My hands dug into his hair, and his palm pressed against my back. We were seeing each other before I left, but no matter how long he stayed here, I couldn't let this get serious. After a short while, he stopped to look at me, his eyes a little unfocused. He said something too fast for me to follow.

"Gil, we won't be taking this further."

He groaned, leaned forward, and kissed me again. "For now." He got up, smiling his sly, crooked smile.

"Go." I half shoved him out of my room while he laughed. Jeez. With one morning together, he'd gotten my guard down. I was in trouble.

Another day at the office meant another day of dress-up. I grabbed my off the shoulder wine-red sweater and black leggings. And what better shoes than my rose Docs? Another day, huh? So why did I feel so self-conscious?

Nol sat at the dining table when I rounded the corner out of the downstairs hall. A *Seattle Times* newspaper lay in front of him. My shoulders dropped. Crap, I never got around to giving him his passport last night. Adulting sucked sometimes. My coat and purse were still on the couch. David had made more than a passport. Inside the envelope was a French passport with a visa, a debit card, and bank account information. He had even put fifteen-hundred dollars into the account. Interesting. I tossed the envelope on the table and walked into the kitchen.

And three, two, one. "I told you to wait." Right. On. Cue.

I shrugged and set the coffee pot down. "I'm reckless, remember?" I picked up my mug, leaned on the counter and blew on my coffee. "Fuck off."

Nol grunted but didn't say anything. Someone steps thumped down the hall way, too heavy for Ray or Charlie and that left only one other person. "What's wrong?" Gil slowed down as he passed Nol's spot at the table.

"Nothing," we both said. I took my first sip and let myself enjoy the simple things.

Gil paused at the peninsula. "Where are your freckles?"

I stopped, my mug halfway to my mouth, not sure how to respond. This was not the phrase I'd expected to hear before heading off to work, especially from the guy I'd just made out with.

"It's called makeup, Gil. She likes to cover them."

Gil came over and tried to press a thumb to my cheekbone. I batted his hand away. "Your freckles are beautiful. Why would you cover them?"

"Because she hates them," Nol answered for me. Again.

I rolled my eyes and went in search of some breakfast. Lucky Charms, Ray's favorite, sat on the counter. "Where's Ray and Charlie?"

"Charlie took Ray to—" Gil hesitated.

"Mateo picked her up, and she's walking them to his car. You took too long in the shower."

I was going to start throwing stuff at him. The jerk didn't even look up from his newspaper.

"Okay guys, I'm back! Everyone ready to go?" Charlie's voice echoed through the house from the back, her shoes click-clacking through the pantry.

"Almost!" I reached for a commuter mug.

Gil gasped. "I didn't know there was a way through there!"

Charlie stopped, her eyes going from one of us to the other, unsure of the problem. I laughed and translated while grabbing a banana and protein bar for Gil and me.

Charlie gave me air kisses. "How are you doing?" she asked to me in French.

"*Bien*...better, thank you." I leaned in and hugged her tightly.

Gil took the lunch bag from me and kissed my cheek before he scooped up my hand, his fingers interlaced with mine. He nodded to Charlie, and we walked out through the pantry together, Nol trailing somewhere behind us.

"*MA ACARIETESSE CARDA?*"

I sighed. "No, for the tenth time, I'm not done yet."

Gil laughed and spun around in my chair again. No matter how hard I tried, my *Aemirin* sounded like crap, and I think he enjoyed my failure. "I've asked five times, and you've been cleaning for over an *hour*. I think I make you nervous." More like fifteen minutes.

Of course he made me nervous. He'd been flirting with me since we'd woken up, and I'd encouraged him at first. I'd folded once; he knew I'd fold again. "I have to make sure my area is clean. I use needles that poke into the skin." Gil didn't say anything for a while, so I looked at him. His eyes scanned the top of my toolbox. "What are you looking for?"

"Needles? I don't understand. Nolan says you paint people, not poke them."

"Yes, paint in their skin with needles."

He still looked confused. "Like what Nolan brought to take our blood?"

"Look." Tossing my rag in the bucket, I grabbed my portfolio from the front and a needle cartridge from my drawer. "This is a simple one, a dragonfly. I used these needles to poke the ink into their skin." I pointed at the tiny tattoo needles in the cartridge. "They stay there..."

I licked my lips, trying to remember the word. "...forever." He slid his hand under the portfolio, into my sleeve, and up my wrist. My hair stood on end, and I shivered.

"Does it hurt?"

I smiled. "Most people say it does."

He took the cartridge from my hand, then set my portfolio on my clients' bench. "Do you have one?" His too-human turquoise eyes roamed over me from head to toe.

"They are forever—people will notice them after I leave here."

"And they will recognize you."

That was the dumbed-down version of it. Best to stick to simple words. "Yes."

"Nolan explained the living amongst humans ruse."

My breath came out in one big rush, grateful not to have to explain further in my choppy *Aemirin*. Gil's eyebrows rose, as if he expected me to say something. His sly smile reminded me of this morning.

My breath hitched, and my pulse beat in my ears. I scrambled for something to say. "What else has Nol told you?"

"*Ai*." He looked up at the ceiling. "Some about Charlie and Ray. He loves your friends. Your art. You have a quick temper—still. Your accent is—"

I scoffed and leaned against my desk, half sitting on the counter. "I'm working on my accent, all right?"

He leaned all the way back in his chair. "Hmm, don't bother. He said I'd get used to it." He smiled an "I know something you don't know" smile.

"Please." I looked away and flicked my hand out. "You couldn't understand me last night."

"Don't fret. Nolan's right. Sexiness outweighs the learning curve."

"Right." I tried and failed to keep my face straight. Gil always said corny stuff like that. "Let's talk about something else."

"We don't have to talk."

I glared at him. The butt. "Funny."

He shrugged. "Your *Aemirin* is more fluid. How did you do that overnight?"

"I don't know. It's still too slow. I listen, and we've been practicing all morning." I pushed myself off the desk and turned to set up my tray, fiddling with stuff.

Gil stayed quiet while I arranged the little ink caps, got the plastic wrap out, and decided which needles I really wanted. The silence made my spine itch.

"You're too quiet."

"I'm enjoying watching you work." The purr in his voice made me look up. In his hands, he spun a purple ink bottle as he watched me. "And I have something to tell you, but I'm not sure how."

I turned around, cocked a hip, and crossed my arms. So that was what that smile was about. "Well, I guess you should just come out and tell me."

He stayed quiet for a while longer, tapping the bottle on his chin. Then he stood up slowly as he set the bottle down and stepped over to me. He placed his hands on my hips and pulled me close. "Last night, watching you sleep, I made a decision." He looked over my head and took a deep breath before meeting my eyes again. "You know I will be here until Charlie gets answers, but when that is over, I want to stay here. With you. If you'll have me." He tightened his hold on me while I stared up at him. Anxiety crept into his eyes when I took too long to process.

"This...this is a big decision. Life changing. You'd resent me in a decade. There are no other *endai* here. No magic. Your beautiful eyes would bring questions. What about the curse?" The more excuses I gave him, the more doubt morphed his expression.

"I'll be with you. That's all I care about." Again with his corny lines.

"You'd be *savilo*. We won't have Nol here. It wouldn't be the three of us against the world like it used to be."

"Don't fuss. I talked to Nolan this morning about it."

My jaw dropped. Nol would lose both of his best friends, and Gileal said Nol was okay with that? He'd be so alone. Gil saw where my thoughts were going and deflated.

"Don't look at me like that. I haven't said no."

His eyebrows shot up, a shadow of that crooked smile showing.

"Would you give me time to think about it? Let me talk to Nol—if he ever talks to me again. You know how hard he takes change. He'll lose both of us, and I'm afraid he's acting brave for your happiness."

"Ours." He rested his palm against my cheek and wiped a stupid tear off my face. Jeez, in the last twelve hours, I'd cried more than when my sister died ninety-eight years ago. "Don't cry. I understand. You know I do."

I realized the small part of me I kept bottled up inside had opened when I agreed to help Nol catch Aswryn, even though Nol pissed me off and annoyed the shit out of me. With them here, I wasn't alone. Even with Charlie, I had to pretend somewhat. She expected me to act older, and I did. But Nol and Gil treated me like my age, except when Nol treated me like a child. That drove me nuts.

"Hallanevaë." Gil's voice pulled me out of my thoughts. He tilted my face up to his. "You make my heart sing. Do you know that?"

I lifted my arms to his shoulders and rubbed his untamable hair between my fingers. He sighed and rubbed the small of my back with his thumbs.

"I don't want to talk anymore," I murmured.

"Well, if that's all it took."

I let out a short laugh and thumped him on the shoulder. He cut my laugh short when his lips touched mine. My body relaxed against his, and the tension in his shoulders loosened. My fingers tangled in his hair while we kissed again. He sat me up on my tattoo bench and pulled my legs around his hips. My heart pounded in my ears. His magic began to flow into me, reaching for mine. Warmth built in my core. Energy swirled around and around but couldn't escape. Too much. I couldn't take a full breath. My stomach twisted. His magic hit a wall and crashed through me, and I felt the full reaction.

I gasped and shoved him back. "Damn it!"

"What's wrong?"

"Magic makes me sick." I held my breath so I wouldn't throw up. I'd told Nol how my body reacted to magic in English.

"I'm sorry. I felt your energy and mine responded."

My eyes flew open, the lights as bright as a two-thousand-lumen flashlight point-blank. Nope, not looking yet. "What do you mean, you felt my energy? I'm blocked."

"I felt something. Didn't you?"

Yeah, but I didn't know how to articulate whatever I felt. "Of course I felt something. It's affecting me, isn't it?"

"Sorry." He stepped away, almost out of my reach.

"Not your fault." My hand found his shirt, and I tugged him close to me again.

Gil slipped his hands around me, his head resting on top of mine.

"You're shivering. What can I do?"

"Stay here for a moment. We have to wait until it passes."

He stiffened.

"What?" I lifted my head.

"What's that noise?"

"Noise?" I stopped breathing to listen. "Oh, that's my cell phone. It's umm...shaking." Like I knew how to say vibrate in *Aemirin*. The phone stopped buzzing, and not five seconds later, the shop phone rang.

Gil let me go, his feet scuffing on the floor toward the shop phone on the front counter. I shivered harder without his warmth. I'd rather he ignore the phone instead of bringing it to me. His quick steps shuffled back, and he handed it to me. Before I even got past "hello," Zack's voice blasted through the little speaker.

"Hally, thank god you're there."

What the hell? "Agent Thomas?" I pulled the phone away from my ear.

"Cops found Katie dead this morning."

"What!" I felt myself start to fall forward, but Gil caught me. My fingers pressed into his arm that held me.

"Ian's prints are all over the place."

"Crap."

"Are the doors locked? Is someone there with you?"

"Yes, but..." My eyes peeked open, and the lights didn't blind me.

Gil stood in front of me, looking down, confused as all hell. He searched my eyes for an explanation. His hands brushed the small of my back to comfort me. Jeez, that felt so good.

"Listen, I'm on my way down. Do not open any doors."

"Agent Thomas? Why did he kill Katie?" My voice warbled.

The rush of Zack's car engine was the only sound. "I don't know."

She'd just been here with her kid. "What about Seamus?"

"First thing I checked. His grandfather has him. Do you want me to stay on the phone until I get there?"

I did, even if it was Zack, but then I remembered. "Oh no. I've got a customer coming in at nine."

"Go and cancel. Hurry."

"O-okay."

"Be there soon." The phone went dead in my hand, but I couldn't let it go.

"Hally? What's wrong? The man is gone. What did he say?" Gil took the phone and set it beside me on the bench, waiting for me to talk.

"Ian's on his way down." I didn't sound like myself.

"Ian?"

My head reeled. Ian had killed Katie, the mother of his child? That rat bastard! Gileal grabbed my hands and shook them. The shake brought me out of my thoughts, and I focused on him.

"Nevie, was that Ian or Agent Thomas?"

"That...that was Agent Thomas. He'll be here soon."

"You're not making sense."

"I have to call Dana and cancel."

"What does that mean?"

Lewis had made the appointment, and I prayed he'd written the phone number down for once. The cubicle panel wiggled when I grabbed it to support my shaky legs. Gil held my other arm at the elbow and pushed open the doors. Our schedule book was in the drawer right under the register. I thumbed through until I found Dana. No last name. No phone number. Damn.

"Hally, please tell me what's going on? You aren't making any sense."

I blinked, still staring at her name. "I can't."

"Yes, you can."

I met Gil's eyes. "No, I mean I can't call her and cancel."

18

Pounding on the back door broke the silence of the shop. The room went blurry for a moment when I spun. We ran to the back, Gil holding my arm.

"Hally!" Zack yelled through the door to be heard. "It's me. Hally?"

My hands shook as I turned the doorknob. Zack stepped in and wiped the frozen rain from his hair. His attention shifted to Gil, came back to me, then he nodded once. "Are you ready to go?"

"Go? Aren't you supposed to stop Ian from coming in?"

"You're not staying here for Ian to find. Let's go."

I frowned. "My phone, it's on my desk."

"Screw that. It stays there."

I sighed, but it really wasn't worth arguing over. As I grabbed my purse, the shop phone rang, and out of habit, I answered it.

"No!" Zack hissed. Too late.

"Hello? Yula's Quill. This is Hally," I said in my most professional cheery voice, also out of habit. No one answered me, but I could hear cars and people talking in the background. The caller ID read UNKNOWN.

Zack glared at me, took the phone, and hung up. "What the hell?"

"That could have been my nine o'clock. I don't have her phone number."

"And you're telling me this now?" Zack got on his walkie-talkie and informed his buddies about this "new development."

"I—I'm sorry. I can't think." I shoved my hair back. "I'm not used to this."

"Yeah, I get it," Zack told me with his walkie at his chin. Where the hell was this nice-guy attitude coming from?

Zack's walkie-talkie chirped. "Thomas, we got a female, blonde hair, about five-ten coming to the front door."

"That must be her!"

"Any sign of Ian?"

"Negative."

"I'm gonna get her. Stay here, both of you." He shoved the break room door open. "I'll be back. Christ."

"I should go with him." Gil pulled away from me. "I could protect him if this Ian shows up."

I tightened my grip on his arm. "This is a human matter. Besides, it's Dana, not Ian."

To help me calm down while we waited for Zack to come back, I explained the situation as best I could. Mostly, Gil asked questions, and I tried to answer them. At least he kept me from spiraling from unanswerable questions. We peeked out of the break room door when the bell above the front door jingled. Dana said something—a question—but they weren't close enough for me to hear.

The person on the walkie-talkie spoke again, too far away to hear anything but "—Ian—coming—door."

"Shit!" Zack yelled. "Why—"

Zack and Dana shoved the saloon doors as they ran toward us. They were past our studios when a bang and shattering glass made us all jump. I pushed the door open all the way. The two dove behind the back of my space on the right and hid behind the printer a mere six feet away from me, but they were stuck.

I jumped again as Ian yelled, his voice too big for my little shop. He couldn't see me thanks to Lewis's saloon doors. "Hally! Get your good-for-nothing ass out here!"

"Dana, come on," I whispered as Ian shoved around the furniture in the lobby. If they ran now, Ian shouldn't see them.

Zack shook his head, his jaw clenched. "Too risky," he whispered. "Get back in there, Hally."

More glass shattered. The display case. The saloon doors slammed against the walls and cracked.

Ian marched toward me. "I am not fuckin' around, Hally." His bloodshot eyes bulged out of his head. Specks of blood spotted his shirt, face, and arms. Ian charged me, and as he passed by, Zack stood up, gun pointed.

"DEA. Ian Jackson, you are under arrest for the murder of Katherine Angelson. Put your hands on your head and get on your knees."

"Thomas, you fucking pig!" Ian snarled, spittle flying. "I didn't fucking kill her. She—she was dead when I got there." Ian's voice faltered.

"On your knees, Jackson. I will shoot."

"Screw you, Thomas!" Ian screamed.

"On your knees!"

Ian leaned forward, then froze. "Fuck!" he yelled and lifted his arms. "Fine!" He refused to kneel, though, so Zack wrenched one of his arms back and pushed on the back of Ian's knee.

My shoulders dropped. I couldn't believe how fast that had ended.

"Go on to the back, Dana. You guys stay there until my agents get their asses in here." Zack proceeded to inform his buddies that he had Ian.

"Hally?" Dana stood up, wobbling a bit. "Are you alright? Tell me what's going on."

I stepped out to meet her. Ian twisted out of Zack's grip when he saw me walking out. Zack turned and held the gun back to Ian's face. I grabbed Dana's wrist and tugged, but she didn't budge.

"Dana, come on."

She was focused on something behind me. I followed her gaze to where Gil stood in the break room doorway. Okay. I turned around and tugged on her again. Dana raised her eyebrows, looking...pleased?

"Hally, what is—" Gil's eyes darted to Ian and Zack, then narrowed in on Dana. "What are you doing with her?"

"What do you mean, what am I doing with her? I'm taking Dana to the back room."

Dana twisted her wrist and clamped down on my arm.

"Dana, are you okay?"

She smiled, but not that friendly one from before. No, this smile made my skin crawl. "Oh, I'm just fine, Hallanevaë." She looked up at Gil. "I did not expect you to be here, Gileal," she said, speaking in *Aemirin.*

Wait...what? Speechless, I stared from Dana to Gileal. What the hell? The hair on the back of my neck stood up.

"Hally, what the hell is going on?" Zack snapped. His eyes flicked to me, then back down to Ian.

"Uh, I'll tell you when I know." My voice shook.

Gil's eyes glowed with utter hatred.

I swallowed. Dana knew *Aemirin.* Dana moved her head in slow motion, a dark, menacing look on her face.

"You? Please don't be..."

Dana began to morph, similar to but more drastic than Gil's spell last night. My vision swam from the use of magic. Her caramel eyes turned yellow with splinters of gold.

The shade of her skin darkened to an almost walnut-shell brown. Her hair lightened from butterscotch blonde to yellow with streaks of white. The planes of her face grew angular, her eyes sank in, and hollows formed under her cheekbones. I gasped.

"Sorry." She cracked her neck. "No Dana here."

"Hally?" Zack called out, still wrestling Ian.

I couldn't stop staring at the evil, smiling *endaë.* My teeth chattered, and I felt nauseous, again. This magic reaction bullshit was getting old. "Um, it isn't good."

"Not for them at least," Dana—or Aswryn, rather, said in English as she turned to Zack.

Dana was Aswryn, and she knew English with only a slight accent. Realization hit. The way she spoke, her understanding of human culture—she had to have visited this realm frequently. I wondered if she'd known everything about me before Nolan came.

"Aswryn, this isn't the way. You can't take her," Gileal said.

She ignored Gil, but to be fair, Gil hadn't moved any closer. Her coat shifted, revealing a scar on her neck: a flaming red orb encircled by a ring of white scar tissue. Looked like she didn't need that tattoo after all.

"I won't let you take her, Aswryn," Gil growled.

This could not be happening. What were we going to do? Aswryn had come while Nol wasn't here. Why was Nol always fucking right?

"Like you can stop me. You aren't strong enough. Nolan is too busy to come protect either of you this time. Come now, Hally." She held her hand out to me as if I'd waltz out the door with her.

"Aswryn, you—" Gil flew back into the bathroom door like a wrecking ball had hit him.

Aswryn's magic washed over me. My knees buckled, and my elbows shook as I used them to sit up. A movement out of the corner of my eye caught my attention. Gil's leg moved, swaying back and forth as he lay flat on the floor, groaning. His hand rose to touch his forehead.

"What the hell?" Ian's shriek tore my attention away from Gil's prone form. He lay on his stomach, his neck strained so he could see us. "Please tell me this is a bad trip."

Zack risked glancing up. He frowned but couldn't stay focused on us.

"Unfortunately for you—" Aswryn turned, her soft leather boots quiet as she spun and stepped toward the humans. I reached for her leg, but my arms were too shaky from the effects of magic. "—this is not a result of whatever you shot yourself up with."

She muttered something under her breath, and with a flick of her wrist, Ian and Zack went flying. Zack flew sideways and hit the printer. Paper exploded everywhere like giant white confetti raining down. Ian skidded backward and his head slammed against the doorframe of the broken saloon doors, and he kept going.

Aswryn kept pushing Ian through the lobby, broken glass scraping the floor. An instant later, his head hit the edge of the couch. Ian's head jerked forward, chin rammed down on his chest, and a disgusting crunch was heard all the way in the back. He didn't move.

"Oh. My. God." Zack scrambled to his feet. "What was that?" The stencil machine fell off the table. Plastic scattered across the tiles, spinning in all directions.

"You'll know in a second," Aswryn said, then muttered the spell again.

She raised her arm, ready to strike, and I dove onto Zack. I expected Aswryn's magic to hit me, but I only felt another wave of nausea for the third time in less than three minutes.

"Didn't you learn your lesson Friday?" Aswryn tsked.

I tried to lift myself off Zack but collapsed after a few inches.

"Don't touch her," Gil croaked.

I opened one eye and saw him kneeling with one hand on the floor for support.

"*Pilassa, Gileal.*" *Shut up.* Aswryn flung a curse, and Gil crossed his arms in front of him, casting a shield. Their spells clashed.

They both wobbled backward from the power they had shoved at each other. Gil scrambled to get to his feet. Aswryn lashed out, and Gil didn't have time to throw a shield. "Stay away, Gileal, or I will kill you. I'm taking her." Aswryn reached for me.

I slapped her hands. Nauseous and dizzy from their damn spells, I didn't have the strength to get away.

"Your magic will amplify my curse and get past the immunity. When I unblock you, that is." Her rough fingers patted my cheek. "Come with me now or I can visit your friends on Queen Anne Hill. That is who's watching your little ginger niece, right?"

My stomach dropped. How did she know where Mateo and Sam lived? Or that Ray was with Mateo, for that matter?

"Now you're getting it. I'm very good at my job, Hallanevaë, and I'm growing tired of catering to you. Come. We can call Nolan on our way."

Something moved under me, against my arm. I jumped before I realized Zack had shifted. Aswryn didn't notice. I tapped two fingers to Zack's back, hoping he got the hint to stay down.

"I don't understand why you would hurt so many people," I said to distract her from noticing Zack's movement.

Aswryn sighed and looked down at her hands. "You won't understand now, but you will later. Let's go."

She yanked on my arm, dragging me to the front. My mind took a second to catch up, until the broken wood of the saloon doors scratched my leg. Then I tried to twist my wrist out of her hand. When we got to the broken display case, I grabbed the metal frame. Aswryn yanked on me, but I refused to let go. Aswryn yanked again and squeezed my right wrist. It popped, and I cried out.

"Aswryn!" Gil shouted.

Gil's spell slammed into her back. Aswryn dropped me. I backpedaled and hid behind the broken case. Aswryn turned, arms up and ready to cast. Gil came out of the back, throwing another spell. His hand spread out wide as he thrust the spell forward.

Aswryn stepped back, her spine curved in as her middle took the blow. Gil met my eyes as he walked by, and in that split second, Aswryn cast a curse. Gil's feet came off the floor before he collapsed into a crumpled pile.

"Gil!"

I jumped over to Gil's side and rolled him over. A heavy hand squeezed the back of my neck, the touch burning my skin like a gallon of rubbing alcohol on a road rash. Power poured into me from Aswryn's fingers; like a puppet master, she pulled me up by the strings. Everything hurt. I couldn't breathe, let alone scream. My foot lifted without my permission, but I fought the urge to take a step.

Dizzy, nauseous, and in pain from various sources, my body was too exhausted to pull away. Instead, I shoved all my weight into her. She stumbled, not expecting me to go forward. Her grip on my neck slipped. My feet somehow got tangled, and I landed on my butt, three feet from Ian.

Aswryn stormed toward me.

I crab walked backward, but she was gaining on me. Tiny slivers of glass cut into my palms with every step. Aswryn kicked the glass shards at me. My ass hit the floor, and I covered my face, but the glass never hit me. Confused, I lowered my arms to find Aswryn's arm stopped in midair.

"Nevie, get behind me!" Gil's voice bounced around inside my skull.

Aswryn yelled as she threw spells at Gil's shield. Their spells slashed against my blocked magic. Pressure built until I thought my body would explode. One last spell hit Gileal's shield, and I felt nothing more, heard nothing more. Silence.

It was like those fight scenes in movies where the main character watches everything happen while music plays and they can't hear a thing. Yeah, that's how it was, except no music.

Gil threw a straight punch into Aswryn's jaw. Fists flying, they fought a few feet away from me. There was less magic now as their energies were depleting. Aswryn got in an uppercut that made Gil stumble backward. She held her palm out, touching Gil's shoulder.

Her curse threw him into one of Lewis's cubicle panels. Aswryn grabbed my ankle, and I kicked her until she let go. She raised her arm to backhand me. I raised my arm to protect myself and squeezed my eyes shut for a second.

Aswryn's hit never came.

Lowering my arm, I found Aswryn three feet away. Her eyes widened a moment, her shoulders heaving, her guard up, and palms facing me, ready to cast.

Her lips moved, a swear word in *Aemirin*, possibly. She stepped back, her arms still up and said something else. Why couldn't I hear anything? Aswryn backed up and raised her arms as if to say, this was your choice. Then she bolted. Oh shit!

"Gil!" I screamed. "Don't let her get away. She's going for Ray and Mateo."

Gil ran past me but stopped in the doorway to look up the hill. He came over and crouched. His lips moved, but all I heard was his muffled voice, like the Peanuts adults. Gil nodded, kissed my forehead, and ran after Aswryn.

19

I STARED AT THE door, blinking. My eyes locked on the empty space where Aswryn had stood. She couldn't vanish. Gileal could chase her down, but he was on his own. Nol needed to know, and we needed to get Mateo and Ray to safety.

I could hear nothing but my heartbeat as I stared through the broken door into the street. Movement beside me took my attention away from the door.

Zack came up and crouched, his feverish, red-rimmed eyes focused on me. He turned his palms up and pulled out some glass shards. His nose twitched when he got the last one out. A dark red streak trailed behind his hands as he wiped them on his jeans. Zack looked at me, his lips moving, but he sounded like a Peanuts adult, too.

His finger shook down at the floor next to me. After another shake, my gaze followed to where he pointed. My hands? I lifted them off the floor and held them in front of me. Glass shards cut into my palms. I couldn't feel them.

He took my left hand and plucked three large shards out. Each one twinkled as he pulled and dropped them on the floor, red-tipped ones beside the clear ones.

The blood started leaking out of my hands in bright red rivulets between my thumb pad and down my wrist. He scratched his ear and left a spot of red behind, like paint. Something about that spot fascinated me, and I reached out to touch it. Zack reared back.

"Damn, Hally. Would you hold still?" Zack's first words made me flinch. "God! Do you want them to stay in here? At least this one isn't as bad as the other one. Don't put your hand back down! There's still glass in it."

Oh. I brought my left arm up to compare it to my right. "This one's bigger."

Zack laughed, one loud huff, and bent over my hand again. "Yeah. You yanked it out of that freak's hand, remember?"

I turned my palm over and back up to watch the liquid roll around. "Is this my blood?"

"No, it's the Pope's. I just pulled out a ton of glass from your hands. Whose blood do you think it is?"

"You said it's the Pope's."

"Oh, wow. You gotta be in shock."

"Really? I thought it was from Aswryn's magic." I set my hand in my lap and looked around the shop. "Ian's dead."

Zack placed my other hand in my lap. "Yes, he is. I felt a massive wave of heat hit us when he flew back, but there aren't any burn marks." He got up and knelt over Ian. His mouth pulled back into a grimace as he leaned back on his feet and placed his arm on his knee.

"Magic doesn't burn." I giggled. "Unless you mean for it to burn, which would hurt."

"Magic?" He pressed a hand on his lower back as he rose. "Yeah, of course, it all makes sense now."

"It does? Oh, good. Then I don't have to explain everything. But maybe you could call Nol? I need to tell him about, um." What was it? "This."

"Right." Zack's walkie-talkie made a noise.

I giggled. "O-o-oh, someone's calling you."

He frowned at me while he talked into the thing. "All clear. Come in."

"Should we tell your friends, too?"

"No. Do me a favor and don't say anything. Can you do that?"

I nodded and mimed zipping my lips. "Oh! But Zack? I remember. She said she was going to visit Mateo—"

"I'll get someone out there soon. Just keep quiet."

"But, no, I mean we have to call Nol." Wait, did he know who Nol was? I paused, trying to reassemble my thoughts.

"Sure, Hally. Just shut up."

"But—"

Zack gave me a stern look and I couldn't remember what we'd been talking about. Shit.

"Not another word."

Sitting there, watching Zack look at the floor, the thought of everyone knowing didn't bother me. My mind couldn't grasp why I had to keep it a secret.

Moments later, his agent buddies came in. I could already see a bunch of lookie-loos watching the action from across the street. Maybe we should invite them in? I almost asked out loud, but I remembered my promise. Right.

"Hell's bells, what happened?" the only female agent asked.

Zack stepped up to the woman, who wore a DEA vest. Was Zack too cool to wear one? The other two agents, wearing DHS vests, checked out the scene. A pair of each.

One of them nudged Ian with his foot. I didn't think they cared that he was dead, except for writing up the report part. Poor suckers. Served them right for taking their sweet-ass time getting in here.

Someone tapped my shoulder. Next to me, the lady DEA agent crouched and smiled a small smile. "Hally?" Ms. Agent kept her voice low and cheerful.

I blinked at her until she wasn't blurry. She was pretty. Lovely cheekbones and the perfect size nose, not too pointy and not too round. If only my nose were nice like hers, but nope. The cornflower blue of her eyes was a shade or two darker than Nol's. They matched her T-shirt, and her brown skin made them more vibrant.

"Can I help you up?"

Sure, why not? I thought.

She grabbed my left elbow and wrapped her arm around my waist to help me to my feet. As I stood, my body began to shiver, and by the time we reached the bathroom, I was shaking enough that Ms. Agent had to help me walk.

"Damn. I can't believe Ian did all this. My name's Agent Conner, FYI." She opened the cupboard under the sink.

I opened my mouth to ask if Zack knew Nol's number—oh wait, I didn't have that number. "Charlie—" I shut my mouth. Zack told me to keep quiet.

"Huh?" She said as she helped me take off my coat and leggings.

I shook my head and focused on the present. My hands got the brunt of the abuse. Bruises decorated the backs of my thighs like cheetah spots with scratches between them. The cut from the splintered saloon doors had already bled through my leggings. Agent Conner pulled out the first aid kit and got to work.

"You're in shock now, but this is gonna hurt like a bitch once you're warmed up. We'll take you to the hospital to get some stitches on your leg and your wrist examined."

Nope, not fucking happening. "N-n-n-no hospi-pi-pital." My teeth chattered too much to say anything else.

Someone knocked on the door, and I swear my heart stopped.

"Conner, I wanna talk to Hally when you're done," Zack said.

"Are you okay to talk to him now?" She scowled at me. She didn't seem to have the highest opinion of Agent Zack-ass either.

I tried to smile but fell short.

"'Kay." Agent Conner helped me get dressed back in my bloody leggings. Having extra clothes was a smart idea; I made a mental note of it for later. She snaked her arm under my shoulders and helped me to the break room, where Zack stood near Lewis's desk.

"Thanks, Conner," Zack said in a soft voice I hadn't known he possessed. "Close the door and guard it, please. I don't want people coming in and scaring her."

"Yeah, in a minute," she told him while she poured some coffee.

Zack glared at her as she moved around.

The microwave dinged, and she brought me a steaming mug. "Coffee should warm you up."

"Th-thanks."

She gave me a quick smile and Zack a threatening look before she walked out.

"I have to call Charlie," I whispered.

Zack sat down and bounced his foot while he waited. He continued to stare at me as I shook. He shifted, rested his chin on one hand, and tapped the table with the other. The whir of the refrigerator competed with his fingers. Tap, tap, tap.

"Zack? Mateo and Ray are in danger."

Zack studied me for a moment. "I'll get a car out there soon."

"No, Zack. Your people aren't safe around her. I need to call Nol. He can handle her far better than we just did."

Zack nodded and cracked his knuckles. "Christ. I need answers."

"I'll give them to you as soon as I'm done with the call."

After knitting his brows for ten seconds, and right before I pushed the issue again, Zack went over and grabbed the work phone. He placed it in my hand, but I stared at it. What was Charlie's number again?

"What?"

"I'm thinking." I looked up at the ceiling, expecting the number to be there or something. "Do you have Charlie's number?"

Zack looked at me like I was stupid.

Oh, for the love of Pete. "Za—Agent Thomas, I can't think straight right now. Your officers won't stand a chance. She killed Ian with a flick of her wrist. Please."

"Is this one as dangerous—"

"Do you have Charlie's number or not?"

Zack pursed his lips as he pulled out his cell phone. He thumbed over the screen. Then, before I reminded him his contacts should be in alphabetical order, he tsked. "It's not under Roux—"

"Bercot-Roux."

Grunting and flipping through his contacts a bit more, he turned the phone to me. Like that was so fucking hard. He set it in my bandaged palm and plopped down on the chair next to me.

Of course Charlie's damn phone went to voicemail.

"Charlie, you need to call Mateo and get him to take Ray to our house now. Call Sam at the office and have him go to our house, too. Then call me. I'll explain everything." I lowered the phone and stared at the thing, white and square with an orange backlight.

Aswryn had thrown Gil around the shop like a dirty rag. Could he stop Aswryn from getting to Ray? Nol and Charlie needed to know now.

"I thought you said you were going to answer my questions?"

I blinked, realizing Zack had been talking for a bit. Staring at the phone wouldn't make Charlie respond any faster, but damn, giving it up and setting it beside me took everything I had. "Yes, I did. I mean, I will. I mean, maybe—"

A knock on the door made us both jump. Agent Conner poked her head in. "They're taking Ian's body. You wanna talk to them before they do?"

"Nah. Thanks, Conner." Zack's phone went off in his pocket. He checked it and winced. "Hally, we've got to make this quicker. My boss needs answers."

"I'll be out here." Conner nodded and closed the door.

Zack crossed his arms and stared at me with his beady eyes. "How did she do that, Hally? And what did you mean by magic?"

My right incisor hooked my lip ring while I looked at Zack's feet. I held up one finger, then picked up my mug with my left, uninjured hand. Luckily, I'm left-handed. Another swallow of almost lukewarm liquid spread inside me. Zack waited, which I'd never imagined possible.

"Do you remember what I told you on Saturday?"

He leaned a bit forward. "Right, right. The two-hundred something old *elf* that likes crepes? I'm assuming Charlie is one, too?"

"Not Charlie, but Gileal and Nol, who is with Charlie, are elves."

"And you expect me to believe that?"

"Don't I, though, after what you just saw?"

He crossed his arms and fidgeted in the seat. "Say you're telling the truth. How many of you are there? A whole population?"

"Just four of us here. The three came here looking for me, like, within the past month." Well, we'd just say a month because I knew that for certain. Although, now I knew Aswryn had been here for much longer.

"What about vampires and werewolves?"

Vampires, really? "No and no. We're just a different species from a different realm where our species can access magic."

"Sure you are. And you can do this? Like that *elf* in there?"

"I used to, but I blocked myself long ago. And would you please stop emphasizing "elf"? You were just thrown across a room by an invisible force. If you can explain that, then by all means, mock me at your leisure."

For a while, he stared at his shoes. Nothing else in his narrow world explained what he'd seen. He believed me, but a lifetime of fairy tales told him magic wasn't real. "Magic and elves. Does the government know?"

I blanched. "They can't. I don't want to end up in a lab."

We sat and waited while he digested all that for a minute. After witnessing everything out there in the lobby, Zack was taking this rather well. I was so proud of the puny DEA agent.

"Zack, Aswryn could be at Mateo's house right now. I don't know what else to do." Why wasn't Charlie calling back?

"I'll put a BOLO out on her."

"No." My heart leaped into my throat as I imagined the damage Aswryn could inflict on more humans. "Don't. If police come in contact with her, you'll have this kind of scenario again. Your people aren't equipped to handle her. You have to give Nol and Gileal room to do their work."

Zack scratched the top of his head. "You're willing to bet Ray's life on that?"

"I trust Gileal and Nol."

He tapped his fingers again and cussed under his breath. "I'll give them forty-eight hours. I need to know the moment they apprehend her. If they can't find her by then, they need more help.

"A BOLO doesn't mean police have to engage. Anyone spots her, they report it, and I'll pass that info on to your friends through you. This is how you can help—use your resources. You're not useless, Hally."

Conner poked her head in again, tapping as she did. "Hey, Lewis wants to come in."

"Jesus Christ." Zack pushed his palms on his knees and stood. "I'll get him before he makes a scene."

"Thanks, Agent Thomas."

20

ANOTHER CALL WENT TO Charlie's voicemail before Zack and Lewis made it back to me. I was tempted to leave another message, but come on! Why wasn't she answering my calls? She always picked up—within reason.

Lewis's voice took up the whole room as he came in, confused about how the hell Ian could have done all this damage. "What do you mean, he landed wrong? That makes no sense."

"When I went to arrest him, he ran and fell on the arm of the couch, and wham! Hit it wrong and cracked his neck the wrong way. I mean he was high and this is Ian we're talking about." Zack leaned against the kitchenette counter and crossed his arms.

Lewis crouched in front of me. "Hey, are you doin' okay? Zack said Ian got you pretty good?"

"Maybe you should get checked out—"

"No hospitals," I shot Zack down.

"Have Yumi do it, then. You trust her," Lewis said.

I pursed my lips. Decades of bad news, accidents, and death had come out of hospitals, giving me a healthy dose of distrust for the inside of those sterile walls.

The latest had been my incident with codeine. I'd told the doctors no medicine, and I almost died because they thought they knew my body better than me. The only doctor I'd ever trusted, my brother-in-law Léon, died in 1925—in a hospital. So, no hospitals.

Zack's phone rang, and he patted his coat down until he found it. "Thomas." Zack's eyes went wide, and he looked at me. "Yeah? You sure?" He pulled the phone away from his mouth and licked his lips. "Hally, I gotta go back to Katie's place."

I swallowed hard and looked into Lewis's knowing eyes. Zack must have told him about Katie on their way back.

"I'd like to get in touch with Katie's dad, let Ray meet Seamus."

"I'll see what I can do." Zack and I locked eyes, and an understanding settled between us. Agent Zack-ass Thomas, of all people, knew the truth, believed it, *and* was keeping my secret. The man I hated with a passion nodded and walked out the door.

"I need to tell—" I licked my lips. "Charlie, but she's not answering. I left a message, but you know she never listens to those."

Lewis wouldn't understand why it was more important to talk to Nol, and he didn't know Gileal. At least forty-five minutes had passed without since Aswryn left.

"I want to text her, but my phone is out there. Could you go get it from my workspace?"

"Workspace, right. Sure, kiddo." He squeezed my bruised knee.

As if on cue, the work phone rang when Lewis left the room. An unfamiliar Seattle phone number popped up on the caller ID. I didn't even get the whole "hello" out before Nol started talking to me at the speed of light in *Aemirin*. How the hell was I supposed to follow that?

"Twynolan! I cannot understand a damn word you're saying. Slow down."

Silence. "Give the phone to Gileal," Nol demanded after twenty seconds.

"Uh." Yeah, such an intelligent answer. Even now he refused to talk to me, and so rude. "I can't," I said.

"*Macon?*" *Why?*

"That's why I've been trying to get a hold of you and Charlie. Did Charlie get my message?"

"Hallë, I do not have time for your games. I must speak with Gileal." He couldn't be this mad at me.

"Games? What the hell is wrong with you?" My wrist twinged, and I loosened my fist. "You're that mad at me that you have to snap at me right off the bat? I'm trying to tell you why you can't talk to Gileal. Fucking-A! And for everything that is holy, did Charlie call Mateo?"

Another thirty seconds of silence.

"Yes. She just hung up on a very confused yet agreeable Sam. They are on their way to your place. Now, tell me what is going on. Why is Gileal's *meril* pulsing? Why is he not responding? And why, by the stars, will you not give him the phone?"

Where to start? "He's not here—"

"He left you? I specifically told him to stay with you." Then he started going off in *Aemirin* again.

"Shut up, Twynolan!" I pounded my hand on my knee. Ow. "Why are you being such a dick?"

He sighed into the phone. "If his *meril* is pulsing, that means he needs help or he needs to talk to me. But when I try to contact him, he does not answer. Where is he?"

"Oh. Before I answer that, I need you to promise to let me explain before you burst into lightning-speed *Aemirin*."

"Hallë, no more bullshit. Tell me." Bullshit was his new favorite English word—I'm not kidding.

"He—We—" I held my breath, just then absorbing the gravity of the situation. How did I explain this? The room went blurry, but I wiped my eyes before any tears fell.

"Hallë, if this is because of last night—"

"No," My voice warbled.

My legs started shaking. Agent Conner had said this would happen after the shock wore off. Perfect timing.

"You were right, okay? You're always fucking right." My throat constricted. "It was Dana. I should have told you, and this...this wouldn't have gone so far. If I hadn't blocked my magic, I would have sensed Dana on Saturday. Or I could have stopped Aswryn Friday, and you'd be done and gone."

"Hallë?" he interrupted, calmer now. "Why are you scared? Is Gileal okay?"

"I don't know. He ran after Aswryn. She told me if I didn't go with her, she'd go to Mateo's house and take Ray. This wouldn't have happened if I'd just told you."

"All right. Hallë, you are not making sense. What would not have happened?"

I tried to breathe and say it right, but everything wanted to come out at once and I couldn't slow down. "Aswryn. My appointment. Dana was Aswryn. She tricked me, and I didn't know, but" I swallowed, "I would have known if I had my magic. She changed. And now Ian's dead. And now she's going to take everyone from me."

"Hally, where d'ya leave it?" Lewis opened the break room door, but when he noticed I was upset—not crying—his eyes hardened. "What's wrong?"

"Nothing's wrong, Lewis." I sniffled. "Things are catching up, is all. The shock, I guess."

Lewis's eyebrows shot up, not believing me for a damn second. Great. "Is that Nolan?"

"Hallë, hand the phone to Lewis, please." This time, Nol didn't bite my head off. He needed to know what had happened and I wasn't saying it right.

"There's no need." I stood and headed to the door where Lewis was still standing. I met Lewis's eyes as I gestured with my chin toward the front and mouthed, "Excuse me."

I needed to get a hold of myself. "Nol, my client today, Dana. She changed, like Gil can. Aswryn threatened to take Ray—" I sucked my breath in. Was that a connection? Gileal was a spy. It was only logical that he'd learned bad guy spells. "Gileal is following her to Mateo's house. You need to find him before Aswryn hurts him."

"Hallë, listen. Mateo and Sam made it to your house. Aswryn does not have them, I swear. Please, calm down."

Fingers touched my right bicep, too soon after Aswryn's attack. I flinched and let out a small scream. For some stupid reason, I raised my arm to eye level. A force of wind went through the room, and Lewis stumbled backward. At the same time, something cracked behind us. Lewis corrected his balance and looked at the closed break room door.

"Sorry, I didn't mean to scream."

Lewis wasn't listening. "How'd that door shut?" He walked up and grasped the knob, but the door didn't budge. He shook the thing, and with one last hard shove, the door flew open. The hinges screeched, and it crashed to the floor. Lewis fell to his knees, having used his full weight to open it. All three hundred plus pounds of him.

"Lewis! Are you okay? Oh crap, your poor knees."

He wouldn't take his eyes off the door as he got up. "Hally, it slammed shut on its own."

Splintered wood flaked off as I brushed my thumb over the crushed frame.

Lewis stumbled over the broken door to the computer chair, where he slumped and stared off into space. He rubbed his bald head and scrubbed his eyes with his palms before he looked down at his beloved computer. "Hally, come look. The computer screen is busted."

"What?" I hurried over. Sure enough, a spiderweb of cracks ran from one side to the other. I went around Lewis and opened up my laptop beside him. The same as the computer. "What the hell?" Nothing else looked disturbed.

"This just happened," Lewis said.

"Yeah, I know. As soon as I—"

"I touched you," he finished for me.

My cell phone chirped, and I looked down at the shop's phone in my hand. No backlight. No ringtone. Crap. The sound of my cell drowned out all other noise in the shop. Or was that the only sound *in* the shop? The microwave displayed no numbers. I went to the fridge and checked that, too. No light.

"Are you gonna get your phone?"

I nodded and marched over to my workspace, where my cell sat in plain sight. Had he even looked? The same number from the shop's caller ID. "Nol?"

"What happened?" he said, less demanding this time. "You screamed, and then you were gone. Are you both all right? Hallë, please, please focus and explain this."

"The door and electronics broke." Yeah, that didn't sound as disconcerting out loud.

"So? Why did you scream?"

"Lewis, um, startled me."

Lewis looked up from his broken computer as I walked back in. "Yeah, and you screamed like I was gonna attack you. All I was askin' is if you wanted me to go get you coffee."

I bit my lip, tapping at my metal ring. "What's happening?"

Lewis swallowed, his brows furrowed as he continued to stare at me. "That's what I wanna know."

"Hallë? Why did you hang up on me?"

"I didn't. The phone broke. I told you all the electronics broke, and the door slammed shut. Lewis had to break it to open it."

"How?" Nol asked.

How indeed. I took stock of our surroundings and myself. As soon as Aswryn left—No, when she'd tried to hit me that last time. My arms had flown up to protect myself, but she never hit me. Gil had thrown up a shield. Then everything had been muffled. Right afterward, I hadn't felt nauseous. The lights hadn't been bright. No dizziness. Zack said I was acting giddy. And I started shivering in the bathroom with Agent Conner.

Both of those were signs of shock. With all their magic, my symptoms hadn't gone away right afterward. Today, instantaneous relief. Besides, what else explained the door and electronics? Nothing.

Impossible.

But it all made sense.

Aswryn had freed my magic.

And as a result I'd almost hurt Lewis. If my magic had used a little more force, he could have died. I mean, look at the computers. My magic had done this without my control or consent. Another accident. Not again. Never again.

"I think she broke through my block." Whether I said that to myself, Nol, or Lewis, I didn't know.

"Charlie and I will be there soon. Wait for me."

"No, if you come it—it'll be your duty to arrest me. I lost control and hurt someone again. Protect my family from Aswryn like you promised you would. Don't follow me, please." I whispered the last part, praying he'd listen. Probably not, but one could hope. I hung up on Nol in the middle of his response.

"Lewis, you're not safe with me. I have to go." Nol would protect them. "Please, this sounds crazy, but take Yumi to my house. Charlie and Nol can explain why. Please."

Would I ever see him again? Or the others? Not with everything they'd seen. Until I blocked my magic, I couldn't be around any-one—if I could even do it again. The last time had been brutal and damn near killed me. How did this happen?

This had been Aswryn's plan all along. The nausea on Friday, Saturday here, and Monday at Westlake with her made sense now. She'd been pushing magic into me all weekend.

But from her reaction when it happened; it must have broken too soon. That bitch. She'd broken *my* spell. No one bested my magic. Absolutely no one. Well, she wanted me to have my magic so badly, she could come and fucking get me.

My foot tapped the door on the floor. I looked back at Lewis's con-fused face. "Goodbye, Lewis. You've been one of the greatest friends I've ever had."

"What do you mean? Where're you goin'?" Lewis stood up behind his desk and called my name again.

"Go to my house, please." I turned, and the back door lifted off the floor and shut when I stepped out. It would stay closed until I left the alley. I stopped and pulled out my phone to give my family the message I'd promised to always give them.

"Purple Ribbon." It was a code we'd established decades ago when Léon's wife gave me a purple ribbon to give back to her when we saw each other again. That ribbon went in her coffin when she died. Before cell phones, I used to mail them an actual purple ribbon. This way was so much easier. Less postage.

They gave me a few well wishes. I'd receive more later or an email.

"*Reste en sécurité, Tante Heléne.*" *Stay safe, Aunt Helen,* Léon texted. My oldest, at ninety-eight, loved to text. He found it much less frustrating than talking with hearing aids.

"Send us a postcard," Léon's grandson, Remi, said from England with a wink and heart emojis.

Amelia, Léon's other grandchild, texted, "Are you all right?" She knew my routine, and this wasn't the right time.

"Later, Amelia," I responded. "Two days."

My phone rang. Charlie's phone number, but she knew not to call. Damn Nol's persistence. At the end of the building, farther into Post Avenue, I opened the door that led to the condos above the shops.

Everything would fall into place. I mean, I'd done this a time or two, for Pete's sake.

First things first. My apartment.

21

If I DIDN'T LIVE with Charlie in my house, I'd have lived here. It was cute, airy, bright, and quiet. Best of all, I worked five floors down.

The last time I had come to my little hidden-away loft I had scared the neighbor who'd refused to believe I owned the apartment. In her defense, I'd looked like a drowned rat.

She'd called the owner of the building, Amelia, in Paris, waking her up in the middle of the night. Amelia had confirmed I lived there and owned half the building with the family.

The neighbor's face had paled, and she'd shuffled right back into her apartment. Bitch. The old lady sold her place a year later. To me. Now I rented that one out to a nice, less judgmental couple decades younger and with much broader minds. I digress.

Up in the loft "bedroom" closet, I dropped to my bruised knees, held my breath for my stupid mistake, then continued. All the shoes fell as I tried to move the shoe rack. I groaned and tossed them shoe by shoe into the other corner. Propped on my right arm and lying on my belly, I dialed the combo to my small wall safe, 1-8-9-4, the year I'd met Emma.

Once inside, I yanked out the first of five small go-bags with passports, visas, bank accounts, credit cards, and US currency cash.

Marguerite Eva Roy from Montreal—not my favorite, but there are a good many Marguerites in Canada, I'll clue ya. I threw the documents into a backpack and changed into clothes I figured fit the personality of a twenty-two-ish-year-old international student.

My phone rang for the umpteenth time since I'd ascended the stairs. Relentless pain in the ass. Right after that call ended, another one began. Groaning, I went to decline the call, but my thumb slipped and answered the freaking thing.

"She's not going to answer, Nolan," Charlie said away from the phone. "I told you, once she sends that message, we cut communications."

I had to smile at her annoyance that I'd felt for days now. I took too long, and Nol realized I'd answered.

"Hallë? *C'yo*, where are you? Your location hasn't changed."

"Nolan! Give me my goddamn phone already."

Crap, I'd forgotten to turn that off. The location hadn't moved since I was still in the building. At least he sounded more concerned now than pissed at me. I guess finding the shop in that state had wiped that pissy attitude right out of him.

I'd never see him again. Even if I blocked myself again, there were no third chances for me. If he arrested me and took me in, they'd kill me. If I died, he'd die. I dropped the phone on the bed and covered my face. What should I do?

"I need you to answer me," he said in *Aemirin*. "Please. This place is beyond destroyed. What happened? Did Aswryn do this, and then Gileal ran after her? His status hasn't changed."

Didn't I tell him what had happened? If Gil's *meril* was pulsing, that meant what? Gil needed to talk to Nol, but for some reason, he couldn't. Neither of us knew why, and speculating wouldn't help.

I lowered myself onto the bed. The scratches still hurt despite the ibuprofen I'd taken in my bathroom with Agent Conner. I clenched my hands, and my wrist screamed. He heard me hiss.

"Hallë?" I'd forgotten to hang up. "*Om quassar.*" *I can hear you.* His voice held that compliance spell from Friday with that hypnotic cadence. Glass crunched in the background. "Don't leave me. Not again," he whispered.

My lip trembled. Everything in me wanted to tell him, to share everything with my *muranildo*, but I couldn't.

"*Nafela vimo utej Muranilde'ai*—" *For the sake of our bond.* "—say something to me, Hallë. I am your *muranildo*. You can tell me anything." He was so not playing fair, calling on our bond.

Lying down near the phone, I sniffled. "I'm not coming back, no matter what you say."

Nol sighed, relieved that I was at least talking. "*Peruda Anara.*" *Thank the Mother Anara.*

"I'll convince Aswryn to follow me and I'll—I'll fix this. Afterward, I'm going to block myself again. It's just the safest choice."

"No, don't block yourself. Are you mad? Charlie said it's been killing you."

"I almost killed Lewis. Look at the door and computer. I broke the fridge! My magic isn't safe. Goodbye, Nol."

"*Sae, mata! Hesëm zentar, Hallë.*" *No, wait. I'll find you.* "Are you listening? If you don't come back here, I'll find you. It is in my job description." He said the last sentence in English.

I smiled at that as I hung up, turned off my location, and silenced my phone. Sighing, I tossed everything that was "Hally Dubois" into the safe.

Second step...

22

"Let me get this straight," Zack said as he took a left on Columbia. "You have your magic back, and now you want to send Aswryn a message so she'll follow you somewhere and you can kick her ass?"

"Yes." I threw my bag and coat into the back seat.

Zack turned on the heater and my seat warmer on high. His little car heater was no match for Seattle weather, though. My winter coat from the apartment had kept my top half dry, but the rain had soaked through my blue jeans and Chucks.

I'd taken Post Avenue to Washington and given my favorite coffee shop a wide berth, knowing Nol would check for me there first. I'd walked over to the DEA office up on Fifth. A mix of snow and rain had started pouring down by the time I got to Second. Not fun. Walking up those Seattle hills wasn't easy any time of year, but adding freezing rain and snow made it damn near torture.

"You're, like, not in control of this stuff, right? Should I even be around you?"

"Um. Yes, you're fine."

"That didn't sound very convincing."

"Well, don't piss me off and you'll be fine."

"I'm not feeling too fine at the moment."

I rolled my eyes. Zack was the perfect person to get me out of here. None of them would believe I'd asked Zack for help. "Head south there's a place not too far southeast we can go. Then when we arrive, leave and you'll be safe."

"Hally, are you sure about this?"

I scoffed. "No. But it's the only thing I can come up with on short notice."

Zack got on I-5 and drove south, while I stared at the squares of glowing yellow through the skyscraper windows as the snow and low clouds darkened downtown. The neon lights of the sports fields turned the haze magenta, green and blue.

Everything had happened so fast and gone so wrong. With my magic free, I would make good use of it. Killing was still off the table, but she'd regret messing with my family and me. Not that I knew any specific spells, but I'd figure something out. I always did.

I rested my head against the seatbelt and watched out the window. This would work. It has to.

I HADN'T MEANT TO fall asleep, but woke up with a thick blanket over me and my seat reclined halfway. Zack hummed an "mm-hmm," agreeing with whoever was on the phone. I decided the person was his boss, with his "yes," "no," and "I'll do that."

"Where are we?" I stretched my legs. My shoes weren't dry, so we hadn't been driving that long "Why are we off the freeway?"

The snow had turned to rain again. Cars lined the road in front of trees on either side. Behind the cars on the right, a wrought iron fence lined a grassy hillside. I sat up all the way and rubbed my eyes. One drove past us, going downhill.

He cleared his throat. "Just trust me, okay?" The car slowed down, and turned left on Judkins Street.

My stomach dropped, and I slowly turned to look at him. "You traitor."

"After you called and asked me to meet you, I tried to call back. When you didn't answer, I tried Lewis. I didn't know you were hiding from them."

"You do realize by bringing me here you're signing my death warrant, right?"

"A little melodramatic, don't you think?"

"Nol will have to take me into custody and bring me to my people's government. They will deem me as a danger to society and sentence me to death. Thanks, Agent Zack-ass." I crossed my arms and pushed back into my seat.

He turned into the back alley and slowed way down. "You're serious?"

"Unless he disobeys his oath, yeah."

"He's gotta make that decision, not you." Zack stopped the car. "You're gonna be okay. Go to your friends. Your buddy will help you figure this out."

"My buddy?"

"Yeah, the one you think is going to turn you in. Which is bullshit. Now get out of my car and into your house."

"If you never see me again, you'll know you were wrong."

Zack tapped his steering wheel. I sighed and got out but turned and knocked on the window. He rolled it down.

"Thanks, I guess."

He looked like he expected me to say more.

"Ya know, for letting me take a nap in your car."

He snorted. "Good night, Hally. I'm still gonna put that BOLO out on Aswryn. So get a fuckin' move on. Forty-eight hours." With that warning, he put the car in gear. The tires splashed through puddles as he drove away. He wouldn't know if I left, but I hesitated.

"Four hours," Nol called out from somewhere close.

All around me was the white noise of heavy raindrops hitting the slush covered cement of the dark alley. I scanned my surroundings. There in the shadow of my neighbor's garage, Nol unfolded his arms and stepped out from under the eave. Cold, calm, and scary as shit, he looked nothing like my Nol.

He came closer—not too fast, but with purpose. Surprise or fear held me to my spot because it certainly wasn't curiosity that made me wait to hear what he had to say. Three steps away from me, he pushed his hair away from his face, mostly dry from his rain protection spell. Boy, I missed that spell.

The muscles in the back of his jaw moved as he ground his teeth. For a moment, I saw his anger, but he closed down, back to his practiced *Zayuri* mask. I stepped back, but Nol took those last three steps and grabbed my shoulders all in one movement.

"Let go." I clenched my teeth. "I'll yell, Nol. I swear."

"Do it. No one will hear you. I cast a ward." I strained to hear his calm, quiet voice above the rain on the pavement. Oh boy, was he angry, but I'd be too if I had to turn my childhood best friend over to the *Amura Ore.*

I looked away. He knew I wouldn't yell.

"Four hours," he said again.

"Why four hours? Take me in now. Maybe Aswryn will follow us back. You do know they'll kill me, right?"

Nol flinched, his neutral mask wavering. His shoulders slumped, and he gave me a flat look. "I had no idea where you were for four hours. You left me. Again. I cannot protect you if you are not with me."

I looked around us. Um, so? "You didn't know where I was for a century. Now you're worried about a few fucking hours?" Nol tried to interrupt, but I kept going. "I told you I can't come back. There are no third chances. You now have a responsibility to take me in."

He sighed, exasperated or maybe just tired. I had no clue if Nol had slept the night before. Friday night, we'd talked until four in the morning, and left before I woke up at seven. He'd spent Saturday night at the precinct. His mouth drew into a deep frown, and the crease between his eyebrows appeared. "Hallë, you will be fine—"

"You're not getting it! *I'll* be fine on my own. I can take care of myself. The problem is protecting my friends from me. I can't let that happen again, and it almost did. Lewis could have died. Stop fighting me on this."

"*Sajé, sitam, sitam.*" *Shh, I know, I know,* Nol whispered coming close enough to keep the rain from pattering on my head.

He leaned over me, far enough for his forehead to touch the top of my head. In a way, he did know, and in another way, he didn't. Nol hadn't seen their faces as my spell took over and killed them before my eyes. The thought of that happening to Lewis scared the shit out of me.

"I have a plan."

"Hallë," he groaned.

"Listen!" I leaned away and looked out into the alley, sorting through my half-assed plan. Water dripped into my eyes, blurring my sight. "Aswryn will follow me out of the city. She can't vanish anymore. I'll incapacitate her, then call you to come get her."

"Oh? Do you know any combat spells? Do you know how to defend yourself against spells?" He shook my shoulders for emphasis or to make me meet his eyes. "Yes, she screwed up when she released your magic in the shop. But even with your magic, you cannot beat her alone."

I shrugged one shoulder and looked down at my rain-soaked Converse. "I can't control my magic. It's better to fight her as best I can with no one else around. That way." I swallowed. "I can't hurt my family."

"You will not hurt them. Your magic is fine."

My hands balled into fists, and I glared at him. "Then explain how my spell continued after the potion evaporated. Tell me why I couldn't stop my own spell and save our friends."

"You were using a traditional spell that you found in the library. You always screwed up traditional ones."

"Gee, thanks." I swiped at the water running down my face.

He shoved his hair back with both hands and puffed his cheeks out. "I think your magic, combined with traditional magic, made the spell too strong for you to stop.

"The spell was also an advanced spell, which did not help matters. The book was written by a notorious *Mellorin endao*. Knowing you and witnessing your struggles in school, that is the best conclusion. You can control your own magic. Just leave traditional spells out of it."

"You have an answer for everything, don't you?"

"Well, I am a genius."

"You're wrong every once in a while."

He tipped his chin up as he fought a smile. "Name one."

"David didn't want sex."

His eyebrows shot up. "What did he want, then?"

"Money. He doesn't want to work with me anymore, though." I held my breath, waiting for him to call me out on my omission.

"I am sorry to have ruined your business relationship."

I tutted. "He creates forged documents. There isn't much of a relationship there." Although, I had invited him to my Fourth of July barbecue the first two years. He never came. "But you do owe me some money for that."

Nol tsked, swooped in, and grabbed me before I had time to react. One arm around my head, the other around my shoulders. He squeezed me tight, then loosened his hold. "*C'yo*, you are a pain in my ass," he mumbled against the top of my head.

"Not as much as you are in mine."

Nol started laughing against me. "I have missed you so much." I didn't have time to respond before he grabbed my hand and spun me toward my house. A second later, he cast a spell to open the gate. "Now come on." He rested his arm over my shoulder. Surprised and a bit dizzy, I walked into my backyard with Nol. "Time to explain yourself."

"What do you mean?" I stopped under the branches of my redwood tree.

"You need to go in and tell your friends everything before we leave."

"We?"

"Yes. *We* must find Gileal, and then *we* will beat Aswryn's ass together. The three of us."

"But—"

Nol pulled me close to the tree trunk. He pressed my cheeks between his hands and tilted my head up so I could see his exaggerated frown. A drop of water rolled down the crown of his head and dripped off his chin. "Aswryn destroyed your shop, yes?"

My cheeks were too squished to answer, so I nodded as best I could.

"Imagine her doing the same to Mateo and Sam's house."

I got his point. They needed to know how dangerous Aswryn was. If I was honest with myself, I knew they needed to know. I was just being a coward.

"And I'm pretty sure Mateo figured it out, or at least a version of it. He pulled me aside and asked if the shop was anything like the wine glass incident."

I pulled on his wrists. He let me go and raised an eyebrow. "Aswryn disguised herself as a human, like an extreme version of Gil's spell," I said. "She knows perfect English. She's been here. A lot. What did she want from that human you saved? Where has she been hiding, and what has she been doing here? Why didn't she approach me before?"

"*Sajé, hytera indem'ar hestë.*" *find peace within yourself.* "We need to focus on what we can control. Like getting out of the cold would be nice." He smirked at me, which made me smile and roll my eyes. Whether our bond, his words, or his smile had calmed me down didn't matter. He helped me see reason. We'd figure it all out.

Nol turned to go up the stairs, but I grabbed his jacket sleeve. "You promised to protect them—"

The white noise of the rain filled the silence as he waited for me to continue. I needed to know if he understood what that meant. How far his promise went.

"Even from me? If you're wrong and I can't control my magic?"

"I will protect them from my short, half-drowned *muranildë.*" He thumped my nose.

This time, I didn't react in any way. "And if you can't?"

"Charlie made coffee..." He gave me a huge grin.

Despite the grave, terrifying circumstances, I laughed. We always found a way to comfort each other in the end.

Nol held out his hand. "*Olentame?*"

Our word of support long ago settled my nerves. I took his hand. "*Olentame.*"

23

Ray knocked straight into me when I opened the back door to the laundry room. Charlie followed close behind her. Instead of scolding Ray this time, I knelt down and hugged her. After all, a few hours ago, I'd thought I wouldn't see her for a decade. Instead of asking me to pick her up, though, Ray went to Nol. She had no clue.

Nol lifted her. She turned in his arms to talk to me. "Tatie, everybody's here. Uncle Lewis didn't bring a pony, though."

"Good. You don't need any more."

Charlie hugged me. When she let go, she held my face in her hands for a second. With tears in her eyes, she looked from me to Nol. "I'm so happy he got you back. I want Ray to have you in her childhood. I take back everything I said last night, Nolan. Thank you."

"Do not take it back, Charlie. I have a temper, and I am sure I will do or say something stupid like that again. You may no longer be here by that time, but I shall remember everything you said and try to live up to your expectations."

I turned and squinted at him. "Did you prepare that speech?"

He shifted Ray and shrugged. "I have had some time to think with the silent treatment Charlie gave me today. Your niece is very wise for her age."

"The silent treatment?"

"Until he stole my phone to call you. Please never go missing again when he's around. He was terrible."

"I was not *that* bad." Nol bounced Ray in his arms a few times and winked.

Charlie took a deep, calming breath. "Let's just say he gets pushy."

"Get in here, you guys! I wanna know why the hell you're not in WITSEC like Lewis said," Mateo called to us from the living room entryway. "I thought that was cool."

I knew he meant to give us an attitude to lighten the mood, but the reminder sent me back to Sunday night. Mother give me strength. This wouldn't be easy.

Charlie walked into the living room ahead of us, Nol in the rear in case I bolted, maybe? Lewis sat in a chair, with Yumi in his lap. She still had her scrubs on, light blue with little candy skulls. Her hair was black with white-tipped spikes this week. Her dark brown, slightly slanted eyes, from her mother's Japanese heritage, still held laughter as she turned toward me.

I moved to go to Yumi, but Nol tugged on my sleeve. I looked up to protest, but he shook his head no. I sighed. He'd promised to stay by me. *Olentame*, indeed. I guessed he was taking that literally.

Nol put Ray down and told her to go to her mother.

Mateo scooted closer to his fiancé. Sam, still in his suit, sat up straight, shoulders back and stiff. He grabbed Mateo's hand, then looked at me and dipped his chin. One nod. He'd listen, but we were on shaky ground. Understandable considering how I'd treated them. I nodded back and broke eye contact.

Mateo looked grim and tired. He hadn't spiked his faux hawk, and he wore blue jeans and a gray T-shirt instead of his normal slacks and button-up. I swallowed the lump in my throat and held my breath. Now for the hard part.

"Hi, guys..."

"Okay, so does that mean things like werewolves?"

My eyebrow rose as I stared at Mateo with his genuine curiosity. "Really? That's your first question?"

"I saw the wine glass. I mean, really." He rolled his eyes and took a drink of the coffee that Charlie had given him. It was the only thing keeping him awake. "That explains so much. Jesus, I was goin' crazy. I knew, *knew* you were witches or something."

I looked up and glared at Nol. The *Zayuri* shrugged, arms clasped behind his back. He stood so close I felt his arm move. No one said anything for a few heartbeats.

"I've had the hardest time keeping this from you. You're closer to me than any others I've met through the years. Please, I need you to understand where I'm coming from."

I glanced at Charlie, sitting up straight in her chair, a hint of worry in her eyes. "I've seen firsthand what governments do to other humans. I was there, watching the SS take neighbors away. I met people who survived and came home after the Allies rescued them from the camps, Charlie's great-grandfather included.

"Almost eight million people were killed because they were Jewish, gypsy, gay, fascist, communist, or offended the wrong person. Imagine what they'd do to me. I'm a two hundred and forty-six-year-old *endaë* who wields magic. They'd study me and take me apart to see how I work. The more people who know, the greater the risk of exposure."

Nol touched my elbow and touched his chest where his *merili* hung on a necklace. "Gileal," he mumbled and walked into the hallway.

Everyone's eyes followed him as he left.

"Would anyone like to see some pictures?" Charlie asked.

"Where did you get pictures?"

Charlie grinned. "Dad sent them over. Just downloaded them to the tablet."

I gasped. "You didn't."

Charlie beamed and pulled the tablet off the table next to her. "He can't wait to talk to you and rub in an 'I told you so.'" She snickered and unlocked the screen.

Mateo grabbed the tablet the second Charlie opened the pictures. "Dear God, woman. Your hair was huge." He lifted it up and showed everyone: me in a yellow bikini and hair up in an eighties hairstyle, feathered and sprayed.

"Nah, you should have seen me in the sixties."

"Dad may have sent some of those. There's the one of his graduation and baking cookies with Tante Amelia and Grand-mére Franny in the sixties."

"*Non,* love, I came back in the seventies when Franny was diagnosed with breast cancer."

"It looks like a sixties hair-do," Charlie said.

Yumi reached over and took the tablet from Mateo. She pointed at one, and Lewis looked down at it. "Okay, so you're an elf—*endaë.* And you guys can really do magic?"

"For now, I can. I'll block myself again later."

"You will not!" Nol blurted from the hall. He came all the way in, his eyes trained on me. "I told you, your spells combined with traditional spells were the problem."

"Nol—"

"How are there two spells," Sam said, "if they're doing the same thing?"

"My magic is different. People usually need a focusing object, word, or potion. I don't. If I understand how it works, I *usually* just make it happen."

No one said anything, digesting, and from their looks, none got it.

"Okay, so for Nol to call something to him, like...the pillow behind you, Sam, he has to use a word or gesture to call it over."

"Now I say it in my head, but when I was little, yes, I would call it to me. But Hallë—"

"I imagine the pillow in my hand." Everyone either jumped or gasped as the little thing came to me.

"Holy fucking shit," Mateo whispered.

"I gotta confess something." Lewis cleared his throat. "After you left the shop, I looked at our security footage."

"What?" My hand clamped over my mouth. "And you let me flounder?" That had never crossed my mind, and we'd need to delete that right after this was over.

Yes, it gave Lewis a concise way to confirm in his black-and-white, right-in-front-of-him world that this was true. But now there was evidence that there were at least three magic-wielding beings in Seattle. Perfect for bureaucrats to use to prove I was dangerous.

Lewis's eyebrows shot up as his bottom lip came out further. "Not my story to tell. Plus, I needed confirmation I wasn't goin' nuts."

"Oh no, sweetie, you're already there." Yumi kissed Lewis's cheek, then squeaked when someone pounded on the door. Charlie cussed, and Nol stared at the door. I sighed and went over. Before I had the door fully open, a dark shadow of a person jetted past me.

"Hally!" Gil picked me up in a tight hug and swung me around in a circle. "How's your wrist? Is that human all right?" He spoke almost too fast for me to keep up. His arms stayed around me as he slid me to the floor. "I'm sorry I took so long. I went to your little shop first to look for you, but no one was there anymore. I understand—"

Nol shot his hand out and grabbed Gil's shoulder. He shoved him against the closed front door. "Where in the starless abyss have you been? Your *meril* has been pulsing all afternoon, and you wouldn't answer any communication I attempted."

"I couldn't. After Aswryn found Mateo's house empty, I followed her through the city." Gil turned to me. "Didn't you tell him what I said?"

I gaped at him. "I couldn't hear anything after you threw that last shield up."

"I didn't throw that up. You did. It gave me the time I needed to call an *evayur* spell."

Right, like I knew what that all meant or how to do it. I went to tell him just that, but Nol groaned and released Gil. He pulled him close and squeezed. "You fucking *nuana*," Nol mumbled. "Wait for an acknowledgment before you run off."

Gil laughed and hugged Nol back. "There was no time, my friend. The trail was already fading as I paused for Hally."

Nol pulled him away from the door. Gil looked quite worse for wear—dirt in his hair and grime on his clothes—and he smelled like rotting seaweed.

"Now that you're done calling him names, can we get back to what happened? Gil, what do you mean, I threw up the shield? I don't know how to do wards and shields."

"Instinct, perhaps? The best part, though, is you have your magic back." Gil bounced on the balls of his feet.

Created a shield? Me? I lifted my arm without thinking and almost tried to form something. I clasped my hands together and squeezed my eyes shut. Yeah, I needed to block myself, no matter what Nol said. "Now you can cast your language spell so I can understand your friends." He beamed at said friends, waving.

Yumi waved back, the others stared, faces ranging from curious to uncertain.

Ray came running up to wrap her arms around Gil's thighs. "You're back."

"Hello, Ray." It looked like someone had been giving Gil lessons this morning.

Ray giggled. "Hello, Gi-le-all."

Not a half-bad try.

"Guys? This is Gileal. Nol's and my very best childhood friend. Gil was our lookout, tattletale, co-conspirator, voice of reason, and other such stuff."

"Hello!" Gil said to everyone, then turned to me. "Hally, will you cast the spell? I would very much love to meet your friends."

"I'm not doing shit, Gileal."

Both *endai* laughed at my attempt at *Aemirin* cussing.

"Hey! It's not funny. Gileal, I am not doing any..." I couldn't cuss back, not in my childhood language. When they laughed again, I spouted off insults in French, threw my arms up, and whacked Gil in the stomach. They shut up as Charlie laughed.

"Tatie, that really isn't fair, is it?"

"Hell yes, it is." I stomped my foot. Damn it! I needed to quit that.

"You don't want a translation for all that," Charlie told them. "I wouldn't make fun of her anymore. You'll regret it in your sleep."

They shut up.

"Why are you so dirty?" I picked up a lock of Gil's mud caked hair. "What happened?"

"I jumped over a tiny bridge onto a beach before Aswryn saw me. But I found where she is hiding. A building by a large lake. I can show you, but if you don't mind, I'd like to change first." Gil leaned over and kissed my forehead. "Do they know about us?"

"Us? There isn't much of an 'us.' We still need to discuss things."

Nol groaned and pushed Gil toward the hall. "He is still so in love with you." And, so that everyone understood, he'd used English.

My friends exploded with questions and comments.

I pressed my palm to my forehead. "Thanks, Nol."

He patted my cheek and left.

"He looks human," Mateo said. "Why?"

"Oh, that's a spell. You'll see later." I bit my lip as I thought about this morning.

"Look at you blushing," Mateo teased.

"Oh, they're cute together," Charlie said. "Apparently, he's a big romantic. You should have seen them."

"You haven't seen us, either, Charlie. He got here last night."

"I saw enough."

She was so full of shit. My smile faltered when I caught Sam's grim face. I pulled up my big girl panties and went over to him.

"Hey?" He scooted closer to Mateo for me to sit down.

"I'm sorry." I held my hand out, palm up for him to take. He didn't move. "For yelling at you, I mean."

His eyebrows rose up into his curls.

"For lying to you, too. I hope you'll forgive me one day."

Sam pursed his lips and looked down at my hand. "So, you were going to leave?"

"I still need to leave, but I have some time."

"You leave and I have to handle Mateo on my own." Sam's lips twisted. "I'm not sure I'm ready for that."

"Dude, you're marrying the guy in, like, four months."

He smiled. "I know. That's why I need his best friend's support."

I sighed. "How long do you think I can pull off being in my twenties?"

"Fifty years or so."

I scoffed and bumped his shoulder with mine.

Sam grabbed my hand and squeezed. His hazel eyes pleaded with me. "Don't leave us."

"People start noticing things like not aging."

"Nah, we'll fake some wrinkles and dye your hair gray. Or we could move with you."

I jerked back and studied Sam. "You would have to give up your practice. I go all over. In fact, my new identity lives in Montreal."

"Hmm, Quebec, huh?" Sam tapped his chin. "Ever been there before?"

"Yep. Lived there a few times."

"Mateo's always wanted to travel. He can work from anywhere."

"What about you?" I asked.

He shrugged. "Meh, I can teach law."

"I don't deserve you guys."

"You got us anyway." Sam side-hugged me.

And then the living room windows exploded.

24

"Ray!" Charlie screamed.

Glass and wood and branches from the front yard littered the living room. Sam and Mateo lay on either side of me. I couldn't see anyone else.

"Mommy?" Ray's voice warbled, on the verge of crying.

"What happened?" Sam asked.

"I think it's who happened," I said.

"Christ. I was afraid of that."

Charlie crouched low across the room and grabbed her daughter near her lab's doors. Ray latched on to her mom's neck. Lewis's and Yumi's chair covered them. They weren't moving.

"What's going on?" Mateo rasped.

"I'm gonna find out." I army-crawled to my other friends.

Lewis's leg stuck out from under the toppled chair. Yumi's head, under Lewis's arm, was closer. Her eyes flew open and focused on me. "I'm good. Check on Lewis. He's out."

I reached under until my palm touched his warm face. We needed to move this chair "He's breathing for now."

"Can you pull me out without moving him? That'll free up some room down here."

I nodded, positioned myself behind her, and hooked my arms under her shoulders. She slid out about an inch. Charlie came over to help, and together, we pulled Yumi out.

"Hally?" Aswryn called from the yard. "I know you're in there."

Nol and Gil came running out of the hallway. Nol walked to the broken front door as Gil crouched next to me. His warm arm pressed against the middle of my back, and his lips touched my ear. "Take the humans to the backyard."

I nodded.

Nol stepped over the debris onto the porch. He leaned forward in a wide stance, both hands gripping his big-ass katana-style sword. The magical metal gave off a faint black-blue glow. "What's your plan, Aswryn? You seem to want the three of us together."

Gil came to stand next to Nol. "And if you touch Hally, she'll blow you across the street. You're outnumbered—"

She laughed, more of a "ha ha" than a real laugh. "I'm stronger than the three of you put together. Hallanevaë, come out before I kill your friends."

"Charlie," I whispered. "Take Ray to the back." I waved for Sam and Mateo to come. Yumi tried to wake Lewis, but to no avail. None of us could pick him up by ourselves. Charlie, Ray, and I crawled toward the hall. I got them a few feet in before Charlie stopped me. "I'm not leaving without them." Her chin pointed back to our friends.

"Fine, but then you must get to the backyard."

From the front, Aswryn yelled, "You have something of mine, Nolan! Give it to me." A thousand bucks said she meant her *va-mameril*.

"Not in a million moons."

"Then I'll come take it."

We had to get farther back before Aswryn reached Nol on the porch.

"Stay here with Ray," I told Charlie.

I scrambled back over to Lewis and picked up one of his thick arms. The other adults came up, and with the four of us together, we dragged Lewis over to Charlie. A loud crash sounded behind us, and Ray screamed. Yellow light flashed across the white ceiling, highlighting Ray's terrified face. The seven of us sat on the floor in the hall, one unconscious. The others looked out to the front at the fighting.

"You guys need to go with Charlie," I said.

Black light flashed on the wall. Nol's sword this time.

"What about you?" Mateo asked. Multiple lights, like emergency lights, illuminated their faces. Yellow, blue-black, and green.

I looked at the front of the house. "I have to help them. Nol said he needed me. Besides, Aswryn forced my magic back. I'll show her just how big of a mistake that was."

"Do you think it'll be okay?"

I scoffed at Mateo's concern. "Hell no. Why do you think I want everyone out of the house?"

Sam grabbed my arm. "We've got this, Hally. Go kick her ass."

I squeezed my eyes shut, leaned forward, and kissed his cheek. "Thanks."

Nol's ward around my house would keep the noise in, but I wasn't sure if anyone could see in. Gil and Nol fought as a team as they backed Aswryn toward the eight-foot-tall cedar fence. When Aswryn had about three feet to go, Nol threw himself forward, sword arcing in the air like some kind of damn anime character. Gil cast a spell right after him. Aswryn threw up a shield before Nol hit her, then she shoved her arm forward, a spell in her palm.

I hopped off the porch against the house and moved slowly, searching for something to throw at Aswryn. Something mundane and unexpected, like the pepper spray. Gnomes next to the house? No. I needed something substantial or distracting. The hose and concrete bench. Charlie always forgot to turn it off, but remarkably, the water wasn't frozen.

With the high-pressure sprayer in one hand and the bench in my awareness, I ran out into the middle of the yard and sprayed water at her. Not prepared for ice cold water in her face, she jumped back in shock, curses forgotten. Less than a second later, the heavy-ass bench came flying around to hit Aswryn dead on. She flew two feet back, landed, and didn't move. I had hoped she'd bounce. Damn.

I looked to see what Nol and Gileal thought of my awesome idea. Both stared at me with matching shocked expressions.

"What?" I shrugged. So the bench had hit her a little harder than I'd intended. How were they surprised? I hadn't used magic in a century. I was not used to this anymore.

Gil snorted and shook his head but jumped into action when he saw Nol move. Nol kept his sword ready as he walked up to Aswryn.

"Hands behind your back, Aswryn." Gil knelt on her back and grabbed her arm. Aswryn wiggled, and Nol pressed his sword against her neck. She winced with her eyes closed.

"Yield and I'll lift my sword," Nol offered. His neutral, trained Zayuri tone made it sound more like a threat than an offer.

Aswryn spat in Nol's general direction.

Gil grabbed Aswryn's other arm. "Not so tough when you can't vanish, eh, Aswryn? Coward. I've got her. The band, Nolan?"

Nol reached under his jacket and tossed Gil connected rings. As soon as Gil went to attach one to Aswryn's wrist, she thrashed around.

"What's wrong?" Nol asked.

"She has something around her wrist. I can't move it out of the way."

Nol growled and lowered his sword.

"Can I help?" All three of them looked at me. Yeah, still here, thanks.

"No, stay back. She's not detained yet."

Well, duh, that's why I offered to help. Gil repositioned himself over Aswryn as Nol reached for her shoulder, sword nowhere in sight. As Nol touched her, Aswryn yelled and twisted, and we all flew backward.

I shook the freezing rain out of my face and got off my ass. I landed farthest away, while Nol and Gil were a measly six feet away from Aswryn in the middle of the yard. As the guys got to their feet, a yellow bolt of energy struck them. Aswryn held her hand out in front of her, the yellow light radiating energy into Nol's and Gil's still bodies. Her *endaen* eyes flashed amber, reflecting the light of her spell. She lifted her other hand toward me.

I raised my arms to protect my head. Hey, it had worked earlier. Yeah, not this time. Aswryn's magic ran through me, seizing every muscle in my body. Her spell tethered me to her. My vision began to fade. All she had to do was wait until we passed out. That downright pissed me off. But how could I stop her? Nol was fucking right again. I didn't know any combat magic. And my plan for her to follow me was half-assed, if that. My vision narrowed.

I envisioned my magic spreading through me, seeping through my pores and creating a barrier between her magic and my skin. My lower back began to tingle, faint at first, then sharp pinpricks as my circulation was restored. My lungs burned. I pushed the spell to go faster, and my magic flickered. Right, no stamina.

My spell oozed out of my diaphragm and hips and, at last, my lungs and knees. Once my barrier reached my head, I looked to check on Nol and Gileal to my right. They weren't doing so hot. My barrier covered my entire body, but her spell still held me like a dry suit in mud. At least I wasn't in pain and I could breathe. I wiggled my fingers and toes, but my legs and arms still couldn't move.

Aswryn stood in the middle of us, hunched over, keeping her weight off her back leg—the side the bench had slammed into. Her hands were out, holding on to our tethers. She took a step back, and her back leg gave out. Our connection wavered as she caught herself. Her chest and shoulders heaved.

If she couldn't breathe, she couldn't cast. At least, it wouldn't hurt to try. My focus narrowed on her. I visualized a barrier, like mine, wrapping around her chest. She still hadn't noticed me; her spell was taking all her concentration. I squeezed and shrank it like plastic wrap in a microwave. Tighter, tighter...

Aswryn's eyes flew open, focused on me. I tightened some more, and her eyes bulged. The energy connecting Nol and Gil flickered out. They flopped once more and didn't move.

Aswryn flung both arms out in my direction. Her spell trickled through my protective layer, but that didn't matter. Any second now, she'd pass out. She had to. Her knees hit the grass, but she didn't let the spell go. The leak grew, and the pressure built. I had to choose which spell to keep. Too late. Her tether broke through my protective layer. The current of her magic seized my lungs and burned my skin again.

One of her hands dropped, and the burning lessened. The other arm fell two seconds later, and her spell broke. We collapsed on the grass, both of us gasping lungfuls of air. I got to my hands and knees, fell over, and landed on my injured arm. Aswryn got further than me.

She snapped her fingers and ignited a spark, tried again, and failed. Fucking A, I needed to suck it up and do...something! But I didn't know how much longer I could go. My heart was racing, and my lungs burned as I sucked in cold air. I needed a very simple spell. We must have done something as kids. When Nol and I wanted to get out of school...something about light orbs. *Crap, Hally, remember.*

I conjured up a light orb spell about the size of a tennis ball and daylight bright. I used to flick them. Okay, so what, then? I sighed and followed the memory. No, I filled them with raw energy. That's right.

While Aswryn was preoccupied with her second attempt at connecting to her magic, my little orb sped across the yard and ignited into a million tiny sparks against the fence. I used to throw them at the school's magical energy grid to short them out! She'd never see that coming. None of our teachers ever did, and only Nol knew. I made another one.

Aswryn succeeded and got her tether spell working, but my orb caught her attention, and she stood there, like a fish mesmerized by the angler fish's doodad light thing. The glowing ball lit up the whole yard, which was its sole purpose. I had to fill this to bursting because she would be prepared for the next one. Aswryn dropped her gaze from the harmless orb a foot above her head to me, and that's when I dropped the damn thing on her head.

My magical energy—as Charlie called it—scattered into a million charged sparks, cascading around her and into the grass where they fizzed and went out. She screamed and fell to the ground again as they burned her. I threw another one as she rolled onto her back. Aswryn deflected the second orb and scrambled up. My third soared right behind the second, and as she looked up, it hit her in the face. She doubled over, her palms over her eyes.

I used that moment to force my ass up off the ground. Aswryn climbed to her feet. The fourth and fifth light orbs went right after each other, but I risked speed over power. They worked for a few seconds. My heart was racing, thudding in my ears, and sweat and icy rain dripped into my eyes. Nol and Gileal needed to wake up. My orbs were just irritating mosquitos, but I had no other ideas.

Aswryn smiled while I bent over to catch my breath. She stalked toward me, shaking her hands out. I tried another light orb, but Aswryn batted that out of the way before I could throw it.

"Aswryn!" Out of nowhere, Nol came up beside her. His sword arced toward her, but Aswryn ducked, and the blade sliced her bicep instead. She came back up, throwing a spell into Nol's middle. He flew back into the ward he'd set up earlier. Green and purple light rippled up and out like the aurora borealis. He slid down into the garden on the side of the house thirty feet away. He wasn't moving.

"Nol!"

Aswryn shook herself, stormed over, and knelt next to him. She reached under his shirt and grabbed his necklace. A dozen or so *merili* scattered across the beauty bark and grass. Aswryn conjured an easy gathering spell and collected them in her palm. She pushed them around, picked one, and dropped the others on Nol's chest. Aswryn held her find and smiled. Shit.

"Hey!" Charlie ran up behind Aswryn with a cast-iron skillet in her hands. "Behind you, bitch!" As Aswryn turned, Charlie swung her weapon as hard as she could, then swung again. Two good whacks to the head.

"Back up, Charlie!" I yelled.

She stepped back but kept the skillet up, prepared to strike again. Aswryn wavered on her feet. You'd think she'd have learned by now. Mundane things hurt, too. Lewis ran up and punched Aswryn in the stomach, then the jaw. She fell, out cold. I couldn't stop smiling.

"Charlie! Help me get to Nol." He still hadn't moved. I got two steps, fell, scrambled to my feet, and fell again. Crap, I was too worn out. As painful as it was, I made myself slow down as I got up and found my balance. Lewis and Charlie came over, grabbed my arms, and helped me kneel next to Nol. Yumi called out something about Gileal, but I didn't know what. My hand shook as I reached for Nol's neck. Gil moved in my peripheral vision. He dropped beside me, his body warm next to mine.

"How is he?" he whispered as he moved my hand to check his pulse.

I focused on Gil instead of Nol. That way, it wasn't real. Not yet. A tear fell down Gil's cheek, and he swallowed. "He's alive, but barely. I was out for Aswryn's last spell. I didn't see what happened."

I turned back to Nol. Barely?

"I can't fix this, Hally. Aswryn must have something holding him down."

This wasn't real. This couldn't happen. For the first time since Nol got here, I reached for our link. There was no response. I rested my forehead on his chest. My hand touched his soft hair I loved so much.

"No," Aswryn growled.

I lifted my head off Nol and turned. Aswryn sat up a good six feet away, blood smeared all over her face and down her arm. Her crazy, bugged-out eyes stared at Nol.

"No! He was my link to the *Zayuri*. I—" She balled her hands into fists and screamed. No one moved to attack her.

I sat up, my hand still on Nol's chest. "He isn't dead. Lift your spell on him."

"I have no spell on him."

"I don't believe you. If you let him die, there is nothing you can take away from me that will help you. Nothing. Now lift the spell and fix him."

Aswryn put weight on her injured leg and fell next to the hydrangea bush. She stared at Nol, her legs sticking out in front. She made a ridiculous spectacle. I didn't know if any of my words had soaked into her horrid, selfish, stupid brain.

"I don't have that kind of power." Aswryn shook her head, blood leaking out of her ears. Her face darkened from a swollen nose and darker splotches from the bruises.

"Wrong answer." I stood and wobbled for a second. "He was your link to the *Zayuri*, right? And you're going to let him die? Just lift the spell you put on him. I know you did it when you grabbed the *merili*."

Aswryn pressed her lips together, jutting her chin out. If she wouldn't release the spell, I needed to make her break it, but I wouldn't back down on my promise not to kill her. How, then? She needed us both; otherwise, all she'd done would have been for nothing. Breaking my block had been pointless, except now I could use it against her. Technically, this was breaking my vow to never use my magic on anyone again, but the intent was justified in my mind.

I lunged forward, knocking her back down into my garden. She didn't hold up much resistance, too weak from all the hits she'd taken. First, I grabbed her *vamameril*, which she had taken back from Nol, from around her neck and shoved it in my pocket. Then I pressed my palms to her temples and started the spell I'd cast on myself a hundred and nineteen years ago.

Gil called my name somewhere behind me but didn't intervene. Aswryn's energy responded to the spell, going frantic. Her eyes bulged as she screamed. Her ME cells began to close, beginning in her belly, where the core of her magic resided. No one had ever heard of blocking magic, their own or someone else's, so it took Aswryn a minute to clue in to what I was doing. When she did, she started to freak. With my hands clamped on her head, I could do nothing to protect myself except tuck my chin in and continue.

Aswryn hit my right arm at an odd angle. My wrist failed, and I released her. She tried to crawl away, but in the scramble, I clamped my hands down on her right arm and sat on her thighs. She panted from the pain. I remembered how much it had burned when my magic closed off. She wheezed as she got her fingers under mine to pry them off.

"Gil, help me hold her down," I called without looking away from Aswryn.

Gil's arm brushed mine as he knelt beside me. He grabbed Aswryn's shoulders.

"You can't do this," Aswryn panted.

"Like hell I can't." I could already feel her magic shutting down. "You should have thought twice before you unblocked my magic. Or did you not realize what a *savilë* is?"

"Gileal," Aswryn pleaded. "Don't let her do this. She's killing me."

"No, I'm not." The last of her magic extinguished, and I let go, nodding to Gil to release her as well. "Now you get to see your curse fail, bitch."

Aswryn lay in the dirt, staring at her hands as she made a gesture and nothing happened. She was so engrossed in searching for her magic that she didn't realize we'd backed away. I tried to stand and get out of the dirt, but I fell back on my butt, my teeth clamping down on my tongue. All the fighting, throwing around spells, and using so much magic to block Aswryn's had exhausted me.

Gil crouched next to me. "Hally? Are you hurt?"

"Check on Nol."

"I have. Hally, there's no improvement. He's dying." Gil's breath shuttered. "I don't know what to do."

I turned to him and leaned over until my forehead was against his. "You have to take them both. Aswryn won't be much trouble. Her magic is gone, and she's weak. But now the *Amura Ore* can't use the curse as an excuse to kill her. Tell them to let her see her failure. The curse is lifted, and now you have to save Nol."

Gil's teal eyes, wet with tears, widened, then focused on mine, an inch away from him. He nodded. "Come then. Help me."

"I can't, Gil. There's no way I'm standing right now." My legs shook, my head pounded, and my wrist pulsed sharp stabs of pain with every heartbeat.

"You must. I will get Nolan home, but this may be the last time you see your *muranildo*."

He offered his hand and helped me to my feet. As he let go, Charlie came and got her arm under mine. The others followed close behind. Lewis picked Nol up and took him to the back, while Sam and Mateo pulled Aswryn out of the garden. Yumi knelt on the ground where Nol had just been while Ray brushed her hands through the grass. Mateo and Sam came up beside Charlie and me, lost looks on their faces. I realized they'd only understood a third of the conversation between Aswryn, Gil, and me. They had no clue what was going on, yet they were helping.

"We need to get Nol home. He's still alive, but barely."

"What did you do to her?" Sam gave no sign of concern, but when his eyes met mine, I saw a hint of fear. Fear of me.

"I blocked her magic. It hurt her badly, but it won't kill her."

"She can't use magic anymore?" Mateo asked. "Like, at all?"

"Not at all."

"Badass," Mateo said.

Aswryn lifted her head and looked at Mateo. "I can still hurt you, little human."

Mateo snorted. "Yeah, but not right now. You can't even stand, bitch."

Aswryn growled, and Sam stepped on her toes.

"Get back there, please, guys. Gil needs to go."

The guys nodded, but as they moved, Aswryn met my eyes. The dull, yellow, haunted eyes held my attention as if by magic. "I will be back for you, Hally. Mark my words, I will get my magic back, and when I do—"

"Yeah, yeah. Get moving." Mateo half dropped her, then lifted her back up until he was level with Sam. Five foot ten to five foot four made a difference when holding a person between them.

Ray ran ahead to Gil and Lewis. Gil picked her up, resting her on his hip. She gave him something and hugged him hard. Gil bound Aswryn with the cuffs Nol had brought, although they could have toppled her over at that point. She had to walk on her own. That was the only way this would work. Yumi, Lewis, and Charlie helped secure Nol to Gil's back, draping him over his shoulders. Gil was about Mateo's height, but Nol stood at around six-four, which made for an uncomfortable walk.

By the time they were done, I could stand on my own, with Charlie beside me, just in case. I checked the knot holding Nol's arms close to Gil, then touched Gil's cheek.

"Hally?" His eyes pleaded with me to understand his doubt about my plan.

"This will work. This entrance is close to the capital. They'll see you right away and take them both off your shoulders. They'll revive Nol, and you can come back and tell me it worked."

He frowned.

"It will work." My eyes bored into him. I needed him to agree. "Tell me."

"He's fading."

"Then go," I whispered. If I spoke any louder, my hope would shatter.

"Say goodbye, please. Say goodbye to your Nol."

Biting down on my lip to keep them from trembling, I reached for Nol's face. His cheek was still warm under my palm. My thumb pressed down on the crease between his eyebrow, rubbing the worry away that wasn't there. That might never be there again. How could he die when he was warm here beside me?

"Hally?" someone asked. I didn't care who.

"Tatie?"

"Hally." Gil grabbed my hand and pressed his lips against my knuckles until I met his eyes. "You have my heart. I'll be back to claim it as soon as I can."

I nodded. "Hurry. There's still time."

Gil frowned at me, but I had to hope. "Hally, I'm sorry."

I shook my head and pushed him, but it was more like pushing myself back into Charlie. My knees gave out as he took the step through the tree that would take them to our realm.

25

EVERYONE WENT BACK INSIDE. Maybe someone helped me, maybe not. I didn't care.

The front of the house was toast: windows shattered, furniture destroyed, appliances and dishes broken. Even Charlie's lab had suffered some damage.

Charlie moved a splinter of wood with her toe. "Do you think insurance will cover this?"

"I..." I cleared my throat. "I'll try to fix some right now, but I've exhausted my magic."

"Tatie, you don't have to."

"The windows won't require that much energy." I closed my eyes and pictured what the windows looked like before. Inside me, my magic pulsed, retreated, then stretched out into the living room. My mind went fuzzy, everything spun, and there was nothing else.

"TATIE, PLEASE DRINK SOME water," Charlie pleaded.

Why?

A straw pressed against my lips. I held it but couldn't find the strength to suck any water up. I let go and turned away.

"Agent Thomas called," Charlie said.

So?

"Tatie, you're so dehydrated. Please?" Again with the straw. Couldn't she just let me sleep? I'd drink when I got up.

"*Ojitos?* OPEN THOSE PRETTY green peepers of yours." Mateo? "We need you back here."

Mateo poked my shoulder, little stabs in my arm. I batted at him. He tugged my hair. I groaned and rolled over. "Agent Zack-ass called a bit ago—again. He wants to talk to you."

The jerk of a cop could wait.

I heard the creak of my door as Mateo left my room.

I HAD TO PEE really bad, but to do that, I had to get up. I opened my eyes. The sunshine screamed through the sides of my closed curtains like some pestering morning person. Ugh. The act of swinging my legs out of the blankets required too much energy, so I dragged them out instead. Once my feet were dangling over my bed, I stared at the floor.

"Here goes nothing," I mumbled or thought. Not sure which.

I slid to the edge, pushed off, and took a step on my shaky legs. Then I proceeded to fall in a heap. My wrist throbbed. With my teeth gritted, I hauled my ass back up and made my way around my room. At the door, I lowered myself to the floor and rested my forehead on the cool wood. After three breaths, I braced myself on the frame, grabbed the knob, and pulled myself up. I needed to move my ass if I didn't want to pee my pants.

"Hally?" Mateo's voice echoed up the stairwell. "You up?" *Stomp stomp* up the stairs.

I tried to get up before he saw me.

"Oh, *ojitos.* Whatcha doing on the floor?" I waved him off, but he tsked at me. "Do not give me any bullshit. What are you trying to do?"

I sighed. "I have to pee."

"Oh. Let's get you over there." He helped me stand and pretended to let me walk. "Okay, you're gonna hate to hear this, but I think I'm gonna have to help you. You can't stand."

I wanted to tell him no or let me try first, but he was right. I'd depleted my energy to the point of passing out. I could have died using that spell for the windows last night. So stupid.

"Fine."

After that was done and never to be spoken of again, he helped me back to my room and guided me to my bed. He stayed there, hands on his hips and tapping his foot.

"That's it. You're changing clothes."

I scoffed. "Screw that."

Mateo disappeared. "Just something comfy. You've been down for two days in the same shirt and undies. It's high time you got your ass out of bed and dressed. We're going downstairs and eating lunch."

"If I can't make it to the fucking bathroom, how the hell am I supposed to get downstairs," I mumbled and got no response.

Mateo came out, a shit-eating grin on his face, holding up a pair of black leggings and a retro My Little Pony jammy shirt that I liked to use as a dress at home. "See? Not bad, right?"

"No."

Mateo dropped his shoulders in exasperation. He steeled himself against my grumpy negativity and got me dressed. I swatted him away when he threatened to change my panties.

"Now I can officially say I've undressed a woman. Ha." And he pushed the shirt on over my head.

"And you can officially go to hell." I snatched my My Little Pony Shirt and pushed my arms through myself.

The asshole carried me down the stairs. I've said before that I'd never get pissed at Mateo. Well, call me a liar.

Daylight spilled in from the cracks between the particle boards nailed over the front windows. Someone had swept up the broken glass and wood. Guess my spell hadn't fixed them after all. I stared at the floor where the old front door had crashed when Aswryn blew it in.

The vision of Nol lying on the ground flashed in front of me. A few times, when everyone left me alone in my room, I'd reached for our bond but only felt emptiness. My *muranildo* was dead.

Mateo slid his hand into mine. I flinched and spun. The room spun the other way, and Mateo grabbed me under my arms to steady me. He helped me to the couch, free of glass and upright once again. The coffee table and one chair were missing. He pulled a blanket out of the cedar chest that used to live in the attic. "I'll make you something to eat. Yumi said nothing too rich."

Why did they bother? No one needed me anymore.

Mateo gave me a mug of tea. "Yumi said no coffee. Sorry, *ojitos*." He sat down next to me and leaned over, almost in my lap. "Things will get better. It doesn't feel like it now, but it'll get easier."

"Don't, Mateo. I know all the fucking tricks. The promises of later. I've outlived my foster parents, sister, brother-in-law, nieces and nephews, not to mention the friends I've killed." And more.

"Well—"

"No. It won't matter. I'll be dead in less than a decade."

"Hally, that's not—"

"Please don't get religious on me. It's a fact. Nol almost died when he was young because we're nine years apart. Our parents didn't know. The day I was born, Nol wouldn't leave my crib. They pulled him away from my side, and he stopped breathing. I screamed bloody murder. They brought him back to me, and he started breathing again. He got better and was walking within a week. We can't survive a decade without each other."

"You were here without him."

"We were both alive."

The toaster popped, and Mateo got up. Sourdough toast does not solve everything. Or at least, I didn't want it to, but teatime with Mateo made me...less negative.

Three cups later, Mateo was in the middle of explaining to me for the third time why Stephen Hawking's theory of time travel was possible.

"It doesn't make any sense. What does it matter how fast you go? It's still a progression of time. How the hell can it get faster?"

"It's the same speed. You go faster. Hally, I swear, woman. How can you have gone to different realms but not believe time travel is possible?"

"My grandmother is…" I took a second to count. "Eight hundred and seventy-seven years old? I think. Don't you think if time travel *was* possible, my people would have discovered it already?"

Mateo choked on his tea. "Really? How long do you live?"

I shrugged. "Around twelve hundred years."

"Then—."

"Listen, it doesn't make sense—" I held up a finger when he opened his mouth. "—to me. I don't care what you say. I'm old and stuck in my ways."

The back door squeaked open. Footsteps thumped, and boots tumbled to the floor. Light from the backyard cut through the dark hallway.

"Hi, Mateo! Ray's grumpy. Go to your room, young lady."

Charlie's socks swooshed on the hardwood. Ray's tiny feet stomped up the stairs. Since I sat closer to the fireplace and Charlie's lab, she couldn't see me yet. "I was wondering if you'd like to stay for din—" She stopped when she poked her head into the living room. "Tatie?" Her voice warbled. "You're up. Mateo, why didn't you tell me?" Charlie came over and hugged me, careful not to knock away my toast.

"I wanted to surprise you. Surprise! And I ordered you Chinese. It'll be here in about thirty minutes." He got up and tucked the blankets around me. "I am going back home to have some *alone* time with Sam. You, old woman you, need to change your attitude."

He leaned over and brought his face an inch away from mine. His brown eyes bored into mine. "Because I give a shit. *We* want you here with us, for however long, because that's all anyone has." With that uplifting speech, Mateo kissed my forehead and walked into the hall. "Ray! Come give me a hug."

"Arguing with Mateo?"

I lifted a shoulder, unsure of what to call that.

Charlie grabbed a throw pillow and sat in the one remaining chair. "Did Mateo tell you to call Agent Zack-ass? I told him what happened, but he wants to talk to you."

"No. Mateo didn't tell me. Well, he didn't remind me." I sighed. "I'll call him soon."

Charlie stared at the floor while she chewed on her lip. "When will Gileal be back?"

"I'm not sure if he will. With Nolan dead, he knows I won't be here much longer. What's the point?"

"To be with you? And are you sure you haven't felt Nolan?"

"Not a whisper."

"Tatie—"

"Wanna get me my phone real quick and I'll call Zack?"

Charlie nodded. Without a word, she popped up and grabbed my phone off the kitchen charger. "I need to look at something," she mumbled with tears in her eyes before she kissed the top of my head.

How bad would this be on her, these last few years with me? I considered going home and spending time with my family, but then I'd be leaving everyone here. Sam had offered to come with me. Maybe they'd enjoy a stay in France.

I sighed and looked down at the phone. First things first: Agent Zack-ass.

26

"Go give Tatie a hug and kiss, Ray," Charlie called from upstairs.

Tiny thumps ran through the house until she flew onto the couch from the hallway. I held my breath and tried not to show how much that hurt.

"Night, Tatie." Ray kissed my cheek, jumped down, bumped my wrist, and ran back to Charlie.

"You okay?" Yumi asked. She'd come an hour after dinner to visit and drink wine. She'd lied, and so had Charlie. Yumi had come over to look at my injuries. The physical ones, at least. The magical energy loss she couldn't do anything about.

"Peachy," I said through clenched teeth.

She took her spot beside me. "You haven't had much soup. Wanna try some now?"

I shook my head.

Charlie came back in, plopped down in her chair, and picked up her wine.

Still tea for me.

"You wanna play Yahtzee?" Charlie asked.

"Please, with how much you've drunk, I'd be surprised if you could keep the dice on the table."

Yumi giggled. Charlie gasped, eyes wide and fake. I pushed the blanket aside and got up.

"What are you doing? You'll fall," Charlie said.

"My bladder is going to burst if I don't go. Besides, I'm feeling better."

Yumi stood, more unbalanced than me.

"Ladies, don't be offended, but I can get to the bathroom my own damn self, thank you very much." I doubted they'd even find the bathroom.

Tired and jealous of their wine drinking, I headed upstairs instead of going back. By the top step, my legs were shaking, and I had to sit, the steep stairs to my left and the hall to my right. I rested my head against the wall and stared down at the landing below. Even if Gil did come back, he'd wait until after the funeral. No way would he not be there for that. Then again, like I'd told Charlie, what would be the point of him coming back?

My shoulders shuddered. I'd been so stupid to think Nol stood a chance. Gil had known it, tried to convince me, prepare me, but I hadn't listened. I couldn't accept my *muranildo's* death, and because of that, I didn't get to really say goodbye to Gil.

I tried to keep the tears in, but they leaked out, silently rolling down my face. As I sat up to wipe my cheeks, the stairs blurred from even more tears, and I almost toppled over and down the steps. Would I die if I fell? Did it really matter if I did? Emma's descendants didn't need me anymore, and I no longer needed to stay alive for Nol's sake. Mateo's words came to mind. They didn't *need* me. Mateo wanted me here. For what?

A crash came from Ray's room like she'd thrown her princess lamp. Rested from my time on the wall, I got up to check on her. Indeed, her princess lamp had fallen and broken. Poor Aurora.

I sat on Ray's bed. "It's okay, *colombe*. We can get you a new one." I scooted over to lay beside her, my fingers feeling for her fuzzy hair. She wasn't there. "Ray?"

Nothing moved in the dark room.

"Ray, come out, *colombe*. I don't have the energy for playing." Had she snuck past me to the bathroom?

"Ray?" I called louder from her open door. "This isn't funny. Come out." After five seconds, when she still didn't respond, I yelled down the stairs, my voice echoing throughout the house, "Charlie! I can't find Ray."

Charlie ran through the house and up the stairs. Yumi came up behind her.

Charlie checked every room. As she came back to us, she pulled her phone out. "Where could she have gone?"

"Guys?" Yumi called from Ray's room.

Charlie hurried in first but moved over when Yumi stepped around her, holding a piece of paper and a strip of leather. "It's for you, Hally."

I shook my head to push down my panic. What did I do with a piece of paper?

"Read it," she told me. She held my hands still. "Read the note, Hally."

Note? Yes, there on the paper, there were words. I shook my head again.

"Charlie, don't call 911." Yumi took the phone away from her. "Read the note."

Hally,
Come get her. Alone. You for her. You'll know where.
Aswryn

"What does that mean? Aswryn is with Gileal!" Charlie screamed, shaking the note. "You blocked her magic. How is she here? Tatie?" She grabbed my shirt. "Tatie, do you know? Why is there a note from Aswryn? Where is my daughter?"

"She—she must have escaped." And likely killed Gileal. Now she had Ray.

"You took her magic, Hally," Yumi stated. "How did Aswryn do this?"

I looked down at the floor, reeling at my own assumption—valid as it was. They were gone. Should I have killed Aswryn?

"Tatie?" Charlie's scared, panicked voice brought me back to the here and now. Her husband's death had broken her, and she'd started having panic attacks. Now her daughter was missing. She needed me, and I would not fail her.

I glanced down to think, taking in Ray's My Little Ponies and dollies lying on the floor. "She doesn't need magic with a *meril*. Magic is contained in them. Honestly, any of you could use one if you learned how."

"How did she get away?" Yumi knew I didn't know, but she liked to brainstorm.

My mind was too worn out for that much thinking.

"Isn't this your bracelet?" Yumi dangled the leather strip in front of me.

I stilled and focused on her calm brown eyes. "Yeah. Where did you get it?"

"It was with the note on the dresser."

I gripped the little metal tag in the middle as tightly as I could. Emma. "I've been looking for this."

"Does she mean for you to put it on?" Charlie asked. "Why would she want you to put on your own bracelet?"

I didn't care if it led us to Ray. "Help me?"

Yumi did as I asked, wrapping it around three times. As soon as she pressed the buckle down, the straps slithered up my arm, crisscrossing like ballerina ribbons.

"What's it doing?" I shook my wrist.

The straps stopped right above my elbow. The strip wound around into an inch-wide band. The original strip that made my bracelet slithered back down and rested on my wrist like normal. Nine met-al-pronged beads as big as my pinky nail grew out of the leather and clamped on.

I screamed as they dug into my flesh. All three of us grabbed the band, but when we pulled, the beads held on. Blood dripped from each one and soaked into the leather.

"What is that?" Charlie went to touch the thing, but recoiled at the last second.

Everyone who might know about this was in *Endae* with no way to reach them. We were on our own. I went to pace the hall but failed. Toast, tea, and egg drop soup didn't make up for two days of recuperation without eating or drinking anything. Charlie dropped to Ray's bed and sobbed. Yumi pulled out her phone and called the others. I went to Charlie's side and rubbed her back.

Lewis got there first, living less than ten minutes away. He let himself in with his key and ran up the stairs. I met him at the top.

"What do we know?" Lewis's calm voice helped calm my nerves.

I threw my hands up, afraid I'd break down like Charlie if I said anything.

Lewis pulled me to him. "Is there a way to contact Gileal?"

"No," I whispered against his shoulder. Lewis had to know Aswryn's reappearance didn't bode well for Gil's survival. Yumi called Lewis over, and he left me. I walked down the hall and sat on the chair in our upstairs family room. The fish tank in the corner whirred and bubbled.

I knew next to nothing about this *endaë*, yet she'd acted as if we were old friends every time—except the last day. Could I have met her before? I didn't know for certain, but I prayed not. How was I supposed to know where to find her? One thing was for certain. It had to be in this realm. Gil told us he'd found Aswryn's place. Next to a lake? That could be anywhere in Seattle—he was unfamiliar with the Puget Sound. Many inlets looked like lakes and lakes looked like the bay.

Nol had fought her at Lake Union, and she had run off somewhere after attacking a human. Why would she do that? What was in South Lake Union? Business buildings, train tracks, and the park. Boats, cars, and planes. Cinder and other bars were close to there. The University of Washington had a few medical labs down there. I shot up so fast I almost fell on my face.

"Charlie?" I caught the railing but didn't have to go any farther. They were all out in an instant. "What happened at your lab?"

Charlie blinked. Anything besides finding her daughter wasn't relevant in her mind right now. "W-what?"

She came and stood in front of me. I placed my hands on her shoulders. "This is important, love. Tell me about the break-in and your friend who went to the hospital."

"He's an intern, but he didn't get hurt at work. I—I'm not sure where exactly. Why?"

"What was stolen?"

"Beakers and tubes, solutions and other chemicals. Everything was back to normal when I got there on Monday. It wasn't that bad."

"Can you find out when and where your intern was hurt?"

"It was a mugging down on the street somewhere. Ernie clocked out of the building at, like, nine twenty. The mugger took Ernie's key card to gain access to the building. Some of the stuff was found in a dumpster in the back alley."

"Could Ernie have been attacked at the park?"

Understanding dawned. "It could have been Aswryn. But why would she want lab equipment?" Charlie gripped my left hand and shook it as she jumped.

"She's working on the curse. Wouldn't she need supplies to experiment on that virus?" Aswryn fought Ernie the intern, which sounded ridiculous when said together, took his key card, got interrupted by Nol, and ran to Charlie's lab.

"Do you think she's at my lab? We have to get there."

Everyone started down the stairs in front of me, talking and clomping, excited to have a clue. Charlie's lab was too easy. No, she'd want me to go where she'd taken those supplies. Her hideaway. But that could be anywhere. Unless she couldn't vanish the loot with her. Or...

"No!" I leaned over the railing. Everyone looked up at me from the bottom. "I don't think she's there. She couldn't vanish after she left the park. Her place is around there somewhere, and I think that's where Aswryn has Ray. We have to figure out where that place is, and driving around South Lake Union won't do anything but waste gas. Charlie, grab your tablet and pull up a map of the area. We need to go over the buildings to see if anything is abandoned or condemned."

We set up in Charlie's lab with easy access to coffee and we had enough room to stay off each other's toes. Sam had his tablet as well.

Mateo used Charlie's computer to pull up Seattle city records and crap. I couldn't do anything except pace and reel in my own head.

What would Nol do? Look at all the facts and data, just like everyone was doing. Take a step back and look for unconsidered angles. He liked looking at things backward, retracing his steps. I set my coffee down and snuck upstairs. No need to involve them in my thought process.

Aurora's porcelain head had rolled under Ray's bed, way back in the corner. I called it to me, knowing full well I couldn't rely on my magic again. No matter what happened after this, I was blocking myself. Yumi had found the note on the dresser across from the bed. Some porcelain dust littered the top where the lamp sat. We'd set the note and bracelet back where Aswryn had put them.

Aswryn had contaminated my only link to my sister—the little luggage tag with our family's address and her name stamped on the metal. My thumb brushed over the worn letters. How dare she tarnish that. She'd used such a precious thing of mine to deliver whatever the hell this was.

I hooked my thumb under the leather band on my arm. When I tried to lift it, the beads dug in, same as before. I snatched up my bracelet and left the room to sit against the wall across from the stairs, the ones I'd thought about falling down just hours ago. I placed my bracelet against my chest and played with the metal tag. Where was she? Which building, or was it somewhere else?

At the back of my mind, something stirred. Not a voice, not a picture, but something less conscious, like a dream. And as in a dream, everything made sense until you woke up confused.

THE SCREECH OF A seagull echoed around the darkness. Between the night and thick mist, nothing was visible. Water lapped from somewhere behind me, but I couldn't turn around. The earthy smell of stagnant freshwater mixed with salt water hung in the air. I stood on a sidewalk looking over a railing down onto a beach. Was this the "bridge" Gil had hopped over to hide from Aswryn? My clothes were soaked, and water dripped from my nose in the light drizzle.

A building with glass windows, so many windows, but not a sky-scraper, appeared out of the mist in front of me. Although I knew I needed to, I was not allowed to go inside. At the far end of the building, a street light turned on over a large yellow sign. My feet made no noise as I ran over to read it.

The public notice sign stated that this building on Fair Something Avenue was being condemned. The numbers and half the words were blurry. I turned back to the ill-fated building, a squat thing in the way of progress.

At the top, just visible, I could make out some kind of towers. The place looked familiar. Across the road from where I stood, the mist pushed back to show me water lapping at the edge of a pier. Old ships floated. Rust sifted away on the wind as one boat started to disappear. A seaplane floated behind the disappearing boat.

I WOKE UP WITH a start. Seaplanes. Lake Union Park had that seaplane company next to the parking lot. I knew where to go.

Alone.

27

SINCE I'D LEFT MY kick-ass rose Docs in the apartment, I couldn't use those in an epic fight. Who was I kidding? Epic my ass. I'd be lucky to get out alive. As long as I got Ray out, I'd be happy. Black Boggs, black leggings, that coat from the apartment, and my black retro My Little Pony T-shirt dress completed my ass-kicking outfit.

Yeah, I wasn't impressed either. Plus, I had to bolt before anyone saw me leave. I snagged a backpack and shoved a pair of shoes and a coat for Ray inside, then some Fig Newtons and a bottle of water from the pantry before I snuck out the back door.

The taxi dropped me off next to the juniper plants and modern art display where Ian had surprised Charlie and me. My breath clouded my vision as I got out and waved the taxi driver off. I hooked my thumbs under my backpack straps.

"Now what, crazy bitch?" I asked under my breath.

I brushed the snow off a park bench and sat down, but the cold seeped through my jacket. Glowing red, blue, green, and white lights reflected off the water, stretched out like a strand of icicle lights on a Christmas tree all around the dark lake. Blank spots from unlit buildings broke up the strand. One right across from me stood out—the old historic steam plant. I remembered when the smokestacks used to belch out clouds of steam onto the lake.

Wait a minute. Smokestacks looked like towers. That damn building had thousands of windows, like a squat five-story skyscraper. I'd been so focused on seaplanes I'd forgotten about everything else in the vision. But now I was on the wrong side of the lake, and the taxi had already left. Fucking-A.

Half an hour later, I got out of my second taxi, my shoes scraping the ice-covered street outside the Lake Union Steam Plant. The lights of Seattle shone through the first floor of the large rectangular building. My armband warmed as I walked up to the closest window. If this was going to turn into the hotter-colder game, the fucking thing better not burn me or I'd really kill her.

I sighed and checked the front door. Locked. How rude. With five stories of glass and a dozen or more sections long, I thought about breaking a window. They had a spare or two. There might be an alarm, though. According to Google, some tech company owned the building, but it had closed down for renovations a year ago. The perfect place for shady *endai* to make exchanges. I'd bet my life Aswryn had left the underground garage open for me. I groaned. How cliché.

Sure enough, as I walked down the ramp to the lower floor, the armband warmed. Not hot yet. The echo of the locked garage gate filled the creepy dark underbelly when I shook it. Resting my cheek against the icy metal, I spotted the entrance door propped open. Gee, who'd have thought?

I fished out my flashlight as I stepped through. Everything the light didn't touch the darkness swallowed. Talk about freaky. Taking advantage of my magic again, I filled my hands with a light orb and sent it halfway across the parking lot, then two more to the right and left. I sent out five orbs in total to brighten the whole area enough for me to see the algae growing down the sides of the walls on the lake's side. The breeze sent over the essence of lake water.

The next orb I kept close and started charging. As the ball filled, a slimy rope slithered from my magical core deep in my stomach and up my body to my arm. The band pulsed in time with my heart, and my magic flowed into it.

I panicked and ripped off my backpack and coat. The band looked normal, didn't hurt, and wasn't warming up. I dropped my spell, and the transfer stopped. After calming down a bit, I filled another orb with energy as a test. Magic started transferring after I'd fed enough energy into the orb to brighten the entire garage. The light dimmed but didn't die out. Okay, I could use some magic. Would the band fill up and fall off like a blood-filled leach? Doubted it.

I extinguished the orbs to save my energy. Into the empty, echoey garage I went. When my flashlight shone on the elevator sign, my band warmed up again. Of course. The least she could have done was leave the fucking elevator on.

My knees gave out on the second to last step before the main floor. In a split second, I managed to twist and land on my butt instead of slamming my knees into the cement. I clicked the flashlight off and sat in the dark, listening to my heart thud in my ears. Even as the cold seeped up into me, my eyes fluttered shut, which was my cue to move. Flashlight on, Hally up.

Mold-dense air, mixed with paint and drywall, overwhelmed my nose and mouth. My boots scraped the cement floor and echoed around the open space. I looked up and imagined the four floors collapsing on me.

With windows in every direction, I shoved my flashlight into a backpack pocket. What now? My boots thumped as I walked across the floor to the windows. Down below, the black water reflected the city lights until my breath fogged the glass, blurring the view.

I turned around to lean against the cold window. Huge diagonal and vertical metal support beams rose up the structure like a skeleton, and the cement core secured each floor like vertebrae. Several doors lined the walls, including the garage entrance and another leading upstairs on the right side of the elevator.

"Aswryn? Show yourself, you sorry excuse for an *enda*." I shivered as my words echoed.

Her laughter filled the empty room, mingling with my voice. I refused to cringe. "It took you long enough."

Her slow steps came from everywhere, giving me no clue as to her whereabouts.

"Do you like your new bracelet? I think it's pretty fashionable. Much better than those boring braided bands they used to be."

"Where are you?"

"Right here." Aswryn stepped out from the left side of the building. "Enough bullshit. Where's Ray?"

Aswryn kept walking toward me, her hips swaying. "Safe."

My chest hurt as I asked the next question, but I had to know. "What did you do to Gileal?"

Aswryn tsked and shrugged one shoulder. "Not so safe. He was quite brave, I'll admit. He kept me from taking your precious *muranildo*...until the end."

Aswryn had confirmed my suspicion. She had no reason to lie. My head spun, but I stayed on my feet and refused to show Aswryn weakness. I could pass out after Ray was back with Charlie. She'd meant to hurt me with her admission, but it only angered me. I let her see my controlled rage.

When so many people die around you, you begin to build tough skin. How many people had I seen die in front of me throughout the years? Too many. How many loved ones had died and left my family mourning? Too many. If I could stand and keep my family together through my own pain, I could damn well make sure Aswryn didn't see the hurt in my eyes from this loss.

Her smile faltered for a second. She strolled around the room, wiping her fingertips on a stepladder. "I don't know how you stand her. That sniveling little brat is always complaining. 'I'm cold. I'm thirsty. I want my mommy.'"

"Let her go. You can't have me until you return her."

Aswryn scoffed. "Dear child, I had you the moment you put on the bracelet. I own you, and you will return my magic."

"You tricked me, giving me my bracelet back with this thing hidden in it. To do what? Limit my magic?"

"Not exactly. That is a slave bracelet. The ancient ones didn't fit your personality. It took me a while to make it right, but I finished it before you blocked me."

I froze. I'd never heard of such a thing, but anything with the word "slave" referring to me did not sound good.

"Yes, now you understand. You will go where I want you to go, come whenever I summon you. Banishment or not, you'll stay with me no matter what realm I'm in."

She was so full of shit. No way could that be possible. "There's no such thing."

"Your government hides so much from its citizens, so much you don't know."

I wasn't going to go down that rabbit hole. I exhaled. "Take Ray home. That's what you said."

"I never said I'd return her. I said you for her, but don't worry. They'll find your precious little snot-face." She shrugged. "I can't guarantee she'll be alive by then, though."

Pissed off to no end, I threw a ball of raw energy at her. My magic hit her in the gut, and she landed on her ass. I threw more at her and stalked forward. After four steps, the band stopped the spell. Stopped. Not pulled. Not diminished. Stopped.

Aswryn got up as I dropped to my hands and knees, panting. Sweat dripped down her face as my magic nauseated her. Now she knew how I'd felt.

She reached out her hand as if she could grab my arm from fifty feet away, and the band started draining my energy, siphoning into her. Aswryn vomited. At this rate, she would break her block within minutes.

The band tightened. I screamed. Aswryn came toward me while the band kept drawing out my magic. She grabbed my backpack and shoved me against the floor. Light exploded in my head as she kicked me in the stomach.

"You stole my magic." A kick accompanied every word. The first to my middle, then my chest. I curled into a ball, and she kicked my back. The last kick was to the back of my neck, where my hands were.

As I lay on the floor, drained of magic, I couldn't defend myself. That didn't mean Aswryn wasn't affected, though. Until her block broke, her body would reject the magic beating against those closed ME cells. But with me depleted she couldn't take anything.

Aswryn fell on me, panting. "You should have killed me, you foolish girl with your high morals. You thought living in exile and taking away your magic to punish yourself would redeem you, but they'll never accept you." She pushed on me to get to her knees behind, grabbed my hair and lifted my head. "*Never.* I would have accepted you. The *Asaidaë'a Metaela* would have accepted you."

The what? *Metaela* was a constellation in *Endae* and the name of the first royal family of our common era. *Asaidaë'a Metaela* translated to *Metaela's* revenge? I'd never heard of that. It sounded like a following of some sort. Odd. Perhaps even a fringe group who had helped her escape after she was arrested.

"What's that? Your little fan club? Sorry, I'm not the groupie type." She'd told me more, in the few times I'd seen her, than anything Nol knew of her. Or what he'd told me he knew. Then again, what could I do about it as her slave? Nothing.

Aswryn raised my head higher and then slammed me into the floor. White light blinded me, then gray spots flickered, and finally, the room came back. She pulled more energy through the bracelet, or tried to, but nothing remained in my system.

"...fully restored. Tests can't commence until both of you are healed more."

I'd missed the first part of her little speech. Like I cared.

"You will obey me." She yanked me up by my hair. "Get up."

"Go screw yourself." I couldn't see through my blurred and starry vision, so I spat where I thought her face was. By her growl, I'd aimed right.

"You little bitch."

Oh, she had no idea. She dropped me, and my wrist screamed when my forearms slapped the floor. The stars blocking my vision receded enough for me to see my arms. Then Aswryn hit the back of my head.

My head bumped into something over and over. With every bump, my brain threatened to explode out of my nose. An artificial light shone on boots as they stepped up the cement stairs above my head. Aswryn had found my flashlight, maybe? On the next bump, my head hit Aswryn's back as she hauled me up the next step. I couldn't move my limbs. The piercing screech of the metal door echoing in the stairwell split my skull in two. Kill me now.

Fig Newtons and Gatorade threatened to come up. "I'm gonna throw up, Aswryn. I'm serious!"

She dropped me from shoulder height, and whatever held me immobilized released me as my shoulders and upper back hit the floor. The impact forced the air out of my lungs. I struggled to breathe, let alone roll over. After a few moments, I opened my eyes. The light from the flashlight and the big bad Aswryn leaned over me. We didn't need the flashlight anymore. The city illuminated this end of the building.

"You've got something in your teeth," I wheezed.

She frowned and touched her mouth before she realized I was fucking with her. "You think you're funny?"

"Maybe." My lungs, shoulder, wrist—Oh hell, most of my body hurt, but I kept taunting her. "Aswryn?" I crooked a finger and as with all creatures of habit, she fell for it. Her hair slid forward and touched my hand. "You're an asshole." I grabbed a fistful of her hair and yanked her down close enough to reach her neck.

I clawed at her throat and shoved the small amount of raw energy that my body had replenished into her. She flew back. The audible thump of her head smacking the floor made me cringe. The light flew to the opposite side of the room. Nothing moved—no brush of fabric or shoes scuffing. Aswryn was out.

Gritting my teeth, I scrambled up, doing my best to ignore my twinging wrist as I crawled to her prone body. My head still pounded as I sat on my heels at Aswryn's shoulders, her head inches from my knees. The chilly air filled my lungs five times before everything settled into place. What the hell was I going to do with her? Was I foolish not to kill her? I shivered as visions of my friends' dead faces filled my pounding head. I couldn't do it.

Aswryn grabbed my wrists. No, she couldn't wake up yet! Before my foggy brain caught up with my reflexes, she had yanked me forward. I tumbled down next to her. She got up and straddled me. Her right hand grabbed my bicep, sucking energy from the band.

"You replenish quickly." She smiled her creepy smile, even as sweat beaded on her forehead.

I'd always been a fast healer. Good for her, bad for me. "You're looking a little green there, Aswryn. My magic won't replenish that quickly if you keep siphoning it." I bucked my hips and punched her.

Blood gushed from her nose. Distracted, Aswryn's grip loosened, and I slipped out from underneath her. I got a few feet away from her, wobbling even on my hands and knees, before I toppled over. My head wasn't doing so well with all the hits it had taken this weekend. This last one might have been the tipping point. Weren't double concussions bad? Gray spots scattered all over my sight.

Aswryn yelled something. I fell and she just laughed. She realized, as I did, that I wasn't getting anywhere far until my head cleared. "I've won, Hallanevaë. Give up."

A second later, Aswryn grabbed my ankles and dragged me down the dark hall, away from the bright city lights. My eyes fluttered closed as my vision went from spotty to gray to black. I lost focus. My body begged me to give in, but I wouldn't until I got Ray home. I would fight until I passed out.

"You're connected to me, Hally. And when I break this wretched block you cast, we will finish my mission."

I had no snarky retort. My head spun too much to think. We stopped at a door, but as she turned the knob, someone pulled it in faster, unbalancing her. They grabbed her around the neck and shoved her as I pulled my legs close in and scooted backward.

"Tatie!" Ray's small voice called from in the room.

Aswryn had someone in there with Ray? One of her revenge members? No, because they were fighting *her*. Another captive.

Between my spotty eyesight and the dark hall, I made out two people farther down the hall. I pushed myself up. One person hit the wall. The other collided with the first. One of them grunted, and skin hit skin.

"Ray? Come to me, *ma colombe*."

Aswryn screamed. A black light arced at a downward angle. A *Zayuri*? Something slid down my arm and passed my elbow. I sat up and hurried to strip off my coat. The band slid down farther, now loose and useless.

Her scream turned to a gurgle, and when she took her last breath, the bracelet clamped down on my forearm. Ray went to my side and wrapped her little arms around my neck. I pulled her into my lap, but I couldn't take my eyes off the dark figure standing over Aswryn's body.

Nothing moved for a handful of heartbeats. Then a light orb appeared. Too bright. The *Zayuri* dimmed the orb enough for me to lower my arm. The *endao* looked so much like Nol that I gasped and fell back. Panicking, I crab walked backward, Ray under my arm.

"Stay back." I held out my injured wrist.

Not-Nol stopped. "It is all right. You are safe now."

This person could *not* be Nol because Nol was dead. Right?

I needed a few seconds to think. Aswryn would have bragged that she had saved him. She'd bragged about killing Gileal. A sob shuddered through me, but I held the rest inside. Gil was gone, but I had to keep it together for Ray.

The *endao* rolled his broad shoulders. Then, with a sigh, he stepped forward slowly.

"Who are you?" I asked.

"What do you mean? I am your *muranildo*."

"Lie!"

This didn't make sense.

"Hallë?"

"Never use that name," I yelled. Why was he doing this? A spell like Aswryn's, maybe, to change his appearance and put me at ease. That wasn't gonna fucking happen. "Nol is dead. And Aswryn was blocked. You didn't need to kill her."

"Look at me, Hallë."

I held my breath. My thoughts were all muddled. I shook my head too fast, and I swear my brain sloshed around. Oh, it hurt so much. "No, you can't be him. He was ...He's gone."

"Hallë, please calm down. You are scaring Ray."

"Ray?" I had to close my eyes to think. I squeezed her tight and rested my chin on her head.

"Think, Hallë." He sounded much closer now.

My eyes flew open. I screamed.

He crouched in front of me, elbows resting on his knees. When had he gotten so close? "*Sajë, sajë. Dairn, Hallë.*" *Find calm, Hallë.* I flinched when he touched my knee. "Be calm and think. No other *endai* knows English. I am your Nol." The back of his fingers touched my face. "You're so cold. *C'yo*, Hallë. You are bleeding." He leaned forward and touched my temple. "What did she do to you?"

I lost it, screaming and kicking until he stopped touching me. "Don't touch me!"

"Tatie." Ray grabbed my shirt in her fists. "Tatie, don't be scared. Nolan's gonna take us home."

"Ask me anything, and I will tell you," the impersonator said.

I shook my head but stopped before my head exploded.

The *Zayuri* licked his lips. "Friday. You asked me if I was mad at you, and I said yes, but I didn't tell you why. I was mad that you jumped between two deadly spells and almost killed yourself. So stupid."

I stopped breathing about the time he got to the "I didn't tell you" part. How the hell was he alive? "Nol?" I croaked.

"Yes, Hallë." His lips curled into a smile, and his dimple showed. I didn't have to reach far. He squeezed me and rested his chin on my head. "Hallë, stop crying. We are all safe."

Nol was right, but it took a great deal of effort to stop crying. The past five days had been hell on everyone. Now everything was over. My emotions were a tad frayed.

Ray wiggled between us. "See, I told you it's Nolan."

I felt Nol shake, then heard his laughter. I pinched him, but not hard enough to hurt. He wrapped one arm around Ray and held us close. We didn't let go for quite some time.

"Can we call Mommy now? I'm thirsty."

Which reminded me. "Ray, find my backpack. I brought some things for you."

Nol kept his arms around me while she went to find my bag.

"Hallë?"

I needed to focus so I didn't pass out on them. They didn't know where we were or how to get out of here.

"Hallë?"

I opened my eyes and saw Ray sitting across from us. My backpack was in her lap, the water bottle in her hands, and she wore her coat and boots. When had that happened?

Nol nudged my arm and held my phone out to me. "Open your phone."

I lifted the phone to my face and saw a huge crack ran down the screen. "Damn it!"

"What?"

"My screen's cracked, and I never bought insurance." I unlocked my phone with my thumbprint and the bright backlight nearly blinded me.

"Unbelievable," he mumbled so low I doubted Ray had heard him.

I ignored him and rested my head on his shoulder. My head hurt too much, and the room wouldn't stop spinning. It was bad enough that the light from the phone was making my headache worse.

"A few more minutes, Hallë." He tucked me under his arm like he used to when we were kids. "Let me try." Nol turned so the screen illuminated his face, but not mine. I saw scratches on his chin and a black eye. His thumb flicked up the screen.

"How did you get here?"

"Aswryn took me from Gileal. I was awake. I just could not respond. I am so sorry I scared you. All of you."

"Aswryn said Gil is dead."

Nol gave up looking at my phone. "She left him to die, but he wasn't dead when she took me. I...do not know if he survived."

My phone vibrated, and he held the phone back up. "Your agent is calling."

"He's not my—hey, don't answer—"

"Agent Zack ah...Thomas?" I had Agent Zack-ass as his contact name. "No, I—I'emm—This is Nolan. Hallë is with me, though. Yes, that'es what Hallë said." Nol was trying his hardest to impress Zack with contractions. Quite cute. Another pause. "Yes, I am. But please, stop interrupting me. Time is important. Hallë is hurt."

As Nol talked to Zack, his voice began lulling me to sleep.

"Hallë?" Nol shook me. "Where are we?"

"Don't have him come."

"Where?" He pulled me up. "Hallë?"

Why Zack? "Union..." I licked my lips. "Steam Plant. Don't have him come."

Nol talked some more. About what, I didn't care. Ray grabbed my hand and asked me something. I wanted this to be over. Why wouldn't he let me sleep?

"All right, you can sleep until we get to the doctor." Nol slid his arm under my knees and stood. I held my breath as the world spun, and my empty stomach wanted to vomit.

"I blocked her," I told him once he started walking.

"You are still mumbling, Hallë. Tell me after the doctor looks at your head."

"No doctor."

Nol scoffed. "Right. This will all go away on its own."

Nol jostled me and I hissed in pain. My shoulder must have been injured when Aswryn dropped me. "Yep."

"You will see a doctor. Do you know how many times you passed out just sitting here?"

I harrumphed. He was such a stubborn brat. "Well, your contractions suck."

"Your *Aemirin* sucks," he countered.

Touché.

28

"So you're the badass Hally was talking about." Zack's shouting woke me.

Nol looked down at me. "Is that good or bad?" I gave him a thumbs-up without lifting my head off his shoulder. I was too damn tired. "I guess so."

"Glad to see you're not dead."

"Yes, it certainly feels good not to be." Nol's smile faltered for a second, and he didn't meet Zack's eyes. They stood for an awkward moment. "Is this your car?"

Zack rubbed the back of his neck. "Yeah." He leaned down to Ray's level. "Come on, Ray. Let's get you in your booster seat."

Ray looked up at me, and I nodded it was okay.

"I didn't know he could be nice," I grumbled.

Nol stopped walking. I raised my eyes to find him looking down at me. "Be nice."

My nose scrunched up. "Why did *he* have to come?"

Nol sighed and didn't answer me. Sure, we got along on Tuesday, but I still hated the guy. Nol hitched me up. I wrapped my arms around his neck, squeaking. Jeez, I was such a wimp. Nol huffed, exasperated with me, and started walking again. "Are you going to be difficult the whole ride?"

"Where are we going again?" I asked.

"Hallë, truly?" He set me down in the back seat. "Hospital. We're going to the hospital."

"I don't want to go to the hospital. I don't need to."

"Do not be ridiculous." He scoffed as he pulled my seat belt around me.

I pushed at him. "I can do that."

He raised an eyebrow and handed me the buckle. I managed to secure the belt after three tries. Nol mumbled under his breath. Ray had a blanket around her and a small teddy bear in her hands. When had that happened? Both guys climbed in, and off we went.

"I called Charlie and told her to meet us at Virginia Mason."

"I don't want to go to a hospital." They ignored me. I rested my head back and closed my eyes. "Nol?" The boys' murmuring stopped. "How did Aswryn get you there?"

Nol didn't respond.

"Nol?"

"*Sajë*, rest for now."

I almost argued but gave up. Instead, I listened to the soft murmurs of their voices. I turned to Ray. She had a phone to her ear but wasn't talking. Who's phone? And when did she get one? Did it really matter? No. I couldn't hear, but I knew she was talking to Charlie by the calm look on her face.

I rolled my head the other way. The traffic light turned red right in front of a dozen neon signs. The red, orange, blue, and green lights blinked and flashed, bright beacons to blind people. They made my head pound. Zack punched the gas.

Oh crap. "Pull over!"

"What? Why?"

"Zack, pull over, damn it!" Zack swerved, and my head hit the window. Maybe I shouldn't have yelled. I moaned and held my head with one hand while fumbling for the handle with my good one. It wouldn't open. "Damn it, what the hell is wrong with your door?"

"Child lock. What's wrong?"

"Get the damn door open before I throw up in your fucking back seat."

"Jesus." I heard one door open, then a burst of freezing air took my breath away.

I managed to get out of the car and took two steps before I fell to my knees in the slushy snow. I wasn't sure which was worse, the dry heaving that wouldn't stop or the bursts of white stars behind my eyelids that accompanied each heave. When my stomach finally settled, I pushed myself off the ground but I tipped forward.

"*Ai!* Hallë, slow down." Nol grabbed me around the waist and steered me back to the car.

Someone handed me a water bottle as I leaned against the door. It was one of those throwaway squirt ones, but I took the lid off anyway. Neither of the guys said anything while I sipped the water. Nol fidgeted in front of me.

Zack leaned his hip against the car and crossed his arms. "Are you good now?"

I took another sip and wiped my mouth. "Think so. Next time, don't ask and don't swerve so hard. My head exploded."

"No, that was your stomach." Zack winked. Huh, that was twice now that he'd joked without being an ass.

"That, too." I leaned over and put my elbows on my knees. "Jeez, this sucks."

"Tatie? Are you okay?"

My cuts stung as I brushed my hand across my forehead. "*Je pense que oui, ma colombe.*" *I think so, my dove.*

I opened my eyes and found Nol on the sidewalk with his arms crossed, watching me.

I frowned. "What?"

"You look like shit." He quirked his lips to give me a smile, but I saw the worry line between his brows.

I pursed my lips so I wouldn't smile. "Shut up. You look almost as bad." I pointed my bottle at him.

He shrugged. "Maybe, but at least I am not getting sick all over the place."

"You know what?" I had to blink a few times to focus. "You shouldn't make fun of me, buddy."

Nol clasped his hands behind his back, still smiling, the worry gone. "Why is that?"

I opened my mouth and took a breath. "I dunno anymore."

He laughed, and I flipped him off.

"You okay?" Zack asked.

"I'll be better when..." I closed my eyes and swallowed. "I um...maybe not."

"Whoa," Zack yelled.

Someone grabbed my shoulders. They lifted my legs and put me in the car. I jumped when they touched my hip. "Don't—"

"*Sajë, dairn.*" *Be calm.* I smelled the spicy clove-scented oil in Nol's leather jacket.

"I'm fine."

My seat belt clicked, and then his warmth was gone. He tapped my nose right before the cold air stopped blowing in my face. I leaned against the door, and the stars stopped dancing behind my eyes. A moment later, or maybe I'd fallen asleep, freezing air blew on my face.

A hand touched my side. "No!"

"Hallë." Nol held my face. "*Hallë, nicam. Olda'ra.*" *It's me. You're safe.*

I grabbed his arm and closed my eyes, counting to ten.

"They'll be here in a sec," Zack said behind Nol.

"Who'll be here?" I asked while I checked on Ray—asleep in her booster.

"The doctors." Nol crouched outside the car.

"I don't want to go into the hospital. I'll be fine after a while."

He looked up at me through his dark cinnamon-red eyelashes. His thumb traced under my eye. "You are hurt, Hallë. You cannot stand on your own and cannot stay awake. You threw up."

"I'm just tired." I grabbed his hand and squeezed.

Nol pursed his lips, frowning.

"I *am*. My head will heal."

"Hallë, you need to let the doctors look at you."

I lowered my voice. "What if they run tests? I don't trust them."

Nol raised his eyebrows, and I squeezed his hand until my wrist hurt.

"I'm serious. They'll give me stuff without telling me. If they find out what I am, they'll keep me. Please don't make me go."

Zack waved his arm. We were under an entrance with lots of too-bright fluorescent lights. I tried to blink away the spots in my vision. Two EMTs in white polo shirts came up behind Nol.

Nol let go of my face and lifted me out of the car. The lights blinded me, and I hid my eyes against Nol's chest. My head pounded. I couldn't breathe. Nol set me down on the stretcher, but when he let go, I held on to his jacket. His arm stayed at my back and his chin on my head.

"Okay, Hally? Can you look at me?" the lady EMT asked.

I shook my head. Everything was too bright, and I knew she wanted to shine a light in my eyes.

"You will be fine, Hallë."

I turned to Nol. "Don't make me go in there alone."

Nol let out a slow sigh. He thought I was overreacting, but he didn't understand. His chin lifted off my head, and I looked up, hoping that if he saw how serious I was, he'd let me stay out here. Nol's eyes crinkled, placating me. "You will not go in alone."

The EMT took the opportunity to look at my eyes. And yes, she used the light. "Most likely a concussion."

Someone unzipped my coat, and I flinched. Then another person said something about a blood pressure cuff. I let go of Nol and hissed as they pulled on my right arm, tugging on my wrist. They slowed down and helped me slide that arm out. My wrist looked like I'd dipped the thing in ink.

None of them thought twice about the slave bracelet, which looked like a simple leather arm cuff to everyone but me. Nol would have freaked if he knew what it was. I didn't know why it had tightened back up, but until this all calmed down, I wouldn't bring it up. We had more immediate problems, like me going into a hospital I didn't want to go into. Besides, Aswryn was dead. It wasn't like she could command me from the grave.

"All right, young lady, we're gonna take you in now." The Velcro from the blood pressure cuff ripped, louder than the EMT's voice.

I shook my head. Not yet, not until Nol understood. Heart racing, I began hyperventilating. Someone grabbed my hand, and we started moving.

Nol wasn't following us. He'd said I wouldn't go in alone, but he wasn't coming. "Nol?"

He jogged over, and the EMTs stopped when he took my hand. "The others are meeting me out here. Once they come, we will be in to see you together. You are safe with these people, I promise."

He didn't understand, and he was letting them take me. I'd never seen anything good come out of hospitals besides babies, and sometimes, they never came out either.

"It's okay, Hally. We'll take good care of you," the EMT lady assured me. "Breathe, sweetie. I'm comin' in with ya, okay? There's nothing to be scared of."

"I...I don't want medicine."

"I'll make it known."

"F...for religious reasons." Best lie ever. They couldn't touch me that way.

They stopped. "Are you serious?"

I peeked an eye open. "Maybe?"

She smiled and shook her head. The other EMT outright laughed.

They stayed and made sure the nurse wrote down my wishes. I mouthed "thank you" to her as she left. They gave me paperwork, tests, and a CT scan, but no one came.

I kept asking and kept getting a no. Two hours, an x-ray scan and a scary concussion diagnosis later, and still, no one came.

Then the threat of medications. Not one person.

Were they that mad at me for leaving? My heart rate monitor jumped up and down and the beeping rhythm lulled me to sleep from the meds they'd talked me into.

SOMEWHERE IN A CLOUD between asleep and awake in the hospital, Nol's familiar magic woke me. His fingertips touched the back of my hand. I felt his hesitance a moment before his fingers wrapped around my left hand. My eyes flew open.

"Hallë?" Nol sat beside my hospital bed, his face hopeful and hesitant as he searched my eyes.

Elation, hurt, anger, and worry twisted inside me.

He frowned, eyebrows drawn close. "Don't look at me like that," he whispered in *Aemirin*. "They wouldn't let any of us come in. They were concerned you were the victim of sexual assault. Yumi went off on them, and they let Charlie in." He tipped his head across from me. Sure enough, Charlie sat in a chair, asleep with Ray. "Mateo will be in here shortly."

I pressed my lips together and glared. Nol didn't lie to me often, but I'd been asking for them for hours.

"*Mahayem.*" *I apologize.* "Charlie explained your fear of hospitals. I didn't take you seriously."

"You probably thought it was some childish fear I needed to get over." I looked at my lap instead of him, answering him in English.

Nol didn't say anything, nor did he deny it.

I took a deep breath. "Tell me what happened. Are you sure Gil is dead?"

"*Sae. Coja juetesëm.*" *No. As I said.* "She left him to die, but he was very close to death. However, I don't know where we were when Aswryn attacked. She used a *meril* to immobilize me in your yard and hid it under my shirt. Ray found it while Aswryn went to meet you."

"Have you ever heard of *Asaidaë'a Metaela*?" I asked him.

He looked down at his hand over my new cast, considering the phrase. "*Sae.*" *No.*

"She said the *Asaidaë'a Metaela* would have accepted me. You're right. She is, or was, working with others. It could be a lead when you go back."

Nol pursed his lips as he stared down at his hands, his brow pinched. I lifted my hand with the oxygen reader and pressed the creases away with my thumb.

"What are you thinking?"

He cleared his throat, shook his head, then met my eyes, his jaw set. "I'm not going back. Not yet." I held my breath as he continued in *Aemirin*. "I completed my mission, and it's over for now."

"I can't let you do that."

"It isn't your decision." He shrugged. "I want to know your friends, meet your family. This is the only time I can do this. Hallë, please support me in this?"

"But have you asked permission?"

He reached for my face and hooked my chin with his finger. "Let's worry about that later, when you're rested."

"Nol," I whined.

"No. The doctors said you must rest to heal. An'di would agree. I can hear her scolding us now."

I gave him a flat look. He grabbed my hand, set it on the bed next to my leg, and rested his cheek on top of it. His blue eyes were dull, and his cinnamon hair was tangled and dirty. Dark bags were visible even under the black eye. Every knuckle was crusted over with blood, as were the cuts on his face, and his bottom lip was cracked. How had he found the energy to kick Aswryn's ass, then carry me down the stairs? And I'd expected him to come with me into the hospital? Damn, I was so selfish.

His eyes fluttered closed as we listened to the beep of my heart monitor for a solid five minutes. I pushed his shoulder. He did a hum-type laugh and switched cheeks, away from me.

"Nol?" I tapped his shoulder. "Hey?" I tugged on his hair again and pushed on him until he turned back to me. I petted his head and played with his hair. "Have Charlie take you to the house and rest. I can't believe you're on your feet, let alone carried me down those stairs."

Nol sat up, inhaling with a frown. "How so?"

"You haven't eaten or drunk anything in two days. I couldn't walk after—"

He waved my concern off. "*Ai*, I'm fine. *Zayuri* have more endurance than most. Plus, as Agent Thomas said, you think I'm a badass." Nol wiggled his eyebrows.

"I didn't call you a badass. Those are his words. More like a pain in my ass."

"Not as much as you are in mine." Nol thumped my nose.

I couldn't stop my smile.

"Hey, you're awake." Charlie groaned and stretched without waking Ray.

"I will leave you two alone. Sleep, Hallë, and I will see you later." Nol spun in his chair and darted around the curtain.

"Hey, love." The IV tugged on my hand as I reached out to her. "Why don't you take Ray and Nol home? You're all exhausted."

She tipped her chin down and glared at me. Oh no.

I couldn't meet her scalding, angry eyes. "I'm sorry for leaving. I wasn't thinking straight, and I got a sort of vision. It happened all of a sudden, and I *had* to go."

"You left us."

I dropped my hands in my lap and played with the IV, pushing on my vein. "I know."

"Abandoned me to run off and fight Aswryn on your own."

I nodded.

"What were you thinking?" she hissed. Out of the corner of my eye, I saw her stand. "We had no clue how to find you. If she'd made the exchange, how would Ray have gotten home?"

I opened my mouth to answer.

She came next to the bed, giving me her sternest mom expression. "*You* are important to us. I would never forgive you for sacrificing yourself—"

"Ray is far more precious."

"We would have figured out a way."

"There was no other way."

"She wouldn't have hurt Ray. That was Aswryn's leverage, the only thing left to use against you. We would have beaten her together."

"All she wanted was me."

Charlie had been so devastated. I couldn't stand to see her that way again, not after she'd lost her husband three short years ago. Losing Ray would have broken her irreparably.

"All? Why can't you see how much we love you?"

"I do—"

"No. You think you're just here to look after us and keep Nolan alive."

Her emotions clouded the truth. I didn't think that. I knew it and so did she. This wasn't for attention, just the bottom line.

"Charlie." I patted the bed and made her sit. "I've never spoken to you about this and never will again. You know from my nightmares what happened, or at least you have a general idea. *Please understand.*" I grabbed her hand with my left, unbroken one and squeezed. "I killed two friends with my magic. It was a prank to evaporate their potions for a school assignment, but it kept searching for moisture, and it found it in them. They were..." I choked and had to take a moment.

Charlie tried to interrupt, but I squeezed again. This was her only chance to hear what she had wanted to know since she was a little girl.

"They were boiled alive. When the potions evaporated, I jumped out of my hiding spot. We laughed, and then they started screaming. Nothing worked to stop it. I have lived with that every day, and while nothing will ever make up for that, I will always live my life for others to atone for it.

"So while I know you love me, there is no way in the realms, in your hell, in the starless abyss, that I would *not* sacrifice myself for one of you. Yes, our family and Nol are what I live for. That is the way it has been. That is the way it will always be." I wiped the few tears I'd shed and licked my dry lips.

"Tatie," she breathed. "I don't know what to say. Thank you for trusting me with that. You don't need to live to protect us or Nolan."

"We must agree to disagree." I shook her hand. "Now would you leave me to rest for a bit and take that little monster sleeping over there home so she can sleep in a real bed? And take that pain in the ass *muranildo* of mine with you?"

Charlie laughed and wiped her own tears. "Yeah. Mateo is supposed to be here in a bit, I think. Or Yumi, or both. I don't know anymore. They're still pissed at the nurses."

"So I hear." I tugged on her hand until she came close to hug and give me cheek kisses.

"Love you, Tatie." She picked up Ray, adjusted her, and moved to the curtain.

"Hello? Are you done in there?" Mateo poked his head around the curtain where he must have been eavesdropping.

"Yes." Charlie hugged Mateo as she left with Ray in her arms.

"My turn to sit with this naughty young lady."

I watched them go and settled in to let Mateo scold me.

"Now you are on *my* shit list, missy. Nolan, though, has told me you've had a talking to from him and Charlie, so you get to rest for a bit." He came over and grabbed my hands. His left hand didn't make it all the way around my cast.

"I understand, and I forgive you." He paused. "For not telling us. You've been to lots of other places, right?"

I nodded.

"And you've never told anyone else. That's what you've always done. Why would you act any differently? It's to keep yourself safe." He leaned in and whispered in my ear, "I've read enough crazy shit to know what the government might do to you if they found out." He leaned away. "And I forgive you for running out like that. Aswryn had magic we couldn't fight. How else were you going to assure our safety?"

At a loss for words, I tipped my chin down in understanding. Setting his jaw, he gave me a sharp nod back. Mateo got up, settled down in the chair Charlie and Ray had been in, pulled out his latest mystery sci-fi book, and let me rest.

Holy shit, I didn't deserve them.

29

I PULLED THE TOWEL off my head and used it to wipe the mirror. If I left my hair to air dry, it would frizz and curl, but who cared? Not me.

My green eyes stared back at me in the fogged mirror. The stitches made me look like an *Edward Scissorhands* cast reject. I hoped they didn't leave a scar. Scars were as hard to hide as my freckles. I didn't want to see the bruises, but some of them were impossible not to notice, like the ones on my jaw, shoulder, and neck. No makeup would cover all this crap, so I decided not to try.

Everything would be better now. Aswryn would never hurt anyone again. I told myself I didn't believe in death as a punishment, so why didn't her death bother me? I touched the band, feeling the metal and leather brush my fingertips. My lip trembled as I heard her words in my head: "I own you."

Why did this thing clamp back down after it had started sliding? I needed to know. What if someone else "owned" me now? The idea sickened me enough that I ran for the toilet. Nothing came out, of course. I hadn't eaten anything since the Fig Newtons. Had that really only been last night?

Once done, I sat against the toilet bowl, holding my wet hair back. The pressure in my head from dry heaving subsided after a while. I checked my Harley Quinn T-shirt and flannel shorts for wet spots. All good.

I needed to eat, but throwing up nothing didn't make eating sound too appealing. If I cooked, maybe I'd feel like eating, and if not, the others could eat it. I got my ass up off the floor, shoved those thoughts I couldn't answer deep down into the pit of my stomach, and left the bathroom.

With everyone asleep, I got some quiet time, somewhat too quiet, in the stairwell. The echo twisted my stomach. But I had to suck it up. Life happened, and if I wanted to keep going, I couldn't dwell on the past. Aswryn was in my past. I prayed my mind wouldn't add her to my nightmares. My mind was a pro at that.

Nol came down just as I was pulling my frittata out of the oven. A pair of green-and-blue flannel pajama pants hung on his hips. The sleeves of his matching blue long-sleeved shirt were pushed halfway up his arms. I wondered if Mateo had gone shopping for him. Not surprising. He tucked his tangled hair behind his ear, and I saw his *Zayuri* ear cuff. Good. He rubbed his eyes, still half asleep.

"Hungry?"

"Not if you cooked it."

I rolled my eyes, set the dish on a hot pad, and pushed the food and a fork in front of him.

"Eat."

He sat on a stool and looked from the eggs to me and back. I set my hands on my hips and waited. Nol grabbed the fork and poked at the food. He lifted a bite to his mouth and blew on it. I glared at him until he swallowed his first bite. His eyebrows rose, and he nodded.

"Hmm, at least it tastes good, even if it kills me."

I threw my oven mitt at him and went about making another one.

"Good morning, Nolan. Good morning, Tatie." Charlie stepped into the dining room in her gray silk pajama shorts and shirt.

"Oh, thank god you made coffee. Hey, you aren't supposed to have coffee with your concussion."

"Take it away and sign your own death warrant."

"I won't." She held her hands up in mock surrender. "I like my life, thanks so much." She scooted past me and patted my shoulder.

I grabbed more eggs and went about chopping more veggies. "Is Ray awake?"

"Yes." Charlie took a sip, still standing in the kitchen next to me. "So? What do you think of her cooking now, Nolan?"

"I must admit, she makes good—what are these?"

Charlie swallowed her coffee. "Frittatas."

"Is there enough for more, Hallë?"

"Yes." I drew out the word. "I'll make more." I pulled out enough ingredients to make a larger one for them all. "Didn't you eat when you got back, Nol?"

"Mmm hmm, I had the leftovers from Sunday."

"And a huge roast beef sandwich," Charlie added. "And he shared cookies with Ray."

"I made those cookies, you know?"

Nol stopped chewing. "Fine, yes." He waved his fork at me. "You can cook. I am corrected."

Ray came running in with two ponies and a doll. She wore a *Tangled* pajama dress and her adorable monkey slippers. Her hair was going to be a bitch to detangle today. I made her slow down to give me hugs and kisses.

"Did you talk to Lewis, Tatie?" Charlie slid onto the stool next to Nol.

"*Oui.* He said I am not allowed to work until I'm one hundred percent healed." I lifted my casted right hand. "But I'm left-handed. I can work."

Nol choked on a bite as we all laughed.

"By the way, Mateo says we're going over to their house for dinner Sunday. Sam isn't too keen on coming back here yet."

Charlie winced. "Yeah, he was a bit shaken up about the whole thing."

I poured the egg mixture into a cast-iron skillet and stared down at the damn thing. There was no way to put it in the oven one-handed. Before I could ask, Nol bumped me out of the way and wrapped his hand around the handle.

"I have it, Hallë. Go sit down and drink your coffee."

That sounded good, actually, so I bumped him with my hip and made myself another cup. Everything seemed okay on the human side.

My friends had forgiven me for running out on them and gave me very pointed looks when I asked for their forgiveness for everything that had happened.

As the sugar granules spilled from the spoon into my black coffee, my mind wandered to what Nol had decided...and to Gil. I slid onto the third stool, not paying attention to whatever they were saying, lost in my own thoughts.

"Hallë?" Nol asked, waving his hand in front of me, eyes wide.

"Hmm? What?"

He chuckled. "Time? I asked you three times."

"What?" I sat up straighter. He could read me well, but not *that* well.

"Your fritta?"

"Oh, shit. Twenty-five minutes."

Charlie rested her hand on the middle of my back. "Are you okay, Tatie?"

"Yeah." I squeezed my eyes shut, open and closed a few times. "The meds, I think."

"Or the concussion." She rubbed my back, then played with the back of my hair.

"Yes, that one," Nol agreed with Charlie.

Everyone got their frittatas. Ray ate most of hers and ran off to the living room again. Nol still looked hungry after his second slice, but he could make his own. After they were done, Nol shoved his sleeves up and folded his arms on the counter. "So, Hallë." Uh-oh, serious Nol voice.

"Wait, a serious conversation isn't allowed with a concussion."

"I promised I would tell you later. You have coffee, and Charlie is here. I think this is a good time."

Charlie rubbed her hands together and leaned back. "Oh, the talk."

"I am staying. Whether it be a month or a year, I do not know. When I am ready, I will go. They owe us this. We saved our entire world. We can have time together."

"But did you get permission? The *Amura Ore* doesn't care—"

"I have not asked yet because I cannot." He paused, knowing me. But I kept my mouth shut. "Aswryn left all of my *merili* with Gileal."

He let that sink in. It took longer for me to grasp than it should have. "You're stuck here? That isn't the same as deciding to stay."

"I decided to stay before I realized where my *merili* were. Now, would you let me talk this time, or will this be like the café?" He raised an eyebrow in challenge.

Yeah, yeah. I slouched and sipped my coffee to shut myself up.

"My plan is for you to talk to your grandmother."

I shook my head but kept sipping.

"She can inform Tolwe of my decision."

I waited thirty whole seconds. "Are you done?"

"No, but this is the quietest I have ever seen you."

Beside him, Charlie choked on her coffee. We both turned as she kept coughing and laughing. "You have not witnessed her silent treatments after you get in trouble. Waiting for your punishment is nerve-racking. Who do you think I learned it from?"

Nol turned back to me, cinnamon eyebrows high. "So much that has changed. I want to see it, Hallë. Please support me in this?"

I swallowed coffee. "What if they don't approve it?"

"This is not for their approval. I am telling them because our bond is very weak and must be repaired before you die."

I scoffed. "And like they'd believe that."

"Charlie can prove it. She showed me your ME cells."

"My *blocked* ME cells," I corrected him.

"Tatie, you have been fading. You don't take care of yourself, and you have lost too much weight. I have pictures."

"I was a chubby child."

"You weren't a child thirty years ago. You've grown paler and more reserved. I'm worried about you. Since Nolan's been here, while you've been annoyed and cranky, I've seen a drastic difference. You care about being heard and standing up for yourself. Maybe it's the bond, maybe something else, but his presence has helped."

I held Charlie's gaze for a moment. "He can't stay here forever."

"You are right, Hallë. This will only be a visit."

I sighed. "What do you have in mind?"

Nol looked forward instead of at me. "You have your grandfather's ability—"

I almost spit out my coffee. "No. Absolutely not—"

"You haven't even heard him, Tatie!"

I pushed my coffee away. "Dream walking is intrusive and wrong. My grandfather even said that. Only in dire times has he used it. Is this that dire to you?"

"Hallë—"

"Dream walking is not the answer."

"*Yánna maca bimecta?*" *Then what is the answer?* Nol asked, standing up and backing away from me, his hands clenched at his sides. "*Donom polten'a wessen, Hallë.*" *I must find a way.* "I'm not strong like you." His shoulders heaved, and he looked down at his fisted hands. "I must have the security of going back. I—I cannot be stuck here," he finished in whispered *Aemirin*. His hands cupped his face, and then he pushed his hair back.

Whoa. Nol was strong, one of the strongest people I had ever known. He did worry easily, though. That was why I hadn't told him about my block in the first place, or about the slave bracelet. He always found the negative and dwelled on it.

I looked at Charlie, who hadn't understood his words but got the meaning. She raised her shoulders, as lost for an answer as I was.

After a minute, I found something to say. "You won't be stuck. We'll find a way, Nol. I promise."

Nol lifted his head, eyes boring into me as his hands clenched and unclenched. "How?"

"What about Aswryn's *meril*? I took it from her the other night. It's in my jeans."

"*Tulaca, sae.*" *Fuck, no.* "That one won't work." He'd reverted to full *Aemirin* in his frustration and anger.

"You don't know that, Twynolan."

"*Ai, alluot.*" *Bullshit.*

Then he spouted off in *Aemirin*. His use of complicated words was starting to piss me off.

"What?"

He gave me a pointed look: *how dare I not understand.* "*Ai*, it wouldn't work. Her *vamameril* is made with her blood. It'll only work with her. Blood *merili* are different—"

I shrugged and tried not to be petty. "Maybe we could make a regular *vamameril.*"

Nol scowled and turned away as he said another word I didn't know. I got the meaning, though. Laughable, ridiculous, or something like that.

"...*iquana.*"

I put my hands on my hips and stomped my foot. "It is not hopeless! If I can make spells you've never heard of, why can't I do this? Do you know how to make a *meril*? At least, the general idea of one?"

"We don't even have material that holds magic."

That part was true. "I will find another way. Just not dream walking. I'm sorry."

Nol jerked and looked down at where Ray was tugging on the hem of his shirt.

"Nolan? Tatie always does what she promises. Please don't be so mad at her."

Nol's face softened, and he knelt down to her level. Charlie and I looked at each other. Her worried face looked about how I felt. Things had gone off track so fast.

"Ray." Nol licked his lips. How would he explain his outburst to a three-year-old? Even a two-hundred-fifty-five-year-old could be called out by a kid. "I...I am not mad at your Tatie."

"You sound mad."

Another pause. "You are right. I should not treat her so. Thank you for stopping me."

Nol stood with Ray in his arms. Her arms wrapped around his neck, and he held her close like he never wanted to let her go. When he opened his pale blue eyes, they were much softer, yet so sad. "I'm sorry," he mouthed to me.

I nodded but swallowed hard and had to look away. His doubt in me hurt. I shoved my hair back and squeezed the back of my neck.

"Do you, um, mind." I swallowed again. "If I take a rest for an hour? I know this is important—"

"Hallë, yes. Please, go sleep."

I tried to smile. "I'll be up in an hour." I could sleep longer after we figured this all out. Sleep was overrated, even with a concussion.

Someone had turned off my alarm. I knew this because my room was pitch black. Pain in the asses. And my phone wasn't on the bedside table to boot. My mouth felt like cotton, and I needed more pain medication. Oh, and some anti-nausea stuff, I discovered when I sat up. The question was where'd I put them? Note to self: bring them into the bedroom tonight. And water. And crackers.

Voices filtered in from the other room. I shuffled into the hallway where the TV lights danced over the white walls on the way to the bathroom. If I played the whole injured card, maybe someone would go bring me some food. I tucked my hair behind my ears and snagged my finger on a stitch. I hated this.

Nothing had changed in my reflection, except my face was paler. My freckles stood out like black pepper. Ugh. I hated my freckles. My eyes looked duller. Two glasses of water later, I headed out to see if anyone would take pity on me.

"Hallë, you are up," Nol informed me in case I didn't know.

I wanted to say something snarky, but my head pounded too hard. Nol sat on the couch under a blanket.

For an answer, I shuffled in and sat beside him. "Where are the girls?"

"Asleep," he said, voice lowered.

"Where's my phone?" I closed my eyes and rested my head back.

"Hidden. You are not supposed to look at screens." Again, low voice. I couldn't tell if he was mad, but at the moment I didn't much care. Someone had taken my phone, and I wasn't happy about it.

"I won't tell if you won't."

"No." Grumpy, and a bit irritated.

I groaned.

"Come here." Nol lifted his blanket.

What did it matter now? Regardless of how distant I tried to be, my heart would break when he left. So I slid over and tucked myself under his arm. He relaxed and pulled me closer. The pressure of his arm behind my head and leaning against him helped dull the headache, and his warmth made me sleepy.

"I'm so glad you're not dead."

"Me, too." He sighed, shoulders heaving. "I'm so sorry, Hallë. For everything."

Hmm. "Well, if you're really sorry..."Nol stiffened against me. "You'd go get me my medicine and water."

Nol laughed. "I think I can do that." He turned, and I tried to cover my face with the blanket, but he tapped my nose before I ducked. The butthead. I'd beat him one day. He came back less than five minutes later with a kettle of water, his sister's tea, and something on a plate. I couldn't tell what in the dark. No medicine, though.

"You think her tea will work better?"

"Yes. I brought food, too." He lowered the plate revealing some butter cookies. How cute. I chose three.

"No matter where you go, cookies and tea are the best pair."

"Fruit, too." He set the plate on the coffee table and handed me a mug.

"You didn't take long."

"I heated the water the proper *endaen* way. However, there is no spell to hurry tea to...What is the word?"

"Steep."

Nol nodded, sat back down, and covered us with the blanket, making sure I could hold my mug and be as close to him as possible.

"You're so funny." I took a sip, but the tea wasn't ready.

"Oh, I am taking all the comfort you will give me."

We sat in silence for a while, watching TV. He was about an hour into *Batman Begins*. Not my first pick to introduce him to movies, but whatever.

I slowly let my breath out, preparing to continue our conversation. "So, you wanna wait 'til the end of the movie or after I drink my tea to start working on ideas?"

"No talking until you finish your pot of tea."

"The whole pot? Before? Nuh-huh, I am quite capable of drinking and talking."

"I am allowing you to sit here with me and watch TV when I know you are not allowed to do anything. Do you want to end this early or not? There will be no other chances."

I grumbled my choice to wait.

Nol chuckled, tugged on my hair, and crossed his ankle over his knee. Back when we were kids, we'd hang out like this, reading, practicing spells, talking, complaining about our parents. So sitting here didn't feel awkward at all. In fact, this felt like the most normal thing we'd done since he got here.

"You need to drink your tea." Nol brought me out of my thoughts.

Wow, talk about history lane. Batman was almost over. We were past Bruce Wayne and Rachel's conversation at the end. Where'd the time go?

"Hallë?" Nol warned.

I sipped my tea, now half gone. "I'm drinking, jeez. You know the movie's over, right?"

"Gordon and Batman are still talking."

I sat up, downing my now-cold tea. Nol grabbed the mug from me and poured more. The credits rolled, and I scooted away to look up at him.

"Well? Are we going to go find a *meril*?"

"Perhaps this should be for a later conversation. You are still healing—"

"I'm done with the other conversation crap," I said.

Nol opened his mouth, closed it, and then turned off the TV. The fish tank was now the only source of light in the room.

"I don't want to argue—"

"Hey! You got the contraction."

Nol frowned. Okay, not the time. I bit into a cookie.

"I don't want to argue, but finding *meril* material over here is impossible." Nol dropped his head back, then looked down at me about ten seconds later.

"Dream walking is non negotiable."

"Yes, I heard you. But if you won't dream walk, what about contacting your grandmother through *Olauvë*?"

30

"You...you mean the same *Olauvë Amura Ore* use for distant communications in government meetings?" I didn't really need confirmation, but was he fucking insane?

"*Ja*." Yes.

"*Olauvë* is not for individual conversations."

"*Sitam*." *I know*.

"But I could never figure it out at home, and it's meant for conferences. I'm *savilë*. Contact with *Aemina* is forbidden, punishable by death—"

"If you get caught."

"Are you that eager to die? I'm not." I got up and wobbled on my feet. Right, concussion. A racing heart rate and panic probably weren't good for that. I took a deep breath and let it out, but my heart kept pounding. "I can't risk your life. The *Amura Ore* would jump at the excuse to never worry about me again."

"We must try because there are two issues. Aswryn's body is in that building. Any human can wander upon it. *Endaen* body, human world, lots of questions will arise."

I stared deadpan as he smirked. He knew that wasn't a huge issue; they couldn't connect me to Aswryn. Her body would remain a mystery.

He took a deep, steadying breath. "They don't know Aswryn is dead, correct?"

I nodded.

"They will begin to wonder why I have not returned with her even though the curse is broken. The longer without me, the more imaginative their minds will go. I also need to report to Tolwe." Nol licked his lips, waiting again. I was beginning to understand, and I didn't like it. "Without a report or any contact, they will consider me dead or gone rogue. *Zayuri* will be sent to find the reason."

I began pacing the room. I felt lightheaded, and my head hurt, but I had to move. I had to do something. "Holy hell."

"*Sitam.*" *I know.*

I quit pacing and dropped down on the bay window, my head against the cold glass as I watched the snow fall. I took a breath in. Let it out. Then another one. I didn't want any *Zayuri* here. "There's no other way."

"Correct."

"You're not helping, you know." I turned around and glared at him. The fish tank light made his hair look brown. He sat, as usual, with his hands across his stomach, his legs stretched out in front of him, relaxed as could be and looking at me with an almost bemused look on his face.

"How can I help?" Nol shrugged. "I cannot use *Olauvë.*"

He had a point. "How will you get her body over there?"

Nol looked at his fingernails. "I will need help, but we *Zayuri* have our ways."

I pursed my lips and narrowed my eyes at him. *Zayuri* secret crap. I slid off the window seat and went to stand in front of him.

Nol drew his eyes away from his hands and looked up at me, eyes wide and waiting. Then he looked down at his lap. "Hallë. Please?"

His pleading tone got to me. "It has been so long..."

"I know, but I have faith in you. What's the worst that could happen?" Nol peeked up at me, a teasing look in his eyes.

I rolled my eyes. Many afternoons had consisted of sitting in my grandmother's living room, failing to learn the special communication and falling asleep. Nol had sat reading in the corner by the fire, snickering to himself. She'd kick his butt out at least three times a week.

"When I do this, I won't be aware of anything here."

"*Sitam.*"

"So…" I twisted my T-shirt in my hands. "Would you stay by me?"

Nol studied me for a moment. "Of course."

"No snickering."

He smirked. "I'll do my best."

I growled in frustration before I sat down next to him. Leaning against him, I pulled the blanket around me. "You won't leave me?" I tipped my head back to see him.

Nol huffed. "I will not leave this couch. There are no doctors to keep me from you."

"That's not funny."

He quirked his lip. I couldn't keep my lips from trembling, and my voice shook. "I thought you were dead."

Nol closed his eyes and slowly let out his breath. "*Sitam.*"

I sat up all the way. "You were lying there. You weren't moving." My throat was getting tight as I tried hard not to cry. "Your pulse was so weak. When Gil didn't come back, I thought you were gone. I couldn't feel our bond." And now Gil was gone.

Nol clicked his tongue, knowing where my thoughts had gone. He leaned over and wrapped an arm around my shoulders, pulling me in. "I am sorry. I know you would rather have had Gileal stay, but that wasn't possible."

I tried to pull up, but Nol kept his arm around me, not done with what he had to say.

"They need to know what is happening, and to be honest, even if they did find out, they would need to find us before they could kill you."

"Yeah, that's so comforting, Nol."

He was right. Again. "May we finish this, please?" His words were muffled against my head. His lips touched the top of my ear, and I felt his warm breath as he whispered, "I will be with you the whole time. I promise."

He lifted his chin as I looked up to see his blue eyes, darker because of the blue light of the fish tank. I wanted to know what had made him think I wanted Gileal to stay, like it had been my idea. Had Gil told him I'd suggested it? Not that having Gil stay would have been bad; it was just that one hundred and nineteen years was a long time to hold on to a teenage romance.

Gileal had continued to love me, but I'd had to let him go. Seeing him again had elated me, comforted me even more than Nol in the beginning. Then again, he had stood by me the entire time. Nol had disowned me, so there was that. Did I still love Gileal? The question shocked me. Did I?

Of course. I had to. Right?

"Hallë." Nol shook my shoulders, interrupting my thoughts. "Quit stalling and go."

"But—"

Nol sat up quickly and thumped my nose. "Go. They need to know."

Well, he was right there. I rubbed my nose and glared at him. "I hate it when you do that."

"You'll get over it." He smiled. "Or not."

I growled in frustration and closed my eyes, relaxing and feeling the room around me. In my mind's eye, I saw Nol beside me. The couch shifted as he pulled his arm back and turned to watch me. "Stop staring at me."

"How did you know that?" There was some surprise mixed with a small amount of humor in his voice.

I pressed my finger to my lips. "Shush."

I let my consciousness drift away. This part I found the hardest, like that time between asleep and awake. Nol fidgeted, and it pulled me back. I smacked his shoulder, and instead of snickering, Nol sat still and shut up. If he'd only done that before, my grandmother wouldn't have kicked him out so many times.

Again, I cleared my thoughts and drifted away. This time, I caught the moment my consciousness separated from my body. The transition between realms was like drifting through one warm body of water, only to submerge into another. Between the realms, the roots of the human realm and *Endae* tangled together.

I saw my realm through my mind's eye, like dreaming, except I was awake...sort of. My energy started to fade. This needed to be done before my body used up everything. Pushing my magic out wide, I searched for my grandmother's *imolegin*. The magic of our realm pulsed, and I sensed the *imolegin* of every *endai* around me, but in some people, something was suffocating them, dulling their energy. The lingering magic of Aswryn's curse. So freaking strong still, so hungry.

To the southwest, there was a touch as light and gentle as a feather against my mind, attracting me to her. The faint smell of the herbs in her garden played on my senses as if I could really smell them. I locked on to that signature and let it pull me to her.

Yalu walked arm in arm with a taller *endao,* down a long stone hallway toward the *Amura Ore* chamber. The small flecks of crystal twinkled in the soft light of torches on the walls, illuminating the patterned swirls and shapes in the carved stone—the famous crystals of the capital buildings.

Yalu had her silver-peppered black hair braided and draped over her shoulder. She wore a long thicker-looking coat, and her dress flowed to the floor. Not that my people wore medieval clothes; Yalu just liked long dresses. The *endao* next to her wore the same *Zayuri* jacket as Nol. They walked past a torch on his side, revealing the gold highlights in his hair.

"Tolwe, wait." Yalu tugged on his arm and stopped. Nol's uncle turned, covering her hand with his. His face caught the light, and I saw the soft smile he gave her.

"Zella, we can't. The *Amura Ore* meeting will start soon."

She patted his hand and shook her head. "Give me a few moments. I need to..." Yalu held her breath and licked her lips "Something's happened. She needs me."

Yalu let go of his arm but didn't walk too far away. Tolwe pursed his lips and went to lean against the wall. He stuck his hands in his jacket pockets and rolled his shoulders back as Nol did. He gave Yalu a sour look, not like Nol's at all. Tolwe looked where they were headed and slumped his shoulders.

"Please be quick, Zella."

"I will." She teased him a little with a faint smile. A few yards away from him, she sat cross-legged against the wall. Yalu rested her palms on her knees, shook her braid back, and closed her eyes. Her awareness touched my thoughts. I wanted to sit back and visit, but there was no time.

"Hallanevaë, my little crow. What are you three up to over there?" Her "voice" held a bit of amusement. "What sort of thing do those boys need my permission for now?"

I would have laughed if only I could. Her face fell when she felt my sorrow, and in an instant, she knew Gileal was dead.

"Yalu, I am sorry. I wouldn't risk coming to you like this if it wasn't the only way."

"Still your mind and let me listen, little crow."

I paused and showed her the events of the week, from when Nol came to Yula's Quill to the time I sat down to contact her. Some moments later, she knew everything, my thoughts and more.

"Nolan is right. I will send Tolwe soon." Her thoughts turned sorrowful. "It was right not to tell Nolan about the bracelet. I know he'll hate it, but don't tell him until I've researched it further. What bothers me is that it tightened back up once Aswryn was dead."

I nodded, but didn't like the idea.

"I'm so proud of all three of you. Gileal's death will be mourned, and we'll search for his body. Nevie, I think you should know, after you left, Nolan drifted, and it was only Gileal and Rajamë who kept him sane. You wouldn't have recognized him. Through your mind, I can see the difference you have made on him already, but he is still hurting. The divide is hurting you both. *Aemina* owes you this. I think I've said more than Nolan would have liked, so I'll stop there. Be patient with him."

I nodded again, unsure of how much of this I could hide from him. One thing still bothered me. "What about that weight suffocating people's *imolegini*?"

Yalu paused. "I'm not sure. No one has felt that before." Another pause. "We will be in touch later. Dream walk—"

"Yalu, I don't think I should."

"Your energy is getting weaker, and dream walking takes less energy. You have my permission. It isn't invasive to me. You are always in my heart and thoughts. Know that forever."

"As you are forever in mine. I miss you."

Yalu pulled away, and Tolwe came to help her up. My magic pulled me back, and the last thing I heard was Tolwe's question: "Did she do something stupid again?"

"Hey!" I covered my mouth when I heard my voice echo through the hallway. Tolwe and Yalu looked as startled as I felt. That wasn't possible. My body pulled me back and I was conscious again.

I found myself lying on the couch under a blanket with my head on a throw pillow. Nol sat on the glider next to the small bookshelf, feet out in front of him, looking outside. I realized he was still in his pajamas from this morning.

"Did you have a good nap?" Nol asked.

I swallowed a few times and cleared my throat so I could talk. "You said you wouldn't leave the couch."

"Oh. Yes, well, I was falling asleep." He got up and came to sit next to me.

More like he got bored. I couldn't have been out *that* long. My arms shook as I sat up. I felt as heavy as a slab of cement, but I managed to move over and rest my head against the couch. I needed more of An'di's tea.

Nol fidgeted beside me, silently waiting, but the charged air in the room said volumes.

I sighed and looked down at my lap. "It worked." I lifted my head enough to look into his eyes but didn't elaborate.

He waited and stared at me, dying for answers.

I realized I was biting the inside of my lip and stopped. "Yalu agrees. *Aemina* owes us this time together, and she said to take as long as you need."

He swallowed and relaxed. Although he'd said they didn't get a say, he'd been worried about my grandmother's opinion.

"Tolwe should be here soon," I added. "He'll take Aswryn's body home."

Nol puffed his cheeks out. He looked away from me for a moment, then let out a deep breath. He stared at the fish tank, knowing there was more.

"Gil never came home."

He held his breath for a moment, then nodded.

"And it's odd. There's this weight on everything. It isn't Aswryn's *imolegin*, but there's a suffocating weight over some people's *imolegini*. Yalu said she didn't feel it, but she'll look into it now."

"Is the curse not gone?"

"Why wouldn't it be? I just felt something weird."

He took a breath to say something but snapped his mouth shut. "*C'yo*, I sense my uncle. I need to go."

Nol ran out of the family room toward my bedroom. He came out a minute later, hastily dressed in his uniform, adjusting his jacket with his *Zayuri* dagger in his hand. The swirling designs glowed the same black-blue light as his *Zayuri* sword. He frowned at me.

"Are you all right?"

He slipped the dagger into his boot. "No, I am not. I hate that I scare you."

I wasn't sure when he thought he'd scared me. In the kitchen maybe? It didn't matter. "You don't scare me."

"Did we not just discuss lying? I know the *Zayuri*—"

"Shut up." I teased, but with a pang of guilt. I needed to tell him about the band no matter what Yalu said. I reached over and pulled him in for a hug. "No more fighting, okay?" I spoke into his shoulder.

I felt him smile against my neck. "I'll try my best, but I cannot promise not to annoy you. You look too adorable when you get annoyed."

Nol laughed, which made me laugh.

"Now, I will be back later tonight." Nol bent back down, touching his forehead to mine again. "*Olentame?*" *Beside me?*

"*Olentame,*" I agreed.

"See, I told you." Nol winked and was out the door before I could ask what he meant.

I stared after him, still in shock about the whole thing. Hell, everything had happened so fast that I was still playing catch-up.

My grandmother felt we needed this time to mourn Gileal together. But I'd already mourned him, and all of them, when I'd had to face a frightening new world alone. So I needed to be strong for Nol and let him stay here and start to heal.

Wow, Nol would stay here. How would that go? The doctors had suggested I suffered more than one concussion, which wasn't hard to believe from the week I'd had. So recovery would take longer. I planned on spending a lot of time sneaking into my art room.

If I was honest with myself, I wasn't as confident as Nol about why I couldn't stop the spell before it killed our friends. Sure, his explanation made sense—using regular spells along with mine always went wrong—but I'd made sure to keep my magic out of it, didn't I? I wasn't certain anymore, but something had gone wrong.

Nol's presence here might help me find out for sure, and if he was right, I might end up keeping my magic. But if I was right, I'd block myself again, even though Charlie thought it was hurting me. I couldn't risk any more lives. In a really twisted way, everything seemed to work out, but would there be something else? I couldn't think of anything, but Nolan and I would figure it out together.

I sighed as my energy drained. My tea was gone, my eyes drooped, and my mind was foggy. I wrote Nol a note and dragged my butt to bed.

31

"Uncle?" Nolan called out from the back porch. As he walked down the steps, he kept his senses aware of everything. Tolwe would not show himself. Where would the fun be in that? But Nolan felt his presence, so he kept his back to the porch. He didn't want to disappoint him by being careless. Tolwe enjoyed testing his nephew, to make sure Nolan didn't become complacent. Even the least trained *enda* could kill a *Zayuri* if they were oblivious.

Nolan was never oblivious, and he worked twice as hard around Hallë. She never paid attention to *anything*. Nolan took a slow breath, keeping his exhale invisible in the cold air. He sank into the shadows, wrapping the darkness around him. Tolwe wanted to test him? Fine. He wanted this done. There were more important things to do, like sleep. He hadn't slept at all since he'd found Hallë.

Nolan slipped through the dark and continued until he stood behind his uncle as he assessed the damage to the front yard.

"Hello, Uncle."

Tolwe chuckled. "Nolan. Good choice, using the shadows along with this realm's magic. I didn't feel you."

"There's no magic here. The energy is similar, but you can't use their energy like our magic. Their technology interferes with our *Zayuri* magic. Intertwining this realm's energy with yours helps."

"Interesting. How long did it take you to distinguish the differences?"

Nolan came around slowly, giving Tolwe a wide berth. His uncle wasn't mean, but he didn't like losing, and Nolan wouldn't put it past him to play dirty. "Not long. Shall we?"

"Momentarily. I am sorry—about Gileal."

"Thank you. It's still hard to believe."

Tolwe looked at him with pity that Nolan didn't want. "So you want to stay? For how long?"

Nolan twisted his lips and loosened his tense muscles. "When I am ready, I will let you know." He rolled his shoulders back to shift his sword's straps back into place.

Tolwe's shoulders dropped, and he shoved his hands into his pockets. "How much does she know?"

Nolan shrugged, adjusting his sword straps again. They were loose tonight. "Most of it."

Tolwe didn't seem too upset or surprised. "Rajamë?"

"No," Nolan growled. Why did he always bring her up?

Tolwe sighed and rubbed his hands together. It was colder over here than it was at home, and the air was heavy and dirty. "Nolan, you need to talk about what happened, and Hallanevaë is the best person to talk to. She is your *muranildë*."

"I am fully aware of who she is to me, Uncle. You don't know her like I do. It would break her heart, and I would do anything to keep from doing that...again."

"She is Zella's granddaughter. She can take it."

"Of course she can take it, but that doesn't mean it would hurt any less. Please, can we go now?"

Tolwe looked toward the house "How is she?"

Nolan fidgeted. "Stubborn, feisty, quick to anger—" Nolan heard Towle laugh and stopped to see what his problem was. "What?"

"In other words, a perfect combination of Zella and her mother."

Nolan choked out a laugh. "*Ai*, yes. She looks like them both, too." "What a handful."

Nol scoffed, laughing. "An understatement of epic proportions. You should hear her accent."

"Oh?"

Nolan nodded. "In any language she's spoken, I can hear it, this small difference. It has an appeal, I'll tell you that."

Tolwe clapped him on the shoulder. "This will definitely be good for you, Nolan. Just remember, she can't go back with you. I wouldn't become too involved."

"It isn't like that. Now let's finish this." They wrapped the shadows around themselves and ghosted to the steam plant. Even in the dark, Nolan saw the blood pooled around the killing wound he'd inflicted on the soulless creature. Nolan heard the rustle of his uncle's clothing upon his arrival, moments after himself. Before he even cast the light, Tolwe had crouched next to the body.

"A little excessive, weren't you?" Tolwe lifted an eyebrow, but Nolan could see the hint of a smile peeking out of the corner of his mouth.

"I wanted to make sure she was dead." He'd struck the killing blow first. Then, before going to Hallë, he'd cast the un-clotting spell and went on to slice her throat for good measure. "Uncle, I'm not making excuses for my actions—"

"I know. Zella told me everything already. Both of your actions were honorable."

"No, I lost my temper when I saw Aswryn attacking Hallë. I'd promised Hallë I wouldn't kill Aswryn and I broke that promise."

His uncle turned away, hands on his hips.

"Was she upset about it?"

"She understood that I lost my temper, but I'd do it again without a second thought."

"I understand your loss of temper. You have always been protective of Hallanevaë. Always. If someone attacked Zella, the body would be unrecognizable."

Tolwe was being generous with his praise tonight. "Still, you've taught me better than that."

"Don't dwell, Nephew. Come help me prepare her body for travel." Tolwe pulled out a bag to carry the body in while Nolan cast the spell to disintegrate all the blood from the floor and inside Aswryn's body. "Too bad we couldn't use Aswryn's *vamameril* to transport her to the capital morgue."

"Nah, builds character."

"Don't steal my lines." Tolwe laughed.

They carried Aswryn's body through the shadows back to Hallë's place. "I expect to hear from you regularly. Make sure Hallanevaë keeps in contact with Zella. She is more than excited to hear from her granddaughter." Tolwe smirked as they walked half in the shadows. "They've already planned their next visit. They will dream walk to have more time and use less energy."

"Hallë hates that." Nolan frowned, remembering their argument that morning. He adjusted his grasp on the body bag. While not heavy, it was awkward holding it with one hand.

"Tell her to suck it up. I hope they make a schedule so I don't have to hear Zella pouting every morning."

"You know you love it."

Tolwe smiled. Within the last few decades, Zella and Tolwe had begun seeing each other. Why they'd waited centuries, Nolan had no clue. Tolwe dropped the body on the roots of the redwood he would travel through, a smaller cousin of the *Coyana* trees in *Endae*.

"Hallë says she senses a weight in peoples' *imolegini?*" Nolan shoved his hands in his pockets. "What do you think that means?"

"The curse was with us for a long time. It may take a while for it to fully dissipate."

Nolan nodded. That made perfect sense. "She thinks I'm mad at her."

"Are you?"

Nolan shook his head. "No. I'm angry...at everything. At Aswryn. Resentful because she's gone and all the people she killed will never return, yet those who are still alive will live on. I'll never see An'di, Rajamë, Camber, and Gileal again."

"You have Hallanevaë still. You'll spend a while with her, and now that the curse is gone, we will appeal again and bring her home."

Nolan nodded again.

"Nephew. Talk. To. Her. With your *muranildë*, you can find comfort, and she'll help you heal."

"Nothing will heal this, Uncle."

"Not if you won't let anyone in. Let her in, Nolan."

Tolwe reached into his jacket pocket and handed Nolan a necklace with seven *merili* attached. "Zella said you may need these. There are a few empty ones in there. Along with your communication *meril* and realm traveling *meril*." Tolwe pinched an amber and then an indigo orb between his thumb and forefinger.

"Thank you, Uncle."

With that, there was nothing else to say except goodbye. They grasped arms. His uncle engaged his *meril* and entered their realm with Aswryn's body through the tree's life force.

Nolan took a deep breath and followed the white cloud of warm air as it floated and dissipated. He could sleep—after he found the best place for his sword and jacket. Not as if anyone could use them besides him, but he needed to secure them.

The whir of the girls' fish tank drifted down to Nolan as he climbed the stairs. A full house again might do him some good. But healing? No, he didn't need healing. Nolan turned the corner and found a note on the table next to the empty pot.

Nol,
This is my note. Just taking a nap. Wake me up when you get back.
Hallë

He smiled and disintegrated the paper. He didn't need to cover his tracks here, but habit prevailed. Nolan turned to her bedroom. They needed to talk, but she needed to rest more. Mother knew he did as well.

He stopped next to Hallë's bed. Still breathing and sleeping. He used to listen to her breathing as she slept. Hallë had spent about half of their childhood sleeping at his house, and the other half he had slept at hers. Their parents gave up nagging them after the first twenty years or so. Nolan couldn't recall a day going by without seeing Hallë. Then she was gone.

How he had survived without her beside him was due to Rajamë and Gileal forcing him to continue. Perhaps Tolwe was right about talking to her. But no, he couldn't bear to tell her about her friend. Raj had tried convincing Nolan where and when she foresaw their paths intertwining, but with too many variables to consider, her precognitions hadn't always been right. Besides, she'd always found the twists and knots of Hallë's fate too tangled to follow.

Nolan lay down in the hammock. His mind wouldn't turn off. The hammock squeaked. The cars on the highway were a constant rush. He rolled over. After another five minutes, he gave up and went out to the couch where the fish tank provided background noise.

At least Aswryn was gone, and with any luck, the aftermath of the curse would be minimal. He stared at Hallë's captive fish to distract himself until he drifted off to sleep. Then he would wake to have another day with his *muranildë* and all her friends. One which did not involve such dire circumstances, just like he wanted.

EPILOGUE

"Call." Nol looked straight at Lewis as he put his chips in.

Anyone except Yumi and I said Lewis had a great poker face. Yumi knew him too well, and me, I was too damn old to be fooled by many humans.

I burned the last card and laid the ten of spades down. Lewis's eyes darted to his cards, widening a fraction. Not good, and Nol just raised an eyebrow. The microwave timer went off, yet none of us left the card table.

Lewis showed us his cards. Ace of hearts and jack of hearts. If I'd have laid down a king of hearts, he'd have had a royal flush. Nol laid his hand down, a queen of spades and ten of clubs—full house.

"God damn it, Nolan. You cheatin' with your magic over there?" Lewis asked.

Mateo clapped once, then went to his kitchen to take out the casserole.

"Lewis, that's rude. Nol wouldn't cheat." I leaned toward Nol. "You didn't cheat, right?"

"No." Nol chuckled. "I thought at least I would have two pairs. Would you like to go again?"

"No!" Mateo called. "Dinner is ready. Get your asses in here."

"The host has spoken," Sam said, getting up.

"Hosts are the people who live there, correct? So aren't you a host as well, Sam?" Nol asked as he pushed in his chair. His contractions were getting more fluid. He was also bugging me more and more about learning French.

"This is all Mateo's cooking. I just happen to live with the most talented cook in America."

"Mm, I like that," Mateo said, coming up and landing a peck on Sam's cheek. "Sit, sit."

Charlie looked around Mateo and Sam's empty living room. Ray wasn't at the table either. We looked at each other, no words necessary. I searched the main floor while Charlie went up to the third.

While the guys's room was off limits, their house offered many other good hiding spots. Ray liked their theater room and Sam's office. I found her on the porch steps leading into Mateo and Sam's postage-stamp fenced-in yard, playing in her own little world.

The sun was low in the sky, reflecting off Puget Sound from their view on Queen Anne Hill. The deep orange made her red hair glow. "Ray, dove, it's time for dinner."

She jumped up. Her feet thumped on the composite flooring as she ran toward me.

"Where're your toys?"

She pushed her tangled hair away from her face. "I didn't bring them out."

"Then what were you doing?"

"Talking to Fea."

"Oh really? Does she want to come in for dinner, too?"

This imaginary friend had appeared Friday and always stayed outside. Ray had played in the backyard most of Saturday and didn't want to go on the playdate we'd set up that morning. She still hadn't slept alone since Aswryn took her, either.

Ray looked back. "No. She doesn't like the smell of Uncle Mateo's cassie roll."

"Oh." I pulled her into my arms for a hug. "What about you?"

"It's okay."

"Okay? You said you wanted it every day last time he made it."

"Well, maybe."

I laughed. She let go of my hand as we got inside and ran through the dark office. I slid the office glass door closed and walked through the hushed room lined with bookshelves.

I paused in the hallway. Everyone was helping and finding their spots at the huge eight-seater table. Mateo, always the cheerful one, laughed at something Yumi said.

Charlie thumped down the open staircase to my left. She made eye contact with me before following my line of sight to where Ray was climbing into the chair next to Nol.

"Thanks, Tatie."

Charlie went over and sat on her other side.

Things were coming together. Zack had dropped me out of their investigation. He had yet to contact Katie's dad for a playdate with Seamus and I was really hoping to make that happen.

Nol and I had repaired most of the damage to the shop and the house. The stained glass windows would need to be replaced. Neither of us could set them right. I'd bought new equipment for Charlie's lab, along with new furniture for the house and the shop lobby. The old stuff reminded us of Aswryn.

Yalu and I had talked twice more that week. Yumi said I should keep dream walking easy while healing from my concussion. The curse was still lingering, and no one had heard of the *Asaidaë'a Metaela*. Yalu hadn't found any information on the slave band, but there was a lot of history to go through.

I told Nol the bare minimum about the slave band, that the thing was dormant, because Aswryn was dead. Yalu would find a way to get it off. I caught him looking at it a few times, but I assured him it wasn't doing anything.

Nol wanted to know everything. He went to Charlie's work whenever she let him, and Mateo was teaching him how to cook. Otherwise, Nol fussed over me. Gil's death had hit him harder than me. Not to say I wasn't mourning him—having Nol beside me helped. I cried sometimes, alone, but I needed to stay strong.

A warm hand on my back brought me back to the here and now.

"Hey, are you okay?" Sam asked.

"Just enjoying the view. What are you doing?"

"Getting wine." His curls shifted as he tipped his head toward the stairs that continued down to the basement and their wine cellar. We watched everyone together, bustling around still. "Do you wanna have lunch sometime? You know, to talk a bit? You seem anxious."

"I do?" My head tilted. I didn't feel anxious. "You'll have to pick me up or stay at the house."

"I know." He slid his arm around my waist. With a bottle poking my side, he leaned his head on my shoulder. "I'm glad you stayed."

I took a deep breath, inhaling the warmth of their home. "Me, too."

"I'm glad Nolan stayed, too. He's a good addition to our perfectly imperfect family."

"Agreed," I said and squeezed him back.

AUTHOR'S NOTE

Enjoyed this book?

I'd be so grateful if you could leave a quick review wherever you buy your books. Reviews help other readers discover The Exile's Paradox — and they mean the world to me.

Thank you so much for reading. The QR code will take you a link to find your favorite place to leave reviews and ratings. Thank you so much for reading.

Don't miss future books! Subscribe to my mailing list at https://subscribepage.io/kristineendsleyand you'll get new release alerts, behind-the-scene sneak peeks, book giveaways, and more. Would you like to know what Hally did that was so tragic? How could she have possibly killed her friends? Sign up for my mailing list and you'll get a free copy of Shattered Fate.

Hally's and Nolan's story continues with book 2, Jaded Loyalties.

ACKNOWLEDGEMENTS

If it weren't for the people here, this would still be a file on my Mac. Thank you.

My critique group at Café Noir in Silverdale. My partner at CritiqueMatch, Rachel. Katie Cross, you are super woman! I wouldn't have done this without your encouragement and advice from you and G.S. Jennson.

My betas! I begged and bugged you to read this and give me your honest feedback. And holy shit, you did! You all rock: Tami, Nikki, Barb, Mary, Liz, Sarah and Cassie.

Adam, I love you. Thank you for coming with me to Miscons; listening to me rant or ignore me when I talk to myself; not complaining when you get up for work and I've just gone to bed and for being my partner for the past twenty-two years.

My boys, you are my world. You amaze me; you inspire me. How did I get so lucky to be your mom? Thank you for being there, for the hugs and Eskimo kisses.

My editors, Elizabeth Darkley and Jennifer Griffin. Thank you for making it look professional, you know it'd be a mess without you.

My cover illustrator/designer, Cristiana Leone, thank you for making this book look so magical!

ABOUT THE AUTHOR

Kristine Endsley lives in Western Washington with her husband and two boys, two old lazy dogs and two wild black kitties. She works as a substitute para-educator to fund her writing habits.

This is Kristine's first novel.